I0604588

Broadcasting Boundaries

Thomas Brant

Copyright © 2025 Thomas Brant.

All rights reserved.

No part of this book can be reproduced in any form or by written, electronic or mechanical, including photocopying, recording, or by any information retrieval system without written permission in writing by the author.

Published by T Brant Publishing

Printed in Great Britain

Unless otherwise indicated, all the names, characters, businesses, places, events and incidents in this book are either the product of the author's imagination or used in a fictitious manner. Any resemblance to actual persons, living or dead, or actual events is purely coincidental.

Although every precaution has been taken in the preparation of this book, the publisher and author assume no responsibility for errors or omissions. Neither is any liability assumed for damages resulting from the use of information contained herein.

Print ISBN - 978-1-0683106-0-7

CHAPTER 1 – Another Show Done
Monday 28th October 2024

"And that's it for another day, I'll be back on Midlands Manic tomorrow for another drive time madhouse. Up next is... Toni bringing you the evening show from Liverpool... oops, did I mean to say that out loud? Of course, I did!" Pete chuckled into the microphone, flashing a grin at no one in particular in the soundproof studio. Pete Smith knew the truth, that only his drive time show, and the breakfast show were truly produced from the Dudley hub of Manic Radio, a quasi-national station that prided itself on being "local" while syndicating its shows from various corners of England.

A 30-year veteran of local radio, joining the predecessor brand, Dudley FM, in the early breakfast slot, making his way round the different shows on the station when it was a true local station. Back then, he was the face—or rather, the voice—of Dudley's morning routines, a comforting presence through breakfast news, traffic reports, and endless cups of tea. Dudley FM was local radio at its purest, proudly small, where Pete could see familiar faces in the streets and hear familiar voices on the phone-ins. But then came the changes, a new owner, a rebrand to Midland Manic with 6 other West Midlands stations, the off peak shows going regional instead of local, another new owner, the breakfast and drive shows going regional and the rest all going to the new Network Headquarters in Liverpool, then two other stations moving into the building complex, East Midlands Vibes, covering the East Midlands, and Northern Vibes, covering Crewe, Stoke and Stafford.

As a resident of Dudley, Pete was well known by the local community. He couldn't walk down the High Street without someone stopping him to talk about the latest drama on the air, or to complain—good-naturedly, of course—that his jokes were getting stale. He always chuckled and deflected the jibes, but secretly, Pete cherished every interaction. It reminded him that, despite the shifting sands of ownership and the impersonal nature of the network's new direction, he was still Dudley's voice.

As the final song, a throwback to 2010 which the network had fed, unlike the days when Pete could pick his own playlist, faded out, he leaned back in his chair and flicked a switch to deactivate his mic. The station jingle bounced through the studio speakers, signalling the end of his slot. He stretched his arms above his head, feeling the satisfying crack of his back, a reminder of his years hunched over microphones and soundboards.

"Another day, another show," he murmured to himself, grabbing his thermos and sipping the last cold dregs of tea.

Stepping out of the studio, he could see Lyra and Al, the Northern Vibes presenters, and Tim and Ellen, the East Midlands Vibes duo, walking out of their studios, their drivetime shows on the quasi-national Manic network having been presented by them for their regions at the same time as his own, show. There was a moment of shared glances and nods—a silent acknowledgment of another shift complete, the solidarity of presenters juggling the quirks of a network that felt both expansive and eerily narrow.

Tim, Pete knew, was of the transitional era, the bit when independent local radio was moving into the Capital and Heart style of national brands. He'd started on Nottingham Radio and been there long enough to remember when radio really was live and local, but he also understood the tightening belts of the industry and the gradual push towards syndication. Pete felt a pang of camaraderie whenever he saw Tim; they shared a nostalgia for a type of radio that was slowly slipping through their fingers.

Ellen, like Tim, was of the same era, having started at Birmingham Star, the former Birmingham local station similar to how Dudley FM had been. She had a quiet, steady style, the kind that made listeners feel like they were having a late-night chat with an old friend rather than just tuning in for updates on traffic and weather. Pete respected her professionalism, the way she could pivot between light-hearted banter and serious news without missing a beat. There was an understanding between them, unspoken but solid, that they were part of a dwindling breed in the radio world—personalities who had honed their craft in local studios before "network" became the buzzword of the decade.

Lyra and Al, on the other hand, were younger and distinctly of the "new breed" of radio hosts. Al, the corporate drone, who believed the brand guidelines were the be all and end all, and Lyra, who was a hybrid of the transitional era and the corporate generation, brought in to inject "youthful energy" into the airwaves. Lyra, unlike Al, was one of those who despite their brand-coach types who had never been in the TSA, the targeted service area, lived and breathed Crewe, her birthplace, and would visit the towns that she broadcasted to on her days off, to at least appear legitimate to the audience.

Al, on the other hand, plugged the network links, the promos and the corporate soundbites with a kind of unyielding precision, as if he were reading off a script. Pete had to admit that while he did keep bullet points to help him keep close to a structure, or at least be able to remind listeners every 20 minutes about the '£500k Money Drop', Al needed a full word by word script to deliver his lines, a safety net he clung to like a lifeboat in the unpredictable seas of live radio. Pete knew that Al, like most presenters his age, wanted that coveted network slot on either Lite Group's Manic Radio, Bauer's Hits Radio, or maybe even Global's Heart. Al saw the regional gigs as stepping stones, each one a rung on the ladder leading him closer to what he believed was the pinnacle of radio success.

The fact that the 3 networks, Manic, Hits and Heart were almost identical and competed in the same markets for the same listeners was a fact Al either ignored or saw as a challenge. Pete had overheard him during coffee breaks, talking about "honing his style" to fit the "national mould" and how he practised hitting the exact intonations for the adverts.

"Pete, a word," his producer, another 'network clone' who was barely old enough to remember what local radio had once been, called out from the door of his office. Greg, his name tag affixed with a slight tilt as if he couldn't quite commit to it, gestured Pete over with an impatient wave.

Pete stifled a sigh, mentally preparing himself for whatever "constructive feedback" was about to come his way. Greg was part of the new guard, a producer brought in from the Liverpool headquarters to "standardise output" and keep everyone in line with the network's vision of a polished, slick brand. Greg had that polished, slightly-too-eager energy Pete associated with people who'd memorised every corporate manual but never spent a day at the coalface.

"Pete," Greg began, not waiting for him to settle. "What the hell was that, calling out that the next show was from Network control in Liverpool? You know we're supposed to keep up the local image, especially during the drive time. We don't need listeners questioning where the shows are coming from."

"It's in the public file that we present Drive and Breakfast from here," Pete said, sighing, "And everything else is either from Control in Liverpool, the Stratford hub in London, the Dundee hub in Scotland or the Huddersfield hub for the North. Hell, we publicise that Al and Lyra's show and Tim and Ellen's show aren't Stone or Allestree presented but are from here in Dudley. Thank goodness for OFCOM Approved Areas and that. You know, it's funny how Network and OFCOM let the Mid Wales, Northamptonshire, Warwickshire and South Derbyshire shows join us here with their heritage brands and then they all share Liverpool's drive, even though they have their own breakfast."

Pete knew that Mid Wales Manic, Warwickshire Stars, Northants Now and Derbyshire Delight, 4 more of the Manic Radio network stations, had gone to the national drivetime, with their Breakfast shows being from Dudley, unlike the service areas they originally served. He felt the irony in it all. Manic Radio was a jigsaw of regions pieced together with corporate strings, and the effort to make it all seem local was, in Pete's eyes, a flimsy façade.

Greg's face tightened. "You know what I mean, Pete. It's about keeping the illusion of locality. We don't want listeners getting the impression that we're just syndicating every show. Which reminds me, Lyra's guesting as your co-host from tomorrow for a week as Network are sending another newbie for the North Midlands show with Al... and you'll have to obey a script, not your bullet points."

Pete's heart sank. A script? A scripted drive-time show? The very thought was an affront to everything he'd built his career on. Radio was supposed to be spontaneous, the space where personality could still crackle through the airwaves, where he could banter about the new chip shop opening down the street or a local match that turned out to be a nail-biter. But a script? He could feel his irritation rising, though he tried to keep it in check.

"Greg, come on. You know that drive-time needs to feel a bit loose, like we're just chatting here. It's part of the charm! The regulars expect that from me. They don't want me reading some prefabricated nonsense written by someone who doesn't know a thing about Dudley."

Greg rolled his eyes. "Look, Pete, I know you're... experienced. But that's the point. This is the new way things are done. Consistency. People trust a consistent voice. They don't care if you're actually here, in Dudley, or if you're reading off a teleprompter. What matters is the sound, the brand—"

"Brand, right, yes." Pete resisted the urge to throw his empty thermos against the wall. "A brand of some faceless 'Manic Radio' juggernaut. Greg, let me ask you, when's the last time you had a local listener call in to chat about the high street or to laugh about a bit of banter between songs?"

Greg looked momentarily thrown but recovered quickly. "That's not relevant. Our data shows that people want seamless entertainment, Pete, not the messy, folksy stuff you keep clinging to. And Lyra's joining you because the network's wanting to... refresh your slot a bit, add a younger dynamic. You should consider it an opportunity."

Pete barely kept a scowl from showing. This wasn't an opportunity; it was a slow erasure. He saw the writing on the wall. Lyra, with her youthful charm and adaptability to the network's demands, was the future, not him. Maybe they were just biding their time before replacing him entirely.

"And if I don't comply?" Pete asked, folding his arms defiantly.

"Pete," Greg's voice softened, though his expression remained unyielding, "I know you think you're holding onto some essence of what radio used to be. But this isn't the 90s. We need presenters who can fit the format, not fight it. You're either on board, or... well, you understand."

Pete clenched his jaw, feeling the weight of the decision pressing down on him. It wasn't just about a script or Lyra; it was about what he'd spent his life building, his connection with Dudley and its people. But he also knew that he wasn't just fighting for himself; he was fighting for the very spirit of what radio had once been.

With a deep breath, he forced a tight smile. "I'll think about it, Greg. But I can't promise I'll enjoy it."

As he walked out of the office, he knew it was going to be a long, challenging week ahead. For the first time in decades, Pete began to wonder if he really had a place in this new world of "radio." But he knew one thing: he'd make his mark, scripted or not.

* _ * _ * _ *

"Alright Pete?" Colin, the former mid-morning host on Midlands Manic said as Pete walked into the local pub. Pete knew that Colin was still out of work, despite his slot having been networked before the Coronavirus pandemic hit. Like Tim and Ellen, Colin was one of those who had joined radio when it was the transition between local broadcasting and the era of syndicated content. He'd been a staple on Midlands Manic's mid-morning show for years, loved by listeners for his dry humour and no-nonsense style. But when budgets were cut and networking expanded, Colin's voice was among the first to be silenced.

"Alright, Colin," Pete nodded, pulling up a stool beside him. "How's the hunt?"

Colin shrugged, swirling his pint. "Bleak as ever. Applied to a couple of community stations, but they can't pay what Manic did. And they don't want someone who'll rattle the cage, you know?" He looked at Pete knowingly. "You've probably been getting the same line."

"More than a line," Pete replied, sighing. "Network's got this new agenda, you know? 'Refresh' my slot. You know Lyra, the lass who does the North Midlands drivetime, the one who's not quite your era but not the corporate drone that most modern presenters have become? Well, she's set to join me for the week as some kind of youthful infusion, apparently to bring a 'fresh dynamic' or something. It's funny how Midlands Manic used to be 5 different stations competing against each other in the same area, Dudley, Shropshire and South Staffordshire, Wolverhampton and Telford, Walsall and Lichfield, Sandwell and Birmingham and Coventry and Solihull each having their own station, and then when Breeze Media came in, they just rebranded it to Midlands Manic, and then sold it off to the Lite Group for a quid because they were going bankrupt."

"Ah, yeah, the old Walsall Radio, broadcasting for Walsall and Lichfield," Colin interjected, shaking his head with a rueful smile. "I remember it well. It was us competing against Wolverhampton FM, Beacon Radio, Dudley FM, Brum's Best and BRMB, all for the same listeners. You'd prank call the Brum stations or Wolverhampton, making their hosts think that a celebrity was in town, and that BRMB and Beacon, overnight would carry Late Night Love with Dave Torrington, while Walsall Radio and Brum's Best had our own networked show, and Wolverhampton, along with a few other stations, would air some American syndicated programme while Dudley just aired pre-recorded specialist music shows on jazz and blues. It was a time, wasn't it?" Colin chuckled, a hint of nostalgia in his voice.

"That it was," Pete agreed, smiling faintly. "I miss that buzz of genuine competition, knowing listeners had a choice, and if you messed up, they'd just flip the dial, and how it was a yearly battle amongst our local 5 to see who could get the rights to the footie. I miss how one year, Dudley managed to snag the exclusive Wolves rights, so Wolverhampton had to settle for Baggies games, and then the post-game calls in where we'd get Baggies fans calling in to gloat after a win, while Wolves fans grumbled about their team's performance. There was a real pulse to it all, a sense that what we did mattered, that we weren't just broadcasting—we were part of the community."

Colin nodded, looking off into the distance, lost in thought. "Remember how the listeners used to call in, not just for giveaways or shoutouts, but just to talk? The voices we knew by name, who'd chat about their day, or complain about the new roundabout by the High Street? I swear, half of Walsall thought they were unpaid correspondents for my show."

"Exactly," Pete said, chuckling. "It was personal. People felt like they owned a piece of it. Now? Now it's all 'stations under the Lite Group banner' and 'brand synergy.' They think the average Dudley listener cares about 'synergy' and 'consistent national branding'—as if any of that's ever helped someone get through the M5 at rush hour!"

They both fell silent, sipping their pints, each lost in memories of a world that seemed to slip further away with each passing year. The pub around them buzzed with activity, the clinking of glasses, laughter from the nearby table, and the occasional booming voice from across the bar.

Pete then noticed, coming out of the office where the landlord usually did his paperwork, a suited and booted corporate type, clipboard in hand, who looked out of place amidst the rustic, cosy atmosphere of the pub. Pete nudged Colin. "What do you reckon he's here for?" he whispered.

"Steve's probably sold up or leased it to some corporate pub chain," Colin replied, shaking his head. "Seems like nothing's off-limits these days. Even the local boozer isn't safe from the takeover."

Pete sighed. "Guess it's all part of the same story, isn't it? Everything's becoming... streamlined. All that talk of brand identity and synergy, taking over every nook and cranny, squeezing out the soul of what used to be genuinely local."

Colin took a long, reflective sip of his pint. "Maybe that's the fate of things now. But it's hard, Pete, when you're from here, and they're telling you your roots, your quirks, and everything that makes you 'you' is outdated. Feels like being told to throw yourself out with yesterday's papers."

They sat in silence for a moment, each wondering how long they could keep adapting before there was nothing left of their original selves. Pete thought of the early mornings, the easy familiarity with his listeners, the banter about everyday things that only someone living there could really understand. And he knew Colin felt the same loss.

"Well, you know what," Pete said finally, his voice firmer than he felt, "Maybe there's still room for a bit of real radio. Even if it's squeezed between adverts and scripted segments, maybe, just maybe, they'll let us get away with a few words of our own here and there."

Colin raised his glass with a faint, wry smile. "Here's hoping. And if not... well, they'll know we won't go down quietly."

They clinked glasses, sharing a silent pledge to keep fighting for the old ways, even as the world shifted around them. They might be relics of a bygone age, but in their hearts, they were still broadcasters—true voices of their towns, holding on to that last spark of local radio.

--*-*

"And don't forget, the £500k Money Drop is happening Friday with Kyle and Sue," the voice of Toni Green on the car radio as Pete climbed into his old, weather-worn Vauxhall, said. Pete knew that the faux enthusiasm of Toni's voice was all part of the script, another cog in the machine pushing the network's latest competition. She didn't even know most of the places in the Midlands where listeners would be tuning in, but she didn't need to. To her, it was just a gig, a slot in the lineup, and Pete couldn't blame her for that. After all, she was just doing what the network wanted, keeping it slick, high-energy, and impersonal. "It's £3 to enter by text or online, or free to enter by phoning us on 0330 880 3601. Terms and conditions apply and it's a competition across the Manic Network, Manic Goldies, Manic Metal, Manic Rock, Manic Soul and Manic Dance networks. Lines close at 3pm on Friday 1st November, and as usual you can see the terms at manicradioplays.co.uk."

Leaving the car park of the Waterfront, a business complex near to the Merry Hill shopping centre, Pete sighed. Having an old FM/AM radio in the car meant that he was restricted to the BBC national stations, BBC WM, Heart Radio, Capital, Hits Radio, the few true local independents left or Manic Radio. Out of all of them, Pete often found himself gravitating to BBC WM, the public service station that, at least to some extent, still held onto that local feel he so missed in his own work, or the new breed of independent stations, like Black Country Radio, the new BRMB and even the new Radio Wyvern.

Turning the dial, Pete decided that Black Country Radio, which was hosting its weekly Soul and Motown hour, was the perfect choice for the drive home. He felt a rush of familiarity as the smooth tunes of Marvin Gaye and Smokey Robinson filled the car. Black Country Radio wasn't like the polished machine of Manic; it had a rough-around-the-edges charm, a voice that still felt anchored in the community.

It was ironic, in a way, that their studio building was the opposite side of the canal at The Waterfront to the old Dudley FM building, which was now the Midlands hub for Manic Radio and its various network channels. The two studios, though close in proximity, couldn't have been more different in spirit. Black Country Radio embraced the local, with its community-driven segments and eclectic playlists, a nod to the area's musical tastes rather than a network-prescribed setlist. It was a holdout, in Pete's eyes, a symbol of resistance to the homogenisation that seemed to be swallowing everything around him.

As the canal shimmered in the twilight, Pete caught a reflection of the old Dudley FM building, now rebranded with the sleek, neon Manic Radio sign, a beacon of all things networked and impersonal. He remembered walking into those same doors over thirty years ago, his heart pounding with the thrill of joining a team that knew Dudley like the back of its hand. Those were the days when even the building smelled of coffee and stale biscuits, a comforting mix of morning show prep and hurried breakfasts on the go. Now, it smelled of cold, antiseptic modernity, stripped of its character and familiarity.

Pulling onto the main road, Pete let the voices on Black Country Radio wash over him, feeling an inexplicable sense of warmth. He wasn't sure how long he could keep swimming against the tide at Manic Radio, especially with scripts and co-hosts being forced on him. But, for now, he could still savour these small pockets of familiarity, the moments that reminded him of why he'd fallen in love with radio in the first place.

He knew the fight was one he couldn't win forever. There would come a time when even Black Country Radio might fall, and community radio, as he'd known it, would be little more than a memory. But maybe, just maybe, if he could keep sneaking in those unscripted moments, those little nuggets of local flavour, he could keep that spirit alive a little longer.

As Pete pulled into his driveway in the Dudley suburb of Pensnett, a council estate which hadn't changed much since he was a kid, he switched off the car and sat for a moment, lingering in the quiet after the soul music from Black Country Radio. The familiar row of houses, each with their small, carefully tended gardens, was a stark contrast to the polished but sterile world he'd just left behind at the Manic Radio hub.

Pensnett might not have the gloss of the new developments springing up all over the region, but it had character, a lived-in feel that he found comfort in. Here, he was just Pete from down the road—not a radio host, not a cog in the machine, just another neighbour. He'd often run into familiar faces at the local corner shop, where the owners had known him since his teens, or at the fish and chip shop, where he'd hear the same old stories from folks who'd listened to his show since the days of Dudley FM.

As he finally stepped out of his car, he felt the chill of the evening settle around him. He glanced up at the night sky, where a few stars managed to break through the haze of light pollution from the nearby town centre. It was a quiet, grounding moment, one that reminded him of the roots he'd planted here and the people he felt responsible to, in his own way.

Stepping through his front door, he saw his son, James, a 21 year old final year Media, Film and Television studies student at Wolverhampton University, reading on his laptop the Manic Radio brand guidelines for staff.

"Hmmm... I bet Kylie can't wait for tomorrow when she hears me with Al on Stoke Drive," Pete heard James mutter as he saw James slouching, and groaned, as it meant that somehow, without Pete knowing, James had been signed by Manic Radio and not told anyone that he was joining the very network that Pete had spent years railing against. The irony was almost too much, and for a moment, Pete considered laughing it off as some elaborate joke. But the way James was poring over the guidelines, eyebrows knit in concentration, told him otherwise.

"James," Pete said, trying to keep his voice steady, "when did you... get hired by Manic Radio?"

James glanced up, caught off guard, and offered a sheepish grin. "Today... Al, Greg and some Network bloke, Ben his name was, did some auditions at Uni this morning. Ben said I sounded like the perfect voice for Manic, almost as polished as Toni, Al, Lyra and Kylie. He said that I might even have a network slot on Manic Dance and Manic Rock soon."

Manic Dance, a EDM and Club and Manic Rock, a classic and modern rock station, were just two of the network's additional channels. Hearing that James might soon be another cog in the same corporate machinery, albeit on the youth-oriented offshoots, made Pete's stomach churn. His son, who'd grown up on tales of local radio's heyday, who'd heard about the glory days of Dudley FM and Beacon Radio—was now poised to join the ranks of those Pete considered part of the problem.

"That's... big news, son," Pete said, trying to keep the conflict out of his voice. "They've got you lined up for Stoke Drive, then? Quite a slot for a newcomer."

"Yeah," James said, his face bright with excitement. "It's just an on-air test, and I'll be working with Al and Ben on the show, as he's covering Lyra, something about her being off for the week."

Pete scoffed, as that excuse was all too familiar. The network's "off for the week" line was often code for testing replacements, covering for presenters who were being temporarily reassigned to cover other regions, or simply part of the endless reshuffling that the network now saw as necessary for supporting their "fresh" branding. The fact Lyra was being temporarily reassigned to join him on the West Midlands drive show and bringing in Ben, one of the network floaters who were also middle management on the Network side of things, to join Al in Stoke just reeked of manoeuvring. Pete knew the pattern too well, having watched it play out countless times in recent years.

"Well, guess that means the Smiths are taking over Manic Radio, eh?" he said with a chuckle, though it lacked his usual warmth. "You'll be rubbing shoulders with all the network big shots in no time."

"Erm... I... won't be going by James Smith on air, Dad," James said with a grin. "I'm going on air as Jimmy Reeves... mum's maiden name."

Pete knew his wife, Sarah, had used her maiden name on air when she was a radio presenter back in the 90s and

00s, and still used it to present syndicated community and local radio shows which were pre-recorded and distributed as filler programming for small, independent stations struggling to keep up with 24-hour content. Having presented both ILR, independent local radio, and Smooth, a Global station which was an adult contemporary network, Sarah had known first-hand the transition from local to corporate-controlled radio. Their other child, Chloe, a 19-year-old Law with Criminology student at the University of Birmingham, did student radio as well as syndicated CHR shows for the various community and local stations that needed content across the country. Chloe had chosen the on-air name "Clo Reeves", and Pete knew that she was aiming for a slot with a brand like Manic, Bauer or Global one day, though she hadn't yet said it outright. Pete could see that the family radio legacy was alive and well, but not exactly in the way he'd imagined.

James and Chloe were part of a new generation that had grown up immersed in the increasingly polished, structured world of network radio. They hadn't experienced the fiercely local spirit of the Dudley FM days, and to them, a career with a major CHR network like Manic or Hits Radio stood for a big break—a path to the "big leagues." Pete couldn't fault them for chasing success, but he couldn't deny the twinge of disappointment at seeing them join the very machinery he found himself resisting.

There was one thing Pete picked up, well two really, and that was James had completely shod his Black Country accent, and also a mention of a Kylie. Pete knew that, well as far as he was aware, James hadn't got a girlfriend, although he often went out claiming he was going to a friends, or that he was stopping overnight with a University mate. But perhaps there was more to his son's personal life that he didn't know—after all, James was an adult now, living his own life in a way Pete hadn't fully anticipated.

A lot was changing, not just in radio but in the very fabric of Pete's family life. The thought of his children adopting new personas, polished and smoothed over, part of the same network mould he'd grown so wary of, felt strange. It was like they were slipping into new skins, ones he barely recognised. Yet he knew that their path was their own, and he couldn't begrudge them for wanting to succeed, even if it meant embracing the very system he resisted.

"Right, Jimmy Reeves it is, then," he said, trying to inject some enthusiasm. "But remember, once they've got their hooks in you, it can be hard to keep hold of who you really are. Don't let them strip away everything that makes you... well, you."

James grinned. "I'll be fine, Dad. This is what I want to do—proper radio, reaching loads of people. Isn't that what you wanted back in the day? Anyway, Kylie's there too, so I'll be seeing her after she's finished her show."

It was then that Pete worked out who James was talking about, Kylie Morgan, one of the Warwickshire Stars breakfast hosts, who had recently graduated from Wolverhampton in the same course as what James had been in, and had joined Manic the previous November, initially doing pre-recorded content for their Manic Dance and Manic Rock sub-brands, mainly the decade stations, having done what James will be doing tomorrow, done an on-air test show, albeit with Tim in the East Midlands Vibes show. She was fresh-faced, driven, and undeniably talented, embodying that new, sleek generation of radio hosts. Pete knew that she was a fan of crop tops, short skirts and fishnet stockings, what most of the female Manic presenters wore to give that "trendy, youthful edge," as the brand liked to say. Kylie seemed to take to it naturally, like a duck to water. Pete had to admit she was good—professional, quick on her feet, and knew exactly how to hit those network beats with ease.

"So, Kylie, eh?" Pete said, raising an eyebrow, trying not to let his surprise show too much. "How long have you two been together?"

"Oh, two years. We've been keeping it quiet, but we're... well, tomorrow we're going Insta official... once my new socials are set up. I've been excused from lectures tomorrow, so I can have my photoshoot, get some promos done and also so some TikTok, Insta and X pics can be taken of Kylie and me."

X, the name that Twitter had adopted the previous year, replaced Twitter's iconic bird logo with a sleek black "X," aligning with its rebranding as a broader social platform. It was no longer just a place for quick, unfiltered thoughts; it was now about curated, stylised content. The idea of James and Kylie going "Insta official" felt like a foreign concept to Pete, yet he could see the appeal for them. They were embracing a world where visibility was currency, and personal branding was as essential as the job itself.

"Anyway, there's a whole marketing thing Manic have about his coupling up, which is why we're going public. They think it'll be good for our image; you know? Show off that we're not just voices on air, but relatable, real people too," James added, sounding almost rehearsed, as if he were already practising his new network-approved persona. "Anyway, want some goss about Al?"

Pete chuckled, shaking his head in a mix of amusement and disbelief. "Alright then, Jimmy Reeves, hit me with the Al gossip. What's the latest from our favourite corporate drone?"

James leaned forward, grinning. "He's banging Toni Green, you know, the evening host from Liverpool. Kylie told me he's a bit of a man-whore, and that Lyra had her boyfriend clean his clock when Al tried it on with Lyra."

Pete chuckled, as he remembered, in the first month of Al being at Manic, he'd appeared the one afternoon with a black eye and a limp, and he knew that Lyra's boyfriend, Si, was a professional wrestler, someone who wouldn't take kindly to someone disrespecting his partner. The idea of Al, so tightly wound in his corporate image, getting a swift dose of reality in the form of Lyra's boyfriend was both hilarious and oddly satisfying. It was a reminder that, underneath all the network polish and protocols, they were still just people, vulnerable to the same blunders and embarrassments as anyone else.

"Figures," Pete chuckled, shaking his head. "Al always did think he was God's gift to radio… and apparently, God's gift to every woman in the studio as well."

James laughed, nodding. "He's also had a few Bauer and Global staff in his little black book of conquests, according to Kylie. He's a smooth talker, Dad, but not as slick as he thinks he is. Still, Manic loves him because he's… what's the word? 'Marketable.' Anyway, Ben and Greg said I've got the network promos down pat."

Pete sighed, sensing the divide between himself and James widening. There was a palpable difference in their understanding of radio—a generational shift that had crept up without him noticing. James saw radio as a high-stakes, competitive arena, where marketability and visibility were just as vital as the voice behind the mic. Pete, however, couldn't shake the feeling that something irreplaceable had been lost in this relentless pursuit of branding.

"Marketable or not, just remember that radios about connection, son," Pete said, softer now. "It's not just about saying the right words or looking good on a promo. It's about making people feel like they're listening to a friend, someone who understands their world."

James looked at him, the confident grin replaced by something subtler—maybe even respect. "I get that, Dad. Really, I do. But the world's different now. People my age, they're looking for… well, for a vibe. They want something that sounds polished and on-point, something to match their Spotify playlists. It's all part of the package. Anyway, Ben and Greg said that I'll be doing, after the Drive, mainly pre-recorded stuff and the odd live show, but I'll still be 'on-air'. My first Network show is on Manic Dance, ironically, on Saturday - it's a pre-recorded Ibiza Classics show, and all I need to do is record the links. I'm using Studio One all day Saturday to build a bank of pre-recorded shows for Manic, Manic Dance, Manic Rock and Manic Metal."

Studio One, Pete knew, was the Midlands Manic studio, his studio for Drive and Kat and Moses's Breakfast show, the prime studio as it was in the centre of the building and so had views of the other 9 studios, each one having a different station in the Manic Radio network come from them, as well as one being for local news that was, unlike the Dudley FM days, pre-recorded, not delivered live. Studio One was where Pete felt most at home, the heart of the station he'd known since its Dudley FM days, where he could still sneak in a bit of himself between network directives. The idea of James using it to pre-record polished, scripted content for multiple Manic channels was a bitter pill to swallow. It felt like watching his legacy transformed into something unrecognizable, tailored to fit the mould that James and his generation accepted without question.

"Oh, and Kylie will be recording this Saturday's show with me, so once the photoshoots finish tomorrow, I'll be cracking on with my first network slots," James continued, his face lighting up with excitement. "The best part is, with these pre-recorded shows, I'll be on air even when I'm not in the studio. Pretty cool, right?"

****

CHAPTER 2 – The Break Room (or a Frat Party)

It was Tuesday, the day after James had told Pete the news that he had been signed to Manic without so much as a hint to his family. Pete was sitting in the break room of the Manic Radio hub at The Waterfront, where the majority of presenters had either finished their post-Breakfast show debriefing, or were getting ready to start their pre-Drive briefings. Of course, with all but 3 hosts being under 30, that meant that the break room was more like a university common room than a professional radio station's relaxation area. Coffee cups and energy drink cans cluttered every surface, and laughter filled the space as presenters compared playlists and scrolled through each other's latest Instagram stories. The room buzzed with the kind of energetic chaos Pete associated more with his son's university than a workplace. He glanced around, feeling slightly out of place.

Lyra sat cross-legged on one of the armchairs, a Starbucks cup balanced precariously on her knee, while she animatedly recounted a story to a group gathered around her. Al, perched on the arm of the sofa with his perfectly styled hair and pristine trainers, was scrolling through his phone, chuckling as he showed something to the others. Pete caught snippets of their conversation—it seemed to be a mix of on-air banter and gossip about who had nailed the most recent TikTok trend.

Pete sat at the corner of a table, nursing his own mug of tea. Unlike the others, he wasn't documenting his every move on social media, but he'd glanced at his phone earlier and seen that both James and Kylie had officially gone "Insta official," just as James had warned. The fact that the photo had been took after Kylie had finished her breakfast show with Tina, the two Warwickshire Stars presenters, was obvious from the backdrop of the Warwickshire studio and the matching outfits they wore—stylish, coordinated, and calculated for maximum impact. That it was obviously staged, with James sitting at the desk and Kylie on his lap, both wearing headsets and grinning into the camera, felt like a world away from how Pete remembered meeting his wife Sarah in a radio studio. Back then, it had been at an event both Dudley FM and Wolverhampton FM had been covering, the two stations having a friendly rivalry but a mutual respect for each other. The photo James and Kylie had shared felt manufactured, staged for the 'likes'—a far cry from the candid, slightly blurry photos Sarah and Pete had from their early days, taken by colleagues who didn't care about the perfect angle or lighting.

Pete knew that James had the day off from Uni, so was having his corporate induction and orientation today, but at the moment was sitting in the corner of the break room, it being lunchtime, his tongue down Kylie's throat at the two were doing more than heavy petting and holding nothing back for the benefit of the younger crowd around them. Pete cleared his throat, more out of habit than in hopes of interrupting, and tried to focus on his tea. It had gone cold, much like his tolerance for the overt display, but he figured this was the new reality of Manic's "fresh dynamic." The days of hushed chats and polite laughs were clearly over.

"Oi, Morgan," Al shouted, a grin on his face, and Pete knew that it was going to turn into a session at the Student Union instead of a workplace canteen.

Kylie glanced up from her spot beside James, her lipstick smudged just slightly and rolled her eyes at Al's shout. "What, Crozier?" she replied with a playful grin, not moving from James's lap. The others watched with a mixture of amusement and curiosity, as if Kylie and James's relationship was some kind of reality show that had suddenly landed in their midst.

"Save some for the air, yeah?" Al smirked, giving James a mock salute. "Jimmy Reeves, the next Manic heartthrob, turning our humble Dudley studio into a scene straight out of Love Island."

"Well, I ain't on 'til brekkie, babes," Kylie said with a grin, "And Jimmy here's got a couple of hours until he's in your show, so we're just... making the most of the break." She glanced up at James, who chuckled, unbothered by the attention. The fact that both Al and Kylie used James's on-air name for effect felt odd to Pete, as though his own son had slipped into a stranger's skin, leaving behind the young man he'd known. This was "Jimmy Reeves," not James Smith from Pensnett, and the transformation seemed almost complete. Pete couldn't help but wonder if his son was genuinely enjoying this new identity or if he was simply caught up in the showbiz glamour Manic seemed so eager to push.

"Alright, let's get a bit of decorum here, yeah?" Pete said, forcing a smile and trying to keep his tone light. "This is a break room, not the Love Island villa."

"Come on, old man, we're twentysomethings, not 'hot chocolate and biscuits, bed by 9," Cody Lane, the newsreader on Midlands Manic, piped up from across the room, grinning cheekily. Cody was dressed in his usual trendy streetwear, effortlessly fitting in with the rest of the young crowd. He leaned back in his chair, one foot propped up on the edge of the table, clearly enjoying the shift from news bulletins to banter. "Anyway, Crozier, looking forward to the weekend mate?"

Al looked up from his phone, catching Cody's eye with a grin that was half mischief, half swagger. "Oh, mate, the weekend's gonna be legendary. Pussy as far as the eye can see," Al began, but quickly caught himself as he noticed Pete's frown from across the room. He shrugged and continued with a less suggestive tone, "I mean, it's going to be good fun. I'm going up to Liverpool to see Toni, maybe have a night with her and some of her mates from Hits Radio... few drinks, bit of blow, you know the drill." Al shot a sideways glance at Pete, whose expression was a blend of discomfort and disapproval.

Pete knew that Al did cocaine and often bragged about it, as if his casual drug use were another badge of youthful rebellion and defiance of the "old guard." It seemed to be a point of pride for Al, a way to remind everyone that he played by different rules, even if those rules aligned suspiciously well with Manic's corporate ethos of "edgy" branding. Pete knew that, back in his day, when he was Al's age, the only vices of radio hosts wasn't cocaine or designer drugs, but rather a pint at the pub after a show or the smoke-filled broadcast studios, where chain smoking was a common sight. As a former smoker himself, Pete remembered how he'd get through a 10 pack of Benson &

Hedges by the end of a particularly hectic shift, puffing away between ad breaks and records. It was a different era, rough around the edges but somehow authentic, rooted in the community it served. The idea of Al's designer drugs and flashy nights out with corporate types from Hits Radio seemed worlds apart from Pete's days at Dudley FM.

"Ah, right, you and Toni, between you and Kylie and James, you've got the 'power couple' slots sorted, haven't you?" Pete said, trying to inject some humour to lighten his growing discomfort. "I guess we're living in the age of 'Insta love' now."

James flashed Pete a sheepish grin, though he didn't seem remotely phased by Pete's disapproval. "It's all part of the game, Dad. You know that. People want a bit of 'real life' from their presenters, yeah?"

Kylie chimed in, still lounging comfortably in James's lap. "Yeah, it's all about that relatability. Listeners don't just want voices—they want to know we're like them, having a laugh, living a bit, y'know? Makes us seem… accessible."

Pete managed a tight smile, though inside, he felt a pang of frustration. He'd always believed that his listeners connected with him not because he shared every detail of his life but because he knew theirs. It wasn't about showing off; it was about being present, being someone they could rely on, a familiar voice in the chaos of the everyday. But this generation seemed to crave a different kind of connection—a glossy, social media-fuelled version of "authenticity" that felt anything but.

"Hey guys!" Liam Price, one of the Mid Wales Manic breakfast hosts, shouted as he pulled out one of his earbuds, "Manic Dance have announced they're dropping a F1 related track in the next 10 minutes on the Lunchtime EDM show. They've given a clue too... '33'."

"The Verstappen track?" James said, grinning, and Pete knew that his son, having done EDM and Club sets at the student union at Wolverhampton would know what the track was because of his interest in dance music. "I know what it is. It's '33 Max Verstappen' by Carte Blanq and Maxx Power, came out last year. Capital would never touch that track in a million years. It goes 'Tu-tu-tu-du, Max Verstappen' for most the song. It's as popular in Holland as Kernkraft 400 is in Germany. It's a big track in the Euro scene, especially after the F1 hype around Verstappen - I mean, he's a triple F1 Champion, his team boss is the husband of Geri Horner, for god's sake. It's not just an F1 track, it's a cultural moment."

Pete groaned, as he knew who Geri Horner, or when she was single, Geri Halliwell, was. He'd followed the Spice Girls' rise to fame as part of the music landscape, but hearing Max Verstappen and F1 culture intertwining with pop stars in the same sentence felt like a sign that he was completely out of touch with the present.

"I haven't watched F1 since Schumacher left Ferrari to retire," Pete said, sighing.

"Mate, you're ancient then. His kid's been in F1 and gone," Liam laughed, grinning over at Pete. "You've missed a whole new generation of F1, it's all about the Verstappen show now. And before you say 'I remember when

Fernando Alonso was a rookie and won his first title,' just know that Max Verstappen is the new king of F1, mate. He's basically the Michael Jordan of motorsport now. You should get in the loop, Pete. Everyone's talking about it."

Pete gave a dry laugh, not sure whether to take Liam seriously or not. "Yeah, right, I'll add it to the list right after I learn how to use TikTok," he said, raising an eyebrow. The irony of the conversation was not lost on him: he, the veteran presenter with thirty years in the game, was now being made to feel like an outsider in a place he used to consider home. Here, the currency wasn't experience, knowledge, or loyalty; it was relevance, flash, and how many followers you could stack up on a social media platform. "I do keep up with some modern programs, like... The Voice and Strictly, and I use X and Facebook. I mean, I'm 52 for god's sake, so I do know some social media stuff, but this TikTok and 'Insta Official' business?" Pete shook his head, "It's a whole new world."

"Don't worry, mate, we'll get you there," Cody teased, raising his mug in a mock toast. "Tell ya what, pass your phone and I'll update your socials for you with Insta and TikTok."

Pete shook his head with a smile, though there was a slight edge of resignation to it. "Thanks, Cody, but I'll pass on that. I reckon I'll stick to what I know for now." His mind wandered back to the old days at Dudley FM, when listeners connected with him over the airwaves, not through curated moments on Instagram or TikTok challenges. Back then, the conversations were raw, unscripted, and, for better or worse, real. You had to show up with your whole self, not just the edited bits that made for a slick social media feed.

Lyra, still perched comfortably with her Starbucks cup, turned to Pete with a sly grin. "Honestly, Pete, you're not that far behind. You could totally pull off a TikTok dance. Just need to get the right angle, and maybe some dramatic lighting."

"Yeah, Dad, I'll do one with you in Studio 1," James said, grinning, "show you how it's done, old man."

Pete snorted, though his chuckle was more out of awkwardness than genuine amusement. The thought of performing some over-choreographed TikTok dance in front of his colleagues—and, more to the point, his own son—was something he could scarcely stomach. Still, the offer lingered in the air, like a challenge he didn't know how to decline.

"Guys, it's on!" Liam said, and the sound of 33 Max Verstappen's pulsing bassline filled the room, and everyone turned toward the speakers, some nodding their heads to the beat, others already pulling out their phones to share the moment. James's grin widened as the track built to its first drop, the sheer energy of it almost contagious.

Pete winced, feeling the weight of the moment settle on him like a heavy cloud. He'd been in radio long enough to know that moments like this were all part of the show— the attention-grabbing tracks, the manufactured excitement, the carefully curated content. But that didn't mean he had to like it.

"Right, well, that's… something," Pete muttered under his breath, trying to appear engaged. He glanced at James, who was now fully in his element, swiping through social media with one hand while the other rested casually on Kylie's shoulder. It was like the world had spun and suddenly Pete found himself living in the outer ring of it all—too old to fully embrace this new wave, but too close to ignore it.

"Oooh, some of the Hits Brum lot have commented on mine and Kylie's Insta post!" James said with a grin as he tilted his phone towards Pete, showing him the growing flood of likes and comments. The post—shot after Kylie and Tina's Breakfast show, with a caption.

@KylieMorganBrekkie: *Chilin' with my man @ManicDanceReevesy in the @WarwickshireStars studio #CoupleGoals #ManicDance #ManicRadio #TotesInLove*

Pete noticed that there were over 15,000 likes and comments already—was one more data point in a world Pete no longer felt part of.

@hitsradiowestmids: *'True power couple vibes!*

James grinned, tapping through the comments like he was scrolling through the latest stock prices. He tilted the phone again towards Pete, like he was showcasing some sort of trophy. Pete didn't need to read the comments to know that this was exactly the sort of "public persona" stuff that made his skin crawl. It wasn't just a picture of two young presenters. It was a carefully constructed brand statement: #CoupleGoals, #TotesInLove, each hashtag calculated to tick all the right boxes. He could almost hear the corporate drone from Manic HQ in Liverpool—Ben Morrisey or some other middle manager—saying "Excellent engagement, guys, keep it up, you're really hitting the target demographic."

"And the other Manic Dance guys have commented on the one on my profile too, Dad. Dr Manic, all the other ones. Looks like everyone's loving it. Pretty mad, right?" James added, clearly proud of the attention.

Pete saw that James's post was similar, but swapping the "my man @ManicDanceReevesy" with "the sexy @KylieMorganBrekkie" on the caption, with Dr Manic, a self-proclaimed 'Doctor of Dance and Trance on Manic Dance', tagging them both with a fire emoji. Pete couldn't help but feel a pang of disconnection. This was the new world of radio: a carefully orchestrated social media machine designed to create buzz, generate brand loyalty, and turn every personal interaction into a marketable commodity. Where once it was the on-air connection that mattered, now it was all about these curated moments, these visible snippets of "reality" that only served to deepen the illusion.

He sighed, leaning back in his chair, trying to push the unease down into some corner of his mind. He had been part of the radio scene long enough to know it was always evolving—some evolution for the better, and some for the worse. But this shift, this embrace of the hyper-polished, influencer-driven approach, felt like a bridge too far. It wasn't that Pete didn't understand the need for relevance, or the importance of keeping up with trends. But the way his son and his colleagues were consuming and feeding into it felt almost… hollow.

"Yeah, mad," Pete muttered, forcing a smile that didn't quite reach his eyes. "So, what's next, James? You getting into podcasting as well, or is that too 'old school' now?"

"Statistically," Cody said with a grin, "Podcasts are ideal for the "long-form storytelling" market, but they're not quite the main event anymore. Everything's about short-form content now—TikTok, Instagram Reels, maybe YouTube Shorts if you're feeling adventurous." He flashed a cheeky grin as if he'd just revealed some secret code. "But hey, don't worry, you can always find your niche, Pete. You're a radio legend, right? There's definitely space for the older demographic too. You know, for the 'retro' crowd."

"Cheers, Cody," Pete said dryly, though he couldn't hide the faint chuckle that escaped him. Retro. That's what he'd become now—retro. The thought stung more than he expected.

The energy in the break room shifted as the track's beat grew louder, and some of the younger hosts began to clap along. Pete sat back in his chair, watching the frenzy of shared posts and inside jokes. It wasn't that he didn't get the value of social media—after all, he had his own accounts. But there was a part of him, a bigger part than he wanted to admit, that felt uneasy about how far Manic had gone in its pursuit of "brand authenticity." Everything was so curated. And it was becoming harder to tell where the lines were between who people actually were, and who they needed to be to stay relevant.

"Hey, maybe we could do a Manic Radio TikTok challenge," James suggested casually, as though he were planning a segment, rather than floating an idea that made Pete's stomach churn, but the others nodding along like the idea was the next big thing.

"A dance challenge?" Abdul Zahir, the local Head of Marketing for Manic's Dudley hub said with a grin. "Hmmm, that'd be good for the socials, get a bit of buzz going. Everyone loves a good challenge." He raised an eyebrow, clearly enjoying the thought of the station's branding splashing across TikTok. "I've got the perfect track for it."

Pulling out his phone, Pete notice Abdul type the name of a song into Spotify and the chords of O-Zone's Dragostea Din Tei started blaring from his speakers. Pete blinked, feeling the absurdity of it all wash over him. The track, a flash-in-the-pan pop hit from nearly two decades ago, had somehow made its way into the current social media zeitgeist. It seemed like a fitting anthem for the world Pete now found himself in—nostalgic, tacky, and somehow still embraced as fresh and viral.

"Ma-ia-hii, ma-ia-huu," Liam, James, Lyra, Al, Tina and Cody all chimed in, singing along with exaggerated enthusiasm. It was like they'd all swallowed the corporate Kool-Aid, effortlessly slipping into the rhythm of the moment, as though the 'hits' of yesterday were somehow still cool and relevant today because they could be packaged into a viral meme. Pete's head spun a little, trying to reconcile the spectacle around him with the radio station he thought he understood.

"Alo, salut, sunt eu un haiduc," James continued while everyone else had stopped, and the others erupted into laughter, clapping and cheering him on. Pete couldn't help but chuckle at his son's enthusiasm, even if it felt surreal. It was a bizarre mix of old and new—a room full of young radio presenters singing a song Pete remembered from his own early days in radio, but now, it was a kitschy anthem of the TikTok generation.

"How do you know-wait, let me guess," Pete said, sighing, "Part of your set lists at the Student Union gigs?"

James grinned, nodding with pride. "You got it, Dad. Throwback tracks like this go down a treat with the crowd! We mix it in with newer stuff, and it's always a winner." He shot a quick glance at Kylie, who was clearly impressed by his little solo. "That and it gets thrown in a lot on Clubland and Stephanie Hirst dropped it on Belters the other night on Hits—so yeah, it's practically iconic now. You should see the crowd when this track comes on."

Stephanie Hirst's Belters, one of Hits Radio's Saturday night shows, had become a cornerstone of mainstream dance music programming. Pete knew her from her independent radio days, prior to her gender transition, a talented presenter who had always been a force in the industry, but this new era, where even nostalgic pop hits were recycled for TikTok challenges and playlist placement, was something Pete hadn't fully wrapped his head around.

"I remember when she was at Radio Aire when she was 16," Pete said with a sigh. "She'd joined the overnight shows there—before all this." He waved his hand around at the chaos in the break room, half out of frustration, half out of nostalgia. "Back then, it felt like we were all part of something real. You know? Not just content machines."

"Wait, you remember when Stephanie Hirst was at Radio Aire?" Al interrupted with a laugh, clearly amused by Pete's comment. "That's ages ago, mate! Bet she was a different person back then, eh?"

"Yeah, she was," Pete said, nodding slowly, a touch of melancholy in his voice. "We all were. The industry felt different. There was more room for the real stuff, you know? Less of this... curated, hyper-polished nonsense. She even did the Top 40 countdown at one stage, you know, Hit40UK, that Capital produced and was on most the networks-GWR, Capital Radio Group, all the other big names. Back then, radio was about the music first, not about chasing the next viral trend." Pete trailed off, a sense of loss weighing on him as the younger generation of hosts continued to laugh and chat around him. He'd been in this industry for long enough to know it would change, but the speed of that change, the way everything seemed to have become a commodity—his own son included—was a lot to process.

"If my memory serves right, Manic was a ILR station in Liverpool called 'Garston's 106.2 Manic FM' at the time, similar to Key 103 in Manchester... the station that became the keystones of their national brands - Lite's Manic Radio and Bauer's Hits Radio. It's like Heart used to be Birmingham's 100.7 Heart FM, but now it's the Heart you hear across most of England." Pete shrugged, looking at the new generation around him. "Everything's connected now, streamlined and branded to within an inch of its life. Back then, every town, every city had its own flavour, you know? You could hear the difference. Garston's Manic FM didn't sound anything like Key 103 or Capital London. Each one had its quirks, its own community—it was radio for the people who lived there, not for some big data demographic."

The younger presenters exchanged glances, a mix of amusement and curiosity flickering across their faces. Pete could tell they viewed his nostalgia as something quaint, a relic from an era long past, but they humoured him, nonetheless, probably chalking it up to his "retro" status.

James broke the silence, his tone almost indulgent. "Yeah, but times change, Dad. People want things faster now, more streamlined. They want to feel like they're in on something big, not just listening to some bloke down the road. It's all about the shared experience now. Everyone, everywhere, tuning into the same vibe."

Pete sighed, nodding slowly as he listened to his son. "I get it, son. I do. I'm not against change, believe me. But sometimes it feels like we're losing the heart of it all—the individuality, the soul. It's like everything's one big playlist these days. Where's the grit, the surprises? Where's the humanity?" His words hung in the air, and for a moment, a hush fell over the break room.

James shifted on the couch, glancing at Kylie for reassurance before looking back at Pete with an empathetic smile. "It's still there, Dad. It's just different now. People like me and Kylie, we're doing it in our own way, you know? Building a brand and connecting with listeners... but in a way that makes sense for today. It doesn't have to be like it was for it to still mean something."

Al, picking up his phone again, raised an eyebrow. "Honestly, Pete, your drive show still gets all the loyal callers... oh yeah, they're stopping that today for you, aren't they? And they're depriving me of the most gorgeous-"

"Crozier, if you want Si to clothesline you again for perving on me," Lyra cut in with a sharp look, her tone a mix of warning and amusement, "keep it up." She sipped her coffee, unfazed, while Al held up his hands in mock surrender, grinning cheekily. "Anyway, he's in Dudley doing a wrestling show at the Town Hall this evening, so Al, if you want to avoid a repeat, maybe think twice before running your mouth."

Everyone burst out laughing, and Pete had to admit it was a good distraction from the heaviness that had settled over him. The room had its moments of camaraderie, even if it was a far cry from the kind he was used to. Lyra flashed Pete a knowing grin, as if to say, we're still here, some of us, fighting the good fight in our own way.

Just as Pete was starting to feel a bit more settled, Greg, his young, corporate-minded producer, strode into the break room, clipboard in hand and a headset perched around his neck. He looked around the room, taking in the scene with a mix of mild disdain and forced enthusiasm.

"Alright, everyone," Greg said, clapping his hands together to get their attention. "Hope you're all enjoying your downtime, but let's remember we've got shows to prepare for. Pete, Lyra—Network wants you both in Studio 1 in ten for a readthrough. It's 1 o'clock, so we've got 3 hours until we're live. James, your lunch is over, and Ben needs to finish the corporate induction."

The energy in the room shifted, and the presenters' laughter faded as Greg's announcement settled over them. Pete caught Lyra's eye, and she offered him a sympathetic smile, her own mood tempered by the call to action. He felt the unspoken solidarity between them, two veterans of sorts in a room buzzing with a new kind of enthusiasm, one that was more fleeting, fuelled by social media likes rather than genuine connection.

James stood up, giving Kylie a quick peck on the cheek before turning to Pete. "Catch you later, Dad. Knock it out of the park with Lyra, yeah?" His tone was upbeat, but there was an edge of awareness there—James knew, in his own way, how strange this whole setup felt to Pete.

Pete nodded, giving his son a reassuring smile. "Will do, son. Good luck with the induction."

* _ * _ * _ *

"60 seconds until segment 1," Pete heard in his headset as he adjusted his mic, the familiar weight of the headphones grounding him in the present. Across the console, Lyra was in her seat, focused but relaxed, her eyes flashing with a mix of excitement and determination. Greg stood outside the studio window, clipboard in hand, nodding approvingly as he watched them prepare for the show.

Pete could see Ben in Studio 2, preparing to do the Stoke drive with Al, and James was there too, as it was his on-air debut as a floating and co-host, giving him a chance to experience the show format in a controlled setting. The sight of James, now in his element, a part of the Manic family, was bittersweet. Pete felt a pang of pride mixed with a hint of sadness—this wasn't the radio world he'd hoped to pass on to his son, but it was the one that now existed, a machine of brand coherence and audience targeting that operated on an entirely different wavelength.

"Alright, here we go," Greg said in Pete's ear as he counted down the seconds. "And... you're live!"

Pete took a deep breath, his fingers instinctively finding the buttons and sliders on the console. The familiarity of it brought a sense of calm, a reminder that, no matter how much had changed, this was still his domain.

"Good afternoon, West Midlands! It's Pete Smith here on Midlands Manic," he said, reading the script that was on his screen, knowing that some Network writer had copied and pasted the other stations scripts and merely changed the localisations to fit the Midlands. "Here to bring you home this grey Tuesday afternoon. First, it's the news with Cody Lane."

As the news cue played, Pete leaned back, eyes momentarily drifting from the script to the scene outside the studio window. Cody's polished voice filled the airwaves with updates, crisply summarising the day's headlines. Pete barely registered the news, lost in his thoughts as he glanced sideways at Lyra, who was scribbling last-minute notes on a tablet, focused on the show ahead.

The buzz in the studio felt surreal. He could see the control room through the glass, where Greg and the production team watched everything, tapping at their screens, adjusting levels, and murmuring into their headsets. On the screen beside him, his next scripted segment blinked, waiting for his attention, a reminder of the rigidity he'd come to resent. The spontaneity of live radio, the essence he'd cherished, felt distant, buried beneath a script designed to standardise him.

"...and now back to Pete and Lyra with your drive-time essentials on Midlands Manic," Cody wrapped up his news segment, cueing them to begin.

Pete leaned forward, glancing at Lyra. She gave him a nod, and he could see a glint of mischief in her eyes—a reminder that she, like him, still found ways to sneak in those little personal touches amidst the corporate structure.

"Thanks, Cody!" Pete began, his voice smooth but carrying an edge of warmth he hoped his listeners would feel. "Right, folks, the traffic looks like its usual Tuesday mess around the M5. But not to worry, we've got some tunes lined up to make your journey bearable. And Lyra, are we sure those roadworks are ever going to end?"

She laughed, playing along seamlessly. "I reckon those cones have become permanent residents, Pete! Let's just accept them as part of the Midlands scenery now. Anyway, what would you do with half a million pounds?"

Pete noticed that the answer was "Retire and buy a place in the countryside," but as usual, he was expected to play along with the competition script. Yet, as he scanned the answer on his screen, he decided to take a small risk, hoping Greg wouldn't notice.

"Oh, half a million?" he replied with a chuckle, deviating slightly. "You know, I'd probably buy a little pub by the canal. Somewhere you can actually hear yourself think. What would you do Lyra?"

Lyra grinned, catching on to Pete's intention to take the question off-script. "A pub by the canal sounds tempting, Pete! But I think I'd buy a McLaren, a nice motor, something to speed through Spaghetti Junction when it's all clear. Maybe throw in a chauffeur so I can enjoy the views without dealing with the traffic!"

Pete knew that that was what the script said for her to answer—a flashy, aspirational response meant to appeal to the dreamers listening in. But in Lyra's hands, it came off with a wink, like she was letting the audience in on the joke. He saw a few heads in the control room shift, Greg and Ben exchanging looks as if they couldn't decide whether Pete and Lyra's deviation was a breach or an enhancement. Pete, however, felt a small spark of satisfaction, relishing the tiny rebellion. It was in these moments, however fleeting, that he could still see a sliver of the radio he loved—the kind that felt connected to the listener, not just regurgitating branded fantasies. "So, Lyra, how do you enter the £500k Money Drop?" Pete continued, glancing over at Lyra, who picked up the prompt smoothly.

"Well, it's simple, Pete!" she chimed, going full professional while giving him a small wink as if they were co-conspirators in some secret. "Just text us at 87106, with the word DROP, visit www.manicradioplays.co.uk or phone us on 0330 880 3601 for your free entry. Lines close at 3pm on Friday, so get in quick if you fancy a chance at the jackpot. Winners are picked from an entry who's listening at any of the Manic Radio stations, Manic Dance, Manic Rock, Manic Goldies, Manic Soul and Manic Metal, as it's a network-wide competition."

The mention of all the Manic sub-brands felt hollow to Pete, a reminder that this contest wasn't really for the Midlands, but for anyone in the network's wide-reaching web. The fact that the legal disclaimer was because otherwise OFCOM would clamp down on the entire Manic network for misleading listeners was another sign of how far radio had drifted from its roots. Local competitions used to be about the people in the town, a chance for a caller Pete might see at the pub to win a prize. Now, everything was stretched across regions and demographics, each entry reduced to a line in a spreadsheet, a "statistic" for Manic's brand managers to present at their next quarterly meeting.

"Calls are free, but texts and web entries are £3, and for today only, as a special offer," Pete said, continuing the promo with fake enthusiasm and manufactured excitement. "It's double entry on texts! So, if you want that extra shot at half a million, now's the time to go for it! Up now its Slim Shady himself, Eminem, with his newest track, Houdini."

As the intro of Houdini began to play, Pete felt the hollowness of the segment settle in his chest. For years, his relationship with his listeners had been genuine and unscripted, albeit with bullet points in the past few years to allow him to stay within the station's format. Now, even his words felt like borrowed phrases, crafted by someone in Liverpool who'd never set foot in the Midlands, who'd never braved the M5 on a rainy Tuesday, and who had no idea what his listeners actually wanted to hear. The audience was just a nebulous "demographic," a set of targets on a spreadsheet, and Pete was just another cog in the Manic machine, there to hit his marks and keep the numbers up.

* _ * _ * _ *

"And that's it for another drivetime," Lyra said as the clock struck 6.57pm, the end of the broadcast drawing near. She gave Pete a playful, slightly conspiratorial smile, and he returned it, grateful for her presence throughout the show. She'd injected just enough personality to make the whole experience feel a little less scripted, a little closer to the kind of radio he loved.

"Yeah, and remember that Toni's up next, and she'll be reminding you how you can win that stunning £500,000 in our network-wide Money Drop competition! Also, up next on Manic Rock," Pete said, reading the promos for the sister stations on the script, "Its a trip to the days of Van Halen, Iron Maiden, and all the classics you love with DJ Savage on the evening show, and Dr Manic is on Manic Dance with the Old Skool Club Mix, bringing you all the hits from the golden days of rave and hardcore." Pete finished the promo with a forced smile, handing over the reins to the network-controlled evening shows. "Here on Midlands Manic though, here's a bit of Calvin Harris with a throwback, 'The Girls'. See you tomorrow for the #HumpDay Drive."

Pete felt like he was going to cringe as the outro music played, signalling the end of his show. The control and personality he once had were slipping through his fingers, piece by piece, replaced with the flashy graphics and network promotions Manic demanded. As soon as the studio light went off, Pete took off his headphones with a sigh, catching Lyra's sympathetic look. She patted his shoulder, a silent gesture of solidarity, and they walked out of the studio together, leaving behind the buzzing control room where Greg and Ben were deep in conversation.

"Thanks for today, Lyra," Pete said, managing a small smile. "You kept it real in there. Made it feel a bit more like… you know, actual radio."

She chuckled softly. "Anytime, Pete. Believe me, I know exactly what you mean. There's only so much brand talk I can take too. We might be outnumbered by 'Team TikTok,' but as long as I'm here, I'll make sure we sneak a bit of the old stuff in." She winked, and Pete found himself genuinely smiling for the first time that day.

As they walked out, the sun had dipped below the horizon, casting a soft, fading light over the waterfront. Pete's gaze lingered on the shimmering canal, where the old Dudley FM studio across the water stood, a shadow of its former self under the cold, neon glow of Manic Radio's rebranding. He remembered the days when he'd leave that very building, his head filled with ideas for the next morning's show, the comfort of a familiar voice filling the quiet airwaves.

"See you tomorrow, Pete," Lyra said, giving him a wave as she headed for her car. Pete watched her go, appreciating her energy, her loyalty to the job even as the industry reshaped itself around them.

For a moment, he stood in silence by the edge of the canal, hands in his pockets, feeling the weight of everything that had changed. Then, with a heavy sigh, he turned back to his own car, the cold October wind brushing past him as he started the engine. The faint strains of Black Country Radio's late-night jazz programme floated through his speakers. He smiled. Maybe, just maybe, there was still some soul left in radio—if you knew where to look.

****

CHAPTER 3 – James
Wednesday 30th October 2024

James strolled through the campus of Wolverhampton University, earbuds in, listening to promos for Ibiza Headbangers, which he and Kylie were going to be hosting on Saturday as a pre-recorded late-night show on Manic Dance. It was just one of the multiple weekend slots he'd landed, his entry ticket into the big leagues of national radio. The energy of the track was contagious, and he found himself grinning as he mentally mapped out the show segments—his favourite EDM mixes, Kylie's throwbacks to 90s dance hits, and the carefully crafted banter Manic's production team had scripted for them.

James knew that the only material done so far was him and Kylie having recorded some links to be used as the promos, following the corporate induction he had had the previous day at the Dudley hub of Manic Radio. He had sat through a series of meetings, presentations, and brand exercises led by Ben, who, along with Greg, had made sure he understood "The Manic Way". The fact Kylie had, a year earlier, when she was recruited in exactly the same way, sat through the same induction had been a relief. She'd given him the heads-up about everything from the "brand guidelines" to the pressure to rack up social media engagement and hit certain "relatability" marks with listeners. With her encouragement, he'd managed to nod and agree through the corporate jargon, eager to impress, but he could tell his dad would have had a very different reaction to it all. Pete was all about unscripted banter and local connection, while Manic seemed obsessed with the "polished package."

"Oi, Jimmy! Heard you and Kylie went Insta official!" called out Mark, one of his course mates, with a teasing grin. "I didn't know you'd landed a slot at Manic? I was ill Monday and Louisa told me some of the Manic folks were here auditioning us for a 'new voice' for their network. Turns out they've signed up 'Jimmy Reeves'!" Mark gave a mock bow, as if James were some celebrity.

James laughed, sliding his earbuds out. "Yeah, mate, it's mad, right? One day I'm just doing the odd student radio slot, the next, its full-on Manic induction, Insta reveals, the lot. Didn't think I'd be doing all that so soon."

Mark looked impressed. "Fair play, you're on the same network as Toni Green now! Everyone listens to her evening show. And you're hosting with Kylie too? She graduated a few months ago from here, and she's a total star already. How did you manage that? She's practically Manic royalty!"

James grinned, shrugging with mock modesty. "Guess I've got the voice they're after," he said, though he knew his relationship with Kylie had been a major plus point in Manic's eyes. "Anyway, we've been dating for a couple of years in secret-"

"Wait... Louise, Martha, Scofe, get over here, seems our Jimmy's got a little story for us!" Mark called out to a few more course mates, who were passing by. They looked curious, their interest piqued as they gathered around James, who grinned, knowing he was holding court.

"Alright, alright, keep it down, yeah?" James said, smirking. "Yeah, Kylie and I have been together for a while. But, you know, with her at Manic and me still in Uni, we kept things low-key. Didn't want the hassle of people making a big deal out of it."

"So, what's it like, then?" Louisa asked, wide-eyed. "I mean, being in that world with the whole 'brand image' thing? It sounds intense!"

James shrugged, slipping back into his casual charm. "It's definitely... different. There's a whole persona they want you to live up to, even off-air. Manic's got this image— young, flashy, always on point. Kylie's been helping me get into the swing of it. But honestly? The real work's in remembering all the script lines and staying 'relatable' enough for social media. Plus, I have to keep up the 'Jimmy Reeves' brand."

"Jimmy Reeves!" Martha said, chuckling. "I knew I recognised that voice when I heard the promos on Manic Dance's Old Skool Breakfast. So, you and Kyles are the new power couple of Manic, yeah?" Martha teased, nudging him playfully. "Have you met Toni Green yet?"

James laughed, taking the teasing in stride. "Nah, haven't crossed paths with Toni yet. I know her boyfriend though. He was here the other day."

"Al Crozier? He's the guy who does Northern Vibes, right?" Mark chimed in, raising his eyebrows. "Heard he's a bit of a character."

James chuckled, nodding. "Yeah, that's one way to put it. Al's... intense. Manic loves him because he's good at sticking to the script and the brand guidelines like it's a religion. Honestly, the guy's a walking, talking promo machine. He'd probably recite the guidelines in his sleep if you asked him to."

Everyone laughed, and James continued, enjoying the attention. "It's funny though. Dad can't stand him. Says he's 'network through and through' and doesn't get what radios really about. Anyway, yeah, he's taking me and Kylie up to Liverpool Saturday."

The group looked even more intrigued, leaning in as James went on. "It's all part of the Manic routine, you know? Big weekend in Liverpool, meet the team, make some content, and, of course, film a few bits for TikTok. My first show's going to be on Saturday night too on Manic Dance."

"Ah, but is it going to be live or recorded," Scofe, a redhead who preferred her nickname to her real name, Skhopia, asked with a raised eyebrow.

"Ah, if I told you that, I'd have to kill you," James said with a wink, as he knew that the illusion of everything being live was a big part of Manic's image, even though a lot of their content, especially late-night slots, was pre-recorded. "You know how it is, with us Media Studies lot, we're always knowing what is live... and what is pre-recorded," he finished, leaving his friends in suspense, and they all chuckled knowingly.

"And will you still be allowed to do your student union sets, or are Manic clamping down on that?" Louisa asked, smirking. "Or are you too 'big time' now for our humble SU?"

James sighed, as he remembered that Kylie had to pull out of doing sets at the SU when she joined Manic. "Yeah, unfortunately, I've got to give those up. Part of the 'brand management'—they want you to keep your presence strictly on Manic. So, no more midnight sets at the SU bar." He gave a mock-sad face, which drew a sympathetic groan from the group.

"That sucks," Scofe said, shaking her head. "But hey, at least you get to do it on a national scale, right?"

"Exactly," James said, putting on a brave face. "And with Kylie there too, it's going to be epic. Besides, I've got the Ibiza Headbangers show with her now, and... well, keep it under your hats, but on Christmas Day, on Manic Dance, I'm bringing some Broad Street Bangers. Anyway, have you lot seen my new Insta?"

"Let's have a look, then!" Louisa said, pulling out her phone, and the others followed suit, eager to see James's social media makeover.

James pulled up his profile on his own phone, showing them his newly curated posts. His profile was slick, filled with polished photos from Manic's promotional shoot: him and Kylie in trendy, coordinated outfits, posed in the studio, a few shots of him in the DJ booth looking deep in concentration, and of course, the famous "Insta official" post that had garnered all the attention. Each post was captioned with hashtags like #IbizaHeadbangers, #ManicDance, and #JimmyReevesOnAir, perfectly crafted to hit the "young and edgy" vibe Manic expected.

"@ManicDanceReevesy? You went with that for your handle?" Louisa asked with a smirk. "Got to admit, it sounds pretty slick, but also a bit... what's the word? Corporate?"

James chuckled, running a hand through his hair. "Yeah, well, that's Manic for you. They're all about brand consistency. So, if I want to keep the gigs rolling in, gotta stick with what the network wants. I've got some merch in my car too if anyone needs some notebooks, pens, power banks or phone cases. They've also given me some codes for the free 1 month nBus tickets that we had a couple of years ago when we were Freshers and also some codes for 12 month Manic Prime app subscriptions."

"Wait, a free bus pass? And Manic Prime?" Louisa asked, her interest clearly piqued as she raised her eyebrows. "I could do with renewing my bus pass as I'm broke and struggling to make it to campus without shelling out on fares all the time. Since they scrapped the free shuttle for this year, it's been a pain in the neck getting here."

James grinned, reaching into his backpack and pulling out a stack of promo codes. "Consider it done, Lou! Honestly, they gave me a bunch to 'share the Manic love,' so help yourselves. And yeah, the Manic Prime app's actually pretty decent—lets you stream all the Manic channels, plus exclusive podcasts and all the network's live shows. Pretty handy if you're stuck on the bus and fancy some tunes."

The group eagerly grabbed codes from him, each one looking pleased with the unexpected freebie. As they pocketed the codes, the banter shifted back to his relationship with Kylie.

"So, this 'Insta official' thing," Mark teased, nudging him. "Does it mean you've gone, like, full-on Manic couple goals? Or are you both just playing along for the publicity?"

James hesitated for a fraction of a second before responding. "It's real, don't worry! But yeah, there's no denying the publicity boost doesn't hurt. Manic love a good story— 'couple conquering the airwaves together' and all that. But we're solid, you know? We've been shagging for ages, and put it this way, she isn't just my girlfriend, she's my partner in all this Manic stuff too," James finished with a grin, brushing off the laughs from his friends. "She's got my back."

Mark leaned in with a cheeky grin. "So, how's it feel, mate? Like, going from DJ sets at the SU to full-on branded, national shows with a 'showbiz' girlfriend? You two are basically the Beckhams of Manic Radio now."

James chuckled, shaking his head. "Alright, let's not get carried away. It's not all glamorous. There's a ton of branding rules—like, don't even think about veering off script, and that ripped jeans, hoodies and band t-shirts are the order of the day."

"That fits you mate," Mark said with a grin, as James often wore band t-shirts, stuff like Kasabian, Arctic Monkeys, and The 1975 even before he joined Manic two days earlier. "You love your rock brands, so you fit right in. Have they put a photo of you on the Manic site?"

James loaded the Manic website and went to the Dance part, before showing the presenters page to his friends.

"Here you go," James said, pointing to the page. "They've got the usual 'Meet Our Presenters' section. Look at this one," he tapped on a picture of himself, taken during a promo shoot at the Manic studio. It was one of him in the Kaiser Chiefs t-shirt he'd picked up at a festival the summer before, standing in front of a backdrop with Manic Dance's signature neon colours. The shot was intentionally casual, but his pose—leaning against the DJ booth with a knowing smirk—gave off a vibe that screamed confident, ready-for-the-big-time, but still accessible.

"Jimmy Reeves, Manic's hottest new hunk, bringing you the Ibiza Headbangers every Saturday night!" Louisa teased, giving him an exaggerated wink. "Is this what they've been training you for, mate? You've got the look down. Next stop, national icon. Do you know the promos yet?"

"You mean the 'Get your phones out, as I'm going to tell you how to enter the £500k Money Drop' stuff?" James replied with a grin, "Yeah. You know I actually made my debut yesterday on Manic, right?"

"Wait, you were already on air?" Louisa asked, her eyes wide with surprise. "And here I thought you were just getting the lay of the land!"

James grinned, feeling a rush of pride. "Yeah, I did a little bit on the Stoke Drive show with Al Crozier. They wanted to get me on air to introduce me to listeners, kind of like a test run. It was just a few segments, but I got to throw in a bit of banter and do some of the competition promos. Nothing big, but it was cool to see how it all works behind the scenes. It's on the app if you want to hear it."

"Wait, so you're already doing live bits and the Money Drop promos?" Mark said, looking impressed. "That's actually big. They're really pushing you fast, huh?"

"Yeah, no pressure or anything," James replied, laughing. "But that's Manic for you. Once you're in, they've got you doing all sorts straight away. They just need you to look and sound the part, you know? And it doesn't hurt that Kylie's already got a huge following—makes it easier for me to ride that wave a bit."

Martha leaned in, smirking. "So, what's it like working with Al, then? He's got a bit of a reputation. We've all heard the stories."

James rolled his eyes but smiled. "Al's... something, alright. He's all about the brand, hitting the marks, sounding flawless on air. I mean, he's got charisma, no doubt. But off-air? He's as much a 'character' as they say, especially when he's talking about his weekend plans. Still, he knows what he's doing, so I'm learning from him. You know he's a Stoke Uni grad, but he was born... in Barking... which is why he sounds like he's come from the Capital Radio School of Presenters. He was brought up on Capital from birth and has aims of getting a national show on there someday. But for now, he's got his sights set on making a name with Manic, and honestly, the guy has a following. People tune in just for him, even if he's a bit... intense."

Scofe snickered. "Intense? So, he's the 'work hard, party harder' type, then?"

James nodded, chuckling. "That's putting it mildly. Al has no problem fitting the whole 'work hard, party harder' image, that's for sure. Manic seems to love it though—he's got this persona that really clicks with the whole 'live fast, laugh louder' vibe they want. And I have to give it to him, he's relentless when it comes to prepping. He's in the studio early, rehearsing everything down to the last detail. He's serious about getting to the top. There again, banging Toni doesn't harm his chances. You know his last girlfriend was a Hits Radio producer?"

"Oh, Al's got that side to him too, has he?" Louisa raised an eyebrow, amused. "Guess that explains the confidence! But seriously, James, this sounds wild. You're right in the middle of all this radio drama and on your way up. Does your dad know what you're getting into?"

James smirked, shrugging casually. "Yeah, Dad knows, and you can imagine he has his opinions. He's old school, thinks radio should be about the listeners, the local feel, not all this social media and brand focus. He's been at Manic Midlands forever and says he hardly recognises it these days. But he's supportive... mostly. Thinks I'm getting caught up in all the 'fancy marketing'—that's what he calls it. He reckons they're more interested in 'image' than radio. Thing is, we all know radio has adapted, and if stations don't move with the times, then they'll get left behind. Look at how Bauer adapted Free Radio when they brought them off Orion, and now it's Hits Radio. There's no room for local radio, and our lecturers know it."

"Yeah, to be fair, it's all about the hits and quick, catchy content now," Scofe finished, nodding. "Our lecturers talk about 'engagement metrics' all the time—keeping listeners hooked so they don't flip to streaming instead. Radio's got to keep up, or it'll be outpaced. Just like that local TV experiment, how they were losing viewers to YouTube and Netflix because they couldn't hold onto their audiences."

James nodded, feeling the weight of that reality. "Exactly. Dad's got this idealistic view of radio, like it was back in the day when every show had a local touch, and every presenter knew the community. You know, a couple of weeks ago, he was going on about how he and Jezza Kyle was on competing stations, Dad on Dudley FM and Kyle on BRMB."

"Let me guess," Scofe said with a grin, "Pete was all about Dudley pride, while Kyle was probably stirring up drama even back then?"

James laughed, nodding. "Pretty much! Dad loved the community vibe, taking calls from locals who'd chat about everything from lost pets to pub football scores. Kyle, though, was already pushing the envelope, more about shock and stirring things up. Then he went on about some Torrington bloke who played sappy love songs at night on Beacon."

Louisa chuckled. "Oh, that Late Night Love? My Mum talks about that show and how it's on some obscure internet station now, playing the same cheesy love songs and dedicating them to couples who've been together for decades. She used to listen to it every night—said it was the kind of radio you don't get anymore. Real people, real stories, none of the fluff we get now."

James couldn't help but smirk. "Yeah, well, that's exactly what Dad misses. To him, radio was this... community thing, not just a bunch of polished playlists and endless promotions. But Manic's changed, the world's changed, and he just doesn't see that nostalgia doesn't pay the bills. If I'm honest, that kind of radio feels like... ancient history now."

Scofe nudged him, smirking. "So does that mean no chance of Jimmy Reeves doing a 'Late Night Love' segment, huh?"

James laughed, holding up his hands in surrender. "Not unless Manic's brand managers have a change of heart! They want high-energy, 'always on' vibes, and that's what I'm here to bring. Though, if we hit it big with the Ibiza Headbangers show, maybe I'll sneak in a slow track or two. Could be a good laugh!"

The group burst into laughter, clearly imagining James sneaking in some soulful ballads between the high-octane dance tracks.

"Alright, Mr. Manic Dance Star," Louisa said, rolling her eyes with a grin, "don't forget us when you're all famous. And keep those promo codes coming!"

James chuckled, his confidence growing with each laugh from his friends. The Manic world was intense, full of expectations and branding guidelines, but moments like these reminded him of why he wanted to be in radio. It was fast-paced, a bit chaotic, and yes, a little scripted, but he was on his way.

* _ * _ * _ *

James opened the door of Kylie's Great Bridge flat, a small one-bedroom flat above a barbers. It was half five in the evening, and having drove to the flat after leaving campus, James felt a strange sense of calm, knowing he could relax with Kylie before they both jumped back into the whirlwind of the Manic Radio world.

"Hey, babe!" Kylie called from the kitchen, where she was busy making tea. She was dressed down in joggers and a cropped hoodie, looking a world away from the polished, on-air persona she maintained. Seeing her like this, just Kylie without the Manic gloss, made him smile.

"Hey," James replied, leaning against the kitchen counter as she poured hot water into the mugs. "Crazy day at uni. Everyone was grilling me about the whole 'Jimmy Reeves' thing, asking if I'd met Toni, and of course, the usual stuff about Al."

Kylie chuckled, handing him a mug. "Let me guess—some were curious, some were just nosy, and a few were probably hoping for free merch."

James laughed, nodding. "Pretty much! I'm all out of the Uni Essentials Packs they gave us when we were Freshers, which they gave me filled with the usual giveaways like Manic pens, notebooks, and the free nBus passes. Honestly, it's like I'm already doing Manic's marketing on campus."

Kylie rolled her eyes, smiling as she took a sip of her tea. "Just like last year when I was at Uni in my final year and joined Manic. They had me handing out those merch packs to every fresher and giving out Manic Prime download codes. I felt like a walking billboard!" She chuckled, nudging him playfully.

James grinned, feeling a shared understanding with her. "Guess that's the price we pay for being part of the Manic brand. But, you know, I kind of love it. You know they've already been airing the promos we recorded yesterday for the Headbangers, even though we've not got the show in the can?"

Kylie laughed, shaking her head in amused disbelief. "Classic Manic! They're all about the hype. As long as the promos are hitting the airwaves, they don't care if the actual show isn't ready. Keeps people talking, I suppose."

James took a sip of his tea, feeling the warmth spread through him. "Yeah, I've got to admit, it's exciting. Everyone at Uni was buzzing about it today. You know some of the lads think we're live on Saturday?"

Kylie grinned, leaning back against the counter. "Let them think that! It's all part of the mystery, right? They don't need to know it's pre-recorded. Besides, it makes us sound like we're in the studio every minute of the day, living that 'always on' vibe Manic's obsessed with."

James chuckled, nodding in agreement. "I guess you're right. Keeps the brand fresh and the hype alive. Even my mates were going on about the 'Ibiza Headbangers' like it's some groundbreaking thing. There again, if it gets listeners away from Hits or Capital, then it's a win for Manic. Plus, word of mouth for uni students is like a goldmine for Manic. If they think they're getting an exclusive, even if it's all part of the brand's image, they'll be tuning in just to see what all the fuss is about."

Kylie laughed, setting her tea down and giving him a playful nudge. "Exactly! Manic knows what they're doing—create a bit of mystique, make everyone think it's live, and suddenly everyone's talking about it. You'll be the campus celeb by Monday!"

James grinned, feeling a rush of pride and excitement. The world of Manic Radio was fast-paced, relentless, and full of expectations, but he was starting to understand how to play the game, and with Kylie by his side, he felt ready for whatever came next. They were the new wave, the polished faces of national radio, and together, they were about to make their mark.

"Anyway, I told Dad I'm crashing here tonight, babes. Fancy a Balti for tea, order in from that one in Carter's Green opposite the clock?"

"Hell yeah, sounds like a plan," Kylie replied, her eyes lighting up at the mention of their favourite curry spot. She moved over to grab her phone, scrolling through the menu with a practised familiarity. "You know, the guy behind the counter there has a brother who runs an offie, and he said if you mention his name, he'll give you some money off whatever booze you buy with your order. He recognises us now since we're in there so often!" She flashed him a cheeky grin, making James laugh.

"Freebies for the 'power couple'—the perks of small-town fame!" James joked, leaning over her shoulder to look at the menu. "I'll get a lamb Balti, extra spice, and we can split a naan. And maybe a few beers to go with it?"

Kylie nodded, tapping her phone to place the order. "Sounds perfect. And hey, if we're going to be the Manic Dance 'power couple,' we might as well treat ourselves now and then, right?"

As they waited for the food, they settled onto the sofa, flipping through the latest social media posts and putting some Clubland, a television channel which broadcasted classic dance anthems, on in the background. The pulsing beats of Clubland's throwback hits filled the room, adding to the relaxed, almost celebratory vibe of the evening. For James, this was the perfect balance: the world of Manic Radio with all its gloss and hustle was exciting, but here, with Kylie, he could enjoy it without the pressure. Just two young people riding the wave of early success, together.

"Ben said to send him an email with what tracks you fancy for the show on Saturday and he'll get Network to give the thumbs-up," Kylie said as she grabbed James's car keys that he'd left in his jacket and put them on the key rack. "I've gone for the usual suspects: Faithless, The Chemical Brothers, and a bit of Darude, because, you know, classic Ibiza vibes. What about you, babe?"

James nodded, leaning back on the sofa, thinking through his set ideas. "Nice. I was thinking some Armin van Buuren, maybe some newer stuff from Calvin Harris to mix it up, and... oh! Gotta have Tiesto in there. Keeps it high-energy, and the listeners will recognise it right away. A bit of Sunchyme and a dash of Satisfaction, the usual bangers, maybe some Blackstreet, some Kernkraft for that retro vibe. A bit of Eminem's deep cuts, like "Without Me" to add a slight edge, and we should throw in a remix of "Insomnia" to keep everyone tuned in. Might listen to last week's Stephanie Hirst's Belters to see what else we can add. There also a few new mixes that are coming of some of RAYE and Dua Lipa's stuff, and a Gwen Stefani/Dua mashup of Physical that's been out a couple of years but isn't getting much airtime in the clubs. And... well, I was thinking that Pete Tong version of Galvanize, Your Love (9PM), Dua's Houdini (Danny L Harle 'slowride' mix) and a bit of Fatboy Slim to round it off."

Kylie nodded with approval, eyes lighting up as James rattled off his list. "Oh yeah, I can definitely see those going down a treat. And if we're pulling the club crowd in, a couple of those Pete Tong reworks will keep them hooked for sure. Plus, if we end on something like Fatboy Slim, it gives the whole show a bit of that classic feel, even with all the newer stuff mixed in. You're thinking like a pro already, Reevesy!" She nudged him with a smile, clearly impressed.

James laughed, enjoying the thrill of planning his first major show. "Well, you're not the only one who knows how to bring the hype! I want this show to feel like a proper night out—high energy, but with some of those nostalgic bangers that keep everyone hooked. And let's be honest, if I'm gonna make a name, might as well start by putting together a killer playlist."

Kylie grinned. "Anyway, Ben says we've got three shows to record Saturday, and then Al's picking us up for Liverpool."

James grinned, as he knew it was all voice-tracked pre-recorded content, but he was eager to bring the same energy as if it were live. "Three shows, huh? Busy day, but it's worth it. And Liverpool with Al... well, that should be interesting." He chuckled, already predicting the "intense" Al experience.

Kylie laughed, rolling her eyes. "Oh, you know Al'll have it all planned to perfection. He'll probably give us a rundown on everything from what to post on socials to how to 'maximize audience engagement' with each promo we do. He takes his brand so seriously it's like he's on-air 24/7. He's got some blow for the after-party at Toni's, and babes, if you fancy drilling some of Toni's Hits mates or Toni herself while we're at her flat, consider it a hall pass. I think I might let Al and you spit roast me too."

James laughed, trying to take it all in stride as he put his arm around Kylie. "Al's something else, that's for sure. Just hope he doesn't overdo it with the 'maximize engagement' talk. And a hall pass, eh? You sure, babes? I mean, we've been together two years, even though we only went Insta official yesterday, and you sure you don't mind me fucking another girl if it's all part of the night out?"

Kylie shrugged with a playful smile. "Babe, we're both in this wild industry now. A bit of fun won't change that we're solid. Besides, this weekend is supposed to be memorable. Let's just enjoy the ride, yeah?"

James nodded, feeling a mix of excitement and surprise at how open Kylie was about the whole thing. It felt like they were truly diving into the world of high-energy radio, where boundaries blurred, and life became a bit of a show itself.

@ManicDanceReevesy: *Balti, naan and a bit of Clubland with my girl @KylieMorganBrekkie—perfect way to unwind after a busy day! Let the prep for @ManicDance #IbizaHeadbangers begin! #CoupleGoals #ManicDance #JimmyAndKylie*

James posted on his Instagram feed, a photo of the two of them snuggled together with the containers of their Balti spread out in front of them, capturing the cozy, yet vibrant vibe of their evening in. Within minutes, notifications started popping up, likes and comments from friends, fellow presenters, and even a few fans who'd stumbled across his account after the big Insta reveal the previous day.

"Nice, Reevesy, looks like people are loving it!" Kylie grinned, scrolling through the comments on his post. "You're practically a pro at this already."

James chuckled, shaking his head as he watched the numbers climb. "Guess I am! I mean, it's strange, though, isn't it? Like, all we're doing is having dinner, but it's suddenly 'content' now. I suppose that's just how it works in the 'Manic Way,' right?"

Kylie shrugged with a smile, reaching for a piece of naan. "Exactly. You've got to show people a bit of everything— behind the scenes, the laughs, even the down-to-earth moments. Makes you feel more 'real' to them. It's what keeps them tuning in. But don't worry," she added, leaning in to kiss him on the cheek, "we've still got our little moments too, just for us."

James smiled, appreciating the balance Kylie seemed to have mastered between on-air personality and real life. They were partners, not just in the flashy world of Manic, but here, in the quiet moments too. He felt lucky, knowing they could navigate this crazy world together.

They settled back, letting Clubland's beats fade into the background as they savoured the meal and unwound from the day's excitement. The journey ahead was bound to be intense, filled with challenges, late-night shows, and endless promos, but for now, James felt ready. With Kylie beside him and the bright lights of Manic Radio on the horizon, he knew they had a chance at making something unforgettable—both on-air and off.

****

CHAPTER 4 – Unexpected Visitors in the Early Morning
Wednesday 30th October 2024

Pete sat up in bed, his senses on high alert as he heard the unmistakable sounds of Chloe's giggles and someone else's muffled voice filtering through from the hallway. He rubbed his eyes, trying to shake off the grogginess as he glanced at the alarm clock beside him—1:02 a.m. He wasn't expecting Chloe home at this time in the morning.

He slipped out of bed, his footsteps quiet as he crept down the hallway, just close enough to catch snippets of their conversation.

"Shhh! If Dad hears us, he'll be straight out here, thinking you're a burglar or something!" Chloe whispered, failing miserably to suppress another burst of laughter.

"Oh, right," the other voice replied, a male voice, low and with a hint of nervousness. "Didn't realise I was going to be dodging security at this hour."

Pete's eyebrows shot up, recognising the voice instantly as Cody Lane, one of three news presenters at Manic Midlands. Cody Lane, known for his cheeky charm and quick wit on air, was the last person Pete expected to find sneaking into his house at this hour, let alone in the company of his daughter, Chloe.

"You know, Cody, I really need your cock in me," Chloe giggled, the 19 year old and the 24 year old advancing up the stairs, clearly underestimating how far their voices could travel in the quiet of the early hours. Pete felt a mixture of disbelief and irritation. He'd always been a protective dad, and hearing his daughter bring home one of his colleagues—someone barely five years older than her, no less—wasn't exactly what he'd predicted for a peaceful night.

Pete noticed that Chloe was wearing a micro dress, the bottom not even covering her. fully, and he felt his irritation rising further. He cleared his throat loudly, stepping into the hallway with his arms crossed, catching them both off guard.

"Chloe. Cody," he said in a voice that was calm but laced with a hint of disapproval. "Mind telling me what you're doing here at this hour?"

Chloe froze, her face flushed with a mix of embarrassment and surprise. "Dad! I didn't think... well, I wasn't expecting you to be awake, especially with James being out."

Pete raised an eyebrow, glancing between the two of them. "Doesn't matter whether I'm awake or not, does it? You still brought home a... guest in the early hours. Care to explain?"

Cody, ever the quick-witted newsreader, tried to muster a confident grin, though it came out more sheepish than charming. "Hey, Pete. Chloe and I just thought... well, I was escorting her home."

"Escorting her home, eh?" Pete folded his arms, looking Cody up and down with a sceptical expression. "Seems like quite the escort service to me, considering it's well past midnight, and you're sneaking in like it's some undercover operation."

Chloe, clearly embarrassed but not quite ready to give up her defiant streak, rolled her eyes. "Dad, relax. It's not that big of a deal. We were just... hanging out, and I missed the last X10 to Mezza, and the last 9 to Stourbridge, so Cody offered to give me a lift. That's all," she finished, but the sheepish glance she shot Cody betrayed that it wasn't just an innocent lift home. Pete sighed, pinching the bridge of his nose as he took a moment to gather his thoughts.

"Right, and the next step after this 'lift' was to sneak past me, was it?" Pete replied, his tone now carrying a hint of the parental disappointment that had made even James think twice about his actions. He looked at Cody, who was doing his best to avoid Pete's gaze, and then back to Chloe. "And, Cody, I'm sure you realise that this isn't exactly... standard protocol when it comes to giving a colleague's daughter a ride home."

"Dad, it's not like James is here... he's probably fucking his girlfriend to some corporate-approved playlist on Manic Dance. Now, if you'll excuse me, I need Cody's cock to fill me as I'm fucking horny and we haven't shagged in a month as his flatmate's mum's moved in and taken over the place," Chloe shot back, her voice filled with defiance but tinged with embarrassment. "She's a bloody Catholic who believes anything less than celibacy until marriage is some sort of mortal sin."

Pete noticed as Cody moved closer to Chloe, his left hand reaching down to the bottom of her skirt. That was enough for Pete.

"Alright, that's it," Pete interjected, his voice firm and no-nonsense. "Cody, you've got two options: either make yourself scarce and leave, or we have a very uncomfortable chat here in the hallway."

"No, Dad," Chloe said assertively. "I pay board, so if I want to bring someone home, that's my choice. Cody's my guest, and we weren't exactly expecting an interrogation. I'm an adult, Dad, not some kid sneaking around."

As she said that, a small bag fell out of her clutch bag, and Pete knew instantly, based on the high-energy work environment, and "party" culture that had seeped into Manic, that it was a certain Class A drug named Cocaine.

"What's that doing in my house, Chloe?" Pete's voice grew colder, his gaze fixating on the small bag of white powder now lying on the carpet. "Since when did my house become part of this Manic 'party culture'?"

Chloe's defiance wavered as she saw the anger in her father's eyes, a flash of guilt crossing her face. "Dad… it's… it's not a big deal, alright? It's just a bit for fun. Zara at Uni got if for me. It's only a sample amount anyway."

Pete knew, however, that it was more like a full gram and that it was enough to keep her going through the night. He took a deep breath, struggling to keep his composure. This was a side of Chloe he hadn't fully seen before, a side shaped by the pressures of university life, the influences around her, and possibly the changing culture of radio that he'd always felt sceptical about.

"Chloe," he said, his tone firmer, "this isn't what I raised you for. I know you're independent, I know you're an adult, but bringing drugs into my house? That's where I draw the line."

Chloe, however, snorted. "Yeah, whatever. Anyway, you know James'll be on it soon enough, right? Cody told me that Liam will hook him up on Saturday when that annoying brother of mine and his girlfriend record their Ibiza Headbangers show at the studio. I mean, seriously, Dad, everyone at Uni for me, and Manic for James, does it. It's not the 90s when you smoked 20 a day in Marlboros, Chesterfields and Bensons, and then went out for a pint after your shift." Chloe rolled her eyes, her words laced with sarcasm, dismissing the seriousness of the situation as she scoffed. "It's just what people do now. It's not some big deal. Anyway, I'm going to my room for a bit of Charlie and a few Players, and Cody's coming with me."

Pete's jaw clenched as he watched his daughter brush past him with a flippant disregard that stung worse than any insult. She was right about one thing—it wasn't the 90s anymore. But that didn't mean he had to stand by and watch his daughter join her uni pals fall into the party-all-night culture that some universities seemed to cultivate. The fact that James was likely to fall into the same culture at Manic, and could soon be heading down a similar path, only made the moment more bitter. Pete's children seemed to be swept up in a world he no longer recognised—a world where authenticity was secondary to image, and indulgence was just part of the "brand."

He exhaled, struggling to shake off the mounting frustration as he watched Chloe and Cody retreat down the hallway, their hushed giggles fading as they disappeared into her room. For a moment, Pete just stood there, the weight of the situation pressing down on him. The home he'd tried to create as a sanctuary from the pressures of work and the world outside now felt invaded by the very culture he was railing against at Manic—a culture that valued the facade of excitement over real connection, and distraction over responsibility.

Turning back to his own room, Pete lay down, but sleep didn't come easily. Thoughts of his children—each entangled in their own version of this flashy, "modern" world—kept his mind racing. James, with his brand-building, scripted banter, and Kylie, with their carefully curated social media presence; Chloe, embracing the fast-paced party culture of university life. And him—Pete—caught somewhere between the relics of an era long past and the shiny allure of the present, trying to make sense of it all.

* _ * _ * _ *

"...smoked a few Players and got that high," Pete heard Cody say as he walked into the break room at the Dudley Hub later that morning. Pete was nursing his usual tea, trying to shake off the sleepless night and his frustration with Chloe. But as he caught the tail end of Cody's boast to Al and Liam about the previous night, his irritation flared anew. Cody leaned back in his chair, grinning as he recounted his antics, clearly unaware of the discomfort etched on Pete's face.

"Fucking hell mate, no wonder you're chipper," Liam said with a grin as he raised his takeaway coffee cup in a mock toast to Cody. "Night like that on a Wednesday? Guess some of us have all the fun!"

Al smirked, leaning in with that familiar air of mischief. "Careful, Cody, wouldn't want the old guard here"—he nodded towards Pete—"thinking we're all about late-night 'extracurriculars.' Gotta keep the brand squeaky clean, yeah? Anyway, after we go to the bathroom, can we go smoke a cigarette? I really need one..."

"But first, let me take a selfie!" Most of the presenters, PR and producers who were gathered in the break room erupted in laughter as Al struck a pose, holding his phone up high with an exaggerated pout. Pete knew it was the lyrics to a song by The Chainsmokers called "Selfie," the one that had become an anthem for the selfie-obsessed, brand-driven culture that had seeped into the very fabric of Manic Radio. Pete felt a sinking sensation in his chest.

He wasn't just tired from the sleepless night, or angry at Chloe. He was exhausted by the sheer weight of the cultural shift he was seeing, not just within his family but in the industry he'd once loved. A world where spontaneity and authenticity were being replaced with calculated poses, curated images, and endless branding.

"Anyway, old man," Liam said, grinning. "Isn't it nap time for the over 50s?"

"Nah, Li, it's pensioners specials down at the Brierley Hop House, so the old man can get his cup of tea and discount lunch," Al chimed in, laughing as he leaned back, clearly relishing the banter. "He's only got 16 years till he gets his old fart pension and granny bus pass. Anyway, Li, thought you were just doing your usual Mid Wales Breakfast."

"Nah, I'm covering the network 1pm slot too, my national debut, so I've got half hour before it's due to air," Liam said, glancing at the time with a smug grin. "Kyle is off so Sue's live from Speke and I'm remoting into the network part to be the second half of the show. Big day for me, mate. Anyway, I've got some stuff in my car you, Cody and Ben'll love. Fresh in from my supplier. I'm sure, Al, you'll need a pick me up for Drive... and when I see Morgan tomorrow, I'll give her a few baggies for Reevesy. Has he and Morgan said they're doing Liverpool, Al?"

"Yeah, mate, they're in. You know, I can't believe she pulled a sickie and didn't come in for hers and Tina's breakfast show. Anyway, I make it half 12, mate, so you've got half hour till your second show. I'll take a dozen bags of whatever you've got, mate," Al replied with a sly grin, glancing around to make sure no one outside their circle was listening. "Better be the good stuff, mind you. Gotta keep that energy up for Drive time." He laughed, as if they were talking about nothing more than extra coffees or energy drinks.

"Good, good. Lane, you need any top ups?"

"Yeah, I've only got £50 though and we don't get paid tomorrow, so any chance you could put some on tab, mate? I'm heading to Clo's again, and Reevesy and

Morgan'll be there, so we're going to get shit faced right under Pete's nose."

Pete's blood ran cold as he heard Cody's last words, the casual tone in which he spoke about sneaking around and getting drunk under Pete's roof sending a wave of disgust through him. He'd had enough. His hand clenched into a fist, but he forced himself to exhale, keeping his composure—just barely. The whole conversation felt like a sickening joke, as if these young presenters had forgotten entirely about responsibility, about the trust they should have as professionals, and about respect for the older generation, their families, and themselves.

Pete didn't speak at once, but the silence in the break room thickened as he walked in, his presence at once commanding attention. Al, Liam, and Cody froze mid-laugh, the easy banter of moments before vanishing as they registered Pete's expression. He wasn't in the mood for jokes, and they could all see it.

"Cody," Pete said, his voice low and measured. "You-"

"I what, old man? Chloe invited me, and as he said last night, she pays board, and her brother's entitled to bring people over too. So, don't go all Dad mode on me, alright?" Cody's tone was defiant, though there was a hint of caution as he looked up at Pete, likely recognising that he'd pushed too far.

Pete took a slow, steadying breath, trying to hold back his growing anger. He could feel the tension in the room thickening as Al, Liam, and the others watched, caught off guard by Pete's reaction.

"Let me make one thing very clear," Pete began, his voice calm but unmistakably firm. "What you choose to do with your time outside of work is your business. But when it involves my family and my home, that's where it stops being just a bit of 'fun.' You think this is all a game—sneaking around, late-night antics, and dodging responsibility? Maybe that flies elsewhere, but it doesn't fly with me."

Cody shifted uncomfortably, his usual bravado faltering slightly under Pete's stare. He glanced at Liam and Al for backup, but neither seemed eager to jump to his defence. Al was already scrolling on his phone, looking for any distraction from Pete's glare.

"Pete," Cody began, his tone slightly more restrained, "it's just... Look, we didn't mean any harm. Chloe's an adult, and it's not like we're causing any real trouble."

"Not causing any trouble?" Pete scoffed, crossing his arms as he fixed Cody with a stern look. "You bring drugs into my house, disrespect my family, and then treat it all like some late-night laugh? Do you even understand what respect is?"

"Disrespect? Man, do you even know why Chloe does those syndicated CHR community radio shows?" Cody said, chuckling. "It's because you're an overbearing old man who still thinks the world revolves around 'genuine radio' or whatever. She does them so she can get noticed by Manic, Bauer and Global, where people actually get ahead, not like you, stuck in some outdated fantasy about what radio used to be. No one cares about the 'good old days' anymore, Pete. Not Chloe, not James, not even most of the listeners you're holding onto."

Pete's face hardened, and he took a step closer, his voice a low, dangerous whisper. "You think you know it all, don't you, Cody? Think you're some hotshot because you can keep up with the latest trends, and Chloe's falling for it because she doesn't know better."

"She knows more than you think, mate," Cody said, grinning. "She understands why stations like Capital, Manic and Hits are popular. They're not about nostalgia or some half-baked idea of 'community spirit'; they're about giving listeners what they actually want—quick hits, excitement, energy. People tune in because it's all happening fast, and it's all on-brand. Meanwhile, you're clinging onto some outdated notion of radio as if it's the 90s, like some relic stuck in the past."

Pete's eyes narrowed, his jaw set. He didn't have time for lectures from someone who barely understood what true connection meant in radio, the very foundation he had built his career on. "You think this 'excitement'—this overblown, brand-heavy act—is the real heart of radio? Let me tell you something, Cody, back when radio had meaning, it wasn't about 'hitting the trends.' It was about serving the people who listened, about genuinely connecting with them. What you're doing? It's just... shallow."

Cody rolled his eyes, a smirk tugging at the corners of his mouth. "Look, Pete, if this is about me and Chloe, just say so. We both know you're just upset because the world moved on, and you didn't. Everyone's got to change with the times."

"No, Cody," Pete shot back, his voice carrying the weight of years spent behind a microphone. "This isn't just about change. It's about respect—respect for yourself, for your work, for your listeners, and, yes, for the people who came before you. You want to make radio your own? Fine. But don't act like you're above it all just because you're playing the Manic game. That game? It's not everything."

The room fell silent, the tension thick. Liam, shifting in his seat, glanced from Cody to Pete, clearly uncomfortable. Al, usually quick with a witty comment, simply looked down at his phone, unwilling to meet Pete's gaze.

Without waiting for a response, Pete turned on his heel and walked out of the break room, his shoulders tense, his mind buzzing. He was tired of the flashiness, the shallow pretences that now filled the industry he'd loved for so long. It wasn't just about changing times or adapting to new trends. It was about holding onto what made radio real—something these kids, with their cocaine-fuelled nights and image-driven antics, seemed to have forgotten.

* _ * _ * _ *

Pete was lying in bed with Sarah, trying to watch a Mel Gibson film called On the Line, an ironic choice as the film was set in a radio station in which host takes a call, where an unknown person threatens to kill the showman's entire family on air. To save loved ones, the radio host will have to play a survival game and the only way to win is to find out the identity of the criminal.

The sound of Chloe and Cody, along with James and Kylie, all in Chloe's room, the various sounds of sex, club music and sporadic laughter seeped through the walls. Pete clenched his jaw, his frustration mounting as he tried to ignore the raucous noise coming from his daughter's room. It felt like a mockery of everything he'd tried to uphold in his home—a sense of stability, respect, and responsibility. Instead, his house had become the centre of a party atmosphere that mirrored the superficial values he fought against at Manic Radio.

"Fuck, Jimmy, pound my arse!" Kylie's voice came through the walls, muffled but unmistakable, as laughter and music mixed into a chaotic backdrop. Pete felt his temples pulse, his patience worn thin by the continued reminders of just how much things had shifted in his family. He glanced over at Sarah, who seemed as uncomfortable as he felt.

"You know Chloe's taking drugs, love?" Pete said as the film continued to play in the background, though neither of them were really watching. Sarah's eyes widened, her expression a mixture of shock and worry.

"Drugs? What… how do you know?" she whispered, glancing toward the wall as if their voices might be overheard.

Pete sighed, rubbing his forehead. "I found a bag of cocaine in her bag last night. She said it was just for fun, some 'uni thing,' but it's not just that. It's… everything. The attitude, the disrespect, the way they all treat our home like some kind of free-for-all. And at work, Liam mentioned how he was going to hook James up with drugs during their Liverpool trip this weekend. It's like everything's spiralling into this… mess of parties, drugs, and image."

Sarah's face fell, a look of deep concern darkening her features. "I don't understand, Pete. This isn't the way we raised them. How did it get to this point? They're so swept up in this… lifestyle, and it's like they're strangers in our own home."

Pete sighed, his frustration building as he looked down at his hands, feeling the weight of the situation bearing down on him. "It's this industry, Sarah. Manic, the culture—everything's just a show. Everyone's out for the next big high, the next piece of attention, and James and Chloe are just falling right into it. I try to be there, to show them there's more to life than this flash and glam, but they just see it as 'old-fashioned' or out of touch."

Sarah placed a hand on his shoulder, squeezing gently. "Pete, I know you feel responsible. But you can't carry this alone. They're adults now, or at least they think they are. We can try to talk to them, but maybe we need to look at this differently."

Pete looked over at her, his eyes weary. "Differently? What do you mean?"

"Maybe we should set some boundaries, love. Make it clear that while they're under our roof, there are expectations. And as hard as it is, we might need to give them a reality check. We can't change the culture they're in, but we can draw a line here."

A faint thud from Chloe's room pulled them both from their thoughts. Pete felt the frustration and helplessness simmering again, but Sarah's words grounded him, giving him a direction.

"Maybe you're right," he murmured, taking a deep breath. "They need to know this isn't going to be just a free-for-all, even if Manic and their friends make it seem like that's the only way to live. I'll talk to them in the morning. I just hope they're willing to listen. Fuck it... mind if I change the film, love? I can't get into this."

Suddenly the stereo from Chloe's room got louder, and Pete recognised the music coming from it as Destination Calabria, the saxophone riff blaring through the walls, mingling with the laughter and chaotic noises that had only grown louder. Pete clenched his jaw, reaching for the remote with a sigh. This was his home, yet tonight, it felt like he was the stranger here.

Sarah gave him a sympathetic smile, rubbing his shoulder. "You know, maybe we should get out for a bit tomorrow. A little break from all this... noise. Take a drive, just the two of us?"

"Can't, it's Friday tomorrow, and I've got drive-time to host. But maybe this weekend? We could head up to Shrewsbury or something, just us." Pete managed a small smile, feeling the first bit of relief all evening at the thought of some time away with Sarah.

"Sounds like a plan, love," she said softly, leaning her head on his shoulder. They sat in silence for a while, ignoring the pulsing music and chaotic sounds from

Chloe's room, each lost in their own thoughts. Pete felt a small comfort in knowing that, even amidst all the turmoil with his children, he and Sarah were on the same page. The two of them had weathered a lot together, and they'd get through this too.

Finally, the noise started to fade, and the sounds of laughter and conversation from the other room dwindled into silence as the night wore on. Pete exhaled, grateful for the quiet, even if he knew it was only temporary. Tomorrow would bring its own challenges, but tonight, at least, he could find a moment of peace with Sarah by his side.

****

CHAPTER 5 – Producer Lily
Friday 1st November 2024

Pete walked into The Waterfront, his Vauxhall being in for a service at a Brockmoor garage, it's annual MOT due just as the first of November dawned grey and misty over Dudley. As the garage had been a short walk from the area where the Manic studios were, being at the back of the Wickes' store on the Wallows, a small residential and trading estate separated Pete from his usual morning routine. The streets were quiet, with only a few delivery vans rumbling past. He sipped his takeaway coffee, feeling the familiar tug of dread mixed with duty as he headed toward the Manic Radio building. The events of the previous night weighed heavily on him, and he wasn't sure how much longer he could keep up with this corporate-driven circus.

As he entered the Manic studios, he nodded to the receptionist, who barely looked up from her phone. He wound his way down the corridor towards the break room, passing posters of Manic's branded shows—loud, bold, and brimming with the 'energy' that the audiences wanted, when he saw what he thought was a 16 year old sitting on the lap of Abdul, one of the PR managers, her arm around his shoulders and giggling in a way that felt out of place in a supposedly professional setting. Pete frowned, pausing in the hallway. This was a radio station, not a playground or, worse, some teen hangout. He approached with caution, unsure whether to step in or keep his distance.

Pete noticed she was wearing knee high socks, a short skirt, a tied up blouse and a skinny tie and her hair was styled in pigtails that gave her an even younger appearance. Pete cleared his throat, stepping closer to get Abdul's attention. "Alright, Abdul," he said, keeping his tone light but firm, "who's this, then?"

Abdul looked up, seemingly unfazed. "Oh, Pete! This is Lily, she's transferred from the Cardiff hub. She's 28 and is one of their Breakfast presenter/producers for Cardiff Vibes. Greg's off today, he's sick, so she's producing your drive show today and Jimmy's shows that he's voice-tracking tomorrow. She's got a lot of experience... trust me..."

Pete noticed that on Lily's upper lip there was some white powder residue, and his suspicions flared. He took a deep breath, pushing down his unease. The last thing he needed was to jump to conclusions, but with everything that had happened recently—his children's behaviour, the culture at Manic—he found it difficult to dismiss.

"Nice to meet you, Lily," Pete said, managing a polite nod. "Cardiff Vibes, eh? They're a bit more relaxed down there, aren't they?" He tried to keep his tone friendly, but his eyes couldn't help but linger on the powder. Lily seemed to notice and quickly wiped her nose, offering him a bright, slightly nervous smile.

"Oh yeah, we're very chill down in Cardiff," she replied, brushing off the moment with a laugh. "I'm really excited to be here, though. Manic's Midlands hub has such a… vibrant energy. Heard so much about it." Her accent had a soft Welsh lilt, and Pete had to admit, she seemed friendly enough, even if her presentation felt a bit off for a professional environment.

Abdul gave Pete a wink, oblivious to his colleague's reservations. "Lily here's a star... in more ways than one. Trust me mate, it's well worth £9.99 a month on... certain sites."

Pete blinked, momentarily taken aback by Abdul's casual remark. He knew the younger members of the Manic team were more attuned to the social media and influencer culture, but this was a new low in workplace professionalism. With the thinly veiled innuendo, it was clear that Lily's "other work" was common knowledge among some of the staff. Pete wondered, not for the first time, if anyone at Manic really cared about boundaries anymore.

"What Abdul means is you can subscribe to my OnlyFans," Lily said, unabashed, flashing a quick, cheeky grin as she adjusted her blouse with a casual nonchalance. "And see the... uncovered truth... about me."

Pete's eyebrows shot up, though he tried to keep his expression neutral. This was a world away from the radio industry he'd grown up in, where professionalism and connecting with listeners were the priorities. Now, it seemed the lines between personal branding, entertainment, and professionalism were so blurred they hardly existed.

"Right," he said, clearing his throat, choosing his words carefully. "Well, Lily, welcome to the Midlands. Hope you're ready for a, uh, different kind of energy here." He couldn't help but feel a slight pang of nostalgia for the old days—days where the biggest worry was a last-minute change to the playlist, not what your producer's online alter-ego might be.

"Looking forward to it, Pete," she replied breezily, flashing a dazzling smile that bordered on flirtatious. "I hear you're quite the legend here."

Pete managed a faint, polite smile. "Let's just say I've been around a while."

Lily turned her attention to her clipboard, all business now. "Alright, so today's show, we've got the usual drive-time fare, but Manic's pushing the £500k Money Drop hard across the network, so they want frequent mentions, about every 10 minutes. Plus, there's a new promo for Jimmy's Ibiza Headbangers show tomorrow night on Manic Dance that we're supposed to plug at least three times."

"Of course there is," Pete muttered under his breath, not thrilled at the thought of turning his drive-time show into a relentless parade of network promos.

"Anything else?" he asked, hoping there might be some real content left for his show.

Lily glanced down at her notes, tapping her pen thoughtfully. "Well, it says here that a Lyra Nott is your co-host?"

"Just for the week, gorgeous," Abdul said with a grin. "Look, Lils, head to the newsroom, would ya? Al and Liam have got some zip if you fancy some."

"Oooh, zip, eh? I could do with some as I was up all night working on a few side projects," Lily chimed with a wink, grabbing her tablet and striding off toward the newsroom without a hint of hesitation.

Pete watched her go, feeling increasingly out of place. The casual talk of drugs, OnlyFans accounts, and the lack of boundaries was miles away from what radio had once represented for him. As he walked towards his own studio, he couldn't help but reflect on how much things had changed. The "energy" Lily had referred to didn't feel like the vibrant, community-driven atmosphere he'd once cherished. Instead, it felt like a relentless pursuit of shock value and self-promotion—a culture that seemed to be rubbing off on everyone, including his own children.

* _ * _ * _ *

"Found out who our producer is," the text on James's phone from Kylie read as he sat in the Hogshead, a pub opposite the main campus of Wolverhampton University, having a quick pint before heading to another Media, Film and Television Studies lecture. It was cold, James knew, but the Manic hoodie and beanie were keeping him warm as he nursed his drink, thinking about the increasingly surreal world he was diving into at Manic. James glanced at the text from Kylie, raising an eyebrow. Their producer? He hadn't expected any changes after Greg had taken him through the induction process.

"Yeah? I thought we were doing them in Liverpool?" James responded quickly, as he thumbed out his reply and took another sip of his pint. The thought of working with a different producer was a bit surprising, especially since

Greg had been all over his induction, getting him in sync with "The Manic Way." He knew that he and Kylie were expected to have their first show polished and ready to broadcast like seasoned pros.

His phone pinged again with Kylie's reply: "Nope, for your shows tomorrow in Dudley. Greg's out sick, and they've got someone from Cardiff stepping in for us."

James frowned slightly, feeling a twinge of uncertainty. "From Cardiff?" he typed back. "Have you met her?"

"Lily Jenkins. And, yeah, met her once at the Cardiff hub last year. She's… well, she's interesting, let's say that." Kylie added a laughing emoji, then another text: "She's in the WhatsApp group you got invited to when you joined Manic, the 'Gals and Geezers' one where we post nudes and all that."

James chuckled, as he and Kylie had posted the previous night a photo of them two, Cody, and James's sister, Chloe, fucking, into the WhatsApp chat, and half the presenters from Dundee to London commented on how hot the photo was and joked about who was next to join in. The whole scene seemed surreal, but it was just one more part of the strange, unfiltered culture at Manic.

Scrolling up, James chuckled when he saw a photo of her, the 'jailbait' looks and the schoolgirl outfit making her look as if she were barely out of her teens. If anything, Lily seemed to embody the "anything goes" spirit that Manic pushed so hard. He felt a mix of excitement and apprehension, knowing that whatever Lily brought to the table, it wasn't going to be a typical professional setup.

He replied, "Oh, yeah, I've seen her posts. Didn't think she'd be the 'producing' type—more like the type to lead a wild night out!"

Kylie replied almost immediately: "Put it this way babes, she'd fuck any bloke and wear them out with her energy. Think she once joked she was born to be a 'team-building exercise' at Manic!" The message was followed by a winking emoji and a laughing one.

James snorted, downing the last of his pint. Working with someone like Lily promised to make his recording session anything but routine. Between her OnlyFans account, her unconventional persona, and the endless rumours circulating on the Manic WhatsApp group, it sounded like she'd add an extra layer of chaos to the already manic atmosphere. He wasn't sure if that was a good or bad thing.

"Sounds like she's gonna make tomorrow interesting, that's for sure," James texted back. "Hopefully, we get the tracks recorded without too many 'extras'!"

Kylie's reply was quick: "Oh, I'm sure she'll keep it professional… in her own way. Besides, we've got a brand to build. Gotta hit that balance between 'relatable' and 'wild,' right? See you later?"

James replied with a thumbs-up emoji, grabbing his bag and heading out of the pub. As he walked through campus, he thought about how much his life had shifted in such a short time—from student union DJ sets to the glittering world of Manic, the chaotic brand culture, and now working with people who saw professionalism through an entirely new lens.

* _ * _ * _ *

"She's such a slut," Lyra said to Pete as the two were getting ready. It was five minutes to four, five minutes until Lyra's stint as Pete's co-host was on the beginning of the end, and Pete, in a way, knew he'd miss the younger presenter's grounded energy and wit amidst the chaotic "youthful" atmosphere at Manic. Lyra's comment pulled him from his thoughts, and he couldn't help but chuckle a bit despite the weariness of the day.

"Yeah, Lily's definitely… something," Pete replied, adjusting his mic and looking over the show notes. "Between her 'side hustle' and the antics in the break room, I'm half-convinced we're running a reality show instead of a drive-time programme."

Lyra smirked, rolling her eyes. "At least I know I won't get roped into some TikTok dance or OnlyFans promo with you as my co-host," she teased. "God, can you imagine Greg and Abdul's faces if you started posting that kind of content?"

Pete snorted, shaking his head. "I think I'd rather walk barefoot through Dudley town centre than stoop to that level. Can you believe this is what radio's come to, though? We used to fight over playlist changes, not whether someone's outfit on-air is going to 'drive engagement' on their personal profile."

They shared a brief look, an understanding between two broadcasters who valued authenticity, though Lyra was well aware she wasn't quite the same 'old guard' as Pete. Still, she admired his dedication to real, meaningful connections with listeners—something the industry seemed to be losing rapidly.

"Look at her, she's taking selfies with her blouse even more unbuttoned and tightening her tie like it's a fashion statement rather than, well, basic professionalism," Lyra muttered, casting a quick glance out the studio window as Lily struck another exaggerated pose with her phone, her laugh carrying through the glass.

Pete shook his head, pulling himself back to the task at hand. "Alright, enough about her. We've got a show to run. Might as well give the listeners some sanity for a change."

Lyra nodded, settling into her seat. "Let's give them what they came for—a bit of normality amidst the madness." She shot him a reassuring smile as they went live.

"Good afternoon, West Midlands!" Pete began, his voice warm and welcoming, even though todays script made him look like a caricature of the very brand he often resisted. "It's Pete and Lyra here on your drive home—bringing a bit of calm to your commute... or at least, trying our best!" he added, injecting a touch of humour that Lyra knew was his way of hinting at the chaos just outside the studio walls.

Lyra picked up smoothly, her tone light but with a hint of sass. "Calm, yes—though we've got a few surprises up our sleeve, like the chance to pocket that £500,000 in the Money Drop. So, if you're feeling lucky, keep your phones handy; we'll be dropping details straight after the news with Cody Lane.

The news sting played, and Cody's polished voice took over, reading the headlines that were relevant to the 4pm slot, the start of the drive home for many West Midlands listeners. Pete took the moment to gather his thoughts, trying to ignore the buzzing phone in his pocket, no doubt a flood of messages in one of the many Manic WhatsApp groups. Pete knew that there were some that he wasn't included in which younger presenters and producers were, with some maybe more risqué than he'd care to imagine. He glanced over at Lyra, who was similarly taking a rare moment of peace as Cody's news segment continued. They exchanged a knowing look, both aware that these brief moments of reprieve were becoming increasingly scarce in the fast-paced world of Manic.

When Cody wrapped up, Pete resumed with the energy he was known for, even if he had to dig deep to bring it out. "Alright, and that was the latest from Cody Lane— keeping us up to date so you don't miss a beat on this misty November evening."

Lyra joined in, her tone warm yet playful. "And speaking of things you don't want to miss, we've got some classics coming up, plus a bit of Calvin Harris to get you through the traffic." She glanced at Pete, her expression wry. "But first, Pete, how do you enter next week's £500k Money Drop draw?"

Pete couldn't help but roll his eyes slightly at the endless plugs for the competition, though he maintained his professional tone. "Well, Lyra, all our listeners need to do is text DROP to 87106 or hop onto our website at manicradioplays.co.uk and click through to enter online. Entries cost £3, but there's also a free entry route, by calling 0330 880 3601, which is included in most phone plans. So, there's your chance, folks—£500,000 up for grabs, and with just a few taps or clicks, you could be in with a shot."

Lyra flashed a grin, seamlessly adding, "Its a network competition across all Manic Radio stations, as well as all Manic Dance, Manic Metal, Manic Goldies, Manic Rock, and Manic Soul shows—so the competition is definitely heating up! Lines close next Friday at 3pm, and Dr Manic from Manic Dance will phone one lucky winner live on-air to make their dreams come true," she concluded with the kind of enthusiasm Pete could only muster for the listeners' sake.

"OMG!" Lily said from the booth on the live feed, and Pete knew that this was a new scripted feature. "Did you hear the latest hot goss about Manic's hot couple, Jimmy Reeves and Kylie Morgan?"

Pete suppressed a sigh, his hands gripping the console as he forced a smile and maintained his composure. He knew this "hot gossip" feature was just another way for Manic to push its brand-friendly narratives and the whole "power couple" image of his son and Kylie.

Lyra jumped in, her tone balancing curiosity and humour. "Ooh, go on, Lily—spill the tea! What's going on with Manic's very own Romeo and Juliet?"

Lily leaned closer to the mic, her bubbly voice full of enthusiasm. "So, I heard that Jimmy and Kylie are planning something big for tomorrow's Ibiza Headbangers show on Manic Dance. Word is they're going all out with some special remixes and shoutouts to their 'super fans'. Also, they might be popping up in a certain Liverpool club tomorrow before the show with none other than Toni Green!"

Pete kept his smile in place, though internally he felt a pang of frustration. Here was another carefully scripted moment, where even his son's love life was being used as part of Manic's brand-building strategy. He could almost feel the distance growing between them, every announcement like this eroding the personal connection he once had with James. But he was a professional, and he'd trained himself to keep his tone upbeat.

"Oh, sounds like a wild night ahead for our Jimmy and Kylie," Pete said, managing to sound genuinely interested. "And for all you partygoers tuning in, don't miss out—it sounds like tomorrow's show is going to be one to remember!"

Lyra shot him a knowing glance, her tone matching his. "Yeah, I'll have to tune in myself, Pete—sounds like they're bringing Ibiza right to the Midlands!" She turned her attention back to the listeners, seamlessly transitioning into the next segment. "But first, let's keep your Friday drive moving with one of the tracks that will be appearing on Ibiza Headbangers, tomorrow at 10 on Manic Dance."

The sound of 'Destination Calabria' pulsed through the speakers, the infectious beat filling the studio. Pete noticed that Lily was taking more selfies, pretending to use her microphone as a saxophone while she danced along to the music. Her exaggerated poses and wide grin gave off the impression that her primary focus wasn't exactly on the job at hand but rather on gathering content for her personal brand. Pete shared a glance with Lyra, who rolled her eyes subtly, acknowledging the absurdity of the situation.

As the track played, Pete leaned toward the mic to prepare for the next segment, trying to keep his frustration in check. He reminded himself that he was here for the listeners, the people who tuned in not just for the glossy entertainment but for a genuine connection—a connection that had become harder to maintain amidst the endless social media antics and scripted hype.

When the song ended, Pete jumped back in with his signature warmth, speaking directly to the West Midlands audience. "Alright, that was 'Destination Calabria'—one of the tracks you'll hear tomorrow on Ibiza Headbangers. But here's hoping your destination is a bit less chaotic than that tune! Now, if you're in a queue on the M5 or inching your way through Birmingham, don't worry; we're here with you to make it as smooth as possible."

Lyra chimed in, "And speaking of smooth, we've got a chance for you to win a pair of VIP tickets to House of Manic at the Utilita arena in Birmingham. Yes, VIP, not just your regular tickets! You'll be right up there with the Manic team, mingling with the crew and even getting to go backstage and meet Busted and Dua Lipa, our headliners. To enter, all you need to do is text HOUSE to 87106 by 6pm and then we'll ask the selected winner 2 questions about our House of Manic headliners. Texts cost your normal standard network rate, and usual terms apply, and we'll be phoning someone straight after in the last hour of tonight's show, so keep your phones close by! Anyway, up now is a bit of Dua Lipa, with her newest single, 'These Walls'.

Pete watched as the automated playlist that was network wide from the Liverpool headquarters cued up the Dua Lipa track, and he felt a slight pang of resentment at how little freedom he had over the music he was playing. Gone were the days when he could tailor his show's soundtrack to suit the mood of his local listeners; now, everything was a meticulously curated setlist decided miles away.

As the song played, Pete allowed himself a brief respite, leaning back in his chair and gazing through the studio's glass walls. He could see Lily bouncing around, while at the same time on the phone, which Pete knew meant that there was someone calling the studio to talk to him and Lyra, but with the network mandate that all calls must not be put through unless approved by Cal, the regional manager, who was currently rejecting 100% of all of the callers unless they mentioned specific keywords from the scripted prompts. It was one more reminder of how little spontaneity remained in his job, everything managed to the last detail, leaving no room for genuine moments with the listeners.

When the Dua Lipa track ended, Pete returned to the mic with a slightly forced enthusiasm, glancing briefly at the blinking "caller" light on the console that would, as always, go unanswered. "And that was the latest from Dua Lipa, taking us right into the heart of your Friday drive home. Its quarter past 4, and Lyra, what's coming through on the WhatsApps?"

The Manic Midlands WhatsApp line, where listeners could send text messages or voice notes that the producer would cut up and the presenters would say things in order to make it look like a live interaction, was running on Pete's screen. He knew this was the one place where they could sometimes catch unfiltered feedback from listeners – provided it passed the producer's checks. Lily, of course, had full control over it, and Pete saw her scanning through messages with a smirk, pausing at ones that seemed to catch her eye. She turned to him, holding her phone as she filtered through the latest messages, and sent Pete a pre-approved script for his next line.

"Got a few good ones here," Lily said, with that familiar flirtatious grin. "Mark in Dudley says that he's looking forward to House of Manic, and that he's entered the competition. He's hoping to win and take his partner to see Dua Lipa live." She giggled, looking at Pete with a mischievous glint in her eye. "He also says, 'Tell Pete he's the real legend—never misses a beat'! Also, we've got Clara on the line."

Pete knew that the 'call' was in fact a pre-recorded message, sent through the system by Lily to mimic live interaction, just like so many "listener calls" at Manic that were crafted to sound fresh and spontaneous. He forced himself to play along, keeping the spirit of live radio alive for the listeners' sake.

"Ah, cheers, Mark!" Pete said with warmth. "Glad to know there's a fellow legend out there! And Clara—what's on your mind today?"

The pre-recorded voice of "Clara" played, cheerful and scripted to the point of being almost unnatural: "Hi Pete, hi Lyra! Just wanted to say I'm SO excited for House of Manic!"

"Nice Clara," Lyra said even though she knew what was coming up next. "What're you looking forward to seeing?"

"Can't wait for Dua! She's so fire, like, I was telling my girlfriends how I'd LOVE to be right up there close to her!" Clara's pre-recorded voice exclaimed. "And seeing Busted too, they're total legends. Hope I win those tickets—fingers crossed!"

Pete grinned at the microphone, going along with the spirit of it all, even if he knew Clara's enthusiasm was likely more a product of Manic's production team than a genuine listener moment. "Thanks, Clara! We'll be pulling for you. And to everyone else, remember—just text HOUSE to 87106 for a chance to join us at the biggest party this side of Birmingham!"

As they wrapped up the segment, Pete leaned back, watching as Lily tapped her phone, no doubt scrolling through more staged messages. The illusion of "live engagement" was all part of the show, but sometimes it felt hollow, a mere shadow of the raw connection he once had with his listeners. Glancing at Lyra, he could tell she felt the same fatigue under her professional smile.

The clock ticked closer to 5 p.m., meaning the first of the three hours of the drive show had been broadcast, leaving two more hours of the same polished, scripted banter, promotional plugs, and carefully managed "listener engagement" to get through. Pete felt the fatigue setting in, a kind of mental exhaustion from having to keep up the facade day after day. It wasn't just the pace; it was the relentless lack of authenticity, the feeling that everything he said had been pre-approved and crafted miles away by people who didn't truly understand what radio was supposed to be.

Lily was at the console, scrolling through more WhatsApp messages with her usual exaggerated enthusiasm. Pete caught Lyra's eye, and for a brief moment, they shared a look of mutual weariness. It was an unspoken acknowledgment, a reminder that amidst the manufactured excitement and perpetual branding, they were still trying to bring something real to the show— even if that was becoming harder every day.

"Right, Pete," Lily said, glancing up with a wink. "The next bit is a promo for tonight's Manic Dance party mix, and then you're meant to talk up the £500k Money Drop again. We've got to keep those plugs frequent!" She tossed her hair back with a grin, seemingly oblivious to Pete's growing frustration.

Pete forced a smile, trying to keep his voice level. "Of course, wouldn't want anyone to forget about that £500k, would we?"

Lily laughed, giving him a thumbs-up. "That's the spirit! And if you need a bit of 'motivation'"—she air-quoted with a wink— "you know where to find me. Just say the word!"

Pete managed a polite chuckle, though the undertone of her comment left him uncomfortable. He looked over to Lyra, who was doing her best to stay professional, but Pete could see the flash of annoyance in her eyes too. It seemed they were both caught in a situation that was quickly veering into the surreal.

The show rolled on, the minutes ticking by with the usual rhythm of scripted segments, networked songs, and more competition promos. Pete went through the motions, delivering each line with the practiced ease of someone who had been doing this for years. Yet inside, he felt as if he were simply playing a part, a figurehead in a broadcast that had lost its soul.

****

CHAPTER 6 – The Big Weekenders Begin

Saturday 2nd November 2024

The morning light was grey as James pulled up outside Kylie's flat in Great Bridge, the industrial skyline of the Black Country stretching around him in a mix of grey skies and neon lights. He was dressed for the night ahead, in skinny jeans, a Manic Dance hoodie, and a beanie, his new "Jimmy Reeves" look carefully curated for both comfort and brand appeal. Today was the first time he and Kylie would record the Ibiza Headbangers show, their much-anticipated slot on Manic Dance, and they were due to head up to Liverpool right after to catch up with Toni and the team.

Kylie greeted him at the door, her blonde hair loose around her shoulders, dressed in a sequined top under her Manic hoodie. "Ready, babe?" she asked, grabbing her duffle bag. "Al said we're going to Toni's first for pizza and pre-drinks, and then we're off to town."

James gave her a quick kiss on the cheek, grinning. "Ready as I'll ever be. This'll be our first real night with the crew. Bit nervous, actually."

Kylie laughed, slinging her bag over her shoulder. "Nervous? You're Jimmy Reeves now, love. Just channel your inner 'Ibiza Headbanger' and you'll be fine!"

They hopped into the car, and as James drove, the radio blared the latest promo for their show, voiced over by a deep, smooth announcer. "Get ready for the hottest beats straight from the heart of Ibiza, brought to you by Manic Dance's new dynamic duo—Jimmy Reeves and Kylie Morgan! Only on Manic Dance, Saturday nights at ten!" James couldn't help but feel a thrill at hearing his name broadcast, even if he knew the high-energy branding was miles from the gritty reality of today's back-to-back recording session.

Arriving at The Waterfront, James pulled up on the double yellows outside the studio building, stepping out into the crisp November air with Kylie by his side. The buzz of anticipation mixed with the faint hum of nerves as they walked through the studio doors. Today was James's first ever voice-tracked back-to-back recordings with Manic, even though he'd done some on his mother's studio setup that was usually used for community and local independent radio stations that brought her syndicated shows. But today was different; today was the big leagues. This was his debut on Manic Dance, a slot that promised national reach and the chance to get his name out there properly.

As they headed inside, they were greeted by Lily, who was on production duty for the morning. She looked fresh-faced despite her wild Friday night out, sporting her signature schoolgirl look with her shirt just a bit more unbuttoned than strictly necessary. She grinned at James and Kylie, giving them an exaggerated thumbs-up.

James could still feel the alcohol and cocaine from the previous night in his system, and the erection he had from seeing Kylie and Lily dressed in their Manic gear made it clear that it was going to be an interesting few hours. He took a deep breath, hoping to keep his focus as he stepped into the booth.

"Alright, lovebirds!" Lily called with a teasing grin, positioning herself at the control desk. "Let's get this party started. First up, we'll run through some quick liners, then dive into the show segments. You know the system, right Kyles?"

Jimmy knew that last year, Kylie had been in his position, joining Manic while in her final year at Wolverhampton Uni, doing pre-recorded voice-tracked shows where they recorded the links, and the computer systems would automatically slot them between the songs and ads as if it were live. Today, though, there was an extra layer of pressure. Their Ibiza Headbangers show was Manic's latest Saturday night push—a pre-recorded slot disguised as a live, high-energy party broadcast, and James wanted to make sure they nailed it.

"Yeah, we're good to go, Lil," Kylie said, adjusting her headset as she flashed James a reassuring smile. "Just follow my lead, babe. We've got this."

They settled into the studio, each taking a microphone. James felt a familiar rush, but this time there was an edge of nervous energy too. He glanced at Kylie, who gave him a small nod and mouthed, "You're going to smash it." Her confidence was contagious, and he straightened, leaning into the mic as Lily cued them.

The red recording light flicked on, and they dove into the first segment. "Alright, Ibiza! It's Reevesy and Morgz here, ready to make your Saturday night unforgettable!"

James began, his voice filled with as much energy as he could muster, his nerves fading slightly as he slipped into the rhythm of it.

"Yep, we're bringing the beats, the bangers, and the absolute best of Ibiza straight to you, wherever you are!" Kylie followed, her voice playful, bouncing perfectly off James's. "We've got everything from the latest Calvin Harris drop to those throwback dance hits you know you love. So, grab a drink, get on your feet, and get ready for a night you won't forget!"

Lily grinned at them from the other side of the glass, giving a thumbs-up. "Nice! That's it—keep that energy up!"

James knew that he wouldn't hear any music, as voice-tracked shows, unlike ones recorded as-live, didn't include the songs in the studio feed. Instead, he and Kylie would record the talking segments separately, and the tracks would be slotted in by the automated system once they were done. It was strange, holding all that energy with nothing but silence in his headphones, but he leaned into it, trying to channel the live feeling he was meant to project.

They went through the motions, recording their intros, outros, and a few cheeky "Ibiza shout-outs" to imaginary listeners, creating the illusion of a bustling, wild night. Kylie took the lead on some segments, her voice smooth and assured, while James threw in some banter about the "legendary Ibiza parties" and their supposed experiences at club nights they'd never actually been to. With every segment, he could feel his confidence growing, his nerves dissolving as he settled into the role of Jimmy Reeves, Manic Dance's new face of late-night fun.

"And this one's for Dr Manic, our resident DJ at Manic Dance, who's no doubt enjoying the Balearics this weekend. It's the TOZA remix of '33 Max Verstappen', for all you F1 fans out there!" James said, throwing in a shout-out that would tie into Manic's corporate push to blend popular culture into their sets. The segment felt punchy, high-energy, and he felt a thrill as he imagined the audience vibing along, even if it was all pre-recorded.

Kylie chimed in, her voice full of excitement, "Oh, Dr Manic, this one's for you, mate! And for everyone tuned in, make sure you stick with us. We've got throwbacks, new drops, and a few cheeky surprises lined up for you tonight!"

Lily flicked off the red light, her face beaming with approval. "Perfect! That's the vibe we need—high energy, good banter, and a bit of mystery. Jimmy, Kylie, you're sounding like naturals!"

They worked their way through the rest of the show segments, filling each link with playful energy and occasional scripted banter designed to make it sound like they were deep in the heart of a live party. As they wrapped up the final segments, James felt the satisfaction of knowing they'd delivered something that would keep listeners entertained, even if it wasn't truly live.

Lily leaned into the mic, giving them a grin. "Alright, lovebirds, that's a wrap for the first one. Take a quick 5 mins before we do the second show. You both absolutely smashed it! The Manic execs are going to love it." She leaned back, checking her phone, undoubtedly scrolling through some WhatsApp messages and leaving James and Kylie a moment to catch their breath.

James looked at Kylie, a grin spreading across his face. "That was… intense. Feels like we're building this whole wild world for people to buy into. Kind of surreal."

Kylie laughed, nudging him playfully. "That's the Manic way, babe. High energy, high drama, and never letting the audience know it's all recorded miles from Ibiza." She took a sip of water and glanced at Lily, who was still absorbed in her phone. "And hey, you're a natural, Jimmy Reeves."

He gave her a mock bow. "Well, I do have a good co-host. You keep me on track." His phone buzzed, and he saw a new message from the Manic team WhatsApp group.

Al Crozier: *"Oi, Reevesy, I'm half an hour from the Dudley hub. Drinks on me in Liverpool later – you and Morgz ready for Toni's?"*

Kylie peered over his shoulder, reading the message with a grin. "Drinks on Al? I'll believe it when I see it." She glanced at him, her eyes gleaming with excitement. "You ready for Liverpool?"

James shrugged, trying to play it cool, but he couldn't hide the spark in his eyes. "Ready as I'll ever be. First time meeting most of the network crowd in person. And with Toni there, it'll be like meeting royalty. Anyway, Lily, we're ready."

They settled back into their seats as Lily queued up the system for the next show's recording. James felt a flicker of nerves as they prepped for another hour of high-energy segments, but he leaned into the moment, mentally rehearsing his "Jimmy Reeves" persona.

As the recording light flicked on, James grinned. "Oi, its Reevesy and Morgz here, and if you weren't here last week, you missed some smashing Headbangers. Honestly, what on earth were you doing, listening to Hits Radio's Belters?"

Kylie jumped in, her tone light and playful, "Exactly, what were you doing? We've got better stuff than Stephanie Hirst and her weekend Belters, so you know you're in the right place now! Forget Hits – this is the real deal. Ibiza Headbangers, coming to you with the biggest tunes of the night!"

"And first up, it's a nice slow track to get you... nah, we don't do slow here on Headbangers, instead we're going in-the-mix! That's right, a whole hour of non-stop Ibiza energy right here on Manic Dance to get you started. We're here until 2am, rocking with you, so let's kick it off with something massive—this is Ibiza Headbangers!" James's voice hit the perfect pitch of excitement, his words spilling over with the thrill of the imaginary crowd they were bringing to life.

Kylie grinned, leaning into the banter seamlessly. "You heard him, people! Buckle up because Reevesy and I aren't slowing down. From the heart of Ibiza straight to your Saturday night, this one's for everyone out there who's ready to get on that dancefloor!"

The recording session continued, each segment an exercise in pure performance. James found himself slipping deeper into the Jimmy Reeves persona with each link, his confidence building as he and Kylie bounced off each other, creating the illusion of a wild, pulsating night that listeners could get lost in.

After wrapping up the final link, they both pulled off their headsets, sharing a triumphant grin. It felt like they had created a show that would keep listeners hooked, even if it was carefully constructed rather than live. Lily gave them a small clap from the other side of the glass.

"You two are absolute naturals. That's going to keep the punters locked in for sure," she said, flashing them a grin. "And don't worry, I'll make sure it sounds seamless. You'll be legends by midnight."

James chuckled, reaching out to high-five Kylie. "We did it! Our first real show on Manic Dance."

Kylie squeezed his hand, her eyes gleaming with pride. "And just think, babe—this is only the beginning."

As they packed up, James's phone buzzed again. It was Al: "Right, I'm outside the hub, ready when you are. Let's hit the road, legends. Toni's waiting!"

James and Kylie grabbed their bags, thanking Lily before making their way to the lobby. Outside, Al was leaning against his car, grinning as he saw them approach.

"Ready for the big night?" Al asked, his tone full of mischief. "This is going to be one for the books."

Chloe had to admit, her microskirt, no panties or bra, and a cropped halter top might have been overdoing it a bit, but she, Cody and a few of their friends from Uni for Chloe and Manic who wasn't going to Liverpool for Cody, were going to Broad Street, and not leaving Birmingham until dawn. They were making a night of it, and as far as Chloe was concerned, there was no such thing as "too much" when it came to a night out. She knew Cody would be glued to his phone most of the time, catching the latest Manic WhatsApp notifications and keeping tabs on what Al, James, and Kylie were up to up north. It was part of the thrill—a shared sense of being in the inner circle of Manic, living the lifestyle their listeners only dreamed about.

"Right," Cody said, slipping his phone into his pocket, "I'm ready for whatever Broad Street throws at us tonight. And from the look of it, so are you." He shot her a cheeky grin, his eyes skimming over her outfit with a nod of approval. "Although, you do look hotter without anything on."

Chloe knew that, although she wasn't a Manic presenter, having a brother who was one and a boyfriend who read the news for the Midlands hub gave her some status. She loved the thrill of the lifestyle, of feeling like she was part of the world her brother and Cody inhabited at Manic. Tonight was another chance to embrace it, and she planned to make the most of it.

Looking on her phone, she noticed a photo from her brother's Instagram page, where he, Kylie and their producer, someone who looked like a schoolgirl, were in the Manic Dance studio, which had been Studio 1, their dad's Midlands Manic drivetime studio.

@ManicDanceReevesy: *Ibiza Headbangers incoming with me and @KylieMorganBrekkie on the decks and @FlowerOfDesire keeping things cool! 🎉 Can't wait for you all to tune in – this one's going to be legendary! #ReevesyandMorgz #ManicDance #IbizaHeadbangers #CoupleGoals*

Seeing the post from James made Chloe grin. She felt a thrill knowing she was part of the same world, even if she wasn't in the thick of it like her brother. The Manic culture was more than a job for him; it was a lifestyle that had pulled them both into a scene full of energy, music, and, yes, a bit of chaos. And tonight, on Broad Street, she was determined to embody that same spirit with Cody and their friends, creating their own night of drama and excitement right there in Birmingham.

"Look at that," Chloe said, showing Cody the post. "Jimmy and Kylie are already getting people hyped for the Headbangers show tonight. Who's that with them?"

"Ah, Lily, one of the Cardiff Vibes producers—bit of a character, that one," Cody replied with a smirk. "Always in the Manic chats, stirring things up. She's definitely on-brand for Manic Dance. Trust me, she's got more 'side hustles' than anyone else at Manic. Makes Jimmy and Kylie look like amateurs. She runs an OnlyFans on the side, as well as a few other subscription services, if you catch my drift." Cody winked, clearly amused by the unconventional career path of his co-worker. "She's the kind of girl that fits right into this Manic world. Proper wild, no limits. Loves taking nudes and posting 'em on WhatsApp!"

Chloe laughed, arching an eyebrow at Cody. "Sounds like she's got the 'Manic lifestyle' nailed then. Can't believe James is working with someone like her. Bet Dad would lose it if he knew."

Cody grinned, chuckling "She was your dad's producer yesterday! Spent more time on WhatsApp and Insta then producing."

Chloe shook her head, amused by the thought of Lily and her dad in the same studio. The idea of someone as wild and uninhibited as Lily rubbing elbows with her old-school dad was almost too much. She could just imagine Pete's exasperated expression, trying to focus on his work while Lily posed for selfies and laughed over the latest Manic WhatsApp banter.

"Well, let's make sure tonight's as wild as they're having up in Liverpool," she said, linking arms with Cody. "I want to make a memory or two that even they'll envy."

Cody flashed a grin. "Sounds like a plan. Besides, you know Broad Street's got its own kind of 'Ibiza' vibe—if you squint and ignore the Brummie accents."

They hopped on the tram to New Street, and Chloe felt the familiar thrill of anticipation bubbling up. Tonight, they weren't just hitting the clubs; they were embodying the Manic energy they'd grown up around, the high-octane lifestyle that had pulled her brother—and to some extent, her too—into its orbit.

As the tram passed The Hawthorns, Chloe saw Cody looking at his phone and then laughing. "Oh, Clo, you'll love this."

Chloe took Cody's phone and saw it was in a WhatsApp group chat called 'Gals and Geezers', and it was a short video of James and Kylie in the back seat of Al's car, having sex while Al was driving. "Who's that filming then?"

"Oh, its Liam, you know, you met him last night, Black guy with red hair? He does the Mid Wales Breakfast show. Loves to document everything when the crew's out. Honestly, I think he gets a kick out of capturing all the madness on his phone," Cody explained, smirking. "The chat it's on is what we call the nudes chat, as it's all about what everyone's getting up to, photos, videos, the lot. It's just part of the… Manic family tradition, I guess." Cody winked as he took his phone back, chuckling at the scene. "It's good when you're at home and you need a wank, as its always full of stuff, you know? Everyone's got something wild to share." He gave Chloe a cheeky grin. "Smile babes!"

Chloe saw that Cody was taking a selfie of the two of them for his Instagram and instinctively struck a playful pose, leaning in close with a mischievous smile. Cody snapped the photo, immediately posting it.

@LaneOClock: *Heading to #Brum with the beautiful @CloReevesRadio for some #BroadStreetVibes #CoupleofClubbers*

Chloe smirked as the likes and comments started to trickle in almost instantly. She felt a surge of satisfaction—this was more than just a night out; it was an extension of the lifestyle she was leaning into, the same lifestyle her brother, Cody, and their whole circle at Manic embodied. The likes, the hashtags, the image—it all tied into the culture she was getting swept up in, a world where moments weren't just lived, but documented and shared.

As they stepped off the tram, Broad Street was already buzzing with energy. The lights from bars and clubs spilled out onto the pavement, and groups of people, young and buzzing with anticipation, lined the street. The thumping beats from nearby clubs mixed with the chatter and laughter of people out to make the most of the weekend. Chloe felt a thrill run through her; this was her scene, her playground for the night.

"Clo!" three people Chloe knew from Birmingham University who were in the same year of Law as here and were her best friends said as she and Cody got off the tram at the new Brindleyplace stop. The night was just beginning, and she was already in her element.

As she and Cody joined her friends, they were greeted with hugs and cheers, each of them dressed to the nines, looking ready to make the night count. Chloe's friends teased her about her bold outfit, and she laughed it off, unbothered. They all knew she thrived in the spotlight, especially on nights like this.

Her friend Jess pulled her aside, a playful smirk on her face. "So, your brother's like a big radio star now, yeah? Hosting some Ibiza thing tonight? That's mad!"

Chloe knew that she shouldn't mention his show was pre-recorded or voice-tracked, as the illusion that it was live was part of the allure Manic Dance promoted. She nodded, putting on a proud expression. "Yeah, Jimmy's doing Ibiza Headbangers tonight on Manic Dance. He's been working with some big names, you know, getting the whole Manic 'star treatment' up in Liverpool." She threw in a little shrug to play it cool, though a spark of pride warmed her.

Jess whistled, clearly impressed. "Must be surreal, having a brother living the 'radio dream.' And here we are, about to conquer Broad Street like it's the club capital of the world!"

Cody joined them, chuckling at the conversation. "Oh, trust me, Clo's brother isn't the only one living it up. Chloe here's practically Manic royalty with her connections. Anyway, ladies, you know there's going to be some Manic folks come here in a bit? DJ Hexx, one of the Manic Metal hosts, is one of my best mates from way back, and he said he might swing by with a few of his crew after their show wraps up." Cody grinned, clearly relishing the chance to keep the night lively with a few "celebrity" appearances of his own.

Chloe's friends looked impressed, and she felt her sense of importance swell. This night was shaping up exactly the way she wanted it: a blend of her own circle and the glamorous, high-energy world that had sucked her brother and Cody into its orbit. She wasn't just living it; she was crafting the experience, making it hers.

* _ * _ * _ *

If James had to say one thing when Toni Green answered the door to her flat, seeing her wear a strap-on under a silky robe certainly wasn't what he'd expected. He exchanged a quick glance with Kylie, who barely suppressed a giggle as Toni gave them a broad grin and motioned them inside.

"Welcome to Liverpool's finest!" Toni announced with a laugh, clearly loving the shock factor. She led them through her flat, which was already buzzing with the other Manic presenters and crew members, along with some from Hits Radio, Heart and Capital Radio, the three competing networks whose own presenters often mingled with Manic's crew, creating a sense of camaraderie amid the competition. Drinks were flowing, and the room was filled with laughter, music, and a general air of mischief.

James looked at Toni, then the strap-on, then Toni again, and then the strap-on again, confused as to why she would be wearing such an outfit for a pre-party, but Toni just winked at him, clearly enjoying the confusion. "Oh, don't look so surprised, Reevesy! Half of us are already drunk or coked out, and the shagging has already started. If you want me to fuck ya, then I'll happily oblige," she teased, her eyes sparkling with amusement.

Chuckling, James knew that his anal cherry had already been popped by Kylie a few months ago, during their 'hidden relationship' phase, and that when it came to women with strap-ons, he was a bit of a submissive to that sort of thing, and that if Toni was offering, then he would happily join in.

Kylie leaned into him, her voice a playful whisper, "Remember, babe, your hall pass is good for the night. Have fun, but don't wear yourself out too soon." She gave him a quick kiss on the cheek, laughing as she melted into the crowd, immediately drawn into a conversation with one of the Capital presenters.

Toni guided James over to the kitchen counter where an array of drinks was set up alongside a few neatly laid-out lines of coke. She poured him a shot, handing it over with a grin. "First night in Liverpool with the Manic crew—cheers to that! And hey, don't worry about keeping up. We go hard, but it's all in good fun."

James downed the shot, feeling the familiar burn as it went down. He looked around, taking in the chaotic scene: Al was in the corner, already locked in a deep conversation with a group of Hits Radio presenters, and Liam was somewhere on the balcony, laughing loudly with a few other Manic DJs. It was surreal seeing all these personalities he'd grown up hearing, all under one roof, letting loose.

Just then, Toni leaned in close, her tone conspiratorial. "So, Jimmy Reeves—living the brand, yeah? You know, you and Kylie are the real deal. Manic's been dying for a fresh duo to light things up, and you two are smashing it. Keep it up, and who knows where you'll end up." She nudged him, her eyes gleaming. "But tonight? Tonight's just for fun. Now, Reevesy, come to my boudoir, and let me show you how we really welcome new talent up here in Liverpool!"

James felt his heart race, a mix of nerves and excitement flooding over him. He exchanged a quick glance with Kylie across the room; she gave him a playful, encouraging thumbs-up, fully on board with the night's anything-goes vibe. Following Toni down the hallway, he was keenly aware of the thumping bass from the main room blending with the muffled laughter and conversations from the party. Toni's flat, with its neon-lit decor and edgy, modern art, felt like an extension of Manic itself—bold, no boundaries, and a little surreal.

As they reached her room, Toni threw open the door with a dramatic flourish. The space was softly lit, with flashes of vibrant colours reflecting off the walls from an LED strip running around the ceiling. She turned to him, crossing her arms with a grin.

"So, Reevesy," she said, slipping her robe off to reveal a glittery crop top and a set of fitted leggings that contrasted sharply with the bold accessory she'd been flaunting, "you've got the voice, the look, and now, you've got the Manic vibe. All that's left is to see if you're up for anything."

James felt a nervous chuckle slip out. "Anything's the Manic way, right? Guess I'd better get comfortable with it." He moved towards her, feeling the thrill of diving into this fast-paced, boundary-blurring world.

* _ * _ * _ *

The line of cocaine that Zara, her best friend, provided made Chloe grin as she snorted feel hornier than she already did. Broad Street was alive, and Chloe was ready to dive headfirst into the chaotic energy surrounding her.

The fact it was only 8 in the evening and she was on her second line, her third drink, and had already had sex with Cody in the toilets in the club that they were in, the dildo she had inserted into herself earlier keeping Cody's seed inside of her, the two having decided not to use condoms or other forms of birth control for the thrill of it, made her feel liberated. She was fully living out the manic, carefree energy that seemed to permeate everything associated with her brother's new world at Manic. Cody was close behind, downing his own drink and laughing as they danced their way through the pulsing crowd, each beat of the music driving them further into the wild atmosphere of Broad Street on a Saturday night.

Chloe noticed Cody's phone buzzing, a new message in the "Gals and Geezers" chat popping up. It was from Toni Green, and it was a pic of James having a strap-on filling his arse while he was eating Caz Lowe, one of the Bee Manic, Manchester's Manic Radio station, out like it was his last meal. Chloe burst out laughing, showing the photo to Zara, who looked on with equal parts shock and amusement. The boundary-pushing world that James was embracing at Manic was something Chloe could relate to. It was outrageous, uninhibited, and so far removed from the world they'd grown up in. It made sense in a twisted way, even if she knew their dad would be mortified if he saw it.

"Fuck, your brother's a right slut, having Toni Green pound him like a pro," Zara laughed, clearly enjoying the wild absurdity of it all. "Hang on, is that his real cock?"

Chloe chuckled, as James was naturally well endowed, with him giving his penis the nickname "tree trunk" due to how it compared to most. She nodded, feeling a strange mix of pride and amusement. "Yep, that's my brother alright, making his Manic mark. Guess he's finally embraced the 'anything goes' vibe they all talk about. He's going all in, just like the rest of them. Anyway, babes, want to try something different next time we have some coke? You see, Cody here can get us into the VIP lounge at our next stop."

"What do you wanna try, Clo?"

"Well, how about snorting it off Cody's cock?" Chloe said with a wink, as she saw Cody, Abdul, and a few of his Manic friends grinning at the suggestion. Chloe felt the energy of the night, pulsing with the promise of more reckless fun, blurring the boundaries between the world her brother had joined and her own sense of freedom. She knew Broad Street would only get wilder as the night went on, and she was more than ready to live up to every moment, fully embracing the "Manic" spirit in her own way.

As they moved through the crowds, Chloe spotted a few familiar faces from uni, friends and classmates who were equally drawn to Broad Street's vibrant atmosphere. They greeted each other with cheers and half-drunken hugs, everyone hyped for what promised to be an unforgettable night.

Cody leaned into her ear, his voice laced with excitement. "You're loving this, aren't you? Living just as big and loud as your brother. Manic would be proud!"

Chloe laughed, linking her arm through his as they headed to the next bar, letting the throbbing beats of music and the electric atmosphere carry them. Tonight, she didn't have to worry about family expectations or her father's stern expressions. In this moment, under the neon lights of Broad Street and surrounded by friends, she was just Chloe, free and unbound, living life on her own terms.

* _ * _ * _ *

"Right, folks," James heard Toni say. It was quarter to nine, and the taxis that would take the 30 strong Manic, Hits, Heart and Capital crew from the Speke flat to the city centre were lined up outside. Toni had just shouted the rallying cry, and the room buzzed with anticipation. James, still catching his breath from the scene in Toni's room, exchanged a quick grin with Kylie, who'd been soaking up the atmosphere with a casual ease that made her look like she'd been doing this for years.

"Alright, Liverpool!" Toni said, her voice echoing over the excited chatter, "tonight we're hitting the town, so let's get in those cabs before they leave us behind!" She pulled James and Kylie aside, her smile a mixture of encouragement and warning. "Remember, tonight isn't just about blowing off steam. Manic's watching, and you two are the faces of the new vibe we're selling. Keep it wild, but keep it memorable, alright?"

James nodded, feeling the weight of Toni's words. The night was more than just a party; it was an opportunity to solidify their place in the Manic brand's world of high-energy, anything-goes culture. They were here to make an impression.

The ride to Liverpool city centre was filled with laughter and selfies, everyone in high spirits as they prepared to dive into the chaos of Saturday night. Al was in the taxi with James and Kylie, leaning forward from the front seat with a mischievous grin. "You two ready to show the Scousers how it's done? Liverpool's got energy like no other, and tonight, we're the main event."

Kylie shot him a grin. "Bring it on, Al. We're ready for whatever Liverpool's got!"

James looked out the window as the city lights flickered past, his mind racing with a mix of nerves and excitement. This was it—the kind of night he'd heard so much about since joining Manic, a night where they could let loose and be themselves, even if that "self" was carefully packaged for an audience hungry for a glimpse into the lives of radio's wildest personalities.

As they pulled up outside the first bar, James noticed Hits Radio's Hattie Pearson, one of the network presenters, leaving with some of the other Hits crew, her sequined dress catching the light as she laughed and linked arms with her friends.

"Hey, Hattie, fancy meeting you here!" Toni said with a grin, stepping out of the cab with James and Kylie following. Hattie turned, flashing a dazzling smile as she spotted them.

"Toni! Well, look who decided to take Liverpool by storm tonight!" Hattie called back, striding over to give Toni a hug, the two networks' presenters sharing an easy camaraderie. Despite being competitors, Manic and Hits both shared a certain kinship, knowing they each fed into the same electrified, fast-paced culture of CHR radio. "Me and some of the Hits gang are going down the Cavern Club. I see you've got some of the Manic lot here. You're not gonna cause too much trouble, are you?" she teased, casting a playful glance at James and Kylie.

Toni laughed, pulling James and Kylie into the exchange. "Oh, you know us! Just a bit of innocent fun, showing the Scousers what a proper Manic night looks like!"

Hattie smirked, crossing her arms. "I'll believe that when I see it! Enjoy, and try not to get yourselves banned from anywhere. Oh, and Toni, you owe Hirsty a fiver when you're next in Manc. She said that Reevesy was probably pre-recording his Headbangers while she does Belters live as the real deal!"

Toni rolled her eyes, chuckling. "Tell Hirsty she'll get her fiver when she manages to get through a whole Belters set without playing 'Rhythm is a Dancer'!"

The two women laughed at that, as Rhythm is a Dancer was a regular on the Stephanie Hirst's Bangers show, the 90s classic having become a running joke among the stations. Hattie gave them a final wave before disappearing down the street with her crew, and Toni led the Manic group towards their first stop for the night—a high-energy, neon-lit bar known for its wild atmosphere called Crystal.

"Right guys," Toni said to the assembled crew from the various CHR stations. "We've got the VIP section reserved at Crystal, so let's make it a night to remember! Drinks are on Manic's tab until midnight, so get stuck in!"

The crew cheered as they streamed into the club, immediately swept up by the pulsing beats and flashing lights. The VIP area was a roped-off section above the dancefloor, offering a perfect view of the crowd below. James felt the atmosphere hit him like a wave, the bass vibrating under his feet as he exchanged a glance with Kylie, her eyes sparkling with excitement.

As they settled in, Al handed them each a drink, his expression one of pure mischief. "Alright, Reevesy, Morgz—tonight's your initiation into the full Manic experience. Show 'em what the Midlands crew's made of!"

The group dove into the night with abandon, drinks flowing, laughter echoing over the music, and every so often, one of them would pull out a phone to capture the moment. James found himself caught up in the sheer thrill of it, feeling both part of something bigger and also oddly detached, as if he were a character in someone else's story. It was the strange paradox of the Manic culture— living life loud and fast, yet always aware that every moment was also part of the brand.

Taking a snort of cocaine, James felt Toni grab him and Kylie, and saw her take a photo of the trio, unaware that on his upper lip, the shadow of the white powder was faintly visible, giving away the wild energy that had already taken hold of the night. Toni posted the photo to her own Instagram, adding a cheeky caption

As the night progressed, the music seemed to grow louder, the lights brighter, and the energy more frenetic. James could feel the buzz of adrenaline and the lingering effects of the coke, making everything sharper, more intense. He looked around at his colleagues—Kylie laughing and dancing, Al with his arm around a Capital Radio presenter, and Toni leading the charge with her usual confidence. It was everything he'd been promised and yet somehow even more chaotic than he'd imagined.

A sudden cheer erupted from their group as the DJ switched to an Ibiza classic, and the crowd responded with a roar. James and Kylie joined in, their voices blending with the crowd's as they threw their arms up in the air. It felt surreal—an unending wave of music and energy that carried them deeper into the night.

But even in the midst of the revelry, James couldn't help but feel a tiny, nagging thought pull at him. He'd dreamed of making it big, of feeling this rush of being at the centre of it all. And yet, with every cheer, every flash of a camera, there was a part of him that wondered if he was living his own dream or merely acting out someone else's version of it.

"Come on, Reevesy!" Al shouted, pulling him out of his thoughts. "No deep thoughts tonight. Just live it!"

James grinned, shaking off the momentary hesitation as he threw himself back into the heart of the celebration.

This was the Manic way—loud, fast, and unapologetically wild. And tonight, he was all in.

****

CHAPTER 7 – The Big Weekenders Conclude

Sunday 3rd November 2024

James woke to a pounding headache, the remnants of the previous night's drinks still swirling in his veins. He squinted at his phone, the screen painfully bright, and saw it was already half eleven. What was more was that Al was still in his arse, fully erect, spooning him at the same time, while Toni's pussy still had his own cock still buried in it, a tangled mess of limbs from the chaotic night they'd barely made it through. The room smelled faintly of stale alcohol and the unmistakable musk of a night that had gone way beyond any boundary James had ever known. He shifted slightly, feeling the weight of Al behind him and the unexpected intimacy of Toni still clinging to him, her soft breath steady, contrasting with the chaotic remnants of the evening.

Looking faintly through the door, he could see Kylie was awake, sucking Liam's black cock like she was starving, and it was the only thing available. Suddenly James felt Al's fingers tease his nipple, the feeling making him even more horny, and his cock cumming into Toni.

"More," Toni groaned, her hand reaching down to where James was firmly plugged into her, and James grinned as he made his thrusts faster.

Suddenly the sound of the landline within Toni's Speke flat rang out, startling everyone in the room from their hazy state. Toni groaned and pushed James back a little, clearly annoyed at the interruption. She reached over to grab the phone, muttering a quick, "Hang on," before speaking into the receiver.

"Yeah?" she said, her voice hoarse from the late night. As she listened, her expression shifted from groggy to giggly. "Oh, Smitty's called in sick, and you need me to do the evening show he normally does on Sundays?"

Toni rolled her eyes, struggling to suppress a laugh. "Yeah, yeah, I'll cover, no worries... what, you want Crozier with me? He's meant to be heading back to Brum, and he's got one of Dudley's breakfast shift with him."

Al stirred behind James, catching bits of Toni's conversation. "What? They want me on the national show? My national break?"

Al's voice cut through the morning grogginess, and James turned, feeling the excitement ripple through Al even in the hazy post-party daze. This wasn't just another day—it was the kind of break people in the industry dreamed about. The national Sunday evening slot was no small gig; it was prime-time exposure, a chance to speak to the whole of Manic's audience and beyond.

Toni covered the receiver with her hand, rolling her eyes at Al's growing enthusiasm. "Yeah, Al, they want you. Apparently, Smitty's down with food poisoning. This is your shot, but let's be clear, you'd better be able to string a sentence together."

Al sat up, gently easing away from James. "Oi, Reevesy, you were my warm-up act," he joked, flashing a cheeky grin as he clambered out of bed, stretching. "Liam's on my insurance, so he'll drive you and Morgan back down to the

Midlands after, yeah? You two deserve a rest. But me? I'm about to make a bloody splash tonight!"

James forced a chuckle, feeling the mixture of pride for his mate and exhaustion from the whirlwind weekend. He could barely think straight, let alone process the idea of Al taking on a national show in their current state. "Knock 'em dead, Crozier," he mumbled, propping himself up on one elbow, feeling a twinge of envy mixed with relief that he wasn't the one who'd be going live.

Toni gave Al a playful shove. "Go on then, big shot, get yourself cleaned up and make sure you don't sound like you've had half of Liverpool's stock of booze." She smirked as she watched Al stumble off towards the bathroom, visibly trying to shake himself awake.

As Al disappeared, Toni turned back to James with a mischievous smile. "You and Kylie did alright last night, didn't you? That Ibiza Headbangers slot's going to make you two the names to watch."

James managed a half-smile, recalling the thrill of recording the show and the surreal energy of their night out. "Feels like I'm living in someone else's life, to be honest. Last night was wild… but then waking up like this," he gestured at the state of the room and the mess they were all tangled in, "it's… a lot to process."

Toni chuckled, leaning over to ruffle his hair. "Welcome to Manic, love. It's always going to be a bit mad, a bit out of control. The trick is to hold onto what you want from it and not let the craziness own you."

James nodded, appreciating the wisdom in her words even if it still felt overwhelming. Just then, Kylie pulled herself away from Liam, wiping her mouth with a cheeky grin, clearly amused by the chaos of the morning after. She crawled over to James, pressing a quick kiss to his forehead. "Come on, babe. Let's grab a coffee and sober up a bit before we head back."

James felt her pussy rubbing against his cock, and he knew that he needed a release otherwise he'd be struggling with the pent-up energy all the way back to Dudley. "Fuck, babe, if I don't cum, I'll be struggling all the way back to Dudley," he whispered with a grin, pulling her close as she straddled him with a playful glint in her eyes.

Kylie chuckled, brushing her fingers through his hair. "Alright, one more for the road, then," she murmured, leaning down to kiss him. Their laughter mixed with the soft murmur of voices from the others in the room, a scene of indulgence that felt both surreal and typical of the weekend's wild rhythm.

As they finished, Kylie slid off him, her face flushed, and they shared a quick smile that held the comfortable intimacy they had developed over time. The whole experience—the recording sessions, the wild night out, the unexpected morning—all felt like a dream, one where he was constantly navigating between exhilaration and exhaustion.

By the time they both cleaned up and found themselves in the kitchen, Al was already dressed and buzzing, glancing at his watch with a look of determination. He clapped James on the back, a triumphant grin on his face. "This is it, Reevesy. Watch me go and steal the show tonight, yeah?"

James smirked. "I'll be tuning in for sure, mate. Don't let them forget the Midlands are holding down the fort."

Al shot him a thumbs-up before heading out, leaving a trail of energy in his wake. James and Kylie settled down with mugs of strong coffee, feeling the reality of the morning finally beginning to set in. Liam joined them, looking surprisingly fresh despite the previous night's escapades, and gave a little nod as he downed his own coffee. "Right, you two, ready for the drive?"

James nodded, his mind still on Al and his big opportunity. He couldn't help but feel the weight of it—how fast things were moving, how quickly he was getting swept up in this world. And yet, sitting there with Kylie beside him, he felt a certain contentment that balanced out the intensity.

"Who the fuck parked a bus outside?" Danny O'Neil, the Manic national drivetime host, who presented the drive shows for Manic Radio's local stations that did not have their own regional drive, like Warwickshire, Northamptonshire and South Derbyshire, as well as some other small regional hubs, shouted from the doorway, looking bleary-eyed but amused. The presence of an articulated bus parked right outside gave an absurd touch to the morning after's haze.

"Rail replacement, innit," Joe Svenson, Danny's producer, said, chuckling. "They've closed the Northern Line from South Parkway to Hunts Cross."

James laughed, unable to hold back his amusement at the surreal sight of a rail replacement bus parked outside Toni's flat after the wild night they'd just had. It was as if even Liverpool's public transport was conspiring to add an extra layer of chaos to their weekend.

"Guess we're not the only ones who had a long night," he said, raising his coffee mug in a mock toast to the stranded commuters outside.

Kylie grinned, nudging him. "Let's hope their journey is less eventful than ours has been."

As they prepared to head out, James checked his phone and found a string of notifications, some from the WhatsApp group, but some on X from a mixture of Manic, Hits, Capital and Heart hosts. One that stood out was from Hits Radio's Stephanie Hirst, who's 'Belters' show had been on at the same time as James and Kylie's pre-recorded Ibiza Headbangers on Manic Dance the previous night. Hirsty had tweeted a playful message, tagging both James and Kylie:

@StephanieHirst: *So, @ManicDanceReevesy & @KylieMorganBrekkie think they can out-bang Belters? Loved the Ibiza Headbangers, you two! But just wait till I bring the bangers next week – live, as always! #BeltersVsHeadbangers*

James chuckled, showing Kylie the tweet. "Looks like we've got some healthy competition," he said, feeling the friendly rivalry add a new edge to their Manic journey. Hits and Manic might be fierce competitors, but the camaraderie between presenters, each trying to bring their best energy to the airwaves, kept things exciting.

Kylie grinned, clearly up for the challenge. "Guess we'll have to raise the stakes next week. If Hirsty wants to bring the heat, let's give her a run for her money."

@ManicDanceReevesy: *Oh, Hirsty, you really had to throw down the gauntlet, didn't you? We'll see if Belters can handle the heat next Saturday. @KylieMorganBrekkie and I have a hella fire show next week... no Rhythm Is a Dancer needed! #IbizaHeadbangers #LetsGetLoud*

James pressed "send" and felt a surge of adrenaline at the thought of this budding rivalry. It wasn't just about ratings; it was about creating an experience that listeners would remember. Hits Radio might be a major competitor, but Manic Dance's Ibiza Headbangers had a distinct vibe they were crafting – and that was something he and Kylie would push to the next level.

Kylie sipped her coffee with a grin, watching as the notifications began to roll in. "This is going to be fun. Let's make next week unforgettable."

Liam glanced over, catching the tweet exchange and chuckling. "Hirsty getting in on the banter, eh? Your old man knows her from way back, don't he?"

James nodded, chuckling as he sipped his coffee. "Yeah, Dad's mentioned her a few times. They were both in radio when it was all about local vibes and live connections. Now, she's still going live and kicking up the nostalgia with her Belters, but here we are crafting the Ibiza Headbangers brand, and it's all… so different."

Kylie nudged him with a grin. "Well, if we're doing something different, then let's do it big. We've got the branding, the hype, and now a bit of competition. And hey, nothing wrong with borrowing a bit of that old-school live energy for our own style."

James felt a surge of determination as he thought about next week's show. He and Kylie were building something exciting – something that blended the flash of Manic's branding with a touch of the genuine enthusiasm his dad always said radio needed.

Just then, Toni came into the kitchen, looking uncharacteristically awake. "Saw the tweets, Reevesy. Those were hella shots fired at Hirsty! The bosses are gonna love that, as Hits is our biggest rival in the CHR game. Keep that spark going, and who knows? You two might be the ones setting the pace for all of Manic!"

James grinned, feeling a surge of pride. The idea of building a legacy on Manic Dance—a fresh new edge to the network's branding—was exhilarating. This wasn't just about being "Jimmy Reeves" for one Saturday night; it was about carving out a space in the CHR landscape, standing out even amidst the scripted, pre-recorded nature of their shows.

As Liam grabbed his car keys and signalled for James and Kylie to follow him out, Toni gave James a final wink. "Let me guess, you've already done next week's show and got a few shots fired at Hits on it?" she teased, smirking as she watched him.

James laughed, nodding. "Yep, something about we've got better stuff than Stephanie Hirst and her weekend Belters."

Toni laughed, clapping him on the back as he headed out. "That's the spirit! You're building a brand, Reevesy—now go back and show 'em what you're made of next week. And make sure your dad hears it too; he'll love knowing his kid is shaking things up in his own way."

James couldn't help but smile as he and Kylie followed Liam out to the car, a mixture of pride, excitement, and anticipation bubbling up inside him. The thought of his dad tuning in to hear his son rival Stephanie Hirst's Belters show was oddly satisfying. Sure, Pete probably wouldn't love the wildness of Manic's brand, but the competitive spirit? That was something they shared.

*_*_*_*

"Woah, that's some shots fired!" Chloe said as she was checking her X feed, Cody's arms wrapped around her chest as the two were in her bedroom at the Smith family home. "Have you seen this, Cody? James and Steph Hirst having a X feud?"

@StephanieHirst: *@ManicDanceReevesy, Oh, firing shots at me, are you? You better bring the tunes then, not just the talk! 😂 Let's see if Ibiza Headbangers can keep up with Belters but remember – live always wins! 🎧 😏 #RadioWars #BeltersVsHeadbangers*

*@**HitsRadio**: Woah, we've got a showdown on our timeline! Who's got the Saturday night moves? 🎶 Is it #IbizaHeadbangers with @ManicDanceReevesy & @KylieMorganBrekkie or our very own @StephanieHirst's #Belters? Let's hear it, folks – which tunes keep you rocking? 🔥 #SaturdayShowdown*

*@**ManicRadio**: So, @HitsRadio has laid down the gauntlet? You hear that @ManicDance? We all know Reevesy and Morgz will bring the heat to Ibiza Headbangers! Saturday nights just got louder – who's tuning in? 🔥 #IbizaHeadbangers #SaturdayShowdown #ReevesyAndMorgz*

Cody chuckled, scrolling through the thread with a look of amusement. "Your brother's really leaning into it, isn't he? A bit of banter with Hirsty is good for him—keeps it lively. And hey, even Hits Radio joining the fun makes it more legit. They're not just seeing him as 'Pete's kid' anymore."

Chloe grinned, feeling a flicker of pride. "I know, right? And he's giving Stephanie Hirst a run for her money. I bet she didn't expect the competition to be so upfront. Manic's always been known for its energy, but now it feels like James is making his mark, not just riding the wave."

Cody nodded, leaning closer to the screen. "And everyone's watching it unfold. Manic's taken the bait, Hits is playing along, and now every listener on X is weighing in. If he plays it right, he could get some real attention—not just from the fans, but the big bosses too. You do realise your brother will probably make a real name for himself with this? He's stepping out of Pete's shadow and into his own." Cody squeezed Chloe's shoulder, clearly enjoying the spectacle that James was creating.

Chloe leaned back, a satisfied smirk on her face. "About time, too. James was always the quieter one, but it's like Manic has given him this confidence boost. And hey, if he keeps up with the Hirsty banter and pulls in the numbers, he'll be more than just a 'radio kid'—he'll be a proper Manic name. Plus, it's nice to see him having fun, even if it's all in Manic's mad style."

They scrolled through more comments and memes, seeing the online audience weighing in on which show was the Saturday night champion. It wasn't just a sibling thing; it was pride in seeing her brother thrive in a way that felt uniquely his own, even in a world she knew their dad would barely recognise.

"Let's just hope he can handle the pressure. But knowing James? He'll probably rise to it," Cody said, placing a kiss on Chloe's shoulder as they settled back. The weekend might have wound down, but the hype around James was just getting started.

* _ * _ * _ *

As the car containing Liam, Kylie and James passed Knutsford services, James glanced out the window, his mind racing with the buzz of excitement from the weekend's events. Despite the exhaustion, he felt a renewed sense of purpose and determination. The rivalry with Hits, the energy of Ibiza Headbangers, and the reaction on X—all of it was shaping up to make his role at Manic something far bigger than he'd initially anticipated.

It was then when James realised where he'd left his car, parked on the double yellow lines outside the The Waterfront studio building back in Dudley. With a groan, he slapped his forehead, catching Kylie and Liam's attention.

"What's up?" Kylie asked, stifling a yawn as she leaned over, concerned.

"My car," James muttered, trying to laugh off the situation, though his stomach twisted at the thought of a ticket. "I parked it on double yellows outside the studio. Bet it's either ticketed, clamped, or towed by now. Bloody private parking lot there."

Liam chuckled from the driver's seat, clearly amused. "Ah, the price of stardom, eh? Hope that national banter with Hirsty was worth it, Reevesy."

James shrugged, leaning back with a resigned sigh. "Guess I'll find out soon enough. If I've got a ticket, I'll just think of it as paying my dues for the Manic life."

Pulling his phone from his pocket, he scrolled through his contacts list to see if Chloe was online on their sibling's WhatsApp chat. Smiling as he saw she was online, he tapped out a message.

James Smith: *Oi, Clo, if you're up and near Dudley, any chance you could check on my car? Left it on the double yellows outside The Waterfront... might have a ticket waiting for me* 😵

He waited, the dots indicating she was typing back almost instantly.

Chloe Smith: *You muppet! That car's probably already got a dozen tickets on it by now! I'll swing by and see what the damage is. You owe me a pint for this, Reevesy.* 

James chuckled, feeling a wave of relief mixed with sibling gratitude. Chloe might tease him, but she'd always had his back. He could almost picture her rolling her eyes as she read the message, her exasperation laced with amusement.

James Smith: *Deal! Thanks, sis, tell ya what, I'll get ya a Nando's for your trouble, meet up with me, Kylie, Liam and Cody?*

Chloe's reply came quickly, her tone teasing but warm.

Chloe Smith: *You're on, Reevesy. A Nando's sounds like fair payment for rescuing your car. See you soon, superstar!*

James grinned, putting his phone down and sharing a knowing glance with Kylie. It felt good to have Chloe's support, even as his own world grew wilder. He leaned back, feeling a strange blend of fatigue and excitement— the exhaustion of the weekend paired with the thrill of what lay ahead.

As Liam's car made its way down the motorway, James closed his eyes, letting his mind drift back to the Headbangers recording and the unexpected Twitter spat with Stephanie Hirst. The playful rivalry with Hits added a new, competitive edge to his journey with Manic. It wasn't just about following orders or filling a slot; he was part of something that could genuinely shake things up.

Kylie nudged him softly, her voice low. "Proud of you, babe. Not everyone would go toe-to-toe with a Hits Radio legend like Hirsty. Shows you've got guts."

* - * - * - *

An hour and half later, Chloe was sat outside the Nando's at the Merry Hill centre, her brother's BMW pulled up next to her in the car park. James stepped out of Al's BMW, looking a bit worse for wear but managing a grin as he spotted Chloe. Kylie and Liam followed, both equally drained yet buzzing with the afterglow of the wild weekend. Chloe, leaning against the car with a smirk, looked between her brother and Kylie, clearly amused.

"Right, Reevesy," Chloe said, folding her arms with a playful glint in her eyes. "I checked on your car, and lucky for you, the parking gods were on your side. No ticket—though I think the security guard outside The Waterfront was about to start writing one when I got there."

James let out a sigh of relief, chuckling. "Dodged a bullet there. You saved my life, sis. Nando's is on me, as promised. Can't beat a cheeky Nando's, eh, little sis?"

Chloe grinned, nudging him playfully as they headed inside. "You're lucky, Reevesy. But maybe next time don't leave your car on double yellows outside a radio station when you're about to disappear for a wild weekend in Liverpool!"

As they settled into a booth, James felt a sense of calm and familiarity. It was a strange contrast to the chaotic energy of the past two days. The smell of grilled chicken and the friendly chatter of nearby diners was grounding after the heady, surreal world of Manic.

"So," Chloe said, looking between James and Kylie with a raised eyebrow, "you two have definitely made a mark with this whole 'Ibiza Headbangers' thing. That tweet war with Hirsty was brilliant—she's practically radio royalty! Mum and Dad are on a 'romantic' weekend in Shrewsbury and aren't coming back until morning."

James chuckled, leaning back in the booth, savouring the comfort of home mixed with the satisfaction of having taken on a legend like Stephanie Hirst. "Yeah, I never thought I'd end up on Hirsty's radar. She's probably been doing this longer than I've been alive!" He took a sip of his drink, sharing a grin with Kylie. "It's weird, isn't it? One minute you're just trying to make your mark, and the next, you're having a full-on Twitter feud with one of the biggest names in CHR."

Kylie laughed, reaching for a chip. "But that's exactly what makes it fun, right? Manic's giving us a real shot, and we're shaking things up. I mean, I didn't expect Hits to take it so seriously, but now we've got a little rivalry going—it makes it exciting!"

Chloe rolled her eyes with a smirk. "Exciting for you two, sure, but I'm just imagining what Dad's reaction will be. First, he's got you and Steph Hirst bickering on social media, then the whole 'Manic Dance' pre-recorded Ibiza show." She shook her head, laughing. "He's in for a surprise when he tunes in next weekend."

James couldn't help but smile, a mixture of pride and a hint of nerves. His dad might roll his eyes at the flashy world of Manic and the rivalry with Hits, but there was still part of James that hoped he'd see it for what it was— a step forward, a chance to build his own identity.

"Yeah, well, you know Dad—he'll have something to say, that's for sure," James admitted. "Although he'd rather listen to that snoozefest Black Country Radio's late-night jazz. But this whole thing… it feels like I'm finally carving out my own place, something different but still, in a way, connected to what Dad's always done. Anyway, sis, got you something."

James handed Chloe a 50 gram bag of cocaine that he had picked up from one of the club promoters they'd met in Liverpool. Chloe's eyes widened in surprise, a mix of intrigue and caution crossing her face as she took the small bag, tucking it discreetly into her purse with a knowing look.

"You sure know how to keep things interesting, big brother," she murmured with a sly grin, leaning back in her seat. "Guess the perks of Manic life come in all shapes and sizes."

Kylie laughed, raising her glass. "To the Manic way! And to making next week's show even bigger."

James clinked his glass with hers, feeling a renewed sense of energy as the night's events settled over them. The weekend had been a whirlwind, but it was also a turning point—a glimpse into the chaotic, exhilarating, and sometimes messy world he was becoming a part of. With the new rivalry brewing, the support of his family, and the spark of ambition driving him forward, he felt ready to make his mark on Manic Radio and the CHR scene, one wild Saturday night at a time.

As they settled into the evening with Chloe and the rest of their group, James realised this wasn't just the end of a wild weekend—it was the start of something far bigger.

****

CHAPTER 8 – Back to the Grind
Monday 4th November 2024

"Pete, love, do you think the kids have had a calm weekend, especially after the lecture we gave them Friday?"

Pete glanced up from his mug of tea as he and Sarah were sat at the breakfast buffet of their B&B that they were stopping in in the Shropshire town of Shrewsbury. Having left their phones, computers and work worries back in Dudley, Pete and Sarah had embraced the rare chance to unplug and recharge over the weekend. The warm, quiet atmosphere of the B&B felt like a world away from the bustling chaos of Manic Radio. Pete smiled at his wife, trying to shrug off the familiar worries that lingered just beneath the surface.

"I'd like to think so, Sarah," Pete replied, pouring her another cup of tea. "They know how we feel about it all, and maybe, just maybe, they'll take that to heart." He tried to sound reassuring, but there was a niggling thought in the back of his mind. James had a way of getting caught up in things, especially with his new role at Manic, and Chloe… well, she had a rebellious streak that even Pete couldn't deny.

Sarah gave him a wry smile. "I suppose. But you know them—they're young, in the thick of it all. Sometimes I wonder if they hear us at all when it comes to that 'Manic lifestyle'."

Pete sighed, taking a sip of his tea as he glanced out of the window. The tranquil view of Shrewsbury's quaint streets was the perfect counterpoint to his usual life. "I know. But we've done what we can, haven't we? Raised them, given them values. The rest, well, I suppose they have to figure that out on their own."

Just then, Pete heard a ping from across the breakfast room. A young couple was glancing at their phones, chuckling over something they'd just read.

"Did you see the photos on Insta about that hunk, Reevesy?" one of the young women whispered to her partner, barely containing her excitement. Pete's ears pricked up, his curiosity piqued at hearing James's alias, Reevesy, mentioned. "He makes those Love Island lot look like they need a work out. I'd love to be a fly on the wall for one of those Ibiza Headbangers nights. Apparently, they had the wildest party in Liverpool on Saturday with half the Manic crew."

Pete felt a familiar tension build in his chest. He'd hoped James's weekend would be a bit more low-key, maybe focused on his new show and not wrapped up in the whirlwind lifestyle Manic promoted. Hearing strangers gush over "Reevesy" didn't help, especially when he knew that James was barely out of university and already being thrust into the limelight.

Sarah noticed his expression shift and placed a comforting hand on his arm. "Pete, let them have their fun. We both know it's hard to resist the excitement when you're young. And besides, it sounds like James is making a bit of a name for himself. Maybe we should give him a chance to figure things out his own way?"

Pete gave her a tight-lipped smile. "I know you're right, love. It's just hard to let go. Radio used to be about connecting with listeners, building communities. Now it's all about who can throw the wildest party or get the most 'likes'. I barely recognise it sometimes."

He took another sip of tea, trying to let the calm of Shrewsbury settle over him. But as they finished breakfast and stepped out for a stroll along the River Severn, his thoughts drifted back to the chaotic scenes he'd left behind at Manic, scenes that he knew were now part of James's world.

On the way back to the B&B to collect their belongings, as Pete was due back at work later on, he noticed a billboard near to the Ravens Meadow Shopping Centre with a new advert on, having been the previous day an advert for Hits Radio.

"Missing the Balearics? Tune in to Manic Dance with Reevesy and Morgz every Saturday at 10!" the advert read, with a photo of James and Kylie that had been took on Tuesday, James's first day as a Manic presenter. The image showed James and Kylie in their "Ibiza Headbangers" personas, dressed to the nines in branded Manic gear, sunglasses perched on their heads as if they'd just stepped off a flight from Ibiza. James's grin was confident, his arm casually around Kylie's shoulder, while Kylie flashed a sultry smile that captured the very essence of the Manic Dance vibe, along with a tweet attached

@ManicDance: *Get ready for the hottest beats straight from the heart of Ibiza! #IbizaHeadbangers.*

Pete stopped in his tracks, a mixture of pride and unease churning inside him. The advert was bold, youthful, and exactly the kind of thing that would catch the eye of any passerby. It was clever branding—he had to give them that—but seeing his son up there, larger than life, felt strange. This was the James he'd raised, but it was also someone different—a curated persona, carefully crafted for the spotlight.

Sarah followed his gaze, her expression softening. "He looks happy, doesn't he? Maybe this is his way of making radio something new, Pete. Just because it's different doesn't mean it's wrong."

Pete nodded, although he wasn't sure he fully agreed. "It's a big leap from the radio I knew, that's for sure. But maybe… maybe he'll surprise us."

The advert then turned around, as it was one of those billboards that could carry 4 different ads, to reveal one for the Mid Wales Manic Breakfast show, one of the shows produced from the Dudley hub serving Shrewsbury and the surrounding areas. The ad featured a grinning Liam, the same presenter who'd been with James in Liverpool over the weekend, and his fiancée, Suzie, a young Chinese presenter who co-hosted the show, the two twentysomethings being part of the clique that James had been swept up in at Manic. Pete studied the new advert, noticing how upbeat and polished Liam and Suzie looked, posed in a way that conveyed energy and friendliness. They were the new face of local radio, bridging Manic's brash style with an approachable warmth, and it was clear they were targeting a younger audience.

Sarah smiled as she took in the image of Liam and Suzie. "They look like they're having fun too, don't they? It's different from our day, Pete, but these kids—they know how to make it work. It's like they've found a way to turn it into something bigger than just radio. It's a whole… lifestyle, I suppose."

It then changed to the national drive advert for Manic Radio, one used in regions like Shrewsbury and Mid Wales where the only local regional broadcasts were the breakfast show. Pete watched as the billboard displayed an advert for Danny O'Neil, the charismatic host of Manic's national drive show, beaming with his trademark grin, one that had become recognisable from London to Liverpool. The ad proudly proclaimed, "Manic Drive with Danny O'Neil – Keeping you moving every weekday at 4!" Danny's image seemed almost larger-than-life, his energetic pose framed against a backdrop of cityscapes that hinted at the network's reach.

The irony was that, in Wellington, Pete would be the advert face, as the Wrekin took the Midlands region feed that he hosted each weekday. As the billboard rotated through its final advert, showcasing one of Hits Radio's campaigns featuring Hattie Pearson, the afternoon network presenter on Bauer's stations, Pete couldn't help but notice the contrast between Hits' polished, slightly subdued style and the bold, edgy look of Manic's ads. It reflected the industry's shifts, the divide between traditional CHR and Manic's more unapologetic, high-energy approach.

Seeing the logo of who owned the totem, Pete had to chuckle, as it was 'Adoors', the sister company to Manic's, part of the Lite Group, who owned it, a competitor to Global's Outdoor division which was the biggest of the main outdoor advertising groups. Manic had clearly been leveraging every bit of Lite Group's reach to make their presence felt in both big cities and smaller towns alike. It was clever, saturating the market not just with radio content but with a brand identity that was hard to ignore.

As they walked back to the B&B, Pete felt a mix of resignation and curiosity. He'd made peace with the fact that James and Chloe were part of a new generation, one that didn't just listen to radio but lived it as part of a social, media-driven identity. He knew he'd see a lot more of James and his colleagues plastered across billboards and social media feeds. It was a bittersweet realisation, but he could appreciate the fact that James was forging his own path—even if that path was one that he couldn't fully understand.

* _ * _ * _ *

A couple of hours later, Pete walked into the Manic Radio hub at the Waterfront to see that there was a new notice on the noticeboard.

MANIC RADIO CHRISTMAS LAUNCHES 1ST DECEMBER 2024 - PRESENTERS NEEDED

NO REGIONAL SHOWS ON MANIC RADIO DURING CHRISTMAS PERIOD - PRESENTERS NEEDED FOR NATIONAL SCHEDULE

LITE GROUP AQUIRES ST JOHNS BEACON AND ONE SNOW HILL LEASES

Pete scanned the new notices, feeling an old, familiar twist in his gut. The phrase "No regional shows during Christmas" hit home with a blunt finality. For decades, Christmas on local radio had been about connecting with the community—charity drives, listener dedications, festive playlists crafted with care. But now, even the holiday season was morphing into something national, homogenised, and devoid of that personal touch he'd spent his career fostering.

The fact that all presenters on full time contracts, which meant everyone bar the cover presenters like James and a few others, would be required to host at least one show during the week and half period that the national schedule would replace the local shows added another layer of frustration. Pete knew that while some of his colleagues might welcome the extra exposure, others, like himself, would see it as a further erasure of the unique flavour each regional station once brought to the table.

"Morning, Pete!" a familiar voice called from down the hallway. It was Lyra, who had been co-hosting with him on the Midlands Manic drive the previous week but was returning to her Northern Vibes drive slot from today. "Want some gossip?"

Pete knew that Lyra's definition of gossip, despite being 26, was different to that of the other staff that were in their 20s, and that it was mainly about schedule updates as opposed to the typical party antics and scandals that often defined the conversations around Manic Radio's younger presenters.

"Sure, Lyra," Pete replied, forcing a smile as she approached, her leather jacket giving her the edgy but professional look she seemed to favour. "Hit me with it."

Lyra gave him a conspiratorial grin. "Al's not here. He's been given the day off... and a bit more... as he was doing the national evening show with Toni Green last night... and swore live on air. Said the 'f' word... just as the show started. Next thing you know, James's Ibiza Headbangers show was playing out instead."

Pete chuckled, shaking his head. "Al swore on air? That's bold, even for him. Sounds like the weekend got the better of him."

Lyra laughed, nodding. "Oh, you should have seen the uproar! Toni tried to cover for him, but he then went on about her 'sleeping with half of Hits and Capital,' and she hit back with some choice words about him being 'a coked-up prat who can't hold his drink'. It was a proper car crash."

Pete winced, imagining the scene. "And they kept that on air?"

"Only for about thirty seconds, but you know how quick that stuff spreads. It's all over X this morning," Lyra replied, rolling her eyes. "They threw Ibiza Headbangers on pretty fast, but not before half the listeners heard it. I'd guess Al's looking at more than just a day off."

Pete looked at Lyra's phone, which had a clip from last night's disastrous show already making rounds on social media. Al's voice rang out, slightly slurred, as he dropped the f-bomb, followed by Toni's frustrated retort. Pete could see the caption someone had added: "When Manic gets a bit too… Manic!" accompanied by laughing emojis and the hashtag #ManicMayhem.

The fact that Hits Radio had also posted a tweet about it—highlighting the chaos with a cheeky jab—only added fuel to the fire.

@HitsRadio: *Looks like Manic had an eventful Sunday night! 🎙 ✴ Let's hope @ManicDance can keep their Ibiza Headbangers running smoothly without any... unexpected language. #RadioWars*

Pete couldn't help but sigh. It was exactly the kind of publicity Manic loved—bold, brash, and guaranteed to go viral. But for someone like him, who valued the respectability and professionalism that once defined radio, it was a tough pill to swallow.

"So, what's the fallout?" he asked, handing Lyra her phone back.

"Well, from what I've heard, they're having a 'sit-down' with Al today. Word is he's..." Lyra made a slashing motion across her neck. "Suspended indefinitely," she said, raising an eyebrow. "I don't think we'll be hearing from him for a while. As for Toni, they're chalking it up to her 'defending the Manic family'—she might even get away with it. Ah well, I'm on my own for the Stoke Drive."

Pete shook his head, a mixture of amusement and exasperation playing across his face. "Only at Manic would something like that become a badge of honour."

Lyra chuckled. "You're not wrong. I mean, they do love a bit of drama, don't they? And Toni, well… she's practically made a career out of 'defending the family' with her wild antics. But still, even she was thrown off by Al last night. He really pushed it too far. Oh, and you've got Lily again. Greg's caught COVID, so he's off all week. She'll be in for production, so enjoy Malibu Barbie."

Pete groaned inwardly at the thought of having Lily in for another week. Her chaotic, unfiltered personality seemed to fit right in with the younger crowd at Manic, but for him, it was like stepping into a parallel universe—one where professionalism had been traded for shock value. He forced a smile for Lyra, who chuckled at his clear discomfort.

"She's a bit of a whirlwind, isn't she?" Pete muttered, trying to mask his irritation. "Guess I'll have to remind myself I'm here to do a job."

Lyra grinned sympathetically. "Oh, you'll manage, Pete. She might be a handful, but she gets things done in her own way. Just don't let her drag you into one of her 'gals' group chats. You'd never hear the end of it. Tim and Ellen's off all week, so they've got one of the Bee Manic crew covering their East Midlands drive show… another of the "23 and dresses like a slapper" crowd. Wanna know the best bit? This Jenny, the cover host… is Lily's sister. Fancy a brew?"

"Only at Manic…" Pete muttered, pinching the bridge of his nose with a mixture of exhaustion and resignation. He had thought this week might provide a small respite after the chaos of last week, but apparently, he was in for more than he'd bargained for. "Sure, Lyra, a tea would be great. Probably need a strong one at that."

The two headed to the break room, where Lily was sat on Abdul's lap, his hand in her skirt band, and the person he assumed was Jenny was straddling Liam, kissing him like he was the only thing keeping her upright. Pete noticed that Suzie, Liam's fiancée, was doing the same with Frankie, the East Midlands producer. Looking at his watch, however, Pete was confused why Liam and Suzie were still here even though it was half past 1 in the afternoon and nowhere near their breakfast show slot. Just as Pete was about to ask, Lyra nudged him with a smirk.

"Liam and Suzie have been doing some voice-tracked stuff for one of the new Manic Prime stations, a Dua Lipa v Katy Perry station," Lyra said, sighing. "Yet another of those curated playlist formats they've rolled out. They've done a Dua one, a Perry one, and a 'Manic Radio Girl Power' station show."

Pete shook his head in bemusement. The concept of having so many niche, curated shows felt a world apart from the days when the focus was on live, interactive radio. It was all part of Manic's relentless push to own every possible listener niche with 'Prime' stations dedicated to narrow themes, where the presenters were more like voice-over personalities than true hosts.

"Dua versus Perry?" Pete muttered, a wry smile tugging at his lips. "That's the future, I suppose – battling pop divas through pre-recorded links."

Lyra rolled her eyes, passing him his tea. "It's all about capturing audiences wherever they are, isn't it? Anyway, this is Manic we're talking about. Nothing stays quiet for long, especially with Lily and now her sister Jenny thrown in the mix." She paused, glancing over at Lily and Jenny, who were now chatting animatedly about last night's antics with Al and Toni. "Weirdly, though, this place would be pretty dull without them."

Pete let out a reluctant chuckle, feeling the faintest twinge of agreement. As much as he despised the chaos, he had to admit that Manic's younger crew brought a certain energy. Yet he couldn't shake the feeling of alienation, especially when he saw the ease with which they navigated this new landscape, where professionalism often seemed to be trumped by a kind of unapologetic hedonism. He took a long sip of his tea, contemplating his place in this strange, new era of radio.

*_*_*_*

"Yo, Reevesy!" James heard as he entered Prestige Barbers, opposite the main Wolverhampton University campus for a quick haircut before heading back to lectures. He'd barely stepped inside when his barber, Taz, greeted him with a grin and a knowing nod.

"Reevesy, mate, caught ya on Manic Dance the other night. Ya sounded like ya were in Ibiza itself how high ya were on air."

James laughed, sinking into the chair. "Cheers, Taz. That's the magic of Manic—they make you sound like you're halfway across the world when really, you're just a few miles down the road in Dudley!"

Taz chuckled, draping a cape around James. "Mate, you're living the dream, aren't ya? Everyone's talking about Ibiza Headbangers. Had a few lads in here saying you and Kylie are giving Hits a run for their money. And that spat with Stephanie Hirst on X? Brilliant, mate. Nothing like a bit of rivalry to get people listening."

James grinned, adjusting himself in the chair as Taz got to work. "Yeah, Hirsty's a legend. Feels a bit surreal, going toe-to-toe with her. My old man knows her from when she was a teen and working at Radio Aire back in the '90s. Bit mad to think I'm having a back-and-forth with someone he looked up to, but it's all part of the game, right?"

Taz nodded, snipping away as he shaped James's hair. "Mate, that's radio for ya. A bit of drama keeps people hooked. Everyone in here was talking about Ibiza Headbangers and saying Manic's the freshest thing out there. And seeing that advert you and Kylie have got up? Mad exposure. Ya hear about Manic's evening show last night?"

"Nah, mate, what happened?"

Taz raised his eyebrows, clearly relishing the chance to fill James in. "Mate, it was a right car crash! Al Crozier and Toni Green were covering the national evening slot, and he starts off with an f-bomb—live on air! Just lets it slip, clear as day. Then, Toni goes at him, calling him a 'coked-up prat' who 'can't manage his booze'... all live. Wasn't even two minutes in before they had to cut to your Ibiza Headbangers show as a quick cover-up."

James's eyes widened as he took it in, stifling a laugh. He remembered how, when he, Liam and Kylie had left Toni's flat the previous afternoon, Al was snorting a line of cocaine and downing a bottle of whiskey, gearing up for what he'd called his "big national break." He hadn't expected Al to actually go live in such a state, though.

The fact that James himself had, first thing that morning, snorted a couple of lines of cocaine to shake off the lingering effects of the Liverpool weekend didn't feel much different from what Al might have done. But seeing how it had turned out for Al, he wondered if he was playing with fire. The Manic brand thrived on pushing boundaries, but there was always a line – and Al had clearly crossed it.

Taz continued, shaking his head in amusement. "Everyone's saying it's the kind of publicity Manic loves, though. The younger crowd? They're lapping it up, sharing clips, making memes. But you know the bosses'll have something to say about it, too."

James grinned, but a hint of apprehension crept in. He knew Manic was all about living on the edge, yet there was a fine line between keeping things exciting and going off the rails entirely. The rivalry with Hirsty had stirred up good-natured competition, and he loved it, but a part of him wondered if he'd eventually slip up the way Al had.

"He'll probably be suspended," James said, sighing. "OFCOM will also probably investigate. If there's one thing radio hosts know is that if you swear on air, OFCOM will come down on you like a tonne of bricks."

"How d'ya mean, mate?"

James shifted slightly in the barber's chair, glancing at his reflection in the mirror before explaining. "It's OFCOM—the radio watchdog. They're brutal when it comes to swearing on air. Doesn't matter if it's an accident; you let the wrong word slip, and they'll make sure you feel it. They hand out fines, impose suspensions… sometimes even threaten licences if they think a station's pushing it too far."

Taz raised his eyebrows, visibly impressed. "Didn't realise it was that serious. So, Al's mess-up last night could cost Manic?"

James nodded, feeling the weight of it. "Yeah, mate. It's not just about the laughs or the memes. If OFCOM gets involved, Manic could end up paying for it, and that'll be on Al. He has aims of going national either on Manic, Hits or another station, and this... it's his career up in smoke. One live slip, and it can all come crumbling down."

Taz nodded thoughtfully, carefully trimming James's hair. "That's mad, mate. Guess it's a real balancing act, then. The stuff that gets people talking, like Ibiza Headbangers and that feud with Hirsty—it's all great until someone crosses the line."

James gave a slight nod, staring at his reflection. Al's slip-up was a harsh reminder of how easy it was to get caught up in the thrill of it all. It was exciting, yes, but it wasn't a game. This was his shot, and while the wild lifestyle was part of Manic's brand, he didn't want it to ruin what he was building.

"Anyway, the goss is that our Manic power couple, Jimmy and Kylie, were in Liverpool this weekend," Lily said. It was half past five, and Pete was presenting his Midlands Manic drive show with Lily by his side in the production booth, repeating what the script had her say. "Anyway, they've got a bit of a feud with someone from the other lot."

Pete tried hard not to yawn as he heard Lily's scripted introduction to the segment, her voice laced with the usual over-the-top enthusiasm. He had to remind himself to keep his tone upbeat, despite feeling disconnected from the high-energy antics that defined the younger Manic crew.

"Yep, that's right, Lily," Pete replied, forcing a smile into his voice. "Our very own Jimmy Reeves and Kylie Morgan have stirred up a bit of friendly competition with Stephanie Hirst over at Hits Radio. It's all in good fun, and it seems like Saturday nights are heating up on the airwaves."

Lily grinned, leaning in closer to the mic, clearly revelling in the chance to play up the drama. "And it's not just friendly rivalry, is it, Pete? Hits threw a few cheeky comments our way, and Jimmy fired back! Love seeing our Manic crew bringing the fire!" She let out a small, knowing laugh, like she was letting the listeners in on an inside joke. "And hey, we all know which station brings the real party. Anyway, it seems that, dear listeners, our Pete knows Stephanie Hirst."

Pete groaned, as, yes, he knew Stephanie Hirst, being in the industry for 30 years and having crossed paths with her more than once, but having that connection brought up in the context of a X spat between Manic and Hits, it felt a bit awkward. Looking at the script, he noticed that he was supposed to take the mick out of Hirst and Hits Radio, but he couldn't bring himself to go through with it. Stephanie Hirst was a respected name in the industry, and Pete knew the challenges she'd faced to build her reputation. The fact that the script would later have him fire shade at Roman and Martin Kemp, the Spandau Ballet legend and his son, who was a Capital presenter, seemed equally cringeworthy to Pete. It was one thing for the younger crowd like James to trade jabs on social media for a bit of fun, but it felt undignified for him to join in, especially when he genuinely respected some of these people. Pete had always prided himself on being professional, and to be part of this forced rivalry left a sour taste in his mouth.

Taking a deep breath, he adjusted his approach, deciding to play it down. "Ah, well, yes, I've crossed paths with Stephanie once or twice over the years," he said in an even tone. "She's done some fantastic work for Hits, and it's good to see a bit of healthy competition among the younger lot. Keeps things interesting for the listeners, right?"

Lily shot him a look that said she knew he was toning it down, but she didn't push it, instead pivoting to the next scripted segment. "You're too kind, Pete! But I'm sure we all know Manic's the place to be on Saturday nights. Sorry, Hits!" She flashed him a grin as she leaned back in her chair, clearly amused by his diplomatic approach.

They continued through the show, Pete managing to steer clear of too much drama while keeping up with the upbeat energy Manic demanded. When the mics were off during a song, Lily glanced over at him with a look which, if it could kill, would have murdered him without hesitation. She clearly wanted him to play up the rivalry and inject some of Manic's trademark edge into the segment.

"Pete, come on," she said, feigning a pout. "You're too old-school! A bit of banter never hurt anyone, and the audience loves it when we poke fun. It's all part of the show!"

Pete smiled, choosing his words carefully. "I get that, Lily. It's just… I've been in this game a long time. Stephanie Hirst, Roman Kemp—they've earned their spots. Hell, Roman's dad is someone I've interviewed and respect not just for his singing but his acting as well. They're people I genuinely respect. I know a bit of banter's part of the job these days, but some things don't sit right with me."

Lily frowned. "Do you want me to get Cal to have you in his office?"

Cal Ellington was the regional hub manager, the person who made the final calls on everything broadcast-related at the Midlands Manic hub. If anyone could pull Pete into line or remind him of his place within Manic's new world, it was Cal.

The fact Cal was in his late 20s and so part of the generation of younger, more commercially minded executives made Pete's approach feel even more precarious. But Pete squared his shoulders, determined to stand by his principles.

"Lily," he said calmly, "I've been on air for three decades. I understand banter, but I also understand respect. If Cal wants to discuss it, I'm more than willing. But there's more to radio than just stirring up drama for clicks."

Lily gave him a knowing look, tapping her acrylic nails on the desk in slight frustration. "Fine, Pete, but just remember, Manic's built its brand on being edgy. People tune in for that energy, that push. You're a legend, sure, but legends need to keep up with the times, yeah?"

She returned her focus to the control board, but Pete could sense her lingering annoyance. He understood the younger generation's focus on engagement, on bold statements and viral moments. But he also knew that radio was more than that – it was about authenticity, something he feared was slipping away in the fast-paced, brand-driven world Manic had cultivated.

As the song finished, Pete knew that the next segment was coming up, and it was more of the same banter-filled script designed to rile up listeners and stir a bit more drama. But Pete wasn't in the mood for it, not after the whirlwind of recent events and his attempts to hold onto some sense of integrity in an industry that was rapidly evolving into something he barely recognised.

The "On Air" light blinked on, and he took a steadying breath. He was about to launch into the next part of the show when he noticed a message pop up on his screen from Cal himself.

"Pete – keep the rivalry angle up, mate. It's good for numbers. Hits are gaining momentum, and we need to keep the engagement rolling. Let's have a bit more edge, alright?"

Pete clenched his jaw but replied with a simple, "Got it." He understood the need to appeal to Manic's core audience, but it felt like he was being pulled further away from the kind of radio he valued.

Lily, seeing the message, gave him a quick thumbs-up, her eyes dancing with the thrill of it all. As they returned to the mics, Pete did his best to add a bit more punch, though his heart wasn't fully in it.

"Alright, folks, as you've heard, Saturday nights are heating up with our own Ibiza Headbangers on Manic Dance, and let's just say Hits Radio's got a bit of a challenge on their hands keeping up," he said, his tone friendly but not quite biting.

Lily jumped in enthusiastically. "Exactly, Pete! We're bringing the Ibiza vibes, the energy, and the party atmosphere—something you're not going to find on Hits. Sorry, Hirsty, but Manic's where the real fun is at!"

They wrapped up the segment, and as soon as the mics were off, Pete leaned back, feeling a bit drained. Lily, however, was clearly buzzing, fully invested in Manic's high-energy, high-drama style. He couldn't deny that this approach worked, that it pulled in listeners and sparked conversations. But deep down, he wondered how long he could keep playing along before he, too, would have to face the choice of either adapting fully or finding a way out.

For now, he'd keep showing up, balancing the demands of his bosses with his own principles. But as he looked over at Lily, who was scrolling through social media with a gleeful expression, he knew that the world of radio was changing, and he'd need to decide how much of himself he was willing to leave behind to stay in the game.

****

CHAPTER 9 – Fireworks of an Annual Contract Renewal Kind
Tuesday 5th November 2024

It was the day Pete was dreading most, the 5th of November, the day of the annual contract renewal he had to have. Every year for 30 years it had been a mere formality, a rubber stamp on another year of presenting, and for most of his career, Pete had barely given it a second thought. But this year felt different, and he couldn't shake the nagging worry that it might be more than just another formality. Manic's world had shifted so radically since 2019, when Lite Group and Breeze Media merged, with Derbyshire Delight, East Midlands Vibes, London Vibes, Midlands Manic and Western Ulster Vibes folded into the new, streamlined Manic Radio network. Coronavirus in 2020, and then the 2022 purchase of 26 different local stations, had only pushed the network toward a homogenised, high-energy, and heavily branded machine. The idea of radio as he knew it had evolved—some might say deteriorated—into a bold, edgy lifestyle-driven brand, where presenters weren't just voices but faces, personas, brands in their own right.

The fact that the 2022 purchases had immediately lost their legacy branding, swallowed into the "Manic" identity with new names, new locations, and a corporate polish, had left Pete feeling adrift. His role, once rooted in community and connection, now felt like it was teetering on the edge of redundancy, especially as he watched younger presenters like his son James embrace the Manic way without hesitation.

Looking at the staff noticeboard, Pete noticed a new notice had been placed:

AL CROZIER RESIGNATION - EFFECTIVE IMMEDIATLY.

That headline itself had made Pete raise an eyebrow, as Al was one of the young 'brand-friendly' presenters who seemed practically made for the new Manic image. Al was the kind who embraced every aspect of the network's edgy, brash style—social media-ready, always on brand, and unapologetically wild. For him to resign without notice was surprising, especially considering his ambition to go national. Pete could only assume that Sunday night's live mishap had led to an ultimatum from management, and Al, rather than face a suspension or worse, had chosen to bow out. A hint of sympathy stirred in Pete; he could hardly imagine what Al would do outside of Manic, a network that had become his entire identity.

The next headline made Pete frown, however

ALL LOCAL STATIONS TO GAIN NEW 'MANIC VIBES' IDENTITY FROM APRIL 2025 - SOME STATIONS TO BE FOLDED INTO NEIGHBOURING STATIONS

The announcement about "Manic Vibes" made Pete's heart sink. He had heard rumours of a rebranding push, but seeing it confirmed brought an uncomfortable finality to the whispers. Since the Lite Group merger, it felt like Manic Radio was on a mission to erase everything that made each local station distinct. The once-familiar names, histories, and connections each station had with its community were systematically stripped away, and now, even the last holdouts would be swallowed up by this new "Vibes" branding. By April, the Midlands hub he'd known and loved would be just another branch of a homogenised Manic Radio.

Looking through the list, Pete noticed that Warwickshire Stars was fated to be folded into the West Midlands feed, with the frequency reallocated to Manic Goldies West Midlands, a new localised feed for the ever-expanding Manic Goldies network. Northants Now, meanwhile, was due to renamed Manic Vibes Northamptonshire, with Manic Radio Three Counties, the Herefordshire, Gloucestershire and Worcestershire station, being eliminated completely as it was a duplicate of the Midlands, West of England and Welsh regional feeds.

The irony that Warwickshire would be flipping to Manic Goldies didn't escape Pete's notice. Manic Goldies—a nostalgia station playing classics from the 70s, 80s, and 90s—was ironically more aligned with his view of radio's purpose than the high-octane, modern Manic brand. He shook his head, torn between frustration and resignation as he realised that the last vestiges of local identity were being sacrificed for a unified "Vibes" image. It was a world away from the days when he'd started out, where each station had a unique character, a community focus, a sense of loyalty to its local listeners.

Then there was Manic Urban, which was a new network aimed at capturing the youth market in urban areas, offering non-stop hip-hop, grime, and R&B in a relentless mix designed for younger audiences who lived online as much as they lived offline. The Manic Urban stations were set to launch in April as well, taking over frequencies in places like East London, North London, and other major city hubs. Pete could barely comprehend how quickly Manic was moving to dominate every niche, every demographic, with their slickly branded, automated feeds.

MANIC GOLDIES TO INTRODUCE REGIONAL BREAKFAST AND DRIVE IN SELECTED REGIONS

That was the final line that caught Pete's eye, one that filled him with a strange mix of nostalgia and irony. It was as if, in a roundabout way, Manic was reintroducing the kind of local connection that he and his colleagues had been fighting to preserve all along, albeit under a more palatable, nostalgia-driven brand. Regional breakfast and drive shows were what Manic Goldies would be introducing, with the new regions being the only stations not taking the current single station programme of an all-day national presenter line-up. But the change wasn't about reviving community-driven radio; it was more about providing a regional flavour to fit the Goldies audience's love for throwback hits. It was nostalgia for nostalgia's sake, carefully curated and branded, rather than the genuine connection that had once defined local radio.

He sighed, rolling his shoulders back as he made his way toward Cal's office, where the meeting about his contract renewal was set to take place. Cal was a competent manager, though Pete couldn't deny that his younger boss's outlook was vastly different. Cal embodied the new Manic Radio vision: efficient, focused on branding, and determined to keep pace with social media-driven trends. For Cal, radio was a product, a package that had to appeal to the largest demographic possible, preferably one that would engage with Manic's digital content.

"Ah, Pete, right on time!" Cal greeted him as Pete entered, gesturing toward a chair across from his desk. The room was stylish, minimalistic, with hints of Lite Group's branding that felt more like a corporate boardroom than a place for radio discussions. Cal leaned forward, his hands folded neatly in front of him. "It's that time of year again—let's talk about where we're going for 2025."

"Right," Pete replied, trying to keep his tone neutral. He was determined not to let his mixed feelings cloud the conversation. He took his seat, mentally preparing himself for whatever changes Cal was about to outline.

Cal offered a reassuring smile, but there was a distinct air of formality that set Pete on edge. "Pete, I want you to know, first off, that we respect the legacy you bring to Manic, especially here in the Midlands. But as you've no doubt seen on the noticeboard, we're in the middle of some significant changes across the network. The 'Manic Vibes' identity is designed to streamline our brand and give listeners a consistent experience, whether they're in London, Dudley, or Dundee. It's about unifying our voice."

Pete nodded, though he couldn't fully hide the tension that crept into his expression. "I understand the strategy, Cal, and I appreciate that Manic wants to capture that younger market. But I can't help wondering where the local connections fit in. The community angle used to be what radio-"

"Woah, before you say anything, we're planning to renew your contract, with a pay increase, on one proviso."

Pete felt a mix of relief and apprehension. A pay increase was welcome, of course, but he knew there was always a catch, especially when it came to the new Manic Radio.

"Alright, Cal," Pete replied, trying to keep his tone even. "What's the proviso?"

Cal leaned forward, hands clasped together, his expression softening in a way that Pete suspected was meant to put him at ease. "We want you to leave the main Manic Vibes station in April and take Lead Presenter on Manic Goldies West Midlands Drive. It's a £5,000 a year increase. It also includes one extra show a week, on a Saturday afternoon. You see, there's a third slot on Goldies that's being opened for local feeds during the EFL season, and it's something you used to do on Dudley FM... a football phone-in... and there's also a new slot opening up on Manic Rock '80s once a week, a 2 hour show beforehand."

Pete was taken aback. A shift from Manic's main station to Manic Goldies was not what he'd expected, though he couldn't deny that part of him felt intrigued. The drive-time show on Goldies would let him reconnect with a more familiar audience, one that valued the same sense of nostalgia he did. The added football phone-in would also take him back to his roots, something he'd once relished during his Dudley FM days. And a show on Manic Rocks

'80s? It felt like a chance to step back into a past he missed. But leaving the main station—Manic Vibes—felt like a final step away from the core of Manic's identity.

He considered his words carefully before responding. "Cal, I'll admit, the idea of Goldies is appealing. It's closer to the kind of radio I've always loved. But leaving Midlands Manic... I can't deny it feels like a step back."

Cal nodded, his gaze steady. "I understand, Pete. But we're looking at a new direction for the Vibes stations, targeting a younger, more socially active demographic. Manic Goldies, on the other hand, is built for a mature audience who values classic hits and a different pace. It's less promos, less celeb gossip, more focus on genuine connection. We think you'd bring a lot of value to the Goldies audience. They're looking for exactly the kind of experience you've built your career around—one with a community feel and authentic engagement."

Pete took a deep breath, weighing the offer. It was true that the high-energy style of Midlands Manic had always been at odds with his approach. Goldies, though more laid-back, felt like it would allow him to connect in a way he hadn't been able to lately. And the football phone-in? That brought a flicker of nostalgia for those Saturday afternoons on Dudley FM when he'd chat with callers about the latest matches, fostering that community feel he'd always cherished.

Cal continued, as if sensing Pete's thoughts. "Look, Pete, we know you've been feeling a bit out of sync with the current Vibes style. And honestly, Goldies is where your talents will truly shine. We're giving you the flexibility to tailor the drive show and the football phone-in, keep that authentic approach. You'd be a leader on the West Midlands Goldies team."

Pete looked up, meeting Cal's gaze. There was something genuine in his tone, and Pete could see that, despite Cal's loyalty to the Manic brand, he respected Pete's legacy. It wasn't just about moving him out of the way; they were trying to find a place where his voice would matter again.

"And the Saturday show on Goldies… the EFL focus is seasonal, but I know you like going up Edgbaston when the Tests are on, don't you? Well, Manic have won the rights to air next season's County for the England and Wales Cricket Boards. That means that you'd be leading the pre- and post-game coverage of Warwickshire and Worcestershire's tests."

The mention of cricket stirred something in Pete, a connection to his roots that felt oddly comforting amid the whirlwind of change. Covering Warwickshire and Worcestershire matches, bringing back that calm and insightful tone to a sport he loved, felt like a return to a world he'd thought was slipping away. The opportunity wasn't just about the drive-time show or the football call-in anymore; it was a chance to anchor himself in something he truly cared about, something that wasn't wrapped in Manic's frenetic branding.

But there was one question he couldn't ignore, and he knew he had to ask. "Cal, if I take this, am I essentially being moved aside from Manic's main platform? I've worked hard here, and it's a big shift to be stepping back, even if Goldies is more my style."

Cal leaned back, thoughtful. "Erm... in a way, yes. Look, Pete, you'd still be part of the Manic family, but the new Goldies regional feeds need experienced hosts. We're moving some of the teams around so they fit the brands that make sense for them. The Vibes platform is evolving, but Goldies is being crafted for authenticity, for voices that connect with listeners on a personal level. That's what you bring, Pete. You'd have freedom over the presentation style, even though the playlists would be common on all the Goldies feeds. I've already spoke to Tim and Ellen, and they're moving to the Goldies East Midlands feed, with Kylie and Tina moving from Warwickshire's breakfast to your slot, if you accept that is."

Pete took a deep breath, absorbing Cal's words. He had known this day was coming, a moment where he'd have to choose between keeping up with a style that didn't suit him or moving to a place that felt more like home, even if it meant stepping away from the cutting edge of Manic Radio. The mention of Tim and Ellen moving to Goldies East Midlands stirred a feeling of reassurance; they were colleagues he respected, people who shared his approach to radio. If they'd seen the potential in Goldies, maybe he could too.

"I appreciate that, Cal," Pete replied, his tone thoughtful. "And I think... I think you're right. Manic Goldies feels closer to what I'd like to be doing. Bringing that personal touch back, even if it's a different demographic."

Cal nodded, his expression one of relief and encouragement. "Exactly, Pete. Goldies needs that genuine voice, the kind of presence that doesn't just fade into the noise. We've done audience surveys, and listeners want the nostalgia, the warmth of a voice that knows the area and connects with them, especially on local issues. And let's face it – no one knows the Black Country and West Midlands like you do."

Pete allowed himself a small smile. The thought of doing a show where he could speak freely, dig into local stories, and bring back a football and cricket focus sounded appealing, almost liberating. After years of battling with Manic's scripted approach, Goldies felt like a door opening to something he thought was lost.

"What about the cricket and the EFL phone-ins, though?" Pete asked. "I've seen Manic's coverage of these things before, and they're usually so… branded. If I'm doing it, I want to make it genuine, bring on local voices, make it feel like the old Dudley days."

Cal chuckled, nodding in agreement. "That's exactly what we're hoping for, Pete. Goldies is allowing for a bit more freedom in style – as long as you keep within Ofcom guidelines, of course. We're not talking about pre-packaged celeb chat; this is real, local sports talk. We're hoping to bring a one-time rival of yours from Wolverhampton FM's phone-in to partner you."

Pete chuckled, as he knew that, of the three presenters on that old show, his wife Sarah, along with 'Big Clive' Tilsey and 'Skinny Pete' Peterson, only Sarah was still in the radio game, Clive having opened a bookmakers and Pete having passed from COVID. This, Pete knew, meant that Manic was planning to bring Sarah to partner him on the new Goldies football phone-in, which would be awkward as she did syndicated pre-recorded radio shows for community and small local stations through her own freelance company. While the thought of working alongside his wife on air was intriguing, Pete couldn't help but feel a pang of nostalgia mixed with excitement at the idea.

Cal leaned forward, his expression turning serious. "Look, Pete, I know this is a big shift, but it's a good one. You'll be in a position to shape the Goldies format for the West Midlands, and yes, Sarah would be joining you if she's willing. We're making an exception with her freelance work; the Goldies team knows how valuable she'd be. You two have that connection people remember, and it's precisely what we're hoping to rekindle in these local feeds."

Pete took a moment to digest it all.. The idea of working alongside Sarah again was both exhilarating and daunting, but he knew they'd make a formidable team. Their dynamic on air was well-remembered, and despite the changes radio had undergone, the chemistry they shared was undeniable. This wasn't just a return to his roots; it was a chance to bring back the kind of radio that had made him fall in love with the job in the first place.

"All right, Cal," Pete said, finally breaking the silence. "I'm in. Let's give Goldies a go. I'll take on the drive slot, the Saturday EFL phone-in, and the cricket coverage. And if Sarah's game, I think we could make it something special. I just have one question - will this be from the new One Snow Hill or the Dudley hub?"

Cal smiled, clearly pleased with Pete's decision. "Unfortunately the lease is up for here in April, and the bosses want to move the Central England hub to Birmingham, which is why they've got a lease on three floors of One Snow Hill, right in the heart of Birmingham. The Central team, including Goldies, will operate from there. It's a more central location, easier access, and, frankly, has the setup we need for both Manic's style and Goldies' more relaxed, localised vibe."

Pete nodded, taking it all in. The thought of moving to a shiny, new Birmingham office was bittersweet. The Dudley hub had been his workplace for years; he knew every corner, every creaky door. But it seemed fitting, in a way, that he'd start this new chapter in a fresh space, with a fresh format. The chance to shape a more authentic radio experience, bringing back a touch of local flavour, was something he hadn't dared hope for in a long time.

"All right, Cal," he said, nodding resolutely. "Let's make it happen. I'll bring everything I've got to Goldies. And... I'll talk to Sarah. I think she'll be up for it."

Cal beamed, extending a hand across the desk. "That's what I like to hear, Pete. Goldies needs a legacy voice with real community insight, and I can't think of anyone better for the West Midlands than you. I just need you to sign the usual contract paperwork, and we're all set."

Pete took the pen Cal handed him, his hand hovering over the paper for a moment. He glanced at the contract, noticing it was worded in the same standard, formal language he'd seen every year, yet this time it felt weightier. He was signing on for a new beginning, a role that allowed him to return to the roots of what made radio meaningful to him.

With a steady hand, Pete signed the contract, feeling a strange sense of excitement mingling with his usual nerves. This wasn't just another year in the world of radio—this was his opportunity to shape a part of the industry that felt genuine, timeless, and rooted in the West Midlands community he loved.

It was then Pete noticed one clause that was new, one he hadn't noticed in his glance.

"The presenter agrees to provide services as an independent contractor and not as an employee of the company."

The phrase caught Pete's attention, and he frowned, feeling a slight twist of unease, especially as he had just signed the contract, and therefore had already committed himself to the terms. This independent contractor clause was new, and it meant he wouldn't be a traditional employee anymore. His benefits, protections, and stability that came with being on payroll would now be gone, replaced by the somewhat precarious world of contracted work. It was a subtle but significant shift in his relationship with the company.

Pete looked up at Cal, who was watching him closely, the polite smile still on his face but with a hint of wariness, as though anticipating Pete's reaction.

"Cal… this independent contractor clause," Pete said, tapping the line with his pen, frowning. "Is this a tax dodge by Manic, or is this part of a bigger shift? What does this mean for my health benefits and job security?"

Cal's smile faltered for a moment, but he recovered quickly, sitting up straighter as he leaned forward. "Ah, I see you're picking up on that. It's part of the wider restructuring, Pete. We're moving towards a more flexible model across the network, and this allows us to offer more freedom for both the station and the talent. You'll still have the same access to resources as before, but as an independent contractor, you'll be more… well, self-managed. It gives you more freedom to take on other projects, if you choose, but it does also mean you'll need to manage your own tax and benefits from now on. Now, I know your wife, Sarah, owns her own production company, right?"

Pete's frown deepened as he absorbed Cal's words. "So, you're telling me this isn't just about the show—it's about reclassifying me as a freelancer? This sounds like another step towards cutting ties with the more traditional aspects of the job. What's next, no pension contributions either?"

Cal cleared his throat, clearly uncomfortable with the direction of the conversation. "Well, Pete, as I mentioned, it's about flexibility. We're modernising, adapting to the changing radio landscape. The industry's evolving, and Manic's trying to stay ahead of the curve. This model is more common now, even with other media companies. The shift to independent contractors gives you the chance to explore more opportunities outside of Manic if that's something you're interested in. You'd have a lot more freedom to work as you see fit, without being tied to a full-time employment contract."

Pete paused, his mind racing as he processed this new reality. The notion of more freedom, the chance to work on his own terms, was appealing, but the lack of security was a bitter pill to swallow. He'd been with the company for so long, had helped build the local brand and community connection, and now, it seemed like all that would be replaced by corporate flexibility. It felt like a final cut—the last step towards stripping away the human element of radio in favour of a model that looked good on paper but left little room for the personal commitment he'd always prided himself on.

The fact that he'd signed without realising that he'd lost his employment status weighed heavily on Pete. His career, built on years of genuine connection with his audience and colleagues, was now entangled in the corporate-driven shifts of the media industry.

"Look, Pete, it's the industry standard. Bauer and Global are already working with this model, and we're just aligning with the industry-wide trend," Cal continued, noticing Pete's hesitation. "Anyway, you've signed the contract now, so as of... 1243 hours, you are no longer a Manic employee."

* _ * _ * _ *

It was ten to four, and Pete was sat in the studio of Midlands Manic, angry. 'Why the fuck didn't I check the contract properly?' he muttered to himself, staring blankly at the control board. His fingers hovered over the microphone, but his mind was elsewhere, still grappling with the revelation Cal had dropped on him earlier. He had signed away his status as a full-time employee without even realising it. Independent contractor. It felt like a betrayal, an undercurrent of change that left him with a sense of uncertainty. He had been too quick to trust, too eager to decide, and now he was left to figure out the logistics of freelancing after decades of stable employment. It didn't feel like freedom; it felt like a final severance.

The last thing he'd expected from his annual contract renewal was this. Sure, he had been prepared for the shift to Goldies, even intrigued by the thought of reconnecting with the audience he once served. But being reclassified as a contractor? That was something he hadn't bargained for. Pete had never seen himself as just a 'voice' for a station. He had prided himself on being part of a family, part of a community. To be reduced to a contractor in a world where everything had become so digital and brand-driven felt like the final straw.

As the countdown on the clock ticked towards his show's start time, Pete forced himself to shake off his thoughts. He had a job to do, after all, and for the next few hours, he would still be part of Manic, still a voice in the Midlands. For now, at least, that was his role.

"Alright, Pete, focus," he muttered to himself. "Get through the show. You've been doing this for decades. The rest can wait."

His mind flickered to James, one of the last to be employed on the old 12 monthly employee contracts the previous week, with the new independent agreements seemingly coming in force for renewals and new talent moving forward. He couldn't help but worry about what this meant for James, especially if he became entrenched in the high-energy, brand-focused world of Manic, only to be tossed aside when the network moved on to the next big thing. The thought left a bitter taste in his mouth, a reminder of the industry's transient nature, and how easily the legacy of his work could be reduced to disposable content.

The light on the board turned red, signalling it was time to go live. Pete flicked the switch, his voice slipping into its familiar rhythm, though the spark felt somewhat dimmed.

"Good afternoon, Midlands," he said, injecting as much energy into his tone as he could muster. "It's your drive home with Pete Smith, taking you through another Tuesday. We've got the news with Lou Jones first, and then it's all about the £500k Money Drop."

Pete knew that he hated the Money Drop promo, a gimmick that embodied everything he felt radio had become—a superficial spectacle, where audience connection was swapped for flashy cash giveaways. But he forced himself to keep his tone upbeat, running through the script with the practised professionalism he'd honed over years. As he glanced at the clock, waiting for Lou's segment to finish, he felt an unexpected surge of rebellion rising within him.

The show returned to him with the familiar, scripted fanfare of Manic Radio, but he paused before diving into the typical high-energy script he'd been handed. Just for a moment, he allowed himself to deviate from the script, leaning into his old, conversational style.

"You know, folks, as we're here on the 5th of November—Bonfire Night—it's a time for a bit of reflection, isn't it? A time when we can think back on what's really important, maybe even a bit of nostalgia," he said, his tone gentler, more genuine. "Which is why... from April, I won't be bringing you home after work."

He took a deep breath, feeling the weight of his words hanging in the silence. The control board, the blinking lights, and even the studio itself seemed to hold their breath. He knew he was teetering on the edge, but he couldn't stop himself from speaking his mind.

"I'll still be here, though," he continued, his voice softening. "Still with Manic, but on a brand new Manic station. You see, from April, Midlands Manic is changing to Manic Vibes West Midlands. Yes, we're losing the name you've known the past 10 years, when Dudley FM, Wolverhampton FM, Walsall Radio, Spires FM and Brum's Best all became part of Midlands Manic, with it becoming one voice across the West Midlands. But now, that Midlands spirit is shifting, and I'm heading over to something a little more... well, familiar. Manic Goldies, from the 15th of April, will be launching a new drivetime show, and I will be the one bringing it to you from the West Midlands. So, if you're like me and you've got a soft spot for the classics, the memories, and maybe a slower pace, then keep an ear out. It'll be a bit of a homecoming for me, and I'd love to have you along for the ride."

Pete then sighed as he knew that Lily was glaring daggers at him through the studio glass, her lips tight with a barely restrained exasperation. He could see her hands flying across her phone, likely messaging Cal or whoever was next in the Manic chain of command to alert them that Pete had gone off-script. But Pete didn't care. The listeners deserved to know what was happening, and after all the years he'd been on air, he felt he had earned the right to speak directly, even if it wasn't perfectly aligned with the new Manic branding.

"And there's other news. As of today, Manic no longer employ me directly," he said, knowing that this would get the older elements of the audience writing and emailing in frustration, their disbelief at yet another shift in the radio world. Pete continued, his voice steady but laced with a hint of the weariness he felt. "No, I'm not gone, and yes, I'm still here for now. But things are changing, as they tend to do. We've all seen it over the years—the names, the faces, the formats. And now, I'm here as an independent contractor, which, well, is a bit of a fancy term for 'freelancer,' really."

There was a pause, as though he were gathering his thoughts, or perhaps preparing himself for the inevitable response from the higher-ups. He knew Lily was already furiously messaging someone in her typical, over-caffeinated frenzy, but he pressed on.

"That means I get some freedom, as the new contract doesn't have a certain clause in it... which means you might see me pop up on BRMB, or Radio Wyvern, or even Black Country Radio doing a show. You see-"

Pete noticed that Lily had deliberately muted his microphone as a song was launching, one of the network fed tracks that allowed no breaks or interruptions. He sighed, letting his frustration simmer under the weight of the situation. He'd barely scratched the surface of what he wanted to say before Lily, ever the vigilant enforcer of Manic's branding, had shut him down.

Through the glass, Lily shot him a disapproving look, her fingers still flying across her phone. Pete knew that Cal or one of the regional managers would soon be on the line, ready to remind him about the brand guidelines, about sticking to the script, about the "consistency" that Manic Vibes was pushing so hard to maintain. But at this moment, Pete didn't care. He'd spent decades connecting with his audience on a personal level, and the thought of his last months at Manic Vibes being reduced to a sterilised, scripted farewell felt hollow.

As the track played, Pete glanced back at Lily, offering her a half-shrug and a faint, defiant smile. He'd said his piece, even if it had been cut short, and he had a feeling the listeners had understood his intent. The phones in the studio had already started flashing with calls—likely listeners wanting to know more about what Pete had hinted at, seeking clarity on why their familiar drive-time host was being shifted to a new station.

Typing a tweet on his own X profile, Pete smiled.

@PeteontheRadio: *Well, the cat's out of the bag - I'm leaving @MidlandsManic for @ManicGoldies from April. If you want me on your local station for overnight shows, email clients@reevesradioltd.radio*

A few moments after posting, Pete's phone buzzed with the first wave of responses. Some were from loyal listeners expressing surprise, others shared disappointment, and a handful were excited to see him on Manic Goldies. Pete could already see the start of a conversation forming around the announcement, fans reminiscing about his early days and sharing stories of how his broadcasts had been a fixture in their daily lives.

Looking over, Pete caught Lily's gaze through the glass, her irritation evident. She tapped her watch pointedly, signalling that he was due back on air soon. Pete straightened up, taking a deep breath and refocusing on the task at hand. Whatever fallout might come, he felt strangely liberated by his impromptu announcement, his first unscripted moment in months.

As the song faded, he resumed his role with renewed energy. "Alright, Midlands, that was a bit of classic Ed Sheeran with his hit track "Shape of You," and let's get back into it! Now, as I was-"

Pete noticed Lily glaring at him before deciding to go to the script. "Well, who wants info on the £500k Money Drop? It's simple to enter. Just send DROP to..."

Pete went through the rest of the show with his usual professionalism, his voice smoothly guiding listeners through each segment. Yet, beneath the polished surface, a current of frustration lingered, a reminder of how Manic Radio's new structure felt like a personal betrayal. The conversation with Cal weighed on him, especially now that he was essentially a freelancer for a company that had been like family for so many years. He couldn't help but feel that the "freedom" Cal spoke of was just another way for the company to loosen their obligations while still profiting off his experience and loyal audience.

By the time he wrapped up, he was ready to leave the studio. Lily was waiting outside, her posture tense, arms folded across her chest. Her expression was a mixture of irritation and exasperation, clearly prepared to give him a talking-to. But Pete was in no mood to be lectured about loyalty to the Manic brand.

"Seriously, Pete? The listeners didn't need to know half of what you shared on air," she said, her voice sharp. "You can't just go off-script whenever you feel like it. Cal's not pleased, and neither are the higher-ups. They're trying to build a brand, and you… well, that was more like a farewell speech!"

Pete met her gaze, unflinching. "The listeners did need to know. These are people who have tuned in to my show for years, Lily. They deserve transparency. Manic can't keep chopping and changing the local stations without any word to the people it affects most—the audience. I know it doesn't fit the polished, predictable 'Vibes' image, but the Midlands crowd? They want more than a flashy, pre-scripted promo. I've got just over 5 months in this slot before I move to Goldies, and my contract has been signed, so if you're expecting me to start behaving like I'm some corporate puppet, well, it's not happening."

Lily rolled her eyes, clearly unimpressed. "Look, Pete, I get that you've been doing this a long time, but radio's changed. It's about brand consistency, engagement, and moving with the times. And as for transparency, that's something we control—Manic's story, Manic's way."

Pete chuckled dryly, feeling the weight of the disconnect between him and the new Manic culture. "If 'brand consistency' means abandoning what radio used to be—a real connection to real people—then I'm afraid that's not my idea of progress."

Lily's irritation softened slightly, though her stance remained firm. "Maybe you're right in your own way, Pete. But times change, and Manic's been built on adapting, on keeping things exciting for audiences who have a million different options every second. They want big prizes, big personalities, and something fast-paced that doesn't feel like it's dragging on."

Pete sighed, feeling a pang of nostalgia for the days when he'd been allowed to slow down, to share stories and take his time connecting with his listeners. "And what happens to the audience who don't fit into the new Manic mould, Lily? They get sidelined, just like the presenters who can't keep up with the pace?"

Lily hesitated, glancing away briefly. "Look, Pete, I didn't make the rules. But people like you, who have a loyal following, well, you've got a chance with Goldies to keep that connection going. It's not the main stage, but it's a platform where people like you can still shine."

He nodded, appreciating her honesty, even if it didn't make the situation any easier to accept. "Well, here's to the future then, Lily. I'll do my time here with the same professionalism I've always given, but don't expect me to pretend I'm something I'm not. Five months left on Midlands Manic and then... well, you're not even my producer, you're just up here from Cardiff this week to fill in for Greg while he gets over COVID," he finished, letting the last word hang. He was not about to mince words or pretend this arrangement suited him. Lily gave him a sharp look, her irritation barely concealed, but there was an understanding in her eyes as well—a fleeting recognition, perhaps, that Pete's resistance wasn't just stubbornness but a genuine sense of duty to his listeners.

"Fine, Pete," she said finally, exhaling as though she'd reached her limit. "Do what you need to for the rest of your time here, but keep it clean, yeah? The last thing anyone wants is more drama. We're here to entertain, not air dirty laundry."

"Understood," he replied, his tone respectful but firm. Pete knew he was walking a fine line, balancing between professionalism and his own integrity, but after today's revelations, he was more determined than ever to stay true to himself. He couldn't control what Manic Radio had become, but he could control his own approach. He wasn't about to let his last months on the main station be reduced to flashy promos and empty banter. He owed his audience more than that.

****

CHAPTER 10 – Sarah
Wednesday 6th November 2024

Sarah sat at her desk in the small, cosy office she had in the home she shared with Pete. Sunlight trickled through the blinds, casting gentle streaks across the room, yet the tension from Pete's account of yesterday's contract meeting hung heavy in the air. Even though they had spoken late into the night, dissecting every line of his new contract, the shock of Pete's forced reclassification as an independent contractor was still raw. It wasn't the world he'd known for thirty years, and it certainly wasn't the world she'd grown up in when she'd started at Wolverhampton FM, the local station that served Wolverhampton, Telford, and ironically Dudley, whereas Pete had joined Dudley FM, which served Dudley, South Staffordshire and Wolverhampton.

Their biggest competitor, apart from each other's stations, had been Beacon FM, a station that had dominated the Black Country and Shropshire airwaves. Beacon had been the powerhouse of local radio back in the day, with its lively presenters, local news, and eclectic mix of hits that appealed to everyone from teens to pensioners. Both Pete and Sarah had held a kind of respect for it, even as they battled it out for listener loyalty. Now, as she sat at her desk, Sarah felt the weight of that era pressing down on her—an era that seemed even more distant with Pete's unexpected contract changes. The warmth of community radio, with its unmistakable local focus, was evaporating in the face of an industry obsessed with national branding and "vibes" over substance.

Looking on Radio Today, an industry website she checked regularly to keep up with developments, Sarah scrolled through the latest updates, her eyes catching on an article that seemed tailor-made to worsen her frustration: ***"Ofcom to remove the vast majority of Key Commitments quotas for community radio stations"***

Clicking on the article, she frowned as she read it.

"Ofcom is going to remove the vast majority of Key Commitments quotas for all community radio stations, following a consultation.

Changes are coming to:

• The types of programming to be broadcast such as the main types of music and speech output.

• The number of hours of original output broadcast each week.

• The number of hours of locally-produced output broadcast each week.

• The languages broadcast on the service.

In return for more flexible on-air content, Ofcom will develop some additional principles for compliance with off-air social gain requirements.

In terms of the music relaxations, Ofcom said the music requirements are not central to the character of a community radio service. In their response, Radiocentre argued that this proposal could lead to 'mission drift' in parts of the community radio sector, with some stations becoming similar to local commercial stations, rather
194

than providing unique services as community radio was established to do.

Ofcom replied saying where specialist music is a particularly important part of a station's character of service (for example genre-based stations), they will ensure that this is reflected in the station's character of service requirements."

Sarah leaned back in her chair, feeling a growing sense of unease. This shift in community radio's Key Commitments would push local stations even closer to the mass-produced, personality-stripped model Pete was now tangled in with Manic. Without the requirement to offer distinctive content, community stations might slowly morph into smaller versions of commercial stations, risking the very essence of local connection and authenticity they were created to uphold.

The headlines of the other articles, **"*Forth 1, Northsound 1, MFR and Tay FM to share breakfast as Boogie in the Morning expands*"**, **"*Evening changes at Magic as Nicki Chapman joins Bauer from BBC Radio 2*"** and **"*Manic to reintroduce regional Breakfast and Drive shows in selected regions on Manic Goldies from April 2025*"** made her pause as she scanned the screen.

The industry was shifting at an alarming pace, and every headline seemed like a nail in the coffin for the kind of radio she and Pete had built their lives around. The thought of more stations sharing the same shows, even across regions with distinct cultures and dialects, felt like a betrayal of radio's core purpose. Each merger, each show consolidation, each tweak to "streamline" content seemed to pull the industry further from its roots in local engagement and listener loyalty.

The fact Bauer had already withdrawn local programming on its Greatest Hits Network a few days earlier thanks to the new Media Act, and now their Scottish stations would lose even more regional identity with the Boogie in the Morning expansion, yet Manic was reintroducing regional shows on Manic Goldies seemed both ironic and bittersweet. The very station Pete was being moved to, despite its nostalgia-driven focus, was reintroducing regional breakfast and drive-time shows, offering a glimpse of the local touch they'd cherished. Yet it was wrapped in the polished, marketable brand of Manic, a bittersweet reminder that local radio was only viable now if it came in the guise of nostalgia. She couldn't shake the thought that they were reintroducing what had been lost, but only for a demographic that the industry now saw as commercially expendable.

Wednesdays, Sarah knew, were HMRC, tax and company director duty days. As the owner of Reeves Radio Ltd, the production company she ran, which employed Chloe for her own syndicated shows for community and small local stations, Sarah often found herself juggling numbers, emails, and invoices on these midweek mornings. Today, however, her mind was elsewhere, dwelling on Pete's predicament and the state of the industry they had both loved.

Reeves Radio Ltd. was a lifeline for Sarah, a way to stay connected to the kind of radio she believed in. Chloe's syndicated show, which focused on contemporary hit music, as well as Sarah's own Soul, Blues, Jazz and

Classic Rock offerings, were the mainstay of their business, reaching community stations that still valued distinct, personality-driven programming. The irony wasn't lost on Sarah that, while Manic and the big networks consolidated, it was the smaller, often overlooked stations that kept radio's original spirit alive.

Her mind, however, kept thinking back to a question Pete posed to her the previous night.

"Love, if I run my services to Manic through your company, under the new independent contract I've signed, would it make things easier for both of us?" Pete had asked, his tone heavy with uncertainty. "Or would IR35 catch up with us?" Pete had finished, referring to the infamous tax legislation that blurred the lines between independent contractors and employees. Sarah knew what he meant. Running Pete's services through Reeves Radio Ltd. might simplify things on paper, but it could also invite scrutiny from HMRC, especially if his work with Manic accounted for the majority of his income. It wasn't a decision to take lightly.

The question lingered in Sarah's mind as she prepared her coffee, the quiet hum of the kettle contrasting with the whirlwind of her thoughts. Pete's suggestion made sense in theory, but in practice, it was fraught with complexities. Reeves Radio Ltd. was structured to give both her and Chloe a degree of freedom, allowing them to take on multiple clients and maintain creative control. Adding Pete's contract into the mix would change the dynamic— and possibly put them all under the microscope.

She returned to her desk and opened a new spreadsheet, inputting some tentative figures. If Pete's Manic Goldies salary was routed through the company, it might actually reduce their overall tax burden, but it would also make Reeves Radio Ltd. overly reliant on one client. That kind of dependency was a red flag for HMRC, especially with IR35 regulations designed to prevent disguised employment.

Although, she knew that Pete's new contract didn't have the exclusively clause in it, which allowed him to work for other stations or clients, as long as it didn't conflict with his Manic commitments. That he'd already advertised on his X post the previous night her company's email address for potential clients only added to her cautious optimism that they might be able to make this work without triggering IR35. If Pete could balance his Manic commitments with work on other stations or projects, it could give Reeves Radio Ltd. more credibility as a genuinely independent production company rather than a disguised employment setup.

But it was still a gamble, especially with HMRC's unpredictable approach to IR35 enforcement. Pete's contract was now as far from the traditional radio employment model as it could get, but it wasn't the freedom he'd hoped for. The freelance route would give him flexibility on paper, yet in practice, he was just as tied to Manic's structure, with little room to recreate the local, community-driven radio he missed so deeply.

The kettle whistled, snapping her out of her thoughts. As she poured her coffee, she allowed herself a small moment of nostalgia, remembering the early days when she and

Pete had met, both fierce rivals on the Black Country airwaves. Wolverhampton FM and Dudley FM had been competitive but respectful, each station proud of its unique voice and the connections it had built within the community. Back then, radio had been about genuine relationships and local influence, not just another cog in a corporate machine. Each station had its quirks, its local heroes, and its loyal listeners who felt like family. That world felt like a different lifetime now, as Pete navigated the maze of contracts and brand mandates, and Sarah found herself wondering if Reeves Radio Ltd. could somehow hold onto that fading legacy.

She took a deep sip of coffee, letting the warmth settle her. Perhaps, she thought, if they structured Pete's new role creatively enough, Reeves Radio Ltd. could function as a bastion of real radio—one that combined Pete's established name with her and Chloe's approaches, catering to the community stations left in the wake of industry upheaval. There was an opportunity here, one that felt risky but exciting. If Pete could balance his Manic Goldies commitments with guest hosting slots or selling syndicated shows or podcasts to other stations through Reeves Radio Ltd., they might just avoid the IR35 regulations and be able to retain the freedom that both she and Pete craved.

Sarah could envision it: Pete as the familiar, steady voice on Manic Goldies, bringing a touch of authenticity to the station's nostalgia format, while also producing and hosting niche shows for smaller community stations through Reeves Radio Ltd. It would be a way for Pete to have one foot in the world of mainstream radio, and another in the world they both loved—the one that valued personality, local culture, and real listener connections.

The prospect made her smile slightly. It wasn't a perfect solution, but it felt like a step in the right direction. Perhaps Pete's move to Goldies, despite the contractual twist, was an unexpected opportunity to create something lasting and meaningful. If Reeves Radio Ltd. could become a small but resilient hub for genuine radio, she might just keep a piece of the radio world she and Pete had cherished alive, no matter how many corporate rebrands the industry threw their way.

*_*_*_*

At half past 3, Sarah sighed when her phone rang. Looking at the caller, she saw that it was Woody Bones, a former owner of Walsall Radio and Dudley FM. Sarah knew he owned Three Towns Radio, a radio station based in Kidderminster that covered the Wyre Forest area, and was also known for its more relaxed approach to the modern radio landscape. Woody had been a fixture in West Midlands radio for years, a figure as local and enduring as the stations he'd built and fought to keep afloat against the tide of consolidation.

"Woody! It's been ages," Sarah said, her voice warm, as she answered.

"Sarah, my dear!" Woody's gravelly voice crackled through the line, as if his energy hadn't faded one bit since the early days of radio. "Look, I need a favour. Our drive host has fell ill, and we need a programme for the 4 to 6 slot. Mind doing a live one for me? You should have access to the remote system as you occasionally do our Blues Brothers special."

Sarah paused, her mind racing. It wasn't unusual for Woody to call her in a pinch—she had occasionally stepped in for Three Towns Radio when they needed a quick replacement, and her Blues Brothers Special was a favourite among the station's loyal listeners. But today, with Pete's situation weighing heavily on her, she hesitated.

"Woody, I'd love to help," she began, glancing at her laptop and the spreadsheet she had been working on. "But I've got a lot on my plate at the moment."

Woody's laugh was warm but insistent. "Come on, Sarah! You know you love the buzz of live radio. And look, it doesn't have to be fancy—just a couple of hours, play some tracks, chat with the listeners. You're still one of the best at this, and the audience would love it."

Sarah sighed, but a small smile tugged at her lips. He wasn't wrong—she did miss the rush of live radio sometimes, the direct connection with listeners that pre-recorded syndication lacked. And with everything going on in her and Pete's world, maybe a couple of hours of pure, unfiltered radio was exactly what she needed.

"Anyway, I noticed your husband's tweet about him no longer being exclusive to Manic. I'd like to commission a 4 times 30 minute podcast from him if possible," Woody then continued. "All about his time at Dudley FM, with you talking about how you and Wolverhampton FM were the competition back in the day. It'd be a cracking listen,

Sarah, and I think our audience would eat it up. Old-school radio rivalry, the glory days of local stations—it's all the stuff people miss now. What do you reckon? Think Pete would be up for it?"

Sarah laughed, the warmth in Woody's voice reminding her of how enthusiastic the local radio community still was, even in the face of all these changes. "Woody, you've got a knack for roping people into things they can't say no to. I think Pete would love the idea, especially given everything going on right now. He could use a project like that, something that feels real and rooted in the kind of radio he actually cares about."

Woody chuckled. "Good to hear it, love. I'll shoot over the details after your drive stint. And hey, if Pete needs any tips on managing this independent contractor malarkey, tell him to give me a bell. I've been doing it for years—comes with the territory when you run a station like Three Towns."

Sarah agreed to both the live drive-time slot and the podcast pitch, her mind buzzing with ideas as she hung up. The thought of Pete diving into a project that celebrated his roots in local radio brought a spark of hope to her day. Maybe this was the way forward—a blend of nostalgia, independence, and creativity that allowed them both to navigate this ever-changing industry on their own terms.

*_*_*_*

15 minutes later, Sarah was up in her broadcasting studio in the spare bedroom, logging into the remote system for Three Towns Radio. It was 10 minutes until she would go

live, and the familiar hum of the equipment felt like a comforting embrace. The spare room, transformed into a miniature studio, had seen its fair share of impromptu broadcasts, but this felt different. Sarah felt a renewed energy, as though stepping back into the world of live radio might help her reclaim a sense of purpose amid the chaos.

Her playlist was ready—a mix of upbeat classics and listener favourites—and she quickly jotted down some notes about local happenings in the Wyre Forest area. Woody had given her the green light to keep it casual, which suited her perfectly. There would be a few call-ins, some chatter about the upcoming Remembrance Sunday events in Kidderminster, Stourport, and Bewdley, and a sprinkling of her signature wit to keep the listeners engaged. Sarah's focus was clear: keep the show lively, personal, and connected to the community, something she knew she could deliver even in her sleep.

As the clock ticked closer to 4 pm, Sarah leaned into the microphone, taking a deep breath. The familiar red light blinked on, and she was live.

"Good afternoon, Wyre Forest! This is Sarah Reeves, stepping in for the brilliant Three Towns Radio drive-time show. I hope everyone's had a fantastic day so far, and if not, well, we're about to turn it around with two hours of great music, local news, and your calls. Let's get started with something to kick things off right—here's Sweet Child O' Mine by Guns N' Roses."

As the track played, Sarah settled into the rhythm of the show. Calls started to come in almost immediately, with regular listeners excited to hear her on air again. One caller, a local florist named Brenda, shared her plans for a Remembrance Sunday flower display, while another, Dave, wanted to reminisce about her Blues Brothers special from last month. The warmth and familiarity in their voices reminded Sarah of why she loved live radio— the immediate, genuine connection with people who shared her passion for community.

Between tracks, Sarah slipped in updates about the Wyre Forest's weekend events, mentioning the upcoming Christmas lights switch-on and a charity run in Bewdley. She kept the tone light and conversational, weaving in anecdotes about her own time in radio when local stations thrived on this kind of direct listener engagement. It felt good to be back in the moment, responding to live feedback and bringing a smile to people's faces.

Halfway through the show, Sarah decided to mention Woody's podcast idea. "You know, folks, I had an interesting call earlier from Woody, the man behind this wonderful station. He's got this idea for a podcast series about the good old days of local radio—think Wolverhampton FM versus Dudley FM, the classic rivalries that made Black Country radio such a blast. And guess who he wants to host it? Me and my husband, Pete Smith. Yes, Manic's Pete Smith, the same one who for 15 years, from the Dudley FM days to now, has been driving people home from their Brum, Wolvo and Dudley commutes. Now, let me tell you, Pete has stories—some that might make you laugh, others that might make you shake your head and say, 'Only in radio!' If you're a fan of hearing how local radio used to be, from the quirky listeners to the hilarious on-air gaffes, this is going to be a treat. Anyway, we've got a bus service update from Diamond Bus - services 8, 15, 125, 292 and 296 are delayed because of the roadworks on Bewdley Bridge... yes, those pesky roadworks are still causing trouble for anyone trying to get across the bridge. Patience, folks— it's just another day in the Wyre Forest! Now, let's get back to the tunes while we wait for things to clear up. Here's a bit of Fleetwood Mac with 'Go Your Own Way'."

As the song played, Sarah smiled to herself. She had slipped into her old rhythm effortlessly, blending local news and listener chatter with timeless music. The text messages kept coming, with a mix of commuters, local business owners, and even a few teenagers chiming in. It felt like the good old days, and for the first time in what felt like weeks, she wasn't consumed by worry over Pete's new contract or the industry's uncertain future.

When the song ended, Sarah picked up where she left off. "Now, who remembers when Beacon FM was the king of the Black Country airwaves? Those were the days, weren't they? Back when Wolverhampton FM, Dudley FM, and Beacon were all duking it out for listeners, and every presenter had their own quirks that made radio feel so personal. I remember Pete and I being on rival stations—he was over at Dudley, and I was holding it down at Wolverhampton. The competition was fierce, but there was always a sense of fun and community. These days, it's all about big networks and national brands, but let me tell you, nothing beats the charm of local radio. Well, on the line is Nigel Freshman, one of Smooth Radio's hosts, who used to present Beacon's breakfast with Jo Jesmond. Fresh, good to have you on the line!"

"Afternoon, Sarah!" came Nigel's familiar voice, full of the warmth that had made him a staple of Black Country radio. "Blimey, it's like stepping into a time machine hearing you on the air in Wyre Forest! This really takes me back."

Sarah chuckled, leaning into the microphone. "Likewise, Nigel. I was just saying to the listeners how much we all miss those good old days. You and Jo on Beacon Breakfast were legendary – made us Wolverhampton FM lot work twice as hard!"

Nigel laughed, a rich, hearty sound that crackled through the line. "Ah, well, it was always a pleasure. I was only thinking last week how things used to be crazy. Especially as the other station in town was a certain one called 107.7 The Wolf."

Sarah laughed, the nostalgia washing over her as she pictured the radio landscape of that time. "The Wolf! Oh, they were the real wild cards, weren't they? Late-night rock specials, local gigs... they had their own vibe, for sure. I think they gave Beacon and Wolverhampton FM a run for their money more than once. They were owned by the Express and Star, weren't they? Had a fierce following, especially with all the local bands they supported. Ah, those were the days – three stations all in one area, all fighting for listener loyalty with personality-driven shows and real community spirit."

Nigel sighed nostalgically. "Absolutely. We all had that sense of pride in our stations. Beacon was loud and proud, The Wolf was raw, and Wolverhampton FM? Well, you were the classy competitor, Sarah. Beacon had the

Tettenhall studios, you lot had studios in the Markets, and The Wolf were tucked away in the Express and Star building, weren't they? A proper mix of local legends under one skyline."

Sarah laughed warmly, memories flooding back. "Exactly! We'd hear a Wolf promo blasting about some local band playing at the Wulfrun Hall, then see you guys on Beacon covering the Dudley fireworks display, and we'd be running a Wolverhampton charity drive for the local food bank. It was like a dance, wasn't it? Each station had its beat, and the listeners knew every step. And the listeners? They'd flip between us all depending on the time of day or who was on – a different kind of loyalty, one built on connection, not just branding."

Nigel's voice softened. "Well, we may not have that same world now, Sarah, but yesterday's news from Manic was interesting, wasn't it. That they were keeping their regional existing breakfast and drive on their main stations, but also adding regional breakfast and drive-time slots to their Goldies network. It's a bit like a nod to the past, don't you think? Trying to bring back some of that local flavour, even if it's wrapped up in a nostalgia-driven package. Anyway, any chance of making a request for a track?"

"Of course, Nigel! What can I play for you?" Sarah replied, her smile audible even through the mic.

"Well, Sarah," Nigel began with a chuckle, "I seem to remember how you and Pete had to fight over who got the right to interview a certain Wolverhampton born soul singer back in the day – the one and only Beverley Knight.

How about 'Shoulda Woulda Coulda'? That song always brings me back to those days."

Sarah laughed, nodding in agreement even though Nigel couldn't see her. "Oh, Nigel, you're bringing back some memories now! That was a fierce debate between Pete and me. Dudley FM and Wolverhampton FM both wanted her on our breakfast shows, and she ended up choosing Beacon! We were both fuming, but you know what? She absolutely nailed it. A legend through and through. Let me get that queued up for you."

As the opening chords of Beverley Knight's classic hit filled the airwaves, Sarah leaned back in her chair, reflecting on the warmth of the exchange with Nigel. It was moments like these that reminded her of why she had fallen in love with radio in the first place. Not the glitzy branding or the relentless push for higher listener numbers, but the connections, the shared stories, and the sense of belonging that came from serving a local community.

When the song ended, Sarah came back on the air, her tone as bright as ever. "There you go, Wyre Forest, a bit of Beverley Knight with 'Shoulda Woulda Coulda.' Thanks to Nigel for that request and for the walk down memory lane. It's so good to hear from one of the voices that made Black Country radio what it was. And you know, maybe we'll convince him to join Pete and me for Woody's podcast. Imagine the stories we could tell!"

The texts and calls continued to roll in, with listeners chiming in about their own memories of those days. One caller, Karen from Bewdley, remembered attending a charity concert Beverley Knight headlined at Wolverhampton Civic Hall. Another, John from Kidderminster, shared how he used to listen to The Wolf on his way to work, flipping over to Beacon when he wanted the local news.

The final stretch of the show passed in a blur of laughter, music, and genuine conversation. By the time Sarah signed off, she felt more energised than she had in weeks. It wasn't just about the radio—it was about the people, the memories, and the small ways those connections still mattered in an increasingly digital, impersonal world.

* _ * _ * _ *

It was quarter to nine, and Sarah watched as Pete's car pulled into the drive of their Pensnett home, and she knew that he had been to the pub for a post-Drive show debrief pint, a ritual that was becoming increasingly rare for him as the pressures of Manic Radio weighed heavier. She could see the tiredness in his posture even as he stepped out of the car, his jacket slung over one shoulder. Pete had always been someone who carried his emotions lightly, but Sarah could read him like a book. Today, there was a mix of resignation and defiance in his demeanour.

She opened the front door before he had a chance to pull out his keys. "You're home later than I expected," she said, smiling warmly as he stepped inside.

Pete gave her a tired smile, leaning in for a brief kiss on the cheek. "Yeah, had a couple at the Bottle and Grape. Bumped into Woody Bones - he mentioned he'd got you covering his Three Towns drive slot today. Said you smashed it, as always. Even mentioned you had one of our pals from back in the day on the line."

Sarah laughed softly, closing the door behind Pete as he set down his bag. "Nigel Freshman, of all people! He called in during the show, reminiscing about the good old days at Beacon. You know, I think he misses it as much as we do. He requested Beverley Knight's 'Shoulda Woulda Coulda' and had me in stitches reminding me of that time we both lost the interview to Beacon. Remember how furious we were?"

Pete chuckled, rubbing the back of his neck as he slipped off his shoes. "Oh, I remember. I think I sulked about that for a week. Beverley Knight on Beacon Breakfast... it was like the ultimate defeat for Dudley FM and Wolverhampton FM combined. That rivalry, though— those were the days, weren't they? Feels like a lifetime ago."

"It does," Sarah agreed, leading him into the kitchen where she had a cup of tea waiting. "But for two hours today, it felt like it wasn't so far away. Woody's listeners were so engaged. Talking about the past, sharing memories of local gigs and stations—it reminded me why we got into this in the first place. Did Woody mention anything that might interest you beyond my stint on air?"

Pete took the cup of tea gratefully, sitting down at the kitchen table with a sigh. "Yeah, he mentioned something about a podcast. Wants us to team up and do a series about the old days of local radio—the Wolverhampton FM versus Dudley FM era, Beacon's dominance, all the madcap stories. Said the listeners would eat it up."

Sarah nodded, her smile widening. "He pitched it to me too. I think it's a brilliant idea. Not just for the nostalgia—it's a chance for us to remind people what radio used to be about. The heart, the community. Not to mention, it gives us a project to work on together. What do you think?"

Pete leaned back in his chair, cradling the mug in his hands. "Honestly? I love the idea. After the day I've had, talking about the days when radio had a soul sounds like exactly what I need. But do you think we can pull it off? Between your shows, my Manic Goldies shift starting in April, and all this new contractor nonsense…"

Sarah shrugged, sitting down across from him. "It's not like we haven't juggled a million things before. Besides, Woody seems flexible. We can record it when we're free, do it through Reeves Radio Ltd., and maybe even pitch it to other stations. A few of those community stations might be interested in picking it up."

Pete's eyebrows lifted slightly. "Through Reeves Radio Ltd.? You mean running it like a proper production company deal?"

"Why not?" Sarah replied. "You're already a freelancer now, whether we like it or not. If we do it through the company, it could make everything simpler—less hassle for you, more credibility for Reeves Radio, and we get to do something that actually feels meaningful."

Pete considered this for a moment, then nodded slowly. "Alright, let's do it. A proper podcast about the good old days. And maybe, just maybe, it'll remind people that radio doesn't have to be all about flashy branding and national syndication."

Sarah reached out, resting her hand over his. "Exactly. We'll make it our way—real stories, real people, and the kind of radio we fell in love with. Who knows? It might even help you feel more at home when you start on Goldies."

Suddenly the sound of a dubstep remix of 'Carol of the Bells' rang through the house from the ground floor bedroom that was James's, and Sarah groaned, as she could hear the sound of sex from the same room.

"Jesus Christ on a bloody motorbike," she muttered as she stood up, rubbing her temples, the Christmas song being ruined by a dubstep remix and the all-too-familiar muffled laughter and moaning coming from James's room. She could feel her patience wearing thin. Pete groaned, leaning back in his chair and rubbing his temples as well.

"That boy…" Pete muttered, his voice laced with a mix of exhaustion and irritation. "You'd think, after all the talks we've had with him, he'd show some respect—especially after last weekend."

Sarah sighed, walking over to the kettle to pour herself a fresh cup of tea. "He's young, Pete. And let's face it, he's in the thick of Manic's madness. It's a world of late nights, brand-building, and… well, whatever's going on in there."

Pete chuckled dryly, though there was little humour in it. "At least we don't have to deal with Chloe bringing Cody back tonight. One over-energetic Manic presenter is enough. You know Kylie's the one who's taking my Manic Vibes drive slot when everything gets rebranded in April. Her and that bloody Tina, her 'best mate'."

Sarah groaned at Pete's revelation, leaning against the counter as she sipped her tea. "Kylie and Tina? Oh, great. The dynamic duo of selfie queens and hashtag warriors. Honestly, Pete, what's the obsession with this glossy, shallow nonsense? It's like Manic's handing the keys to the studio to the next Love Island cast."

Pete smirked, a glimmer of humour breaking through his weariness. "It's what they want, Sarah. Big smiles, social media presence, and no drama—well, except the kind they script. Kylie's polished, Tina's got the 'bestie banter' vibe, and they're young enough to keep up with whatever 'Manic madness' the bosses cook up next."

Sarah sighed, shaking her head. "It's like they're handing over the soul of radio to a team of influencers. Do they even care about the listeners, or is it just about building their personal brand?"

Pete shrugged, sipping his tea. "It's all about the metrics now. Engagement, followers, TikTok trends. Radio's just another stage for the brand they're building. To them, listeners are just numbers on a spreadsheet. And honestly, Sarah… it's exhausting. You know that bloody Lily that I've got producing my show while Greg's off sick—she's a walking Instagram post. She's more concerned about her selfie angles than the sound quality of the show. I miss the days when producers actually cared about content, not just hashtags and trends."

Sarah nodded sympathetically, leaning against the counter. "And it's not like you can do anything about it. The bosses eat it up because it brings in the clicks and shares, but it's hollow. The listeners might follow their socials, but they're not connecting with the show itself. Not like they used to."

Pete let out a weary sigh, swirling the tea in his mug. "It's just another reminder of how far things have drifted. But you know what, Sarah? If this podcast idea pans out, maybe we can show people what radio used to be—what it still could be, if they stopped chasing numbers and started focusing on people again."

Sarah reached out, placing a reassuring hand on his shoulder. "We will, Pete. And who knows? Maybe it'll catch on. Nostalgia's a powerful thing, and if we play it right, we might even inspire a few people in the industry to think differently."

Pete chuckled softly, his expression softening as he looked at her. "You always were the optimistic one. Alright, let's do it. Let's remind everyone that radio used to be about heart, not just hashtags."

As the dubstep remix of Carol of the Bells shifted into a Nightcore version of Slade's "Merry Xmas Everybody, Sarah groaned louder, her patience snapping. She stomped towards James's room, muttering under her breath. Pete winced, knowing what was about to happen but made no effort to stop her.

She flung open the door without knocking. "James Smith, for the love of all things decent, can you turn that racket down?! And while you're at it, explain why I have to hear the entire soundtrack to your 'power couple' antics with Kylie when I'm trying to have a civilised evening with your father!"

James, caught mid-laughter with Kylie sprawled on the bed beside him, froze like a deer in headlights. Kylie, in her usual glamorous-yet-casual style, managed to look unbothered, though a faint blush crept up her cheeks.

"Mum, it's just a remix!" James protested, reaching for his phone to lower the volume.

Sarah crossed her arms, fixing him with a glare. "A remix of Christmas songs in November, accompanied by sounds I'd rather not hear coming from my son's bedroom! Honestly, James, can you and Kylie take your… festivities elsewhere?"

James groaned, rubbing his face in embarrassment, while Kylie, ever the PR expert, smiled sweetly at Sarah. "Mrs Reeves, I mean Sarah," Kylie corrected herself with a practiced grin. "We're just brainstorming playlist ideas for... well, we've been given a Christmas Day show on Manic Dance."

Sarah raised an eyebrow, her expression hovering somewhere between disbelief and irritation. "Brainstorming playlist ideas? Really? Is that what they're calling it these days?"

Kylie's grin faltered slightly, but she held her ground, brushing a lock of perfectly styled hair from her face. "Absolutely! Christmas is all about creating the perfect vibe for the audience. You know, something upbeat, festive, and on brand for Manic Dance."

Sarah sighed, pinching the bridge of her nose. "I get it, Kylie, I really do. But can you 'brainstorm' a little more quietly? This house isn't a recording studio, and your 'vibes' are interrupting mine."

Pete appeared in the doorway, a faint smirk tugging at the corners of his mouth as he took in the scene. "Well, Sarah, it looks like the next generation's already got Christmas Day sorted. Though, James, you might want to remember that soundproofing works both ways."

James groaned again, his cheeks flushing. "Alright, alright! We'll keep it down. Sorry, Mum, Dad."

The next thing Sarah knew, the sound of Dua Lipa's 'Physical' came from the studio upstairs, where Chloe was recording her syndicated show for Reeves Radio Ltd., providing yet another layer of sound to the already chaotic household. Sarah closed her eyes briefly, muttering under her breath about the irony of being surrounded by a family of radio presenters and yet feeling like she lived in the middle of a live broadcast.

"Right, that's it," Sarah said, turning to face Pete with a resigned sigh. "This house may be filled with presenters, but it's not a 24/7 Manic production suite."

****

CHAPTER 11 – Awards Time
Saturday 9th November 2024

The Dakota Manchester exuded the kind of opulence that made Pete feel slightly out of place. The grand chandeliers, polished marble floors, and meticulously dressed staff seemed a world away from the humble studios of Dudley FM, where Pete's career had begun all those years ago. Sarah, on the other hand, seemed to glide effortlessly into the atmosphere, her elegant emerald green dress turning heads as they walked towards the reception desk.

"The Island Awards," Pete mused under his breath as they waited to check in. "Why do all these ceremonies have to sound so... fancy? Back in the day, the only awards we cared about were listener ratings."

Sarah shot him a teasing glance. "Well, darling, times change. Besides, it's not every day we get to stay at The Dakota. Try to enjoy yourself for once."

Pete smirked but didn't reply. The truth was, he wasn't entirely comfortable with these industry events anymore. The awards ceremony was a joint affair for radio professionals across the UK and Ireland, celebrating everything from innovative programming to audience engagement. Manic Radio had a strong presence this year, with multiple nominations, including "Best Digital Content Strategy", "CHR Station of the Year", and "Best Regional Drivetime", which Pete was one of the nominees for. The nomination had come as a surprise to Pete—an acknowledgement of his decades of work, even as he felt increasingly out of step with the direction the industry was heading. But deep down, he couldn't help feeling a flicker of pride. Perhaps it was validation that, despite everything, his voice still mattered to someone.

As they reached the check-in desk, a polished attendant greeted them with a smile. "Mr and Mrs Smith, welcome to The Dakota. We have your suite ready for you. Please let us know if there's anything we can do to make your stay more comfortable."

"Thank you," Sarah replied with effortless grace, collecting the key card. Pete followed her towards the lift, his eyes scanning the opulent lobby. He spotted a few familiar faces from the industry—presenters, producers, and executives from stations across the UK. A few nodded in recognition, though Pete couldn't tell if their smiles were genuine or merely polite.

"Pete Smith, is that you," a voice he recognised from behind him said, and Pete noticed that it was none other than Capital Radio's Roman Kemp, the son of Spandau Ballet legend Martin Kemp, and a prominent voice in the CHR world. Roman's broad grin and easy charm had made him a fixture on Capital's breakfast show, and he exuded the kind of confidence that Pete had never quite managed to muster in these settings. "Dad said you'd be here, but I didn't actually expect to run into you in the lobby! How are you, mate?" Roman's enthusiasm was infectious as he strode over, extending a hand.

Pete shook it firmly, though his smile was more subdued. "Roman, good to see you. I'm… well, let's say I'm surviving these days. Yourself?"

"Thriving, mate. Capital's been buzzing—we're up for a couple of awards tonight. You know how it is: big prizes, big tunes, big personalities," Roman said, his grin widening. "And hey, congrats on the nomination for Best Regional Drivetime. That's no small feat these days, especially with all the changes going on."

Pete chuckled dryly. "Changes is one way to put it. But yeah, thanks. I suppose it's nice to still be in the running for something."

Roman nodded knowingly, his gaze flicking briefly to Sarah, who stood beside Pete with an amused expression. "And you must be Sarah. I've heard stories about you two—Black Country radio royalty, right?"

Sarah laughed lightly, shaking Roman's hand. "Well, I don't know about royalty, but we've been around the block a few times. How's your dad? Still trying to convince you to play more Spandau Ballet on Capital?"

Roman rolled his eyes in mock exasperation. "Every time we're at a family dinner, he's like, 'Why don't you drop a bit of Gold on the breakfast show? The listeners will love it.' I keep telling him it's not exactly what the kids are into these days."

Pete smiled faintly, finding a sliver of common ground in the generational tug-of-war that seemed universal. "Well, Roman, if you ever want to sneak a classic in, I'm sure your dad would appreciate it."

Roman laughed, clapping Pete on the shoulder. "You know what, maybe I'll dedicate one to you during Christmas week. A little nod to the legends of radio."

As Roman was called over by one of his Capital colleagues, Pete and Sarah then noticed the BBC Radio 1 Breakfast host Greg James, Greatest Hits Radio's mid-morning host Ken Bruce, Heart's Amanda Holden and Jamie Theakston, along with Hits Radio's Fleur East, deep in conversation near the bar. The sheer variety of presenters from different stations, each representing their own slice of the radio landscape, underscored just how fragmented—and competitive—the industry had become. Yet there was a palpable camaraderie in the air, a shared understanding among them all: despite the changes and challenges, they were still part of the same extended family.

"Look at that lot," Pete murmured to Sarah, nodding towards the group. "Radio royalty in their own right. Makes you wonder where we all fit in these days."

Sarah squeezed his arm reassuringly. "You've got your place, Pete. Just remember, they're probably thinking the same thing. The industry's evolving, sure, but some things never change. People like you are the heart of it all."

Pete smiled, though her words didn't quite ease the self-doubt gnawing at him. "Maybe. Or maybe I'm just the relic they're too polite to phase out entirely."

Before Sarah could respond, one presenter Pete recognised who, like him, had been in the industry for decades, came over - Stephanie Hirst, the Hits Radio presenter that his son, James, was in a X feud with over dance/club-themed shows. Stephanie was all smiles, her energy as effervescent as ever. "Pete Smith," she said, extending a hand. "Look at you, hobnobbing at The Dakota! It's good to see you here."

Pete took her hand, offering a polite smile. "Stephanie. It's been a while. Still keeping the Hits crowd dancing, I see."

Stephanie laughed, a warm and hearty sound that filled the space around them. "Oh, you know me. If they're not moving, I'm not doing my job. But hey, congrats on the nomination. Heard you're up for Best Regional Drivetime. How does it feel to be in the running?"

Pete shrugged, his modesty kicking in. "Bit surreal, to be honest. I'm not sure I fit into the mould of what's winning these days."

Stephanie tilted her head, her expression softening. "Oh, come on, Pete. You're one of the best out there. And don't let anyone tell you otherwise. The industry may be changing, but voices like yours are what keep it grounded."

Sarah smiled at Stephanie, appreciating her words. "That's kind of you to say. Pete's been feeling a bit out of step with all the branding and metrics these days."

Stephanie nodded, her expression thoughtful. "It's a whirlwind, no doubt about it. But you've got a legacy, Pete. A lot of us younger ones—well, younger-ish," she added with a laugh, "owe a lot to folks like you who paved the way. Don't let the corporate circus get you down."

Pete chuckled, his tension easing slightly. "Thanks, Stephanie. And hey, while you're here, tell me—what's this Twitter spat with my son all about? James seems to think he's Ibiza's new king."

Stephanie's eyes sparkled with mischief. "Ah, Jimmy Reeves. He's got energy, I'll give him that. I don't take it personally, Pete—it's all in good fun. Honestly, it's nice to see the next generation so enthusiastic. Even if they think they've invented the wheel."

Pete laughed, genuinely amused. "That sounds about right. I'll have to remind him that Ibiza was around long before he started curating dance playlists. He's over at the Piccadilly Gardens studios today with his girlfriend, recording a batch of 4 more Ibiza Headbangers episodes for Manic Dance, and a couple of Manic Rock '20s shows."

"Rock as well as Dance? Are Manic trying to make him the Swiss Army knife of radio?" Stephanie quipped with a raised eyebrow, her grin widening. "It's bold, I'll give them that. But hey, if he's got the chops, why not? Just tell him to stay humble. The industry has a way of teaching lessons when egos get too big."

Pete smirked, nodding. "Don't worry, I'll keep him grounded. Or at least try to. He's got a good heart under all that flash. You doing Belters after the ceremony?"

Stephanie nodded, her grin not wavering. "You know it. Straight back to the Hits studio for Belters, as always. Live radio waits for no awards ceremony. But hey, if we're lucky, maybe I can squeeze in a cheeky mention of tonight's winners—assuming you've got your acceptance speech ready, Pete."

Pete chuckled, shaking his head. "Speech? You're assuming I'll win. I think my chances are about as good as James playing a smooth jazz set on Manic Dance. Anyway, I need to apologise for his idiocy, starting a spat on X with you over 'Belters'—he gets carried away with this 'Jimmy Reeves' persona. Sometimes, I'm not even sure he remembers who he really is under all that branding."

Stephanie waved it off with a laugh. "Oh, don't apologise, Pete. It's water off a duck's back. Honestly, the banter keeps things lively. If James wants to take on the queen of Belters, I say let him try. I've been in this game long enough to handle a bit of cheek."

Sarah chimed in, her voice light with amusement. "Well, Pete might not think much of James's antics, but the boy's certainly got flair. And let's be honest, Stephanie, a little competition isn't bad for anyone. It keeps things interesting, doesn't it?"

Stephanie nodded, her smile warm. "Absolutely. And honestly, Pete, it's good to see the next generation so enthusiastic. It might not be the way we did things, but passion is passion. Just don't let him forget to respect his elders—or his dad."

The three of them shared a laugh before Stephanie excused herself to join the Hits table. Pete felt a little lighter after the exchange, even as he noticed more familiar faces milling about. He spotted Capital Midlands's Tom & Claire talking to BBC 1Xtra's DJ Target, deep in conversation about the latest trends in music broadcasting. Across the room, Heart's Mark

Wright appeared to be swapping jokes with Radio 2's Rylan Clark, their laughter cutting through the buzz of pre-ceremony chatter. Pete couldn't help but marvel at the sheer diversity of radio personalities under one roof—a reminder that, despite its challenges, the industry still held an undeniable vibrancy.

As the three-course dinner began, Pete and Sarah found themselves seated at a table with a mix of industry veterans and rising stars. One of their tablemates was Fleur East, the effervescent host from Hits Radio, who immediately brought a burst of energy to the group.

"Pete, Sarah—how's it going?" Fleur beamed, her infectious enthusiasm lighting up the table. "You two look like the calm in the storm tonight. Guess that's what experience brings, huh?"

Sarah laughed, raising her glass. "Oh, we're just here for the show. It's all a bit of a circus, but we wouldn't miss it. And congrats on your nomination for Best National Breakfast, Fleur."

Fleur grinned, raising her glass in return. "Thank you! Honestly, just being nominated feels like a win. The competition is fierce, but I'll take a good party and some great company any day."

Pete chuckled, swirling his wine. "Well, Fleur, if you're looking for calm, you might want to swap tables. I'm sure the night'll get lively soon enough. Noticed over the way is Manic Dance's national Breakfast duo, Ali & Tom?"

Fleur glanced over to the table Pete pointed out, as it was arranged so, instead of each station occupying a table each, presenters and producers from various stations, from community and local to national, were mixed to encourage networking. Ali and Tom, Manic Dance's vibrant breakfast duo, were unmistakable with their high-energy gestures and constant laughter. Fleur smirked, leaning back in her chair.

"Ali & Tom, eh? Those two could power a small city with their energy. If anyone's going to keep things lively tonight, it's them. Do they ever run out of steam?" Fleur asked, her tone amused.

Pete chuckled, shaking his head. "Nope. Mind if I let you into a little secret about them?"

Fleur leaned in, her curiosity piqued. "Go on then, Pete. What's the secret?"

Pete glanced over at Ali and Tom, who were now animatedly chatting with a producer from Radio 1. He lowered his voice slightly, as if letting her in on a trade secret. "Like most of the young Manic talent, they have a love for a certain white powder. No word of a lie, most of the under 30s at Manic, either producers, presenters, engineers or PR, are hooked on caffeine, energy drinks, and sometimes... well, let's just say substances stronger than espresso." Pete's tone was light, but his underlying concern was unmistakable. "You heard the other week my son, James, joined Manic, yeah?"

Fleur raised an eyebrow, her expression a mixture of surprise and understanding. "I heard. Jimmy Reeves, right? Making waves already, from what I've seen. But... are you saying he's getting caught up in that scene too?"

Pete sighed, taking a sip of his wine. "Yep. He's already caught by that bug. It's like there's a reason that Al Crozier resigned from Manic too."

Fleur's expression sobered, her cheerful demeanour giving way to a flicker of concern. "Al Crozier? The one who was practically the poster boy for Manic's new wave? I heard rumours about him leaving, but no one seemed to know the full story. What happened?"

Pete hesitated, glancing at Sarah, who gave him a subtle nod of encouragement. "Al's resignation wasn't exactly voluntary," Pete admitted, his voice low enough not to carry beyond the table. "He got caught in a bit of a mess—on air, no less. Swore during a live show, clashed with Toni Green, and word is, there were… let's say 'extracurricular substances' involved. Management gave him a choice: suspension with a very public apology or walking away quietly. He chose the latter."

* - * - * - *

"Alright Manic Rock, this is Reevesy here, bringing you 3 hours of the hottest '20s rock and a sprinkle of nostalgia for the true classics. Whether you're cruising down the M6, lounging at home, or prepping for a night out, I've got your soundtrack covered. Coming up, we've got Arctic Monkeys, Yungblud, and maybe even a little Paramore to spice things up. But first, let's kick things off with The 1975—this one's 'Part of the Band.'"

James chuckled as he was doing another batch of pre-recorded voice-tracked shows, some for Manic Dance and some for Manic Rock, all at the Manic hub in Manchester's Piccadilly Gardens. Knowing that his dad was sucking up to other industry professionals at an awards ceremony while he was here recording yet another batch of segments didn't bother James one bit. He relished the hustle and the attention his new "Jimmy Reeves" persona was drawing. Besides, the sleek studios of the Piccadilly Gardens hub were far more his vibe—bright, modern, and alive with the energy of Manic's ambitious young talent.

The reason James was at the Manchester hub and not the Dudley one for this batch of recordings was simple - the Dudley hub was closed for the weekend as the studios were being painted, which was ironic as they would be leaving for Birmingham's One Snow Hill, a city centre property which Barclays Corporate was currently the lease holder of 3 of the floors, with Lite Group taking on the remaining Barclays term plus an additional 10 years, ensuring a modern, centralised facility for Manic's expanding operations in Central England. The irony of refurbishing a soon-to-be-vacated space wasn't lost on anyone at Manic, but as always, the network was full steam ahead, balancing logistical changes with its relentless programming demands.

James leaned back in his chair, the glow of the soundboard reflecting off his polished shoes. He adjusted his mic slightly, flicking through the playlist with a confident swipe on the touch screen. This wasn't just a job for him—it was an opportunity, a platform to carve out his own identity in a sea of seasoned voices like his dad's. He was ambitious, sure, but in his mind, ambition wasn't a flaw; it was a requirement.

"Right, next segment," he muttered to himself, clicking into the queue. "Gotta get this done before Kylie's back from the café."

His voice took on a playful, energetic tone as he hit record. "Alright, Rockers, that was The 1975, and we're just getting started tonight. Coming up, we've got Yungblud, Paramore, and some classic Killers for good measure. But first we've got a new track from Amyl and the Sniffers, an Aussie punk rock band tearing up the scene right now. This one's called 'U Should Not Be Doing That,' and trust me, you'll want to turn this up. Let's go!"

James hit the "record stop" button, leaning back in the chair with a self-satisfied grin. His segments were crisp, energetic, and perfectly timed—just the kind of content Manic expected from its rising stars. He flicked his wrist, checking his watch. Kylie would be back soon, likely carrying an overpriced latte and an update on the latest Manic gossip. Until then, he had a moment to do a quick line of coke on the studio desk, a practice that, in his nearly 2 weeks of employment with Manic, was becoming more easier than he ever thought possible. James's initial shock at the casual use of drugs within the Manic culture had quickly faded, replaced by a sense of normalization. Everyone around him—producers, engineers, even some of the older presenters—seemed to partake, and it felt like a rite of passage, a way to cement himself as part of the group. The manic energy Manic Radio demanded wasn't entirely natural, after all.

He tapped the desk nervously, though his outward confidence never wavered. He knew his dad would flip if he ever caught wind of this, but James brushed the thought aside. "It's just part of the job," he muttered, convincing himself as much as anyone else. "Besides, it's not like I'm the only one."

The studio door creaked open, and James quickly swept the remnants of the line into a tissue, slipping it into his pocket. Kylie walked in, her blonde hair perfectly styled, holding two coffees and a croissant bag.... as well as an Ann Summers bag.

Placing the items down, James noticed that inside the Ann Summers bag that Kylie had brought in was a pair of crotchless panties and a new toy which James liked the look of, a pair of lace handcuffs with a matching blindfold, hinting at her mischievous plans for later. Looking at her, he also noticed that she was wearing a new pair of hot pants, and that her ones that she had worn as they had drove up from Dudley were in the Ann Summers bag, alongside a receipt that hinted at her impromptu shopping spree during her café stop. James raised an amused eyebrow, leaning back in his chair with a smirk.

"Well, well," he teased, "looks like someone had an eventful coffee break. Is this for our... post-recording debriefs?"

Kylie grinned slyly, setting the coffee down in front of him. "Nah, more like for now... if you bend over."

James noticed the bulge in the hot pants and grinned, as it was the telltale sign of a strap-on, which was his Achilles heel, as that was the only time he turned submissive towards his girlfriend.

"Fuck, Kyles, you got any lube, or you just gonna go straight into that mode?" James smirked, leaning back in his chair with a mock-casual air, trying to cover the slight unease that crept into his tone.

Kylie's grin deepened, her eyes glinting mischievously as she lowered her hot pants, to reveal that she was wearing no underwear and that, as well as the strap-on for James, she had a dildo inserted into herself to maintain her own pleasure during their "debrief". The fact that the strap-on was curved, and by James's measurements at least 10 inches and thick, meant that Kylie had clearly come prepared for more than just a casual studio session. Her daring approach was nothing new, but the combination of professionalism during the day and the unapologetic intimacy they shared after hours kept their relationship electrified.

"No, Reevesy, no lube this time. I want you to feel all of it." Kylie's voice was a mix of sultry command and playful defiance. James smirked, his usual cocky bravado faltering for a brief moment as he glanced at the studio door. The soundproof walls of the Manic hub gave him some comfort, but the thought of someone walking in on this "debrief" was enough to give him pause.

"Alright, Kyles, you win," he said, standing up and gesturing towards the desk. "But let's at least lock the door this time, yeah? I don't fancy explaining this to the Manic higher-ups—or worse, my dad."

Kylie laughed, tossing her hair back as she strutted over to lock the door. "Relax, James. This isn't my first rodeo. Besides, don't pretend you don't love the adrenaline."

James noticed that, while Kylie was turned to face the door, she was wearing an anal plug as well as the rest of her daring ensemble. Her boldness was nothing short of intoxicating, and despite his initial nerves, James couldn't help but admire her confidence. Kylie turned back to face him, the glint in her eye making it clear she was in full control of the situation.

"Well, Reevesy," she teased, placing her hands on her hips. "Are we doing this, or are you going to stand there staring like it's your first time?"

James let out a chuckle, shaking his head. "Alright, alright. You've made your point. But if anyone asks why the next batch of voice tracks is delayed, I'm blaming you."

Kylie smirked, stepping closer until they were just inches apart. "Deal. Now, less talking, more… cooperating."

Dropping his ripped jeans and boxer shorts, James felt his own larger than average erection stiffening as Kylie proceeded to close the distance between them, her playful dominance evident in every movement. James leaned forward against the studio desk, the glowing lights of the soundboard casting a surreal glow on their impromptu escapade. As Kylie positioned herself, the atmosphere crackled with a mix of excitement and tension, their shared dynamic balancing professionalism with unapologetic intimacy.

"Reevesy," she murmured, her voice low and teasing, "I think you're about to learn why I always win our little games."

James smirked, a mixture of nervousness and anticipation washing over him. "Alright, Kyles. Just don't break me—I've got another show to finish."

Feeling her as she turned him around and bent him over, so his face was mashed against the control panel, James let out a sharp gasp as Kylie inserted the first inch of the strap-on into him. The initial sensation was intense, a mix of discomfort and exhilaration, but he bit his lip and relaxed, allowing Kylie to take control. The cool touch of the desk beneath him contrasted sharply with the heat building between them, and James couldn't help but marvel at how unapologetically bold Kylie was, not just here but in everything she did.

"Relax, Reevesy," Kylie teased, her tone a mixture of command and affection. "You've got this. Besides, I think you're enjoying it more than you're letting on."

James chuckled through his breaths, turning his head slightly to glance back at her. "You know me too well. Just don't—" He let out a sharp exhale as she pushed further. "Don't get too carried away. We're still in the studio."

Kylie smirked, leaning down so her breath tickled his ear. "Oh, don't worry. I've got it all under control. But you, Reevesy, might not be so lucky."

* _ * _ * _ *

"And the award for Best National Drivetime goes to... 'The Simon Mayo Drivetime Show'," the host, a well-known comedian, announced, his voice echoing through the grand ballroom of The Dakota Manchester. A round of applause erupted as Simon Mayo, a stalwart of British radio, made his way to the stage with a warm smile and a polite wave.

Pete knew that there were 5 awards left, the Regional Drivetime, the Best National Station, Best Regional Station, the Ed Doolan Lifetime Award and an award for the Best Radio Group. Of those, Pete knew he was in the running for the Regional Drivetime, but there were rumours that the Ed Doolan Lifetime Award might be going to someone unexpected this year—perhaps a nod to a veteran presenter who had weathered the storm of the ever-changing radio landscape.

Pete clapped politely as Simon Mayo gave his acceptance speech, a heartfelt reflection on his long career and the joy of connecting with listeners across generations. It was a poignant reminder of what radio used to be about and what Pete feared was slipping away. Sarah nudged him gently, her eyes sparkling with pride. "Whether you win or not, Pete, you've done something incredible with your career. That's worth celebrating."

Before Pete could reply, the host returned to the microphone. "And now, onto the award for Best Regional Drivetime. This category celebrates the presenters who keep us company on our commutes, bring communities together, and remind us why local radio still matters."

Pete straightened in his seat, a mixture of anticipation and anxiety bubbling in his chest. He glanced at the other nominees on the screen—talented presenters from stations across the UK, including the Capital Midlands Tom & Claire, his main rival for the West Midlands drivetime, to Garry Spence on Clyde 1, one of Bauer's Scottish powerhouses. Each name represented a different corner of the UK's radio landscape, and Pete couldn't help but feel a pang of nostalgia for the days when regional radio was defined by unique voices rather than homogenised playlists.

The host continued, his tone playful but measured. "This year's nominees have faced tough competition, but their energy, creativity, and connection with their audiences have made them stand out. And the winner is…"

The room seemed to hold its breath as the host opened the envelope, drawing out the moment for dramatic effect.

"Garry Spence, Hits Radio Scotland."

A thunderous applause erupted as Garry Spence rose from his seat, his trademark smile beaming as he made his way to the stage. Pete clapped politely, leaning back in his chair and letting out a quiet sigh of relief. He hadn't expected to win, but hearing someone else's name called still stung a little. Sarah, ever perceptive, placed a reassuring hand on his arm.

"You've done amazing, Pete," she said softly. "Just being here, being nominated—it's a testament to everything you've done."

Pete managed a faint smile, appreciating her words even as a flicker of self-doubt lingered. He watched as Garry took the microphone, delivering a gracious speech that blended heartfelt gratitude with light humour. Garry's energy and charisma filled the room, and it was clear why he'd won—his connection with his listeners, his vibrant personality, and his ability to bridge the old and new in radio.

As Garry left the stage, the host returned, moving quickly to the next award. Pete allowed himself to relax a little, sinking into his chair and taking a sip of his wine. The night wasn't over, but he already felt the weight of the evening beginning to lift. For a moment, he allowed himself to drift into thought, reflecting on the long journey that had brought him to this point.

It wasn't just about awards or accolades. It was about the listeners who had tuned in every day, the stories he'd shared, the laughs and the moments of connection that had defined his career. Even if the industry had changed beyond recognition, those memories remained untouchable.

"And next up, it's the Ed Doolan Lifetime Award. This award is for presenters who have served the nation, either in a regional, local or national capacity with distinction. The nominees are Pete Smith of Manic Radio West Midlands, Stephanie Hirst of Hits Radio, Les Ross of BRMB, Ken Bruce of Greatest Hits Radio, Emma Bunton of Heart and Jo Russell of Hits Radio East Midlands."

Pete knew that, like him, the other nominees had been in radio for decades, building careers that had left lasting impressions on their listeners and communities. The room hushed as the host continued, his voice taking on a more reverent tone.

"This award honours the legends of our industry, the voices that have stood the test of time, adapting to changes while staying true to what makes radio so special—connection, authenticity, and passion."

Pete's heart raced as the nominees' faces appeared on the large screen, their achievements briefly summarised. Stephanie Hirst, who had been a trailblazer in commercial radio; Ken Bruce, a voice synonymous with warmth and wit; Emma Bunton, a national treasure who had transitioned seamlessly from pop stardom to radio; and Les Ross, a local legend in Birmingham's radio history. Then there was Pete himself—a veteran of local and regional radio, who had weathered the transition from Dudley FM to Manic's corporate structure.

"And the winner is…" The host opened the envelope with deliberate flair, pausing just long enough to make Pete feel his pulse in his ears.

"Pete Smith, Manic Radio West Midlands!"

For a moment, Pete froze. The applause that erupted around him felt almost distant, like a wave crashing in the background. Sarah's hand on his arm brought him back to the present, her face lit with pride. "You did it, Pete!" she whispered, her voice thick with emotion.

Pete rose from his seat, his legs feeling unsteady as he navigated his way to the stage. The applause grew louder, joined by a few cheers from familiar voices scattered across the room. As he reached the microphone, he took a deep breath, steadying himself.

"Wow," Pete began, his voice wavering slightly as he adjusted the mic. "I honestly didn't expect this. In fact, it's ironic, as Ed Doolan was one of the people who I grew up listening to as a child on BRMB, and then as a teen on BBC Radio WM. I'm sure Les, like me, would admit that he was one of the best of us—an absolute legend who set the gold standard for what local and regional radio could be."

The room was silent, hanging on Pete's words as he found his stride. His initial nervousness began to fade, replaced by a quiet confidence.

"I started in this industry over thirty years ago at Dudley FM, back when radio was about connecting with people, with communities. It was about the stories, the music, and the magic of live broadcasting. I won't lie to you—there have been times when I've wondered if I still fit in this new world of metrics, branding, and algorithms. But tonight, this award reminds me of something important: radio isn't about the size of your audience or the reach of your platform. It's about the connection. It's about making someone feel a little less alone on their drive home or putting a smile on their face after a hard day."

A ripple of applause filled the room, giving Pete a moment to gather his thoughts. He glanced at Sarah, her eyes glistening with pride, and smiled.

"I couldn't have done any of this without the people who believed in me—my colleagues, my family, and especially my wife, Sarah. She's not just my biggest supporter but also one of the best radio voices I've ever heard. And yes, sometimes my fiercest critic," he added with a wry smile, drawing a laugh from the audience. "But that's what keeps me grounded."

He paused, letting the moment sink in. "This industry is changing, and sometimes it feels like it's moving too fast. But I believe there's still room for authenticity, for storytelling, and for those moments of humanity that make radio so special. To anyone out there who feels like the world's moving past them—whether you're in radio or not—remember this: your voice matters. Your stories matter. And what you bring to the table can't be replaced by an algorithm."

****

CHAPTER 12 – Remembrance
Sunday 10th November 2024

It was seven in the morning when Pete woke up, and despite having only had 6 hours of sleep, the awards ceremony part of the event having concluded at half past 9 in the evening but the bar, dance and networking segments extending well into the early hours, he felt unusually refreshed. Winning the Ed Doolan Lifetime Award the previous evening had given him a sense of validation that lingered even as the industry around him continued to evolve in ways he struggled to embrace. Beside him, Sarah was still asleep, her steady breathing a reminder of the grounded support she always provided.

Pete slid out of bed quietly, not wanting to wake her. The early morning light filtered through the heavy curtains of their suite at The Dakota Manchester, casting a warm glow over the polished furniture and neatly arranged awards programme on the desk. Pete picked up the programme and thumbed through it idly, pausing on the page listing the nominees for the Lifetime Award. Seeing his name printed there, alongside legends like Ken Bruce and Les Ross, brought a small smile to his face.

He made his way to the coffee machine, its sleek, modern design feeling out of place against his preference for a simple kettle. As the aroma of fresh coffee filled the room, Pete's mind drifted to the day ahead. It was Remembrance Sunday, and he and Sarah had agreed to attend the commemorative service at Manchester Cathedral, a decision that felt especially poignant given the reflective mood he was in.

First, however, was breakfast, and Pete knew that Sarah would want to head down to the buffet that was included in their stay. He smiled to himself, recalling how Sarah could never resist a hotel breakfast buffet, particularly when it came with an array of pastries and fresh fruit. He decided to let her sleep a little longer before gently waking her, knowing they had enough time to enjoy a relaxed morning before the solemnity of the Remembrance service.

By eight o'clock, Pete was dressed and ready, wearing a navy blue suit that Sarah had insisted he bring, along with the poppy pin neatly affixed to his lapel. He quietly roused Sarah, who groaned softly before smiling up at him.

"Alright, alright, I'm up," she said, sitting up and running a hand through her hair. "You're far too chipper for someone who spent half the night talking shop over whisky."

"It's the award," Pete admitted, unable to keep the pride out of his voice. "Maybe it doesn't mean much in the grand scheme of things, but it's nice to know that what I've done over the years still counts for something."

Sarah smiled warmly, leaning up to kiss him on the cheek. "It means a lot, Pete. You've given your heart to this industry, and it's about time someone recognised that."

After Sarah got ready, they made their way down to the dining room. The buffet was as extensive as Pete had anticipated, with everything from full English staples to continental options. Sarah immediately gravitated toward the pastries, while Pete stuck to his usual—scrambled eggs, toast, and black coffee. They found a quiet corner to sit, the hum of conversation around them a pleasant backdrop to their own murmured exchanges.

"I noticed James and Kylie haven't come down," Sarah said, looking at her watch and noticing it was quarter to nine. "I did specifically tell James to be down here for now so we could all head to the Remembrance service together," she continued, a faint note of exasperation creeping into her voice.

Pete chuckled softly, sipping his coffee. "Knowing James, he probably convinced Kylie to sleep in after a late night. Or worse, they're brainstorming some Manic 'Christmas Day Special' nonsense over overpriced lattes and dubious playlist ideas."

Sarah shook her head, a small smile playing on her lips despite her irritation. "That boy needs to learn a thing or two about priorities. Today isn't about hashtags or 'vibes'. It's about showing respect."

Pete nodded, his expression growing more serious. "I'll give him a call after breakfast. If he doesn't get a move on, he can answer to you—and that's scarier than any boss at Manic."

Sarah laughed, the sound lightening the mood. "You're not wrong there. Now, let's finish up. I want to make sure we're at the Cathedral early enough to find good seats."

Suddenly James, dressed in a Kerrang! t-shirt and his usual ripped jeans, and Kylie in a mini-skirt and a cropped jumper, strolled into the dining room, looking far too casual for the occasion. James's hair was tousled, and he had the unmistakable air of someone who had barely rolled out of bed. Kylie, holding an oversized coffee cup, seemed unbothered, though her outfit drew a few glances from the more conservatively dressed guests.

"Morning, Mum, Dad," James said cheerfully, plopping down at their table without waiting for an invitation. "You both look very... formal."

Sarah raised an eyebrow, her lips pressing into a thin line. "We're going to a Remembrance Sunday service, James. Formality is kind of the point. Anyway, are you dining?"

James looked at his mother, and Pete noticed the telltale signs that he and Kylie had just had another line of cocaine in their room before coming down—slightly jittery movements, dilated pupils, and a barely concealed energy that didn't match the early hour.

"We're good, Mum," James replied a little too quickly, waving off the suggestion of breakfast. "Just needed a quick coffee before we head out. Right, Kyles?"

Kylie nodded, sipping her latte with a casual smile. "Yeah, we'll be ready to go in no time. Just thought we'd grab a quick one and meet you here."

Pete exchanged a look with Sarah, who raised an eyebrow but refrained from commenting. Instead, she simply gestured toward their outfits. "I hope you're planning to change before we leave. This isn't the kind of service you attend looking like you're heading to a festival."

James glanced down at his clothes, then shrugged. "What's wrong with what I'm wearing? Kyles and I are heading over Toni's in Liverpool, we're gonna skip the service and go straight there. Besides, Clo's back at home, probably shagging Cody."

Pete sighed heavily, setting down his coffee cup with deliberate care. "James," he said evenly, his tone measured but firm, "I'm not sure where you got the idea that today is optional but let me remind you: it's not. Remembrance Sunday isn't about us. It's about paying respect to those who gave everything so we could have this... comfortable, chaotic life."

James squirmed slightly under his father's gaze but quickly masked it with a cocky grin. "Look, Dad, I get it—Remembrance Sunday is important and all that. But honestly, do you think anyone's going to care if Kylie and I skip out? It's not like the veterans are going to notice two fewer people. Anyway, it's not as if its compulsory for Manic staff to go. Anyway, I'll see you later... unless Kyles and I get a train home."

James then stood up and Pete noticed that he was limping slightly, as if he'd spent the night in discomfort or had been involved in something more physical than he'd care to admit. The fact that Kylie had also stood up, and had her hand on James's lower back in a supportive gesture didn't escape Pete's notice. He exchanged a pointed glance with Sarah, whose expression mirrored his concern, but both chose not to press the issue. At least, not yet.

Seeing James then stumble up the step that led from the buffet to the main foyer of the hotel's dining area, Pete noticed something circular rubbing against the inside of

James's jeans at the rear, something that he presumed was some kind of lingering "memento" from whatever activities James and Kylie had been up to the previous night. Pete pinched the bridge of his nose, inhaling deeply to steady his rising irritation.

"You know what he's going to say if you press on it, love," Sarah said, and Pete sighed, as he knew that his son was nearly 22, and so not someone he could ground or order around like a teenager anymore. Pete also knew that any confrontation would likely escalate into a pointless argument, one that wouldn't change James's behaviour in the slightest.

"Yeah, I know," Pete muttered, shaking his head. "He's going to say it's his life, his choices, and he's an adult now. And technically, he's right. But that doesn't mean I have to like it."

Sarah rested a reassuring hand on his arm. "We'll talk to him later, Pete. Right now, let's focus on the service. It's important, and I don't want anything overshadowing it."

Pete nodded, taking another sip of his coffee and trying to push the image of James's dishevelled appearance out of his mind. He glanced at the clock on the wall. It was approaching nine, and they'd need to leave soon to make it to the Cathedral on time.

* _ * _ * _ *

"Fuck," James muttered as the couple got back to the room. "That anal plug almost fell out when I tripped over that step. Could've been a right mess in front of Mum and Dad." He winced as he collapsed onto the bed, his casual bravado faltering slightly. "Especially after you invited both Ali & Tom and let them fuck me raw. I must admit, babes, I enjoyed fucking you while they double banged me though."

Kylie giggled, and James noticed her recalling the memory of the previous night's escapades with a gleam in her eye. "You're such a trooper, Reevesy," she teased, tossing her jacket onto a nearby chair. "Though, maybe next time, we skip the breakfast charade and just head straight to Toni's. Your dad looked like he was about to burst a blood vessel."

James groaned, covering his face with a pillow. "Yeah, well, he's always been Mr. Traditional. I don't think he's ever missed a Remembrance Sunday in his life. But honestly, Kyles, how am I supposed to sit through a service with this thing still in me?"

Kylie laughed, sitting down next to him and ruffling his hair. "Consider it a lesson in stamina. Besides, you're the one who said you wanted to push boundaries. You're doing great, babe." Her tone was light, but there was a flicker of genuine affection as she handed him his coffee. "Drink up. You'll feel better once we get to Liverpool."

James took the cup with a reluctant grin. "Yeah, yeah. I suppose Toni's place is the perfect spot to forget all this family drama for a while. Al texted me earlier. He's handed in his keys to his Birmingham apartment and is moving in with Toni full time, now he's resigned."

"He's actually handed in his keys already? I thought he was keeping that place as a backup," Kylie said, raising an eyebrow as she stretched out beside James on the bed. Her carefree posture didn't quite mask her curiosity. "Toni must really have a pull on him, eh? Or maybe he's just diving headfirst into this new phase of his life."

James shrugged, sipping his coffee and wincing slightly as he shifted his position on the bed. "I guess. But I don't blame him for ditching the Birmingham flat. Manic's been running him ragged, and you know how Toni is—makes you feel like you're part of something bigger, even if it's just a madcap party every weekend."

Kylie smirked, her eyes glinting with mischief. "Well, Toni does have a way of turning chaos into an art form. Pity she's been suspended while OFCOM do their investigation of that late-night show mishap. I heard she's been laying low, but knowing her, 'laying low' probably involves some wild party in Liverpool with all the usual suspects."

James chuckled, shaking his head. "Sounds about right. She's a magnet for trouble and fun, often at the same time. Honestly, though, I'm glad Al's got her. She might be the only person who can keep him grounded after everything that's gone down."

Kylie leaned in, resting her chin on James's shoulder. "You know, for all the madness, it's kind of nice, isn't it? The way we all look out for each other, even if it's in our own messed-up way. Anyway, we've got an hour and half until our train, so, Reevesy..."

James noticed the grin on his girlfriend's face and chuckled. "The mind's willing but the body 's still recovering from last night," James finished with a smirk, pulling Kylie closer despite his mock protest. "You're insatiable, you know that?"

Kylie laughed, her voice low and teasing. "That's why you love me. Besides, we've got time. Who needs boring Sunday morning traditions when we've got our own?"

James rolled his eyes but couldn't hide the grin tugging at his lips. "Alright, fine. But if I miss the train and have to explain why we're late to Toni, I'm blaming you."

Kylie gave him a playful shove. "Deal. Now, let's make the most of that hour and a half."

* _ * _ * _ *

Meanwhile, at Manchester Cathedral, Pete and Sarah took their seats among a growing congregation. The grand interior was filled with a solemn energy, the kind that only Remembrance Sunday could evoke. The faint strains of the organ filled the air as people murmured quietly, each lost in their own thoughts.

Pete adjusted his poppy, glancing around at the faces of those gathered. Many were older veterans, their medals glinting in the soft light filtering through the stained glass windows. Others were families, children shifting restlessly in their seats as parents whispered reminders of why they were here. Pete's mind wandered to his father, a man who had served in World War II and whose stories of courage and camaraderie had shaped Pete's own sense of duty and respect.

Sarah placed a hand on his knee, bringing him back to the present. "You alright?" she asked softly.

Pete nodded, though his expression was pensive. "Just thinking about my grandfather. He would've loved a service like this. Simple, heartfelt, focused on what matters."

Lionel Smith, Pete's grandfather, had died during the Coronavirus pandemic in 2020, leaving behind a legacy of quiet resilience and dedication to family. Pete often thought of him during moments like these, especially on Remembrance Sunday. Lionel had been a man of simple values but profound wisdom, and Pete found himself wishing he could have one more conversation with him, to share everything that had happened in his life since.

Sarah gave his knee a gentle squeeze, her understanding shining through her eyes. "He's here in spirit, Pete. You carry him with you every day."

Pete smiled faintly, nodding. "Yeah, I suppose you're right. He'd probably be telling me to stop moping and focus on the service."

The organ music swelled as the congregation rose to their feet. The first hymn, O God, Our Help in Ages Past, filled the air, the hauntingly beautiful melody echoing through the cathedral's ancient stone walls. Pete joined in, his baritone voice blending with Sarah's lighter soprano, both of them immersed in the reverent atmosphere.

As the service progressed, Pete found himself reflecting not just on the sacrifices of those who had served in the armed forces, but also on the sacrifices he and Sarah had made in their own lives—pouring themselves into their careers, raising their children, and weathering the storms of an ever-changing industry. It wasn't the same kind of service, but it was meaningful in its own way.

As the service ended five minutes prior to the eleventh hour, the congregation moved silently outside to the Cathedral Gardens for the two-minute silence. The crisp November air carried a chill, and Pete pulled his coat tighter around himself as he and Sarah joined the gathering crowd. The distant tolling of a bell signalled the approach of the eleventh hour, and the hum of conversation faded into a solemn hush.

Pete found himself standing next to an elderly veteran, his chest adorned with medals that gleamed in the weak sunlight. The man stood with quiet dignity, his gaze fixed on the cenotaph as though lost in memories of comrades long gone. Pete glanced at him briefly, a sense of respect and gratitude washing over him. It reminded him of why this moment mattered so deeply—not just for those who served, but for those left behind to remember.

The Last Post sounded, its haunting melody slicing through the stillness, followed by a silence so profound that Pete could hear the faint rustle of leaves in the breeze. He bowed his head, the weight of the moment settling over him. Thoughts of his grandfather, of the countless lives lost, and of the sacrifices made filled his mind. He felt Sarah's hand slip into his, a steady presence grounding him as the two minutes passed in quiet reflection.

"When you go home, tell them of us and say, for your tomorrow, we gave our today," the voice of the officiant rang out, carrying the weight of the timeless words through the gathered crowd. The silence lingered for a beat longer before the soft strains of *Reveille* broke through, signalling the end of the two-minute silence and a return to the present.

Pete looked up, his eyes catching the faint glisten of tears on Sarah's cheeks. He gave her hand a reassuring squeeze, feeling a similar sting in his own eyes. It wasn't often that Pete allowed himself to be swept up in emotion, but Remembrance Sunday had a way of cutting through the noise of daily life and reminding him of what truly mattered.

The veteran beside him turned slightly, catching Pete's eye. "Beautiful service," the man said, his voice low and gravelly but tinged with emotion. "Reminds you of all the good men we've lost, doesn't it?"

Pete nodded, his throat tightening as he responded. "It does. And of the responsibility we have to honour their memory."

The veteran gave a small, knowing smile, his gaze returning to the cenotaph. "That's all we can do, son. Remember them, live well, and teach the next generation to do the same."

Pete glanced at Sarah, her eyes still focused on the cenotaph, then thought of James and Chloe. He hoped, despite their current chaotic lives, that one day they would truly understand the weight of days like this. It was a hope he carried quietly, tucked away in the same place where he kept the pride he felt for them, even when their choices frustrated him.

As the service concluded, the crowd began to disperse, the solemnity giving way to hushed conversations and the rustling of coats as people made their way back into the city. Pete and Sarah lingered for a moment, taking in the scene around them. The Cathedral Gardens, with its mix of old stone and fresh flowers, felt like a sacred space, a reminder of continuity in a world that often felt fragmented.

"Ready to head back?" Sarah asked gently, her voice breaking the spell. "We don't check out until tomorrow. We could head to a restaurant and have a quiet lunch, maybe talk about the week ahead. You know, it's funny how, yesterday, you told James we'd be leaving today, but we're actually here until tomorrow. Maybe we should keep that to ourselves, enjoy the peace and quiet for once."

Pete chuckled softly, appreciating the opportunity to spend some uninterrupted time with Sarah. "Sounds like a plan. Let's find somewhere decent to eat, and maybe I'll even let you pick the wine."

Sarah smiled, slipping her arm through his as they walked away from the Cathedral Gardens, blending into the quiet murmur of the dispersing crowd. "Only if you promise not to spend the entire meal dissecting the state of the radio industry. Just for one afternoon, Pete."

"I'll try," Pete replied with a wry grin. "But I'm not making any promises. You know what I'm like."

They strolled through the streets of Manchester, the city alive with a mix of solemn remembrance and the usual Sunday bustle. Pete found himself relaxing in the cool autumn air, the weight of the morning's reflections beginning to lift. The sight of couples and families walking arm in arm, the occasional street musician playing soft melodies, and the distant hum of city life all felt strangely comforting.

As they turned a corner, Sarah pointed to a small bistro with warm lighting and a chalkboard menu outside. "That looks nice. Let's try there."

Pete nodded, holding the door open for her as they stepped inside. The bistro was cosy, its walls adorned with vintage photographs of Manchester, and the soft hum of conversation created an inviting atmosphere. They were seated at a corner table near a window, the perfect spot for people-watching while they waited for their meals.

Over lunch, the conversation flowed easily, shifting from light-hearted anecdotes about the awards ceremony to more personal reflections on the morning's service. Pete found himself marvelling at how, even after all these years, Sarah could make him feel grounded and understood.

"You know," Sarah said, swirling her glass of white wine thoughtfully, "I've been thinking about what that veteran said earlier. About teaching the next generation to honour the past. It's something we've tried to do with James and Chloe, even if it doesn't always stick."

Pete sighed, setting down his fork. "It's hard, isn't it? Watching them go through life in a way that feels so… disconnected from everything we tried to teach them. But then again, maybe that's just part of being young. We made our mistakes too."

Sarah nodded, a small smile playing on her lips. "True. And they've got good hearts, even if they're a bit lost right now. James especially—he's got your stubbornness, you know. He'll find his way eventually."

* _ * _ * _ *

The Northern train between Manchester Piccadilly and Liverpool South Parkway hummed steadily as James and Kylie found themselves in a quieter carriage, tucked away from the prying eyes of Sunday morning commuters. The remnants of their chaotic morning lingered in their minds, but the familiar rhythm of the train offered a brief respite.

James leaned back against the window, his expression a mix of contentment and fatigue. Kylie sat beside him, scrolling through her phone with an air of detached curiosity. She glanced up at him after a moment, her smirk breaking the silence.

"Still sore?" she teased, nudging him with her elbow.

James rolled his eyes but couldn't help the small grin tugging at his lips. "You could say that. Thanks for the… adventure, Kyles. My dad already thinks I'm a walking disaster—this would just confirm it."

Kylie laughed, tossing her hair back as she leaned closer. "Oh, come on. Your dad's got bigger things to worry about than your… extracurricular activities. Besides, he's got that shiny award now. He's probably too busy basking in his glory."

James chuckled as, suddenly, a group of teens with their phone blaring, the sound of his voice from his Ibiza Headbangers show which was obviously being played via the Manic Prime app, saw the couple and immediately recognised James. The teens, dressed in trendy outfits and sporting a carefree vibe, approached with excitement.

"Oi, blud, it's Reevesy and Morgz, the pair who's smashing it on Manic! Oi, Reevesy, your Ibiza Headbangers show's proper lit, fam!" one of them exclaimed, their accents a mix of urban slang and Northern twang. "The Manic couple themselves. Yo, Kez, get a photo!"

James shifted uncomfortably, trying to straighten up while hiding the lingering soreness from the morning's activities. Kylie, ever the PR-savvy one, flashed a dazzling smile and waved at the teens as though they were her adoring fans.

"Thanks, mate," James said, his voice a blend of casual cool and feigned humility. "Glad you're enjoying the show. Got some big tracks lined up for the next episode, so keep tuning in."

"Reevesy, you're a legend!" one of the teens said, holding up their phone for a selfie. "And Morgz, you're fire on those shows, too. You guys should do more stuff together!"

Kylie leaned in, effortlessly slipping into her on-air persona. "Well, keep an eye out—we've got some exciting plans in the works. Manic's always about giving the fans what they want, right?"

The teens erupted in cheers, their energy infectious. One of them asked, "Reevesy, yo look stoned as hell, mate. Big night or what?"

James smirked, leaning into his cheeky "Jimmy Reeves" persona. "Nah, just running on vibes and bangers, you know how it is. Late nights, early mornings—it's the Manic way."

Kylie playfully nudged him, her grin unwavering. "And maybe a little too much coffee," she added, winking at the group.

The teens laughed, clearly eating up the banter. One of them, a girl with a Manic logo on her phone case, gushed, "You two are proper goals! Saw your Insta pic this morning of you two laying on your hotel bed. You look cute together."

James glanced at Kylie, who gave a subtle smirk in response. The teens' enthusiasm was both amusing and slightly overwhelming, but he wasn't about to let the opportunity slip. Playing to the crowd was second nature by now.

"Thanks, appreciate it," James said, giving a casual shrug as if it was no big deal. "Gotta keep things fresh for the fans, right?"

One of the boys piped up, "Yo, Reevesy, you gonna take Ibiza Headbangers live one day? Like, proper live at a club? That'd be sick."

James glanced at Kylie, his mind spinning at the thought. "You never know," he replied, his tone teasing. "If Manic's up for it, maybe we'll make it happen. What do you reckon, Kyles?"

Kylie, ever the strategist, leaned in conspiratorially toward the group. "Let's just say, we've been talking about some... big ideas. Keep listening, and you might see something epic soon."

The teens cheered, taking a flurry of selfies with the pair. As the group finally moved back to their seats, chatting excitedly about the encounter, James slumped back into his, exhaling deeply. He shot Kylie a sideways glance.

"'Big ideas,' huh?" he muttered. "You're gonna get me in trouble with my dad if we start hyping stuff that isn't even on the cards."

Kylie smirked, completely unbothered. "Trouble's part of the brand, Reevesy. Besides, you've got to keep them guessing. It's what makes you interesting."

James rolled his eyes but couldn't hide his grin. Kylie had a knack for spinning even the simplest moments into something bigger—a trait that both impressed and frustrated him.

The train slowed as it approached Liverpool South Parkway. James adjusted his jacket, wincing slightly as he shifted in his seat. Kylie, ever observant, leaned over and whispered, "You need to watch out, babes, especially as I've got work in the morning and you've got uni."

James smirked at Kylie's remark, brushing off the soreness he felt. "Uni's just a tick-box exercise these days. It's all about Manic. And anyway, aren't you the one who convinced me to party like it's Ibiza every night?"

Kylie rolled her eyes, her playful grin never fading. "You'll thank me when your 'Jimmy Reeves' brand is the hottest thing on the airwaves. Just remember who's steering the ship."

As the train pulled into Liverpool South Parkway, the pair grabbed their bags and stepped onto the platform. The crisp November air greeted them, its bite a sharp contrast to the warmth of the train. Kylie linked her arm through James's as they navigated their way out of the station.

"You reckon Toni's already started?" James asked, referring to their mutual friend and Manic presenter Toni Green, known for her legendary house parties.

Kylie snorted, pulling out her phone to check the time. "It's Toni. She's probably already three cocktails deep and orchestrating some sort of dance-off in her living room."

James laughed, though his thoughts momentarily drifted to his parents at the Remembrance service. He shook it off. Today was about unwinding, not dwelling on guilt—

or the stern words he knew were waiting for him when he eventually saw Pete and Sarah again.

* _ * _ * _ *

Pete and Sarah strolled through the quiet streets after their lunch, the weight of the morning's reflections gradually giving way to a lighter, more relaxed mood. The small bistro had provided the perfect setting for their conversation, and now they found themselves enjoying the rare luxury of uninterrupted time together.

"Do you think we should call James later?" Sarah asked as they turned a corner, the bustling city sounds a backdrop to their walk. "Just to check in. Make sure he got to Toni's safely."

Pete sighed, his expression thoughtful. "I suppose. Though I doubt he's in the mood for a parental check-in. He's probably too busy playing the Manic golden boy."

Sarah chuckled softly. "You mean Jimmy Reeves, the next big thing in CHR radio? Let him have his moment, Pete. He'll figure things out—eventually."

Pete shook his head, a wry smile tugging at his lips. "You've got more faith than I do, love. But I suppose that's what keeps this family from completely imploding."

As they reached the entrance of their hotel, Pete paused, glancing up at the elegant facade. "You know, Sarah, I've been thinking. I'm going to stay at Manic, do the Goldies show, but I'm going to do a couple of syndicated shows on my days off... maybe break out a new name for those shows."

Sarah raised an eyebrow, intrigued by Pete's sudden thought. "A new name, eh? Something edgy like 'DJ Pete Legend'? Or are we going for something more nostalgic like 'Smith on the Wireless'?" she teased, a playful grin spreading across her face.

Pete chuckled, shaking his head. "Not quite, love. I was thinking of... well, you remember that '70s and '80s rock show I wanted to do years ago, the DJ Strangelove thing'? Might dust off that old idea, give it a proper go this time. Something different from the polished Manic vibe—more raw, authentic. Reckon there's still an audience out there for it, especially on the smaller stations."

Sarah's eyes lit up with a mix of surprise and approval. "DJ Strangelove! I remember you bringing that up back in the Dudley FM days. It's a great idea, Pete—quirky, memorable, and a proper throwback to what radio used to be about. You could even tie it in with Reeves Radio Ltd., make it a full production. Community stations would love it."

Pete smiled, a flicker of excitement replacing the weariness that had been gnawing at him. "Yeah, that's what I was thinking. Run it independently, maybe sell it as a weekly syndicated show. Something for the stations that still care about connecting with listeners instead of just chasing trends."

Sarah nodded enthusiastically, already brainstorming. "You could start small, maybe five or six stations to test the waters, and build from there. Plus, it gives you a creative outlet—something that's fully yours, no corporate scripts or branding mandates."

Pete's smile widened, the idea taking root in his mind. "You know, love, I think this could be exactly what I need. A way to stay in the game without losing sight of why I got into radio in the first place."

Sarah reached out, giving his arm a gentle squeeze. "Then let's do it. We'll map out a plan when we're back home. And Pete—just so you know, I think your grandad would've loved this idea."

Pete's expression softened, a mix of pride and nostalgia flickering in his eyes. "Yeah, he would've. He always said radio was about heart, not flash. Maybe this is my way of honouring that."

They stepped into the lobby of the hotel, the warmth of the interior a welcome contrast to the chilly November air outside. As they made their way to the lift, Pete glanced at Sarah, his expression lightening. "And who knows? Maybe I'll even let you guest-host an episode or two."

Sarah laughed, her eyes sparkling with amusement. "Oh, please. The listeners would love it—you and me bickering on air like the old days. Wolverhampton FM versus Dudley FM all over again."

Pete chuckled, the weight of the day lifting further with each shared laugh. As the lift doors closed, he felt a renewed sense of purpose. Winning the Ed Doolan Lifetime Presenter Award had reminded him of his legacy, but this idea—this return to his roots—felt like a chance to shape his future on his own terms.

Back in their suite, Pete and Sarah settled in for a quiet evening, the city lights twinkling outside their window. Pete made a note on his phone: DJ Strangelove – pitch ideas for syndicated show. He glanced at Sarah, who was already engrossed in a book, and smiled. For the first time in months, he felt like he was moving forward—not just with his career, but with his life.

As the night deepened, Pete couldn't help but wonder how James and Kylie were faring in Liverpool. Whatever chaos they were diving into, he hoped they'd eventually find their way—just as he was beginning to find his.

****

CHAPTER 13 – Fractured Frequencies

Monday 11th November 2024

The light drizzle of a Manchester morning was a stark contrast to the warmth and reflection of the previous day. Pete woke to the familiar buzz of his phone vibrating on the nightstand. Sarah, still curled up in bed beside him, mumbled a sleepy protest as Pete reached for the device.

Looking at the time, he noticed it was half past 9, and that a text from Chloe had been received. "Dad, they've organised a trip for uni, so I need a loan."

Pete knew that his daughter, who was studying Law with Criminology at the University of Birmingham, often sent messages like this. They were usually followed by vague details about the trip and little else. Pete sighed, rubbing his eyes and sliding out of bed. He stretched and quietly moved to the small desk by the window, opening the curtains to let in the grey light of the morning.

He began typing a response:

Chloe, what's the trip for, and how much do you need? And before you ask, it's coming out of your birthday money if it's anything extravagant!

Setting his phone down, Pete glanced at Sarah, who stirred slightly but didn't wake. He decided to take a quick shower before heading downstairs for breakfast. His mind was already wandering back to the events of the weekend—winning the Ed Doolan Lifetime Presenter Award had been a highlight, but his thoughts kept drifting to James and Kylie's behaviour. Skipping the Remembrance service hadn't surprised him, but it still gnawed at him. He didn't want to push them away, but his patience was wearing thin.

"It's to the Royal Courts of Justice in London, Dad," Chloe's reply popped up on Pete's phone as he finished getting ready for breakfast. "And it's for a full day of sessions with legal professionals. I need £75 for the train and expenses. Pretty please?"

Pete sighed, slipping his phone into his pocket. He made a mental note to transfer the money later but decided not to reply immediately. He'd deal with Chloe once he and Sarah had arrived back in the Midlands. The fact that James, on the other hand, had not messaged him since yesterday afternoon with a photo that, if Pete was honest, something that a 21 year-old might think is funny but a 54-year-old dad would find less than amusing—a nude photo of Kylie, Toni Green and a Manic Radio Liverpool host named Penny Lane with Kylie and Toni using strap-ons to dominate the scene, while Penny wore a cheeky grin, holding a drink aloft as if it were a casual house party snap. Pete had glanced at the image, shaken his head, and promptly deleted it, his patience fraying at the edges.

As Pete made his way down to breakfast, Sarah joined him, now awake and dressed in a smart-casual outfit. She carried the air of someone ready to take on the day but not in any particular hurry. They entered the dining room, choosing a quiet table near the window overlooking the damp city streets.

"Chloe again?" Sarah asked as Pete checked his phone one last time.

"Yeah, another loan request. It's for some legal thing in London. Proper educational trip, apparently," Pete replied, adding, "£75 for train and expenses. Said it's coming out of her birthday money, though."

Sarah smirked over her coffee. "Sounds fair. And James? Still off gallivanting with Kylie?"

Pete shook his head. "No word since yesterday, aside from... something I'd rather not describe. Let's just say he's living up to the 'Manic lifestyle,' and leave it at that."

Sarah sighed, her expression softening. "He'll come around, Pete. They both will. It's just going to take time."

Pete wasn't so sure, but he appreciated her optimism. Their breakfast passed in comfortable quiet, the sounds of other diners and the occasional clatter of plates filling the space. Pete mentally prepared himself for the day ahead—his drive back to the Midlands and, more importantly, a meeting with Manic management later that afternoon to finalise the terms of his move to Manic Goldies in April.

* _ * _ * _ *

Walking into the Manic Dudley hub at The Waterfront, Pete knew it was 1 in the afternoon, a collision on the M6 causing tailbacks and making him late for his meeting with Manic's regional manager, Cal Ellington, who Pete knew was a former producer at Bee Manic and, in his late 20s, was now a regional manager overseeing operations in the Midlands. Cal was a sharp, ambitious figure who

embodied the energy of Manic's younger generation—
dynamic but often dismissive of traditional radio values.
Pete braced himself for what he anticipated would be a
conversation laced with corporate jargon and not-so-
subtle condescension.

Cal was the same person who, the previous week, told him
that he was no longer a salaried employee of Manic's
following the annual renewal of his contract. Instead, Pete
had been reclassified as an independent contractor, a
move that meant losing benefits like a pension and
holiday pay while gaining a so-called "flexible work
schedule." Pete had seen it for what it was—a cost-cutting
measure that left him feeling disposable, despite his
decades of service.

Pete knew, as a local of Dudley, that his roots in the area
made him more in tune with the listeners than someone
like Cal, who treated the Midlands hub as just another
stepping stone in his career. Walking through the familiar
corridors, Pete noticed the smell of fresh paint and the
faint hum of activity. The Dudley hub was in the middle
of renovations, a bittersweet reminder that it would soon
be replaced by the state-of-the-art Manic Midlands
facility in Birmingham's city centre.

Pete reached Cal's office, where the younger man was
already seated behind his sleek, minimalist desk, scrolling
through a tablet. He looked up with a professional smile
that didn't quite reach his eyes.

"Ah, Pete," Cal said, standing to shake his hand. "Sorry to
hear about the M6. Let's get started, shall we?"

Pete took a seat, resisting the urge to comment on Cal's overly polished demeanour. "Sure. Let's talk about this Goldies transition."

Cal nodded, leaning back in his chair. "Right. So, as we discussed, your new role will be on Manic Goldies, weekdays 4 to 7 PM, starting April. We're excited about the nostalgic edge you bring—perfect for the 35 to 54 demographic. Of course, your current drivetime slot here will remain in place until then, giving us time to audition replacements. We're aiming for someone who can match the energy of our CHR branding. You understand."

Pete nodded, though the phrase "match the energy" grated on him. He knew it was code for finding a younger, flashier presenter to appeal to the network's obsession with the under-30 market. "And as an independent contractor," Pete said carefully, "I assume that means I'll be managing my own pension and holiday arrangements from now on?"

Cal's smile tightened. "That's correct. It's a more flexible arrangement for talents like you. You will have to conform to certain things though."

Pete raised an eyebrow, his patience already thinning. "Conform to what exactly, Cal?"

Cal's polished exterior didn't falter, but there was a faint flicker of discomfort in his eyes. "Just the usual. We want you to dress more like Smooth's Nigel Freshman and less BBC-like."

Pete raised an eyebrow, barely masking his disbelief. "So, let me get this straight. You want me to trade in my usual smart-casual wardrobe for something a bit more... Smooth presenter chic? Is that supposed to help me connect with listeners, or just tick a box for corporate branding?"

Cal chuckled lightly, though his tone carried an edge of condescension. "It's about aligning with the Manic Goldies image. We want to project warmth and relatability. Your voice already does that, but the visuals matter too. Think open collar shirts, jeans, maybe a leather jacket. That sort of thing."

Pete smiled, as Cal had spelt out exactly what Pete himself had planned to wear for his upcoming role—as a way to update his image whilst sticking true to his respect for the days of Ed Doolan and other 1980s and 1990s radio icons. "Fair enough, Cal. Though I hope you're not expecting me to start posting TikToks of me doing air guitar in the studio. Let's leave that to James and the Manic Dance lot, eh?"

Cal laughed politely, though the slight tension in his expression betrayed his discomfort. "Of course not, Pete. We know your strengths lie in connecting with the audience in a way that feels authentic. That's what we're counting on for Goldies."

Pete leaned back in his chair, crossing his arms as he studied the younger man. "Good. Because authenticity is about more than just how I dress or what tracks I spin. It's about knowing the people you're talking to. And I've spent my entire career doing just that. Anyway, I'm also going to be doing some shows outside of Manic, now I'm an independent contractor. I assume there's no conflict of interest if I syndicate a couple of niche programmes to community stations? Something like… oh, I don't know, DJ Strangelove—a throwback rock show with a bit of edge."

Cal frowned. "You do realise that Manic Rock exists for rock enthusiasts, right? And community stations? They're only good for filling gaps where commercial radio can't make money," Cal finished, his tone dismissive. "But if you're keen on working with them, I suppose there's no formal conflict, provided you don't use Manic resources or clash with your Goldies schedule."

Pete resisted the urge to roll his eyes. "Don't worry, Cal. I wouldn't dream of borrowing Manic's TikTok ring light or studio time. My wife has her own studio at home, so I'll be perfectly capable of handling production independently. And as for community radio, let's not forget—those stations often hold onto the kind of connection with listeners that big networks have forgotten how to nurture. There's still value there, even if it doesn't come with a shiny profit margin."

Cal's expression tightened slightly, but he managed to maintain his polished smile. "Fair enough, Pete. Just remember, Manic Goldies is your primary commitment, and we'll be monitoring audience engagement closely. It's a competitive market, and we want to make sure every show delivers."

Pete gave a short nod, his patience nearing its limit. "Understood, Cal. Anything else?"

Cal's smile widened, the corporate mask slipping back into place. "That's everything for now. Looking forward to seeing how you bring your unique touch to Goldies."

The meeting concluded with a handshake that felt more obligatory than genuine. Pete left Cal's office feeling both resigned and determined. The corporate structure of Manic might have pushed him to the sidelines, but he wasn't about to fade quietly. If anything, the constraints only made him more committed to proving his worth on his own terms.

* _ * _ * _ *

"It's Monday, four o'clock, and here's the news with Cody Lane," Pete said as the clock struck 4 in Studio 1, his Midlands Manic drivetime slot opening with its usual professionalism. Pete leaned back in his chair, listening as his daughter's boyfriend read the headlines from the broom closet Studio 9, where the news was recorded as-live, with, off peak, all 7 stations at the Dudley hub receiving hourly pan-Central England and Mid Wales news update, and during the peaks recorded local half hourly news segments tailored for each station. Cody's calm, authoritative voice filled the studio as he detailed the latest updates, including regional transport disruptions, a council proposal for new housing developments, and a feel-good story about a local football team reaching the semi-finals of a national tournament.

Pete's attention drifted for a moment. The contrast between his steady approach and the chaotic energy of the newer generation at Manic was stark. Cody, for all his professionalism on-air, was one of the younger staff who seemed firmly entrenched in the Manic party culture—a fact that didn't escape Pete, especially given Cody's relationship with Chloe.

As the news segment ended, Pete knew what was coming, a new competition that Manic were pushing, the 'Manic £100k Daily Drop', while the '£500k Money Drop' was being rested until after Christmas. The irony, Pete knew, was that the weekly competition paid out half a million, while the new daily £100,000 competition was designed to generate daily buzz, with smaller but more frequent payouts spread across the week. Pete had his reservations about the relentless competition-driven format, but he kept those thoughts to himself as he prepared to deliver the slick promo.

"Right, we've got a new competition for you folks," Pete said, reading the script and leaning into his professional tone. "The Manic £100k Daily Drop—your chance to win big every single day. All you have to do is text the word 'DROP' to 87106—texts cost £5 per entry, or you can enter for free by using WhatsApp—01632 960459 is the number you need to WhatsApp your answer to. Suzie Wang, who's in for Toni Green, will be phoning one lucky winner after 7pm when the lines close, so get in quick if you fancy a chance at the jackpot. Winners are picked from an entry who's listening at any of the Manic Radio stations, Manic Dance, Manic Rock, Manic Goldies, Manic Soul and Manic Metal, as it's a network-wide competition. Full terms, conditions and restrictions, are on our website, manicradio.co.uk"

Pete knew that he needed to add that bit of legal disclaimer before continuing with the script. "Anyway, who fancies a throwback? Here's Fast Food Song by Fast Food Rockers. That's right, we're taking it back to 2003 with a track that's as cheesy as a double pepperoni pizza—and just as addictive. Turn it up, sing along, and don't forget the ketchup!"

Pete knew that the playout was nationwide, and that the Speke hub's systems would take over seamlessly for the next link while he readied his own local segment after the track ended. As the bouncy, cheesy beats of the Fast Food Song began to play, Pete leaned back in his chair, half amused at the irony of the throwback juxtaposed with the corporate polish of the Manic network.

The playlist had been chosen to appeal to the nostalgia of twenty-somethings now raising kids while also amusing those who remembered its original run. Pete, however, couldn't help but notice the frequency of these gimmicky throwbacks—another tactic to keep the network feeling "relatable." He appreciated a good nostalgic track as much as anyone, but the corporate over-engineering of the playlist grated on him.

* _ * _ * _ *

Chloe, despite her public appearances, hated her brother. The two had been best friends, partners in crime, until July 2019, when he was taking his GCSEs, when he had started dating his first girlfriend, Sophia Khan, a Northfield born girl whose family had moved to Pensnett and quickly taken to the Smith family. Chloe had initially been thrilled for James, excited at the prospect of a new friend and ally in their teenage mischief. But things soured when Chloe discovered James had used her to cover for his secret meetings with Sophia, letting Chloe take the blame for sneaking out while he gallivanted around Birmingham and Wolverhampton.

Then James went to college, and split with Sophia, whose family had moved to Cotteridge, and Chloe had two years left in her secondary school to stew in the bitterness of her brother's betrayal. By the time James moved on to university and began his ascent into the Manic Radio world, Chloe had transformed her resentment into a subtle but persistent undercurrent of competition. She wasn't content to let him dominate the family narrative as the golden child of media while she played second fiddle, even if their parents insisted that they were equally proud of both.

The final straw happened two weeks ago, when James had, by a chance of luck, got signed to Manic and its world of high-energy, brand-driven chaos. Pete and Sarah had celebrated his achievement with the same enthusiasm they'd shown for Chloe's acceptance to study Law with Criminology at the University of Birmingham, but the family dynamic shifted subtly. Chloe couldn't shake the feeling that James was being elevated as the "fun" sibling, the one who had it all figured out, while she remained the serious, responsible one—hardworking, but ultimately less exciting.

Chloe's simmering resentment reached a boiling point during a family dinner, where James had breezily mentioned that his "Jimmy Reeves" persona was getting him noticed by management and listeners alike. He had playfully teased Chloe about her legal aspirations, joking that she'd "end up being the family lawyer when I inevitably get sued for slander on-air." The comment was meant in jest, but it cut deep, further fuelling Chloe's determination to carve out her own identity—one that didn't involve her brother.

"It's meant to be me getting the Manic slot, the fun, glamorous life that comes with it," Chloe had muttered under her breath later that evening, nursing a glass of wine while scrolling through James's Instagram account. Every post, every story, was a carefully curated showcase of his new life—late-night recording sessions, cheeky grins with Kylie, and candid moments with other Manic Radio personalities. Chloe couldn't help but roll her eyes at the relentless self-promotion.

It wasn't just envy; it was frustration. Chloe knew she was smarter than James, more disciplined, more grounded. Yet here he was, waltzing into the limelight while she slogged through lectures, legal case studies, and late nights in the library. It felt unfair, and Chloe hated the bitterness it brought out in her.

****

CHAPTER 14 – Manipulations Start
Wednesday 20th November 2024

James knew something was starting to get odd, especially as, over the past week, Kylie was starting to get... distant. It wasn't anything he could put his finger on, but he felt it in the way she looked at him when he walked into the room, how she seemed a little more preoccupied with her phone than usual. Kylie was never far from her phone, but lately, it felt like she was absorbed in something he wasn't privy to. He knew she was always calculating—she was sharp, knew how to work a crowd, get the right angles for social media, and push the right buttons to keep the Manic brand buzzing. But now, there was something colder, more deliberate about it.

The sex was great, as, after all, the two had been dating for the past two years, albeit for all but three weeks of it in secret and their relationship still had that raw energy of something new, thrilling, and rebellious. But lately, it seemed like even their most intimate moments were coloured by a growing sense of distance. Maybe it was the constant pressure of their respective roles at Manic, or perhaps the unspoken competition between them. James couldn't quite tell, but he couldn't shake the feeling that Kylie was losing interest in the things that used to matter to her. And worse, she was starting to prioritise something else — something that felt like it didn't include him.

"Are you even listening, James?" Kylie's voice broke him from his thoughts. She was sitting across the room, her fingers scrolling rapidly on her phone as she tapped out a message. "We're doing a live Ibiza Headbangers preview on my Warwickshire Stars breakfast show tomorrow."

James blinked, the sound of Kylie's voice snapping him out of his thoughts. She'd been speaking for the last few minutes, but he had barely caught a word of it. His mind was still preoccupied with the subtle changes in their relationship, the growing tension that had settled like a thick fog between them.

"Sorry, babe, what did you say?" he asked, rubbing his eyes. He hated how easily distracted he'd become, but he couldn't shake the sense that things weren't right. He'd always been in tune with Kylie's moods, but right now, she felt more like a stranger than the woman he'd fallen for.

Kylie didn't look up from her phone, her fingers still furiously typing. "I said we're doing a live preview of Ibiza Headbangers on my breakfast show tomorrow," she repeated, as if he should have known that already. "It's a big deal, James. They're promoting the hell out of it— sponsored slots, on-air shout-outs, the works."

He nodded, forcing a smile as he sat up in his chair. "Right, yeah, sounds great. I'll be ready for it."

But even as he said it, a feeling of dread crept over him. Kylie had always been ambitious, driven by the adrenaline of being at the centre of the Manic storm, but there was something different in the way she spoke now. The passion was there, sure, but it felt more like a business transaction than a celebration of their shared success. It felt like she was running a race—and he was just a participant, not a partner.

Kylie finally looked up, her eyes flicking over to him for just a second. She seemed distracted, almost as though she was sizing him up. There was a brief flicker of something in her gaze, but it disappeared before he could place it. "You are ready for it, aren't you, James?" she asked, her voice cool. "Because you know, there's a lot riding on this. Manic's expecting big things, and if you're not as sharp as you've been promising, it could backfire."

James opened his mouth to respond, but the words caught in his throat. "I've been sharp, Kyles. You know that. It's just... lately, it feels like everything's about... well, I feel like I'm being stretched six ways to Sunday... and... well, my arse hurts."

Kylie's lips curled into a brief, amused smile, but it was hollow, like she was humouring him rather than sharing the joke. She shifted in her seat, leaning back against the plush chair, her eyes not leaving her phone. "You're being dramatic, James. It's all part of the job. We're all busy, and if you can't manage it, maybe it's time you took a step back and re-evaluated. And as for your arse, it's because you're a slut for my strap-on."

James grinned at the last bit, as, he had to admit, whenever Kylie whipped out her collection of strap-ons and anal plugs for him to use, he took to them with great enthusiasm. As he saw Kylie stand up, he felt himself getting hard, seeing her head towards the bedroom, where she stored the sex toys that formed a significant part of their private life. But James hesitated. The thought of another wild night with Kylie—a welcome escape from the constant buzz of Manic—was tempting, but it didn't erase the nagging doubt in the back of his mind.

"Kyles," James began, standing up and catching her before she disappeared into the bedroom. His tone was softer, more earnest than he intended. "Are we… I mean, are we good? You seem distant lately, like there's something you're not telling me."

Kylie stopped in her tracks, her hand on the doorframe. She didn't turn to face him immediately, and for a moment, the silence felt unbearable. When she finally spoke, her voice was even, almost too controlled. "James, don't overthink it. Anyway, I think it's time we started trying for one."

* _ * _ * _ *

Kylie was in the Dudley hub, speaking to the manager, Cal Ellington, who was, at the time, having sex with Lily Jenkins.

"Kylie, I.... love your idea," Cal said with a muffled breath as he adjusted himself on the couch, pulling away from Lily momentarily. The room carried an air of unprofessional chaos, but Kylie, ever composed, ignored the scene unfolding before her. She crossed her arms, leaning casually against the wall, her eyes focused on Cal as though nothing unusual was happening. "Getting pregnant with Reevesy's child would solidify your position at Manic. He's the rising star right now, and if you're tied to him in that way, it could create a power dynamic that ensures your influence both on and off-air."

Lily, sprawled on the couch with a casual smirk, chimed in, "Not to mention, the headlines would be pure gold. 'Manic's Golden Couple Expecting!' The PR department would eat that up. Throw in some Instagram stories and a few on-air mentions, and you've got a narrative that's not just a ratings boost but a cultural moment."

"You know, there's another Manic presenter who did it three years ago, got preggers with her husband and made a whole social media buzz during COVID," Cal said with a grin. "It kept her in the spotlight during a quiet period for the station, and the audience loved it."

Kylie knew who Cal was talking about - Toni Green, then a Bee Manic presenter, who had used her pregnancy during the early pandemic to maintain her visibility and leverage her family narrative into continued relevance and ultimately a Network slot, a position every Manic presenter, apart from the likes of Pete Smith and a few others, was angling towards. Kylie, sharp and ambitious, had been silently studying Toni's trajectory. She recognised how the Manic ecosystem thrived on personal narratives—especially the ones that blurred the lines between the professional and the personal.

Kylie smirked, playing with the hem of her cropped jumper. "That's the point, isn't it? Reevesy and I aren't just presenters. We're a brand. If we control the narrative, we control the future. And let's be real, Cal, Manic loves a good story. A golden couple expecting their first child while juggling top-rated shows? That's not just a boost— it's a bloody empire."

Cal adjusted his shirt, grinning at her vision. "You're thinking three steps ahead, as usual. I'll admit, Kylie, it's genius. But what's Reevesy's take on this? Does he know where this is heading?"

Kylie waved dismissively, her grin sharp and calculating. "James doesn't need to know the full picture yet. He's still finding his footing. I'll let him think it's his idea when the time's right. Anyway, he's been itching to settle into the whole 'power couple' vibe since we went Insta Official. He'll go along with it. Men are easy to nudge when you play your cards right."

Lily laughed, picking up her phone and scrolling aimlessly. "Classic. Honestly, Kylie, you're wasted on breakfast radio. You should be running the whole bloody network."

Kylie flashed her a smile, but her eyes remained fixed on Cal. "One step at a time. First, we lock in the public perception. Then, we make moves. Speaking of which…" She leaned forward slightly, her tone shifting to one of playful seriousness. "Make sure this doesn't leak, Cal. If word gets out before I'm ready, it'll ruin the timing."

Cal nodded, the weight of Kylie's words sinking in. Despite her sharp wit and charm, there was an underlying edge to her that made it clear she wasn't to be underestimated. "Of course. You've got my word. Just keep doing what you're doing, and we'll back you."

Kylie straightened, smoothing her jumper and flipping her hair. "Good. Now, I need a good fucking. Reevesy may have a big cock, but sometimes a gal needs a little more variety." She smirked at Cal, her tone dripping with playful provocation as she headed closer to him, kissing him.

Kylie knew that, despite dating James, she had slept with other Manic presenters and network staff before, often to cement alliances or manipulate situations to her advantage. To her, relationships were as much about strategy as they were about intimacy. With Cal, it was no different—he had the power to influence her career trajectory, and she wasn't above using whatever tools she had to secure her future.

As Cal pulled her closer, Lily rolled her eyes and reached for her phone again. "You two are like a live version of Love Island," she quipped, not bothering to hide her amusement. "Just don't let Reevesy find out—unless you plan to spin this into some wild storyline."

Kylie smirked against Cal's lips before pulling away slightly. "Reevesy's too caught up in his own hype to notice anything. Besides, I'm the one steering the ship in this relationship. He'll go where I need him to. Which reminds me, handsome, I need some more coke."

*_*_*_*

Chloe grinned at the text that Kylie had sent her. Despite being James's sister, she was forming an unexpected alliance with Kylie. The text read: "Clo, we both know James is a mess, but he's useful for now. I've got bigger plans, and with your legal smarts, you could help me secure the next move. You in?"

Chloe read the message twice, her grin fading into a thoughtful expression. She wasn't particularly fond of Kylie, but there was something intriguing about the offer. For years, she had resented James for overshadowing her, and now Kylie was presenting an opportunity to subtly outmanoeuvre him.

She tapped out a cautious reply: "Depends on what you're planning. And what's in it for me?"

Within seconds, Kylie responded: "You'll get your own spotlight, Chlo. You've got the brains, I've got the connections. Together, we can control this narrative. You want a job at Manic as a host, right?"

Chloe knew that her brother's girlfriend had a point, and that, as someone who was ambitious herself, she couldn't overlook the potential benefits of aligning with Kylie. Chloe had always wanted to break into the world of CHR radio, and she knew that her syndicated shows that she did for Reeves Radio wasn't going to sustain her ambitions. Aligning with Kylie, while morally ambiguous, could give Chloe the leverage she needed to carve out her own path in the competitive world of radio.

Chloe smirked as she typed back: "Fine. I'm in. But this better not blow up in my face, Kylie. And I want more than promises—I need guarantees."

Kylie's reply came swiftly, her confidence palpable even through the screen: "Relax, Clo. Cal told me that there's an open audition for a host position coming up after Christmas and I've already put your name forward. Play your cards right, and you'll have a shot. Plus, I'll make sure James stays too distracted to even realise what's happening. Consider this the start of something big for both of us."

Chloe knew from her boyfriend that Cal Ellington, the regional manager for Manic Midlands, held significant sway over hiring decisions, and if Kylie had indeed put her name forward, it wasn't just empty talk. This was a real opportunity—a chance to step out of James's shadow and claim her own space in the world of CHR radio. She mulled over the implications, knowing that aligning with Kylie was risky. Kylie's manipulations had a habit of leaving collateral damage, but Chloe had learned to navigate treacherous waters in her own right. If she played it carefully, this could work to her advantage.

* _ * _ * _ *

"Chloe, James, tea!" Pete said as soon as he walked into the house after another drivetime show at the Dudley hub. It was half-past nine, and he was looking forward to unwinding after a long day. Chloe was already at the dining table, her textbooks spread out as she sipped tea and tapped on her laptop. James, however, was nowhere to be seen.

Pete set his bag down and poured himself a cup of tea. He glanced at Chloe, noting her unusually focused demeanour. "Where's your brother?" he asked, his tone casual but laced with a hint of irritation.

Chloe didn't look up, her fingers still flying across the keyboard. "He's gone to the hub, Rehearsals for House of Manic Live."

Pete knew that James, as a fill in and cover presenter for various Manic stations, would get drafted to cover various shows, but House of Manic Live was a high-profile event, the season ender for Manic where they, like Bauer's Hits Live and Global's Capital Jingle Bell Ball, showcased the biggest stars in pop music alongside their top presenters. Having James at rehearsals for it, even though he'd only been with Manic less than a month, was highly unusual. Pete raised an eyebrow, sipping his tea thoughtfully. "House of Manic Live? Didn't know he'd been bumped up the pecking order already. He's not exactly Greg James or Fleur East."

Chloe smirked, her eyes still on her laptop. "Apparently, Kylie pulled some strings. You know, leveraging the whole 'golden couple' image. Since Toni Green resigned after the Sunday evening mishap with Al Crozier swearing on air a couple of weeks ago... well, James said to me that Cal has been assigned to find someone for the Birmingham show who's 'brand consistent', meaning him and Kylie.

Pete knew that there were 4 shows running over two weeks, with Toni Green having been slated to be the host, and regional presenters slated to be the 'backstage hosts' for behind-the-scenes segments, interviews with artists, and audience interactions. There had been rumours that Manic Dance's Ali & Tom would be the main hosts, a reshuffle from Toni doing all the shows, and that Kylie, as a 22-year-old and host of the Warwickshire Stars Breakfast, would be doing the backstage segments. The fact that James had not been mentioned at all in the original lineup raised alarm bells for Pete. It seemed suspiciously fast-tracked, even by Manic's standards, to have James involved in such a major production so soon. Kylie pulling strings made sense, but Pete couldn't help but feel like his son was being set up as a pawn in someone else's game.

Pete leaned against the kitchen counter, studying Chloe, who was still focused on her screen. "You seem awfully clued in on all this. Something you're not telling me?"

Chloe finally looked up, her expression carefully neutral. "Dad, I'm dating Cody, remember, so he tells me all sorts of things about what's happening at the Dudley hub. Anyway, I'm off to bed once I've finished reading this case study as I'm not hungry."

Pete knew that his daughter had an appetite that was up-and-down, as she was a cocaine user, and that she'd likely spent the day snacking while working on her assignments. He sighed, choosing not to press the issue. Chloe had always been fiercely independent, and he respected her space—even if he had lingering doubts about her priorities.

"Alright, love," Pete said, taking a sip of tea. "Just make sure you're not burning the candle at both ends. And tell your brother not to stay too late at the hub if you hear from him."

Chloe gave a noncommittal hum in response, her eyes already back on her laptop. Pete shook his head, a mix of frustration and resignation settling over him as he headed into the living room with the pizza that he'd brought for him, Chloe, Sarah and James, a 20 inch ham and pineapple one as he knew that the family loved those.

Pete sat down in the living room with his tea and pizza, letting out a weary sigh as he glanced at the framed photographs on the mantle. One was of a much younger James and Chloe, arms slung around each other, their grins carefree and mischievous. It was a stark contrast to the tension he felt between them now. The family had drifted—subtly at first, but now the divide seemed impossible to ignore.

He opened the pizza box, the scent of ham and pineapple wafting through the room. Picking up a slice, he flicked on the TV and turned to BBC News 24, and saw Sarah going through programme notes for one of her syndicated shows that she sold via Reeves Radio Ltd. She glanced up at Pete as he tucked into the pizza and grabbed a slice herself.

"Bloody snow's a pain in the backside. It was a pain leaving The Waterfront when I finished," Pete said as he grabbed one of the garlic sauces that was in the corner of the pizza box. The faint hum of the television filled the room as Pete spread the sauce across his slice, the tension of the day slowly melting away in the warmth of their home.

Sarah leaned back on the sofa, her programme notes resting on her lap. "Snow in November. You'd think we'd be used to it by now, but it always catches people out. It was clear in Dudley when I nipped up to the library there earlier."

The previous night, the temperature had dropped to -3, and a light dusting of snow had coated the streets of the West Midlands, leaving the roads slick and treacherous.

Living in Pensnett, not far from Dudley and Brierley Hill, meant that the Smith family had to navigate some of the steep hills that often became a challenge in icy weather. Pete chuckled at Sarah's comment, his focus shifting back to the warmth of the living room. "You'd think the council would be quicker to grit the roads, but no. Still, it wasn't as bad as the M6 today—pure chaos. I had WhatsApp messages from listeners to say that there had been 4 collisions between Stoke and Rugby... and the Distressway was closed as a lorry had decided to take a nap on its side, blocking all lanes. Typical Monday madness spilling into Wednesday. You know it's going to snow tonight and tomorrow evening?"

Pete watched as Sarah grab the odd sauce out, a pot of chilli sauce which he knew she preferred for her slices. She dipped the edge of her slice into the sauce and took a bite, letting out a small contented hum as the spice hit her taste buds.

"Snow and chilli sauce," Pete said with a smirk, gesturing to her unconventional choice. "You've got a funny way of staying warm, love."

Sarah chuckled, her eyes crinkling in amusement. "Keeps me sharp, doesn't it? Besides, I'm not the one driving in this mess. You're the one who has to brave it to get to The Waterfront and back."

Pete grinned, but his thoughts drifted back to James and the uneasy feeling that had settled over him since hearing about his son's sudden involvement with House of Manic Live. "Sarah," he began, his tone more serious, "don't you think it's strange that James is already being pulled into something as big as House of Manic Live? He's only been with Manic for, what, three weeks?"

Sarah nodded thoughtfully, wiping her hands on a napkin. "It does seem quick, but you know how Manic works. They love a good narrative, and James being with Kylie—it's an easy sell for them. Young, ambitious couple making waves? That's catnip for their audience."

Pete frowned, his expression troubled. "But is it good for him? I mean, he's still finding his footing, and it feels like they're throwing him in the deep end."

Sarah set her slice of pizza down and leaned forward, resting her elbows on her knees. Her expression softened as she looked at Pete. "He's young, Pete. And, honestly, I think he thrives on this chaos—for now, at least. But you're right to be worried. The way Manic operates... they chew people up and spit them out. If James isn't careful, he could burn out before he even hits his stride."

Pete sighed heavily, running a hand through his hair. "It's not just the pressure at work. It's Kylie. There's something about her lately that feels... off. She's always been ambitious, but now it feels like she's steering James, not supporting him. It's like he's just a piece in her game."

Sarah's gaze hardened slightly, her protective instincts kicking in. "Do you think she's manipulating him? Using him for her own gain?"

Pete shrugged, picking at the edge of his pizza crust. "I don't know. Maybe. But James doesn't see it—or maybe he doesn't want to see it. He's so caught up in this whirlwind of attention and success that he's blind to the bigger picture."

Sarah leaned back, crossing her arms as she considered Pete's words. "Then we need to keep an eye on him. Let him know we're here if he needs us. But he's an adult now, Pete. As much as it pains us, we can't fight all his battles for him."

Pete nodded, though the weight of the conversation lingered in the air. "I just hope he doesn't get in too deep before he realises what's happening. Manic's a tough place to navigate, even for someone as sharp as James."

Sarah reached over and placed a comforting hand on Pete's knee. "He's got your resilience, love. He'll find his way. And if Kylie is up to something, it'll come to light eventually. People like her can't keep their schemes hidden forever."

Pete gave her a faint smile, grateful for her steady presence. "I hope you're right."

****

CHAPTER 15 – Hits v Manic
Friday 22nd November 2024

The irony that today was Hits Live, the seasonal showpiece event for Bauer's Hits Radio Network, wasn't lost on Pete as he walked into the Dudley hub of Manic Midlands. The air was thick with the kind of competitive energy that only came around during major events like these. For all its corporate polish and carefully crafted branding, Manic Radio still had a fierce rivalry with its closest CHR competitors—Hits and Capital—and today, that rivalry would be on full display.

Pete sat down in Studio 1, the hub of his afternoon drivetime show, knowing full well that Hits Live would dominate the day's headlines in the CHR world. The event, held at Birmingham's bp pulse Live arena, the former Resorts World Arena boasted a star-studded line-up that had been hyped for months, and Pete had no doubt that the Hits presenters would milk it for every ounce of airtime and social media engagement. Manic wasn't about to be overshadowed, though. The network had its own ace up its sleeve: House of Manic Live, which was running at the Utilita Arena in Birmingham City Centre, or as Pete remembered from when it opened in 1991, the National Indoor Arena. It was ironic, Pete thought, that Birmingham was hosting two of the year's biggest CHR events on the same day, separated by just a few miles but worlds apart in branding, style, and audience.

The fact the main Manic Radio network feed would be broadcasting their drive show from the Utilita, while areas like the West Midlands, East Midlands, Stoke & Cheshire,

Manchester, Liverpool and other key markets were having their normal drivetime shows, with Ali Hussain and Tom Lode, the two Manic Dance presenters, hosting the special event broadcast, didn't sit well with Pete.

Even worse was that his own son and Kylie Morgan were hosting opt-outs for the regional feeds that were still airing their regular drivetime shows, covering backstage interviews and behind-the-scenes segments at House of Manic Live. Pete couldn't help but feel a pang of frustration. Not because James was getting the opportunity, but because it felt like the network was trying to outshine Hits Live in the most disjointed way possible—using a fragmented strategy that pitted its regional feeds against its national identity.

As Pete adjusted his headphones and prepared for his first link of the day, he caught a glimpse of a promo image on the studio monitor: James and Kylie grinning brightly, framed by the neon glow of the House of Manic Live branding. The tagline beneath read: "Your golden couple, bringing you closer to the action!" Pete shook his head. It was a far cry from the raw, authentic radio he'd built his career on.

Pete noticed Greg was sitting in the production booth, more interested in chatting on the studio to outside broadcasting rig setup teams, as, even though it was a network event, Midlands Manic was being classed as the host broadcaster for some weird reason. He wondered whether Greg had even noticed the absurdity of the situation. It seemed like Manic was trying so hard to be everything—edgy, polished, corporate, but also fragmented in the process.

Greg's voice broke through the intercom as he directed some minor adjustments to the satellite link for the live feed, completely oblivious to Pete's internal conflict. "Pete, we're going to be throwing it to James and Kylie at about 4:20. They're doing the backstage interview with some of the artists coming in, so let's get that transition clean, yeah?"

Pete's jaw tightened. He nodded, not trusting himself to speak. The idea that his son, James, and Kylie were getting so much airtime during this big event while Pete himself was relegated to his usual drivetime slot in Dudley, felt like a slap in the face.

"Yeah, sure," Pete finally muttered, adjusting his mic. He wasn't one to argue with Greg. Not today. Not with everything else going on. Still, the frustration lingered. Manic had spent years selling itself as the alternative to the corporate giants, but here they were, trying to play the same game in their own convoluted way. How was this 'manic' energy supposed to shine through when they couldn't even keep their identity straight?

The studio buzzed with activity as the clock ticked down to the start of Pete's show. He had been at Manic for years, longer than many of his colleagues, but the changes over the past couple of years felt like they had torn the place apart. It wasn't just the merger with Lite Group or the looming rebranding to Manic Vibes. It was the identity crisis that came with those changes—how to balance corporate demands with the need for real, authentic radio.

As the clock hit 4 PM, Pete opened the mic, pushed the frustration to the back of his mind, and launched into his show.

"Good evening, Birmingham, it's time to finish work for the weekend as we've got..." Pete said, reading from the script, leading into an automated sweeper that announced that it was 3 hours until House of Manic Live.

Pete took a deep breath, staring at the studio monitor as the sweeper rolled into the background music. The next few hours would be a blur of pre-recorded segments and live breaks, but the weight of the day's rivalry was already settling on his shoulders. House of Manic Live was a massive event, and he couldn't help but feel like it was all a bit too much. The energy, the lights, the cameras—it all felt like it was designed to push Pete into the background.

"Alright, Birmingham, we've got a packed show tonight," Pete continued, forcing enthusiasm into his voice. "In just three hours, we'll be live at the Utilita Arena for House of Manic Live, and if you're not there yet, what are you waiting for? Tickets are flying out the door—join us as we bring you everything you need to know about tonight's biggest event. First, though, its Cody Lane with the news at 4."

Pete settled back into his chair as Cody Lane's voice came through the studio speakers, delivering the 4 PM news with his usual calm and professionalism. As Cody wrapped up the headlines, Pete found himself caught in the whirlwind of the day's events—juggling the expectations of his drivetime slot while knowing that his son, James, and Kylie were stealing the spotlight at House of Manic Live. He couldn't shake the feeling that Manic Radio, under the guise of building a strong brand, was making the same mistakes the corporate giants had made—selling itself out in the process.

The news bulletin ended with a final mention of the Manic £100K Daily Drop, and Pete took another breath, preparing himself to speak. He stared at the promo image of James and Kylie again on the studio monitor. They looked so... polished. So perfect. Pete couldn't help but resent how they were being packaged as the golden couple of radio, playing to the Instagram crowd and the corporate narrative. It didn't sit right with him, not when he had worked so hard to build an identity of authenticity and connection with the audience.

"Alright, let's get back into it," Pete muttered to himself, adjusting the mic and trying to shake off his inner turmoil.

"You're listening to Midlands Manic drivetime with me, Pete Smith, and we've got, for one day only, exclusive, behind the scenes, interviews with Charli XCX, Billie Eilish, Ella Henderson, The Weeknd, Sophie Ellis-Bextor, Dua Lipa and the Midlands's own... Ellie Goulding, all who'll be performing live at House of Manic Live tonight! I'm telling you, folks, this is going to be one for the history books. We've got the stars, the music, and all the backstage drama you won't get anywhere else."

Pete knew that classing Ellie Goulding as a Midlander, even though she was born in Hereford, was pushing it a bit, as his audience was the West Midlands county, not the wider West Midlands region in which Herefordshire was located. But it was all part of the script. Manic was nothing if not skilled at spinning a narrative, even if it bent the truth a little. He glanced at the clock—4:15. Just five minutes until he had to hand over to James and Kylie for their backstage segment.

The track faded out, and Pete hit the button for the next link. "Right, coming up, we've got a throwback from the queen of pop herself, Dua Lipa, and some fresh hits from Olivia Rodrigo. But first, let's head over to the Utilita Arena, where our very own Jimmy Reeves and Kylie Morgan are giving us the inside scoop on all things House of Manic Live. What's the vibe like over there, guys?"

* _ * _ * _ *

"2 minutes to go," James heard through his earpiece. The nerves were starting to kick in, though he tried his best to keep his cool. He adjusted his blazer and glanced at Kylie, who was effortlessly poised, scrolling through notes on her phone. She looked every bit the polished professional Manic needed her to be—radiant, confident, and in control.

James, on the other hand, felt the weight of the moment. He wasn't just representing himself or his career—he was part of a carefully curated narrative. The "golden couple" image, the pressure of hosting a major backstage segment, and knowing his dad was listening all compounded the nerves bubbling beneath his surface.

The fact they were doing not local individual links, but one national network link, so when his dad was cutting to him, he couldn't even personalise his responses to make it feel more authentic for the Midlands audience. It was all about the national brand, the wider audience, and the polished facade Manic Radio demanded.

"30 seconds, guys," the producer's voice crackled in his earpiece.

James gave Kylie a small, nervous smile. "You ready for this?" he asked, adjusting his earpiece.

Kylie didn't look up from her phone, her voice steady and confident. "I was born ready, Reevesy. Don't overthink it. Just smile, hit your marks, and keep the energy up. We've got this."

James nodded, trying to steady his breathing. The countdown in his earpiece ticked down to zero, and the producer's voice came through again. "You're live in 5... 4... 3..."

The fact that they were on radio, as well as recording some clips for the Manic social media platforms, made James hyper-aware of how he carried himself. The red light above the camera blinked on, and Kylie, ever the professional, launched into the segment with the kind of polish that had become her signature.

"We're here at the Utilita Arena in Birmingham, where the excitement is absolutely electric for House of Manic Live!" Kylie's voice carried a perfect mix of energy and charm as she gestured to the bustling scene behind them. "The stars are arriving, the fans are buzzing, and this is shaping up to be the event of the year!"

James stepped in seamlessly, his nerves masked by the upbeat tone he'd honed during his short but intense tenure at Manic. "That's right, Kylie! We've got an incredible lineup tonight—Dua Lipa, Billie Eilish, Ellie Goulding, and so many more. Plus, we'll be bringing you exclusive interviews with the artists, live reactions from the crowd, and all the behind-the-scenes action you can't miss. Now, we're out here in the car park of the Utilita Arena, and we'll be roaming round the crowds and backstage areas to give you an exclusive peek at all the buzz building up to showtime! The energy here is absolutely unreal—let's just say, if you're not here, you're missing out! We've actually got a group of early comers gathered outside the arena, braving the chilly Birmingham evening to get the best spots when the doors open."

James knew he was lying, but the script demanded he say there were fans there when in reality, as it was ten past 4 and the doors weren't scheduled to open until 5:30 for a 7pm start, the only people milling around were event security staff who were getting ready to deploy, a few people walking along the canal and the odd delivery van pulling in with last-minute equipment. But that was the Manic way—crafting a narrative even when reality didn't quite align. Kylie took over effortlessly, leaning into her role as the face of the event.

"Absolutely, James! The buzz is incredible, and you can just feel the anticipation building. We'll be catching up with the stars as they prepare to take the stage, so stay tuned. Remember, this is the only place to get the inside scoop on House of Manic Live!"

James smiled as Kylie wrapped up her perfectly delivered introduction, her charisma filling the airwaves and the Manic social media livestreams with ease. For a moment, he admired how seamlessly she embodied the brand. But that admiration was tinged with a growing unease—how much of this was real, and how much was just a performance, both for Manic and for him?

The producer's voice crackled again in their earpieces. "Great energy, guys."

As the two walked inside the venue, James pulled his phone from his pocket and did the obligatory "couples selfie" that was getting demanded by Manic's social media team. He plastered on his best smile, holding the phone up to capture both him and Kylie with the glow of the arena behind them. Kylie leaned in, her expression effortlessly radiant, and in seconds the photo was snapped and uploaded to Manic's Instagram Stories with a caption.

@ManicRadio: *The golden couple bringing you the inside scoop at House of Manic Live!* 🎤 ✨ *#ManicLive #HouseOfManic*

The post went live almost immediately, and James could already see the likes and comments rolling in. Fans gushed over their chemistry, their outfits, and the energy they exuded. But James couldn't shake the feeling that he was playing a part in a show he hadn't fully signed up for.

Pulling out his earbud case that linked to his mobile phone, James inserted one into the ear that was free because of the other one that had his live feed from the Manic network. Deciding that he wanted to hear something else, he tuned into the Rayo app, the one that Hits Radio uses for its stations, and tuned into Gemma Atkinson & Mike Toolan on Hits Radio Birmingham, what used to be Free Radio until earlier in the year when it was rebranded to align with Bauer's Hits network. The voices of Gemma Atkinson and Mike Toolan filled James's ear as they hyped up Hits Live, their enthusiasm palpable and refreshingly authentic. Unlike the polished, almost hyper-scripted energy of Manic, there was something more grounded about Hits' coverage. They didn't seem to be overplaying the glamour—it felt more like they were genuinely excited to be part of the moment.

Mike's voice rang out clearly: "We're down here at the bp pulse Live Arena, and let me tell you, the vibe is absolutely buzzing! The fans are already lining up, and we've just spotted Tom Grennan sneaking in through the back entrance. He's promised us an exclusive chat before he takes the stage later tonight."

Gemma chimed in, her tone warm and inviting. "Oh, and we've got Becky Hill on the way too—Midlands-born and bred, so you know she's gonna bring it tonight! Plus, we'll be checking in with Joel Corry and Sam Ryder. If you're not here, you're seriously missing out."

James couldn't help but compare the natural flow of their banter to his own meticulously planned script. While Hits leaned into their presenters' personalities, Manic's approach felt more like a relentless push for branding. The contrast made James question whether he was losing his voice in the cacophony of corporate radio.

"Reevesy, what's with the smile?" Kylie's voice broke through his thoughts as she glanced at him curiously.

James quickly removed the earbud, slipping it back into his pocket. "Nothing, just thinking about how surreal all of this is. A month ago, I was just some university student juggling assignments, and now I'm here, doing this."

"Ah, right. We've got twenty minutes until the next link, so fancy a line or two?" Kylie said, and James knew, as he'd become addicted to the cocaine-fuelled party culture of Manic, that she wasn't talking about rehearsing their script. James hesitated, glancing at Kylie, who had already begun rummaging through her bag for the small tin she carried everywhere. He had promised himself he'd cut back, especially after the late-night disasters of the past few weeks, but the pressure of tonight—the cameras, the expectations, the image he had to uphold—was enough to weaken his resolve.

"Fine," James muttered, glancing around to make sure no one was watching as Kylie expertly prepared a line on the back of her phone case. He hated how easily he gave in, but he didn't have the energy to fight it tonight. Kylie handed him the makeshift tray, her eyes sparkling with a mix of mischief and control. James bent down, snorting the line quickly before wiping his nose and straightening up.

"That's the spirit," Kylie said with a grin, quickly taking her own line before stashing the tin away. "Now, come on. We've got a job to do, golden boy."

James nodded, feeling the immediate rush hit his system, sharpening his senses and pushing the nagging doubts to the back of his mind. He followed Kylie into the backstage area, where a small crew was setting up for their next segment. The producer waved them over, checking his watch as he rattled off instructions.

"You're live again in ten. This time, focus on hyping up the crowd outside. We've got the pre-recorded fan reactions ready to roll, so play into that energy. And remember—big smiles, lots of buzz, keep it fast-paced."

James nodded automatically, the cocaine buzz already helping him lock into the polished persona Manic expected from him. Kylie leaned in, her voice low and teasing. "See? You're a natural, Reevesy. Just stick with me, and we'll own this place."

*_*_*_*

Pete could sense the difference between his son's first and second links, how the first was full of faux energy, and the second was more... well, Duracell Bunny like, as if James had just been supercharged with a sudden burst of energy. Pete's decades in radio had taught him how to spot when something wasn't entirely genuine. He didn't want to jump to conclusions, but he couldn't shake the niggling feeling that James's newfound energy wasn't just down to excitement.

Pete leaned back in his chair during a song break, his fingers drumming on the desk as he stared at the monitor. His own show was ticking along, with the usual mix of scripted links, traffic updates, and cheeky banter, but his mind kept drifting to James. The "golden couple" narrative was being played out on every platform, from the live links to social media, and it was starting to feel less like a radio event and more like a carefully orchestrated PR machine.

As Dua Lipa's Houdini started to finish, Pete got ready, as the traffic report was due to be delivered live, and it would need to run smoothly before he could cut back to the national link with James and Kylie at quarter to 5.

"Alright, Birmingham," Pete began, slipping back into his professional tone, "let's take a quick look at your Friday rush hour. The M6 southbound is still crawling past Walsall after earlier incidents near junction 10, and the Expressway heading into the city is no better—so, if you're on your way to House of Manic Live, you might want to leave the car at home and hop on the tram or a train. In Dudley, the Birmingham New Road at Burnt Tree is backed up all the way to Tipton due to ongoing roadworks. So, if you're heading towards Birmingham, you might be best off going a different way. The Keyway in Willenhall is closed due to a police incident near the roundabout with Wolverhampton Road East, so expect heavy delays in the area. If you're planning to head into Birmingham for House of Manic Live, maybe consider public transport—it's looking like the easier option tonight. Anyway, we're off to Jimmy and Kylie at the Utilita Arena, who are talking to Ellie Goulding."

Pete knew that this segment was timed for 8 minutes, as Goulding was scheduled to do a live song in the 'green room' for the radio listeners, a feature being live-streamed on Manic's social media, so he knew he had enough time to stretch his legs, pour a fresh cup of tea, and mentally prepare himself for the rest of the show.

As the feed switch, he looked into the Northern Vibes studio next door, where Lyra was standing up, as all of the drive times that were locally produced, which in the case of Dudley was the East Midlands, West Midlands and Stoke & Cheshire ones, cut to the Utilita Arena feed, seamlessly transitioning to James and Kylie's next segment.

Walking out of the studio, he saw Ellen, one half of the East Midlands team, leaning against the kitchenette counter, pouring herself a cup of coffee. Pete offered a nod, and Ellen flashed him a quick smile.

"How's it going in Studio 1?" she asked, stirring milk into her cup.

Pete shrugged, grabbing a mug for himself. "The usual. Trying to keep the chaos under control while everything else is focused on House of Manic Live. You'd think they'd just send us all to the arena instead of splitting the feeds like this."

Ellen chuckled, taking a sip of her coffee. "I know. Tim's fed up of the constant switching between us in Studio 3 and those in the arena. It's like they're trying to juggle 50 things at once and hoping the audience doesn't notice when a ball drops. But hey, that's the Manic way—make it look like it's all part of the plan."

Pete smirked, pouring his tea. "More like make it up as we go along. You know, I get it—it's a big event, lots of moving parts. But sometimes I wonder if we're just overcomplicating things to outshine Hits Live."

Ellen raised an eyebrow, her curiosity piqued. "You think we're overreaching?"

Pete leaned against the counter, stirring his tea thoughtfully. "It's not just that. It's this obsession with branding—'golden couple this, influencer strategy that.' When did radio stop being about the connection with the listener and start being about the image? We're so busy trying to compete with Hits and Capital, we're losing sight of what made us different in the first place."

Ellen nodded, her expression pensive. "It's true. We're caught up in the race to be the flashiest, but there's something to be said for authenticity. That's what listeners connect with—real people, not just polished PR campaigns."

"Anyway, only 5 months left, and we'll be on Manic Goldies, with the young ones replacing us on the main network," Pete added, his tone laced with a mix of resignation and bitterness. He took a sip of his tea, the warmth doing little to temper the chill of his thoughts. "Have you seen Radio Today?"

Ellen raised an eyebrow, pulling out her phone. "No, what now? Another rebranding leak? Or has someone at Hits or Capital started taking potshots again?"

Pete chuckled dryly, shaking his head. "Nothing quite that dramatic. They're closing down the Midlands Manic transmissions on 87.7FM. Its flipping to Goldies from April, meaning my new show won't be on AM, but will be on 87.7. OFCOM have approved Manic to use the 87.7 frequency for the wider combined WM Goldies service, so Hereford, Worcester, Warwick and even Stafford will be able to hear it."

"Ah, so that's why theoretically Manic Vibes won't be available on FM in Birmingham?" Ellen asked, smiling. "I must admit, I heard one of the engineers muttering about how they're having to prepare to change the 88.3FM frequency in Warwick to the new WM Vibes broadcasts, so the puzzle pieces fit now. It's all part of their grand reshuffle."

Pete nodded, sipping his tea. "Exactly. They're moving all the CHR focus to the digital platforms—DAB, the app, and smart speakers—while keeping FM for the 'heritage' Goldies brand. It's a smart move on paper, but you and I both know it's going to alienate listeners who still rely on FM and aren't ready to jump to digital."

Ellen shrugged. "Times change, Pete. But yeah, it's a shame. FM has that old-school charm. There's something satisfying about knowing you're broadcasting to someone in their car, on a basic radio, no frills. Pure connection."

Pete sighed, glancing at the clock on the kitchenette wall. "Yeah. I just hope that connection doesn't get completely lost in all this rebranding chaos. Anyway, I'd better get back in before Greg starts chirping about timekeeping."

Ellen smirked as Pete knew she'd be having to get back to Studio 3 to do the East Midlands version with Tim of what he was doing with his West Midlands drivetime show. "Good luck, Pete," Ellen said, giving him a playful wink as she grabbed her coffee and headed off.

Pete walked back into Studio 1, placing his tea next to the console. The live feed from the Utilita Arena was still running, with James and Kylie chatting to Ali and Tom as a quartet about the upcoming show, with Tom hyping up the sound checks that he and Ali were doing in the main arena bowl.

"So, Ali, mate," Pete heard Tom say as he switched his headphones back on, "what's your prediction for the highlight of tonight's House of Manic Live? We've got Dua Lipa, Ellie Goulding, and Billie Eilish all on the lineup—who's stealing the show?"

The conversation lasted another few minutes, and Pete could see the WhatsApp messages from the West Midlands audience that he had been monitoring light up the screen. Some listeners were engaging with the hype, excited about the big-name artists, while others sent more sceptical messages, poking fun at the manufactured enthusiasm or questioning why the station was leaning so heavily into the national event when local listeners wanted their regular Friday night escape.

One message caught Pete's eye:

Pete, love the show, but what's the point of all this House of Manic hype when it's just a fancy competition with Hits Live? Can't we just have our regular music and banter without all the glitter?

He sighed. It was a sentiment he felt himself but couldn't say aloud—not while he was still on the air and under Manic's corporate umbrella, even though he was now classed as an independent contractor. He crafted a diplomatic reply, knowing full well it wouldn't satisfy the listener entirely but would keep things professional.

Hi there, thanks for the message! House of Manic Live is a big event for us, and we're excited to bring you all the behind-the-scenes access, but don't worry—we've got plenty of your favourite tunes and chat coming up, too. Stick with us, and we'll make your Friday night feel just right!

He sent the reply, wishing he could be more candid. The tension between his personal frustrations and the corporate demands of Manic felt like a weight he was constantly carrying. Pete took a deep breath and glanced at the clock. It was 4:55, and his next link was coming up soon.

Pete leaned back in his chair, glancing at the studio clock as it ticked closer to the end of the Utilita Arena segment. His tea had gone cold, and the glowing screens around him hummed with the frenetic energy of a station trying to juggle too many balls at once. James and Kylie's voices filled his headphones, their polished banter almost too perfect, too rehearsed. Pete knew the signs—it was the Manic machine working overtime, and his son was deep in it.

"Thanks, Ali and Tom! We'll catch you guys later on stage!" Kylie's voice sparkled with faux spontaneity on the split link, which Pete knew meant that while Midlands audiences would hear that, those listening to the national feed would hear Ali saying the opposite to set up his excitement for the evening ahead. It was the classic corporate radio split-feed trick, where different audiences got tailored versions of the same moment to make them feel uniquely included. Pete couldn't decide whether to admire the cleverness or loathe the artifice.

"Alright, Birmingham," Pete said, smoothly picking up the energy, "that was Ali, Tom, Jimmy and Kylie giving us the latest backstage buzz from House of Manic Live. If you're heading there tonight, you're in for a treat. And if you're staying in, you can subscribe to the Manic Prime app and tune into 'Live from House of Manic', our exclusive radio station which will bring you action life from the stage, or stick around here on Midlands Manic as Ali and Tom are live all night with the show, spinning the latest tracks and exclusive interviews."

Pete let the automated sweeper take over as he prepared for the next segment, his mind spinning. The disparity between the seamless, high-energy production of the House of Manic Live feed and the reality of what radio used to be kept nagging at him. The listener who messaged earlier wasn't wrong—this event was little more than a glitzy competition with Hits Live, a flashy bid to outdo their rivals in the CHR world. But at what cost?

As he waited for the network to play the next song, Pete found himself wondering how much longer he could navigate this new era of radio. It wasn't just the corporate mandates or the fragmented identity of the station. It was the creeping sense that, in trying to be everything at once, Manic was losing what had once made it special.

The sweeper faded out, and Pete's voice slipped into its usual cadence. "Coming up next, we've got Olivia Rodrigo with Get Him Back! and a cheeky throwback from Shania Twain's Man! I Feel Like a Woman, just to keep the vibes rolling as we gear up for the big night. And don't forget, the Manic £100K Daily Drop is still open— get your entries in before 7 PM, and you could be our lucky winner tonight! First, however, here's the news with Cody Lane at 5 PM."

*_*_*_*

It was midnight by time James got home from the Utilita Arena, and he was, after 8 hours of being in Birmingham, worn out. The fact that he had been consuming copious amounts of cocaine and energy drinks throughout the night didn't help. His heart raced, his hands trembled, and his mind felt foggy despite the chemical high. He tossed his bag onto the sofa and collapsed next to it, kicking off his trainers.

"James, is that you?" the voice of his mother came from the kitchen, where a faint light spilled into the dark living room. James groaned, as, before he had left the Utilita, he, Sam, Tom and Kylie had engaged in group sex, where he had been dominated by Kylie, who always knew how to take control, while Sam and Tom added to the chaos with their own indulgent antics. The wild, drug-fuelled escapade had been another chapter in the Manic lifestyle he was getting pulled deeper into. It had been thrilling in the moment, but now, as he sank into the sofa, the weight of exhaustion and self-reflection settled on him.

"Yeah, Mum, it's me," James called back, his voice hoarse from hours of performing, shouting over music, and straining to maintain the high-energy persona Manic demanded of him. He winced at how raspy he sounded. His mother didn't respond immediately, and he wondered if she would press him about his late arrival. The light in the kitchen flicked off, and Sarah appeared in the doorway, her expression a mixture of concern and weariness.

"Big night?" she asked, folding her arms as she leaned against the doorframe. Her eyes scanned him carefully, noticing the slightly dishevelled look and the faint redness in his eyes.

James nodded, forcing a smile. "Yeah, Mum. Big night. House of Manic Live went well. Everyone was buzzing. Lots of hype, lots of good vibes."

Sarah stepped closer, her maternal instincts kicking in. "You look knackered. Have you eaten anything since you left this afternoon?"

James hesitated, trying to remember. He'd nibbled on some snacks backstage but hadn't had a proper meal since breakfast. "I think I grabbed something earlier," he lied, not wanting to admit he'd been running on adrenaline, coke, and caffeine. "I'm fine, though. Just tired."

Shuffling, he found that his anal passage, where the other three had used to get their own pleasure, was painful in the new seating position. Wincing, he quickly adjusted himself, hoping his mother wouldn't notice. But Sarah's keen eyes caught the flicker of discomfort.

"James," she began, her tone soft but probing, "are you sure everything's alright? You've been running yourself ragged lately, and I'm not just talking about work."

James looked away, the exhaustion and guilt weighing heavy on him. He didn't want to worry her, but the strain of balancing the high-energy, party-fuelled Manic lifestyle with his personal life was starting to take its toll. "I'm fine, Mum," he said quietly, avoiding her gaze. "Fuck it, I'm going to bed. Thank God I'm not due in the studio until tomorrow afternoon as I'm covering Manic Rock '20s Sunday Top 20."

James trudged towards his room, which fortunately was in the former study downstairs, with the one upstairs bedroom being the studio setup that his mother used, while his sister Chloe occupied the smaller room next to their parents. He knew that his family could sense something was off, but he wasn't ready to unpack the mess that had become his life. Not tonight.

James slumped onto his bed, kicking off his jeans and collapsing onto the mattress in just his boxers. He stared up at the ceiling, the events of the night replaying in his mind like a chaotic montage. The lights, the energy, Kylie's calculating smiles, the cocaine-fuelled highs, and the rawness of what had happened after the show—it all blurred together, leaving him feeling both exhilarated and empty.

His phone buzzed on the bedside table, the screen lighting up with a message from Kylie:

Kylie Morgan: *You were amazing tonight, golden boy. Couldn't have done it without you ♥ Sleep tight. Big things coming for us x*

James read the message and tossed the phone aside without replying. Kylie's words felt hollow, a scripted reassurance that didn't address the growing distance between them or the complexity of their relationship. He closed his eyes, hoping sleep would come quickly, but the cocaine still lingered in his system, keeping his mind restless even as his body ached for rest.

****

CHAPTER 16 – A Golden Opportunity

Friday 6th December 2024

The buzz of excitement in the newly minted One Snow Hill studios was palpable. The space was sleek and modern, a testament to Manic's investment in their upcoming rebrand as Manic Vibes. James couldn't help but feel a surge of pride as he stepped into Studio 4, one of 30 studios spread over three floors in the building. The equipment gleamed under soft LED lighting, and the soundproofed walls bore the signature neon glow of the Manic logo. This was the future of radio, he thought—or at least, that's what the company line proclaimed.

"Alright, Jimmy, we're assessing the new kit," came the voice of a technician through the control room's intercom. "Let's hear you do a quick intro."

James adjusted his headphones, leaning into the state-of-the-art Neumann mic. "You're listening to Manic Radio, the sound of today—and the vibe of tomorrow. I'm Jimmy Reeves, and we're bringing you all the hits, all the time. Coming up, we've got brand-new tracks from Olivia Rodrigo, Becky Hill, and—of course—the Manic £100K Daily Drop. Stay with us!"

The red recording light blinked off, and the technician gave him a thumbs-up. "Sounding good, mate. You're a natural on this kit. Can't wait to see what you do with it."

The fact that the new studios wouldn't be in service until April didn't stop James from feeling the rush of being among the first to experience the cutting-edge facilities. It was a glimpse into what his career might look like in a few months—polished, futuristic, and at the heart of the Manic brand. He took off his headphones, a satisfied grin spreading across his face as Kylie stepped into the studio.

She looked effortlessly glamorous, her blonde hair perfectly styled and her outfit a carefully curated blend of edgy and chic. "Not bad, Reevesy," she teased, leaning against the doorway. "You're getting the hang of this 'future of radio' thing."

James laughed, but his chest swelled with pride at her approval. "It's hard not to feel inspired in a place like this. Can you imagine doing one of the first shows from here?"

Kylie grinned as she sauntered further into the studio, her heels clicking softly against the polished floor. "Oh, I can imagine it," she said, her voice low and confident. "Picture it: 'Broadcasting live from One Snow Hill, it's Kylie Morgan and Jimmy Reeves, your golden couple, taking you into 2025 with the biggest vibes in radio.' The audience would eat it up."

James chuckled, shaking his head. "Golden couple, eh? Is that what we are now?"

Kylie raised an eyebrow, a sly smile playing on her lips. "We're whatever we need to be to stay at the top, Reevesy. That's the game we're in. You know this will be my studio for when Tina and I take over your dad's slot in April on the Vibes Midlands Drive. You and I are CHR now, but this is just the beginning. The golden couple narrative?

It's not just about being cute for Instagram. It's about being indispensable."

James couldn't argue with her logic. He'd seen how quickly the tides shifted at Manic. Staying relevant wasn't just a bonus; it was a necessity. But the idea of Kylie already plotting their next move, even as they were still settling into their current roles, made him uneasy.

It was then he saw what was poking from Kylie's microskirt, and he grinned, as he saw the head of the strap-on she loved using on him, his grin widening as he recognised Kylie's playful provocation. She caught his glance and smirked, her confidence radiating as she leaned closer to him.

"Focus, Reevesy," she teased, her tone a mix of flirtation and authority. "We've got bigger things to manage than your fantasies right now. Like the national New Year's Eve show we've just been offered."

James blinked, his thoughts snapping back to reality. "Wait, what? A national slot? For New Year's?"

Kylie nodded, her excitement tempered by her usual calculated demeanour. "Yep. It's huge, James. Prime-time, network-wide, and they want us to be the face of it. We'll be live across every Manic station that's on the CHR roster, me, you and two hours of non-stop music, banter, and countdown vibes. It's the kind of opportunity that doesn't come around twice."

James's stomach flipped at the news. A national New Year's Eve show was a career-making slot. The pressure would be enormous, but the exposure could catapult them into the upper echelon of the Manic hierarchy. "That's... wow. That's massive, Kylie. How did you—"

"Cal put our names forward," Kylie interrupted smoothly, brushing a strand of hair from her face. "He says we've proven ourselves with Ibiza Headbangers and the House of Manic Live segments. Plus, the 'golden couple' angle is too good for marketing to pass up. Anyway, if you agree to it, babe, I'll let you try and breed me again like the hunk you are."

James laughed nervously at Kylie's remark, though her casual way of mixing business and intimacy made him pause. She had a way of making everything sound like a game they were playing together—a game where she was always a step ahead.

"Breed you again, eh?" James quipped, trying to match her playfulness, though his mind raced at the implications of the offer. "You're making this sound like a done deal. What if I wanted to spend New Year's with my family for a change?"

Kylie tilted her head, her smile turning sharper. "Reevesy, be serious. This isn't just a show; it's the show. You think your dad got to where he is by turning down opportunities like this? This is how you make your mark. Besides, your dad's got his own slot during the Christmas holidays... he's doing the Manic Rock Early Breakfast on Christmas Eve."

James hesitated, her words sinking in. A national New Year's Eve slot was an undeniable milestone, especially as he had only been with Manic for a month and half, and he was already being, despite not fully established, given opportunities that many of his colleagues could only dream of. But the idea of sacrificing his family time for yet another step up the corporate ladder gnawed at him. His dad had always emphasised the importance of balance—something James felt he was losing sight of.

"Kylie," James began, choosing his words carefully, "I get that this is a massive opportunity. And yeah, it'd be amazing to have our names on something like this. But doesn't it feel like… I don't know, like we're rushing? I mean, we've barely caught our breath since House of Manic Live."

Kylie's eyes narrowed, her confident smile slipping slightly. "Rushing? Reevesy, this isn't something you can afford to hesitate on. The second you start holding back, someone else takes your spot. That's how this business works. And let's be honest, you're not the type to settle for second best... otherwise you'd be dating that slag in your year at Uni, that Paula Hamilton who dropped out last year when she got herself pregnant with twins by some bloke she met at Pryzm. Look at where you are now, James—this is what you've worked for."

James couldn't help but chuckle at Kylie's sharp dig, but her intensity left him uneasy. She was right in a way—he didn't want to miss the opportunity. Yet, he couldn't ignore the nagging voice in his head that wondered whether this relentless climb was costing him more than he realised.

"Alright," he said slowly, trying to find a middle ground. "Let's think this through. If we take this slot, we've got to deliver something huge, something memorable. We can't just do the same old countdown playlist and banter."

Kylie's smirk returned, her sharp instincts already kicking into gear. "Oh, don't worry. Network will sort that out, we just have to show up, bring our A-game, and keep the energy high. Now, push me against the window and fuck my brains out."

James froze for a moment, caught off guard by Kylie's brazen demand. Her mix of intense ambition and playful irreverence was something he had always admired, even if it sometimes left him scrambling to keep up. But today, her sharp pivot between career talk and personal intimacy felt like a reminder of the double-edged sword their relationship had become.

"Kylie," James said with a nervous laugh, stepping back slightly, "maybe we can focus on the New Year's gig first, yeah?"

"Oh, come on James, I've only got one more day until I'm at that point in my cycle where I turn into the Witch of Bitch Hill," Kylie quipped, her laughter echoing around the studio as she stepped closer to James, her expression softening just enough to lighten the mood. "I'm serious, babes, I don't want another monthly visitor for at least 9 months," she teased, trailing her fingers down his arm with a grin that was equal parts charm and mischief.

James couldn't help but laugh, though the tension in his chest remained. Kylie's ability to switch between playful and commanding was something he admired, but it also kept him off balance. He leaned against the desk, taking a moment to collect his thoughts.

"Alright," he said, his voice softening. "Let's take the gig. But we've got to be careful, Kylie. This isn't just about climbing the ladder. If we don't pace ourselves, this whole thing could come crashing down."

Kylie's grin widened, and she leaned in to kiss him on the cheek. "That's my golden boy. Don't worry, Reevesy—I've got this. We've got this. Trust me, by the time that ball drops at midnight, the whole country will know who we are. Now, get a line sorted for us to snort, and then fuck me like you've got something to prove."

James couldn't help but shake his head with a mix of amusement and resignation. Kylie's relentless energy was intoxicating, but it was also exhausting. He reached into his bag, pulling out a small metal tin containing the cocaine they both knew had become a staple of their manic lifestyle. As he set up the lines on the back of his phone case, he wondered—not for the first time—how much longer they could keep up the pace without breaking.

* _ * _ * _ *

"You're listening to Manic Linkin Park!" James said as he was sat in the Warwickshire Stars studio at the Dudley hub a few hours later, pre-recording a batch of links for Manic Linkin Park, one of the new Manic Prime app based stations which was a 'curated playlist with links', which basically meant that the tracks were played on repeat, with links from a presenter interspersing between tracks, sometimes being generic station idents, and some talking about the history of a specific song.

Like his Ibiza Weekender show, James didn't get to listen to the tracks that were set to be played, but instead worked off a script provided by Manic's music team. In a way, James liked it that way, as it meant that he could do more shows, and therefore get more airtime in his less than 2 month career at Manic, even if some of those shows weren't truly "live" or reflective of his personality. It was all part of the game—maintaining visibility, building his profile, and proving his worth to the network. As the final link for the session wrapped, James leaned back in his chair, the faint glow of the studio lights casting shadows on his tired face.

The pre-recording gave him a moment of quiet to think about the New Year's Eve show. The opportunity was massive, but the pressure felt equally colossal. Kylie's confidence was unshakable, her ambition contagious, but James couldn't shake the feeling that their rapid ascent was built on shaky ground.

"And that was Numb, which has been in the charts for over 850 weeks since its release in 2003. Stay tuned to Manic Linkin Park for more of the hits that defined a generation. Up next is The Emptiness Machine, released in 2024. Now, this comes from their eighth studio album, From Zero, which was released a few weeks later."

The red light blinked off as James finished his final pre-recorded link. He stretched in his chair, feeling the dull ache of exhaustion creeping into his shoulders. The Dudley hub, even at this late hour, buzzed with the low hum of distant voices and the occasional clatter of footsteps in the hallway. It was a world that rarely slept, fuelled by caffeine, adrenaline, and, for some, less savoury stimulants.

"Right, Jimmy, you've just got the voice-tracking for the 'Manic Rock Early Breakfast' to do, and then you're done for the night," Shane Tipton, the producer for this session, crackled through his earpiece, and James smiled, as he saw one of the technicians walk into the studio with several cans of Red Bulls and some spliffs, the drug of choice for some of the technicians whose job was to work around the clock maintaining Manic's relentless broadcast schedule. James thanked the technician with a nod, though he avoided the spliffs—it wasn't his vice of choice, and after the night he'd had, the Red Bull would suffice.

Sitting back in the chair, he glanced at the list of voice tracks he needed to record for the early breakfast slot. It was a simple task: upbeat, noncommittal links to keep listeners company during the pre-dawn hours. But the monotony of the job made James think about the excitement of what lay ahead. The New Year's Eve gig loomed large in his mind, a mix of anticipation and dread.

"Let's get this over with," James muttered, leaning into the mic and starting his first link.

"You're up early, and so are we! This is the Manic Rock Early Breakfast, getting you through the morning with tracks from Foo Fighters, Royal Blood, and classics from Green Day. Stick around—there's no better way to start your day than with a bit of rock to get you moving."

He ran through the next few links with practiced ease, his voice chipper and energetic despite the fatigue pulling at him. James had become good at compartmentalising—putting on a polished facade for the mic while keeping the creeping doubts at bay.

But as the session dragged on, his thoughts kept returning to the conversation with Kylie. The pressure to keep climbing, to maintain their status as the "golden couple," felt suffocating. And while Kylie thrived in the cutthroat environment of Manic, James couldn't help but wonder if he was cut out for it. The cocaine-fuelled highs could only carry him so far.

"Alright, mate, that's a wrap," Shane's voice crackled through the headphones after James finished his final link. "Good work tonight. You've got tomorrow afternoon off, right? Make sure you get some rest."

"Yeah, will do," James replied, removing his headphones and leaning back in the chair. "Cheers, Shane."

As James left the studio, the familiar glow of the Dudley hub's corridors felt almost eerie in the late-night quiet. The adrenaline from the session and the lingering effects of the cocaine buzzed faintly in his veins, but the exhaustion was beginning to outweigh it. He made his way to the car park, his thoughts heavy with the decisions ahead.

* _ * _ * _ *

Chloe had to admit, the new flat that her boyfriend, Cody Lane, one of the Manic Dudley newsreaders was renting in Birmingham's Allegro Living, a new development on

Priory Queensway in Central Birmingham, was impressive. The sleek, modern apartment overlooked the bustling city below, and the floor-to-ceiling windows offered a stunning view of the skyline. Chloe stood by the glass, sipping on a glass of wine, her Law with Criminology notes spread out on the coffee table behind her. Cody was in the kitchen, fiddling with a cheese board and a bottle of Prosecco, his way of unwinding after a long day of reading endless bulletins in Studio 9 at the Dudley hub.

Sitting opposite her, however, was Kylie, and like Chloe and Cody, was dressed in very little clothing, the trio having had a cocaine fuelled threesome. Over the past week, Chloe had moved the last parts of her belongings from the family home to Cody's flat, and it felt liberating to be away from Pete and Sarah's constant scrutiny. She was carving out her own life—one that didn't involve being overshadowed by James or answering to her parents. But tonight, her focus wasn't on her own ambition. It was on Kylie's plan.

"You're sure James doesn't suspect anything?" Chloe asked, setting her wine glass on the table and fingering herself as she adjusted her position on the plush sofa. Her tone was casual, but her sharp eyes betrayed her curiosity and the flicker of doubt that lingered in her mind.

Kylie smirked, leaning back lazily against the armrest, swirling the last of her own glass of wine. She looked effortlessly composed, her calculated demeanour unwavering even in the aftermath of the indulgent escapade the three had just shared. "James? Suspect me? Please, Chloe," she drawled, her voice dripping with confidence. "He's too caught up in the whirlwind to notice what's really going on. He trusts me, and that's all that matters right now."

Cody walked over, setting down the cheese board with a flourish and pouring fresh glasses of Prosecco for the women. "I still can't believe he's getting a national New Year's Eve slot," he remarked, shaking his head. "Guy's been with Manic for, what, six weeks? Talk about jumping the queue."

Kylie raised an eyebrow, her smirk deepening. "That's the beauty of branding, darling. It's not about time served— it's about the narrative. Plus Cal has been very... accommodating."

Kylie's words hung in the air as Chloe smirked knowingly, running her finger along the rim of her glass. "Accommodating? Let me guess—Cal's as easy to manipulate as James is. You've got half of Manic wrapped around your little finger, haven't you?"

Kylie laughed, the sound rich and carefree. "Well, when he got Toni Green preggers when she was 14 and he was 16, and she kept it quiet all these years, let's just say Cal's been very eager to ensure certain... favours are returned. Besides, it's not manipulation, Chloe—it's strategy. You of all people should understand that."

Chloe rolled her eyes, but she couldn't argue. Kylie's ambition was undeniable, and her ability to weave herself into the fabric of Manic's power structure was something Chloe begrudgingly admired. She reached for a slice of cheese from the board and leaned back on the sofa, letting the cool night air from the open window brush against her skin.

"So, what's the next step in this grand plan of yours?" Chloe asked, her tone tinged with curiosity as she glanced at Kylie. "You've got James all hyped up about the New Year's Eve gig, but what happens when he starts asking questions? He's not completely clueless, you know."

Kylie shrugged, swirling her glass of Prosecco. "He won't. Not for a while, at least. Right now, he's too focused on keeping up with me and proving himself to Manic. The pressure's enough to keep him distracted. And if he does start getting suspicious, I'll manage it. That's what I do. Anyway, he's going to have a big fall... which will make your dad kick him out... straight into my arms."

Chloe tilted her head, studying Kylie with a mix of admiration and wariness. "You're ruthless," she said, her lips curling into a small smile. "But I suppose that's why you're winning. What happens if he does fall, though? You're banking on controlling the narrative, but James isn't exactly predictable. He might surprise you."

Kylie smirked, setting her glass down on the table. "Chloe, darling, that's the difference between you and me. I don't leave anything to chance. James thrives on approval—whether it's from me, his dad, or Manic. Once I pull the right strings, he'll have no choice but to rely on me. And when he does? That's when the real fun begins. Has Cody ever told you about the 'Manic Office Cum Dump' position?"

Chloe leaned back, smirking at Kylie's remark while Cody's laughter echoed through the flat. Despite the crude joke, there was an underlying tension in the air—an unspoken acknowledgment of how much was at stake in Kylie's grand scheme. Chloe's initial intrigue in Kylie's plans had turned into something deeper: a cautious alliance.

"Let me guess, you're going to make him be the receptacle for every Manic presenter, producer and tech's cum that you decide is worthy of your... pet?" Chloe said, knowing that the revenge on her brother would be poetic, considering how much he had overshadowed her. Kylie laughed, the sound low and sharp, as she reached for a slice of cheese.

"Exactly, babes. The position is known to most within Manic, apart from about 4 or 5 people. Your dad, Nott, Tim and Ellen. They don't know what happens to those who fall out of favour with Manic. The rest, well, they know that the 'Hub Cum Dump' is just one of the ways we maintain order. Of course, I won't actually take it that far unless James really screws up, but the threat is useful. Keep him on his toes, make sure he understands his place in the hierarchy."

Cody raised an eyebrow as he leaned against the counter, swirling his own glass of Prosecco. "You've really thought this through, haven't you? Turning him into a pawn, a spectacle for your gain. It's genius in a twisted sort of way."

Chloe chuckled darkly, shaking her head. "It's almost poetic. James always had everything handed to him on a silver platter—Dad's approval, Mum's doting. You know, they paid for most of his Uni fees, while I'm having to get Student Loans and navigate everything on my own. Now, seeing him under your thumb? It's like karma finally caught up."

Kylie leaned back, the glint of satisfaction in her eyes unmistakable. "That's the game, darling. Radio, relationships, life—it's all about knowing how to play your hand. And trust me, by the time I'm done, James will be exactly where I need him."

Cody raised his glass in mock salute. "To the master strategist. You're wasted on breakfast radio, Kylie. You should be running this network."

Kylie smirked, her expression unflinchingly self-assured. "Oh, don't worry, Cody. Give it a few years, and I will be."

As the three laughed, the atmosphere in the flat remained thick with the tension of manipulation and ambition. For Chloe, it was a heady mix of vindication and apprehension. She had always resented James for the golden boy treatment he received from their parents after he had secured his spot at Manic. Now, watching Kylie systematically pull him into her web, Chloe couldn't help but feel a twisted sense of justice. Yet, there was a nagging voice in the back of her mind—one that questioned just how far Kylie was willing to go, and whether aligning with her was a mistake.

"Do you ever think about what happens if it all goes wrong?" Chloe asked, breaking the momentary silence.

Her voice was quieter now, tinged with something that sounded almost like doubt.

Kylie tilted her head, her sharp gaze cutting through the dim light of the flat. "What do you mean?"

Chloe hesitated, swirling the wine in her glass as she searched for the right words. "I mean, if James catches on—or worse, if Dad does. You know he's no idiot. He's been in this game longer than any of us. If he figures out what you're doing…"

Kylie's smirk grew. "Pete won't catch on. He's too busy trying to fight the system to know that his precious son will be servicing cock for the rest of his career at Manic if he falls out of favour. Besides, your dad's too distracted by his own battles with management, his nostalgia for the 'good old days,' and his struggle to stay relevant. By the time he realises what's happening, it'll be too late to stop it. He'll see James as just another casualty of the cutthroat world of CHR radio—and maybe, deep down, he'll blame himself for not warning him sooner."

Cody raised an eyebrow at Kylie's confidence but couldn't resist adding his own sceptical twist. "You're playing a dangerous game, Kylie. Pete might be out of touch with the new Manic culture, but he's sharp. And if he catches wind of this, he won't go down quietly."

Kylie shrugged, her demeanour unflappable. "Let him try. The beauty of this game is that everything looks like it's happening naturally. To the outside world, James is the ambitious rising star, the golden boy pushing himself to the edge to prove his worth. If he cracks under the pressure, that's on him—not me. And if Pete wants to make a fuss? Well, we'll just frame it as an old man struggling to accept the modern reality of radio."

Chloe watched Kylie with a mix of awe and unease. As much as she relished the idea of her brother being taken down a peg, she couldn't ignore the ruthlessness in Kylie's approach. It was exhilarating to be part of something so calculated, so powerful, but it was also a stark reminder of just how far Kylie was willing to go to secure her position at the top.

"You've got this all figured out, haven't you?" Chloe said, her voice tinged with admiration. "What happens when you've gotten everything you want? When James is out of the picture, and you're running the show?"

Kylie leaned back, a satisfied smile playing on her lips. "Oh, James will be in the picture all the time... as... well, you know that feeling a woman has when, a few weeks after having sex, she might not be having her period soon?"

The tension in the room grew thick, Cody choking slightly on his drink as Kylie's implication hung in the air. Chloe's smirk faded, replaced by a mixture of shock and scepticism.

"You're joking, right?" Chloe asked, setting her glass down as she leaned forward.

Kylie's smile didn't falter. She swirled her glass of wine, her tone dangerously nonchalant. "Not at all. A baby changes the game. It ties James to me forever, cements the 'golden couple' image, and makes me indispensable to the

Manic brand. Besides, nothing screams 'relatable' like a glowing mum-to-be hosting the hottest shows on the airwaves. It worked for Toni Green, didn't it? Her career skyrocketed after she had her kid. This just takes it up a notch."

Chloe stared at Kylie, a grin on her face. "Cody, dear, go downstairs to Maccies and get us something, there's a good lad. Kylie and I need a bit of woman talk."

As Cody grabbed his coat and keys, Chloe kept her gaze locked on Kylie, the grin on her face still lingering. "Don't forget to bring back extra fries," she called after him as he stepped out of the flat.

The door clicked shut, leaving the two women alone in the spacious living room. Kylie swirled her wine glass lazily, the confident smirk never leaving her face. Chloe leaned back against the sofa, crossing her legs as she studied her brother's girlfriend with a mix of fascination and calculation.

"So, a baby, huh?" Chloe finally said, before bursting out laughing. "You know, I'm looking forward to seeing James's face when he does find out that we've been moving against him, and he's forever connected to you."

Chloe's laughter filled the room, echoing off the sleek, minimalist walls of Cody's flat. Kylie tilted her head, letting the laughter play out, her smirk unfaltering as she sipped her wine. Chloe's amusement only fuelled her confidence; she knew the audacity of her plan was its own weapon, a strategy so bold most people wouldn't believe it until it was too late.

"Oh, his face will be priceless," Kylie replied, her voice cool and steady. "But the beauty of it, Chloe, is that he won't even realise what's happening until he's so deep in, there's no way out. That's the key to all of this—control the narrative, control the outcome. And a baby? That's the ultimate trump card."

Chloe leaned forward, resting her elbows on her knees as she regarded Kylie with a mix of admiration and scepticism. "You're not worried he'll catch on? James might be naive, but he's not stupid. If he figures out you're using him—especially for something like this—he might push back."

Kylie's smirk sharpened into something more calculating. "That's the beauty of James. He thrives on approval—mine, your dad's, Manic's. He's desperate to prove himself, to live up to this 'golden boy' image everyone's crafted for him. If he starts to push back, all I have to do is dangle the right carrot—or, if necessary, remind him what he stands to lose. He'll fall in line. They always do. Anyway, did I tell you about the one unofficial perk of working for Manic... the 'Baby Bonus'?

Chloe raised an eyebrow, leaning back with a smirk as she swirled her wine. "Baby Bonus? Go on, enlighten me. Sounds like something out of a dystopian HR manual."

Kylie chuckled, setting her glass down on the sleek coffee table. "Oh, it's very hush-hush. Cal let it slip during one of our... productive conversations. Turns out, if you're part of the on-air talent and you have a baby while working for Manic, they cover a ton of expenses. Maternity leave, childcare assistance, even a media-friendly 'family announcement package'... and an extra £2k a year extra in your pay for every year the child is alive until they're 18. Cal mentioned that they introduced it during COVID."

Chloe's eyes widened, her wine glass pausing mid-air. "Wait, so you're telling me they'll literally pay you extra for having a baby on the payroll? And they keep it quiet? That's... insane. Genius from a PR perspective, but still insane."

Kylie leaned back on the plush sofa, crossing her legs with a self-satisfied grin. "Welcome to the Manic way, darling. It's all about optics. Imagine the headlines: 'Manic's golden couple expecting their first child.' It's not just great press for me—it's a boost for the brand. They get to paint themselves as family-friendly, progressive, and relatable. And I get to cash in while cementing my position at the top. Everybody wins."

"So, if my audition goes well, and suddenly I find Cody got me up the duff?" Chloe said, grinning.

Kylie's smirk deepened, her eyes gleaming with intrigue as she leaned forward, elbows resting on her knees. "Oh, Chloe, now that would be a power move. Imagine the headlines: 'Sibling rivalry heats up as Chloe Reeves joins the Manic roster—and prepares for her next chapter with Cody Lane.' It's practically a ready-made soap opera, with you and James battling for airtime, all while the 'Manic family' narrative plays out perfectly for the network."

Chloe laughed, shaking her head. "I'd probably have Dad's blood pressure through the roof if I pulled something like that. But hey, if this baby bonus is real, it's not the worst deal in the world."

Kylie raised her glass in mock toast. "Exactly. It's all about playing the long game. You and I both know this industry doesn't reward the passive—it rewards the bold. And if you've got the guts to shake things up, you'll find that Manic is more than willing to pave the way for your success."

Chloe sipped her wine, letting Kylie's words sink in. She couldn't deny the appeal of the idea, though it also came with its share of risks. She'd always been ambitious, but aligning herself so closely with Kylie—and potentially throwing her brother under the bus—was a gamble. Still, the thought of carving out her own space in the Manic world, independent of James, was intoxicating.

"Alright," Chloe said, setting her glass down with a determined glint in her eye. "If this audition of mine goes well, and I get a foot in the door at Manic, we'll see where things go. But just so we're clear, Kylie—if this backfires, I'm not going down with you."

Kylie's smile was razor-sharp, her confidence unshaken. "Chloe, darling, nothing's going to backfire. By the time we're done, you'll have your spotlight, I'll have mine, and James will be exactly where he belongs—doing what I tell him, when I tell him. It's a win-win."

The two women clinked their glasses, the room charged with a shared understanding of the high-stakes game they were playing. Cody returned moments later, carrying a bag of McDonald's and shaking off the cold December air.

"Alright, ladies, I bring sustenance," Cody announced, setting the bag down on the coffee table. "So, what did I miss? More plotting? Or have you finally started planning James's retirement party?"

Chloe and Kylie exchanged a knowing look, their laughter filling the room. Cody, oblivious to the deeper layers of their conversation, handed out burgers and fries with a grin.

"Let's just say," Chloe said, unwrapping her burger, "the future's looking very... Manic."

****

CHAPTER 17 – A Tale of Two Christmases

Thursday 25 December 2014

Twelve-year-old James Smith sat cross-legged on the living room floor of the Smith family home, the soft crackle of the recently rebranded Midlands Manic playing in the background. The Christmas tree glimmered with multicoloured lights, and the scent of pine mingled with the warm aroma of mince pies cooling on the kitchen counter. James was clutching his brand-new iPod Nano, a gift he'd unwrapped just an hour earlier, his headphones resting around his neck as the radio played the familiar tones of Pete's Christmas Day special.

"Good afternoon, and Merry Christmas! This is Pete Smith, keeping you company on this festive day with all your favourite holiday tunes. Coming up, we've got Mariah Carey, Slade, and a bit of Band Aid to keep those Christmas vibes going strong."

James grinned. His dad's voice filled the room, warm and cheerful, and for a moment, James felt like Pete was right there with him, even though he was broadcasting live from the Dudley hub. Pete had spent the morning at home with the family, rushing off after the presents were opened to host his annual festive show.

"Turn it up, Mum!" James called out to Sarah, who was busy in the kitchen.

Sarah smiled as she dried her hands on a tea towel and nudged the volume up a notch. "Alright, but don't forget—dinner's in an hour, so don't go stuffing yourself with chocolates!"

James laughed, leaning back against the sofa as he let the music and his dad's voice wash over him. For him, it was the perfect Christmas—simple, warm, and filled with the sound of radio, a constant presence in the Smith household. Chloe, then only ten years old, was curled up in an armchair nearby, flipping through her copy of Harry Potter and the Prisoner of Azkaban. The occasional giggle escaped her as she lost herself in the world of wizards and magic. The family dog, Pippin, a scruffy terrier mix, lay sprawled by the fire, snoring softly, adding to the cosy scene.

Pete's festive cheer continued through the speakers, punctuated by the occasional pre-recorded caller wishing loved ones a Merry Christmas.

"Next up," Pete's voice boomed, "a little something for the big man himself, St Nick, who's currently back home at the North Pole enjoying a well-earned rest after his busy night. Here's 'Santa Claus Is Coming to Town' by The Jackson 5!"

James hummed along, tapping his fingers on the iPod. He glanced over at Chloe, who was now giggling at something in her book, and then at the tree, laden with baubles, tinsel, and an array of handmade decorations from years past. For James, this was Christmas: family, music, and the warm familiarity of his dad's voice on the radio.

"Mum, when's Dad next at work?" James asked, turning the iPod on and scrolling through the playlists he'd already loaded onto it.

Sarah poked her head out of the kitchen, a wooden spoon in hand. "Tomorrow morning, love. He's covering the Boxing Day breakfast show, but he'll be back in time for lunch. Why do you ask?"

James shrugged, still fiddling with the iPod. "Just wondered. Do you think he'd mind if I went with him?"

"Yeah, me too?" Chloe asked, and James groaned, as he knew his sister would find a way to tag along no matter what.

"Alright, you two," Sarah said, stepping into the living room and resting a hand on her hip, "it's not really up to me, is it? You'll have to ask your dad when he gets home later. But don't get your hopes up—Boxing Day shows are usually pretty hectic."

James nodded, already imagining what it would be like to sit in the studio with his dad, surrounded by the buzz of the station, the flashing lights on the mixer, and the excitement of live radio. Chloe, ever the opportunist, smirked at her brother. "If you're going, I'm going. It's only fair."

"Fair?" James shot back, rolling his eyes. "You don't even like radio. You'd just sit there playing on your DS the whole time."

"Would not!" Chloe retorted, sticking out her tongue.

"Enough, you two," Sarah said, her voice carrying just enough authority to settle the bickering. "It's Christmas. Enjoy the day and stop worrying about tomorrow."

James reluctantly let the subject drop, focusing instead on the upbeat music filling the room. He tapped his foot along to the beat, already lost in his own world of playlists and imagined radio shows. Chloe, undeterred, went back to her book, occasionally sneaking glances at her brother with a mischievous glint in her eye.

****

Thursday 25th December 2024

James was sat in his ground floor bedroom, his iMac open, his headset wirelessly connected as he was working on a remix of Dua Lipa's Houdini which was themed as a New Years style anthem for his upcoming national New Year's Eve show. The glow of his screen reflected off the darkened window, and faint sounds of Christmas celebrations filtered through from the living room, where his mum and dad were hosting a small family gathering.

The contrast between this Christmas and the one a decade ago couldn't have been starker. Instead of the simple joys of presents, music, and family, James now felt the weight of expectation and ambition pressing down on him. His career at Manic had rocketed, but with it came pressures that seemed to follow him even on days like this.

"James, dinner's almost ready!" Sarah called from the kitchen. "Are you going to join us, or are you glued to that computer all night?"

"Nah, I'm alright," he said, pulling a bag of cocaine from his pocket, tipping some onto a CD case and preparing it for a quick line. He hesitated for a moment, staring at the white powder under the dim glow of his desk lamp. The festive decorations outside his room and the faint sound of laughter from the living room felt like echoes from a different life—a simpler, happier time. James knew he should go join his family, but the pressure to keep pushing forward, to stay ahead in the cutthroat world of Manic, felt like a suffocating weight on his chest.

He bent down and snorted the line quickly, wiping his nose with the back of his hand before straightening up. The rush hit him instantly, momentarily silencing the doubts and exhaustion gnawing at the edges of his mind.

Ping

James looked to see the 'Gals and Geezers' group chat lighting up his phone screen, with Penny Lane, one of the Liverpool hub hosts who James had slept with during his first weekend as part of the Manic team, posting a raunchy selfie in a Santa hat with the caption

Penny Lane: *Merry Christmas from Liverpool's naughtiest elf . Especially to my baby daddy... Reevesy!*

The photo was accompanied by another one which had a pregnancy test and the dreaded words.

Penny Lane: *Positive. Congrats, Reevesy* ♥"

James grinned, not realising that the next message, one from Kylie, would change his life. James's grin faded as the notification for Kylie's message popped up in the group chat. He hesitated for a moment, his heart pounding as he opened it.

Kylie Morgan: *Well, Reevesy, looks like Santa came early for you this year. Hope you're ready for the responsibility of being a daddy, golden boy. And no, this isn't just about Penny. Merry Christmas* ♥.

Accompanying the message was another pregnancy test, this time from Kylie, with the test showing the same unmistakable result: positive. James's heart sank as the reality of what he was looking at hit him. The rush from the cocaine was no match for the whirlwind of emotions now spinning through his mind.

He stared at his phone screen, the silence in his room now deafening. The group chat exploded with reactions—cheering emojis, shocked faces, and a few playful jabs from colleagues who clearly found the situation entertaining. Penny was laughing it off with a string of winking emojis, but Kylie's tone was sharper, more deliberate.

Ping

James's phone buzzed again, this time with a notification from the "Dudley Hub Chat," a group dedicated to the Midlands team at Manic. His stomach churned as he opened the app, the festive veneer of Christmas Day cracking further with each new message.

But then he noticed why.

Zara Love was leaving.

The unofficial 'hub cum dump' was leaving for Bauer, having got a job at Kiss. James knew that the person who held the position of 'hub cum dump' was basically the person who was free for any Manic presenter to exploit sexually whenever they pleased, a dark and toxic underbelly to the Manic culture that he had reluctantly become aware of during his short time at the company.

James had to admit that Zara had been really compliant when he and her had hooked up during a late-night afterparty at the Dudley hub on his second week of working for Manic, and they had not worn protection, as Zara had said that she was allergic to latex. The memory of that encounter now resurfaced with uncomfortable clarity, layered with the growing unease that came with the realisation of what his workplace culture truly entailed. James's head was spinning—not just from the cocaine, but from the overwhelming chaos that his life seemed to have become.

He threw his phone onto the bed, running his hands through his hair as the gravity of Kylie's and Penny's announcements began to sink in. He was going to be a father—twice, if the messages were accurate—and both children were the result of relationships that blurred the lines between personal life and the toxic culture at Manic. The excitement he'd felt about his career just a few hours ago now felt hollow, replaced by a heavy knot of dread in his stomach.

It was then that another photo appeared on the 'Gals and Geezers' group chat that made James's erection salute as if it were standing at attention during a military drill. The photo was of Lily Jenkins, the 28 year old Cardiff hub producer who looked 16, dressed in just a pair of heels and thigh high socks, sitting on a desk with her legs wide open and a 3 foot dildo between them, the tip placed right against her sex, which, James could see, was wet and exposed in a way that was clearly intended to provoke reactions. The chat exploded with lewd comments and emojis, the toxic camaraderie of the "Gals and Geezers" group in full force.

Undoing his jeans, James knew that his horny state wasn't just from the photo of Lily, but also the cocaine making him hypersexual and impulsive, a dangerous combination on a night where his emotions were already running high.

*_*_*_*

Chloe had to chuckle at the contract that she had, three days earlier, signed, it being in effect from the 5th of January, which would make her a part-time Manic presenter, acting as an independent contractor. As someone who was studying Law with Criminology, seeing the contract and the fine print was a mix of professional curiosity and personal excitement. Manic Radio had an infamous reputation for contracts with clauses that could make even seasoned lawyers raise an eyebrow, but Chloe saw it as a challenge—a game she was ready to play. She'd already spotted loopholes and grey areas that she could use to her advantage if the need ever arose.

Chloe smirked as she leaned back in her chair at the small table in the apartment that she and Cody shared in Birmingham, seeing how there was several loopholes that any lawyer worth their salt could exploit. One clause, in particular, caught her attention—a vaguely worded intellectual property clause that seemed to claim ownership over any "creative output" made while under contract with Manic Radio. She knew that James liked making his own remixes of tracks and would, when he was doing Student Union gigs, play his own remixes in his sets. If James hadn't noticed this clause, he might unknowingly hand over the rights to Manic if he continued creating music while contracted.

Chloe's smirk widened as she considered the implications. She might not be close to James, but this was a card she could keep up her sleeve if she ever needed leverage—either against her brother or against Manic itself. It was all about knowing the game and playing it smart.

Behind the contract, however, was one that Chloe had written herself, two really, one for Cody to sign as he had, earlier, asked her a question that required it, and one which would make James, until he left Manic, the 'hub cum dump.' Chloe had carefully crafted the latter contract, inserting clauses that played into the toxic culture she knew Manic thrived on while also tying James into an inescapable situation if he fell out of favour with Kylie and the rest of the Manic hierarchy. It was a power move, designed to keep James in check and give her an edge in her new role.

She knew Cody would eagerly sign the first contract. His question three nights earlier—asking if she would consider marrying him—had caught her off guard but also presented an opportunity. The contract she wrote for him was a pre-nuptial agreement designed to protect her interests while ensuring Cody's commitment to their relationship remained ironclad. It was a pragmatic move, blending her legal acumen with the personal excitement of their future together. She hadn't shared the second contract with him yet; it wasn't time for that part of her plan to come to light.

She knew that Kylie, on the other hand, was aware of the contract as she had come up with the idea of drafting such a document in the first place. Chloe's collaboration with Kylie had evolved into an unholy alliance—a merging of ambition, cunning, and mutual disdain for James. Kylie had even suggested specific clauses for the "hub cum dump" contract, ones designed to exploit James's vulnerabilities and tie him deeper into the toxic web of Manic's culture.

"Herein the party of the second part consents to fulfilling any requests made by on-air talent, production staff, or other employees of the Manic Radio Group for non-professional services deemed appropriate under the 'community-building ethos' of the organisation. Such obligations may include, but are not limited to, personal companionship, private entertainment, or morale-boosting activities, as requested by the Party of the First Part or their representatives."

Chloe leaned back, her fingers pausing over the keyboard as she admired her work. The "hub cum dump" agreement was as much a psychological weapon as it was a legal one. Every clause, every subpoint, was tailored to amplify James's humiliation should he fall out of Kylie's favour or stumble within Manic's toxic hierarchy. It was cruel, yes, but Chloe rationalised it as poetic justice for all the years James had overshadowed her, all the moments he'd been the golden child in their parents' eyes.

"Cody, babe," she said with a wide grin on her face as Cody walked in with two mugs of tea, his usual easy-going expression lighting up as he set them down on the table. "Thanks, love," she said, sliding her laptop to the side. "I've been going through some stuff for work, but I think we should talk about something a bit more exciting."

Cody tilted his head, a curious smile playing on his lips. "Oh yeah? What's that?"

Chloe leaned forward, resting her chin on her hands as she studied him. "You remember the other night when you asked me that question?"

Cody chuckled, rubbing the back of his neck. "Hard to forget. I was half expecting you to laugh me out of the room."

"Don't be daft," Chloe said with a soft laugh, reaching for his hand. "I didn't laugh, did I? I've just been thinking about it, and... well, I've drafted something that might make things a bit easier for us going forward."

She opened a folder on her laptop and turned the screen toward him, displaying the neatly formatted prenuptial agreement she'd written. "Just click on this and type your name, babe," she said as she smiled sweetly, sliding the laptop closer to Cody. Her tone was playful, but her eyes carried a calculated gleam. Watching, Chloe noticed that Cody did what she asked and signed it without reading further, a testament to the trust—or perhaps the lack of suspicion—he had in her. She smiled warmly, her exterior all sweetness and charm, even as her mind ticked over the next steps in her plan.

"You know, Clo, I'd have signed a prenup anyway, no need to trick me," Cody then said, and Chloe laughed, brushing a strand of hair behind her ear.

"I wasn't tricking you, babe. I just wanted to be sure we're on the same page. It's not about mistrust—it's about being prepared, right?"

Cody leaned over and kissed her forehead, his easy-going demeanour unchanged. "I know. Anyway, your OneDrive syncs with my laptop, and you'd saved the draft there as well. I had a peek earlier and saw what you were up to. You're thorough, Chloe, I'll give you that."

Chloe froze for a moment, her smile faltering before she quickly recovered. "You sneaky sod! And here I was thinking I'd surprise you."

Cody grinned, sipping his tea. "Well, I like to keep you on your toes. Besides, I know you've got a sharp mind— I wouldn't want to be on the wrong side of it."

Chloe chuckled, the tension easing. "You've got nothing to worry about, babe. As long as you stay on my good side, that is."

The two shared a laugh, but Chloe's mind was already spinning with the implications of Cody's discovery. If he'd looked through her OneDrive files, he might have seen the second contract—the one for James. The thought sent a flicker of unease through her, but she pushed it aside, reminding herself that Cody wasn't the type to dig too deeply.

"Anyway," Cody said, setting his mug down and pulling her into a hug, "prenup or no prenup, I'm in this for the long haul. And yes, babe, I know you and Liam have shagged, but I don't care, as you know I'm firing blanks. If you want to use any of our colleagues to take advantage of a certain unofficial Manic benefit, you have my blessing. As long as we're solid, that's all that matters to me."

Chloe blinked, momentarily thrown by Cody's candour. He knew more than she'd given him credit for, and his laid-back acceptance of her schemes—and the complexities of their relationship—was both a relief and a challenge. If Cody was this perceptive, she'd need to tread carefully in the future.

"Thanks, Cody," Chloe said softly, resting her head on his shoulder. "You're one in a million, you know that?"

Cody chuckled, stroking her hair. "I try. Now, come on, let's enjoy the rest of Christmas without any more plotting. You've got plenty of time to take over the world in the New Year."

* _ * _ * _ *

Lyra Nott was sat on her bed at her Alsager house that she shared with her boyfriend, Si Wilcox, a wrestler who was part of the independent UK wrestling scene. Lyra scrolled absentmindedly through her phone, her thoughts drifting between the chaos at Manic Radio and the relative peace of her Christmas morning. The soft glow of fairy lights around the room reflected off her festive pyjamas, a stark contrast to the high-energy world she inhabited during the week.

Unlike her colleagues, she didn't believe in the hedonistic lifestyle that had become synonymous with Manic Radio. Lyra treasured moments like these—quiet, grounded, and filled with genuine connection. Si, dressed in a Santa hat and his usual laid-back attire, sat on the floor, wrapping a last-minute present for one of Lyra's nieces, Clarice, the daughter of her elder brother, Theodore, a lawyer who lived in Wolverhampton and dealt in criminal defence cases. Clarice was six and the apple of the Nott family's eye, her energy and charm bringing light to every family gathering.

"Did you see this?" Lyra said, scrolling to the latest gossip in the Gals and Geezers group chat. She rolled her eyes as she handed her phone to Si, who took one look and shook his head.

"What a slut," Si said, as Lyra showed him the photo of Lily with the three-foot dildo. "And they call that professionalism?" he added, chuckling darkly as he handed the phone back to Lyra. "Honestly, I don't know how you put up with that lot."

Lyra sighed, setting her phone down. "I don't either sometimes. Pete, Ellen, Tim and Clive are the only few sane ones left. The rest are either too far gone in the Manic culture or just trying to survive it. And then there's Kylie… I swear, she's the queen bee of chaos."

Si smirked, placing the wrapped gift to the side. "It's a circus, Lyra. And yet, here you are—still holding your ground. That's why I'm proud of you. You've not let it drag you down, even when it's trying its hardest."

Lyra smiled, leaning over to kiss Si on the cheek. "Thanks, Si. It's not easy, though. Every time I think I've found my footing, something—or someone—tries to knock me off balance. And then there's James."

Lyra noticed that Si frowned when she mentioned James, as he was wrought to do. There was a reason that he despised hearing James's name, and it wasn't just professional jealousy. Lyra suspected that Si despised James as he was jealous of the younger presenter's connection to her. It wasn't something Lyra had ever acted on—she'd always kept her relationship with James professional, despite their occasional camaraderie and how he was cute, despite being the son of one of her colleagues and a colleague himself.

To Lyra, relationships with colleagues were complicated at best and destructive at worst, especially in an environment like Manic Radio. Yet, James's situation tugged at her conscience. She saw him as more than just a naive newcomer caught in Manic's whirlwind. Beneath his bravado and the "golden couple" façade with Kylie, there was vulnerability—a sense that James was drowning in a toxic culture that celebrated excess and discarded anyone who faltered.

And that he was good looking.

And that she had walked in on him and Zara once and saw that he made a horse look like it had a micropenis.

And that-

Damn it Lyra, stop focusing on that. You're dating Si, and even though you haven't slept with him-

Why not? He's a bloke and you're a human woman with needs, aren't you? Lyra sighed, shaking her head to clear her wandering thoughts. The last thing she needed was to complicate her already tangled feelings with thoughts about James, especially on Christmas. Her relationship with Si was stable, even if it lacked the physical intimacy that some might expect. Stability mattered more to her than fleeting passion—or so she told herself.

But Si can't even get it up, and if James isn't using aids to make his 10 inch-

"No, stop it!" she muttered, and Si looked at her with a mixture of concern and curiosity.

"Stop what?" he asked, setting aside the present and scooting closer to her on the bed.

Lyra forced a smile, brushing her hair back from her face. "Just… thinking too much. About work, about everything. Christmas is supposed to be a break, but my brain doesn't seem to get the memo."

You've got it bad for James, girl.

But he's a cokehead, the rational side of her brain interjected. *And he's wrapped up with Kylie Morgan— manipulative, toxic, and willing to do anything to maintain her throne at Manic.* Lyra took a deep breath, shaking off the internal argument. It wasn't the time or place for these thoughts.

Si gave her a sideways glance, leaning back against the headboard. "Thinking about work on Christmas? That's a crime, Nott. Should I call the festive police?"

Lyra laughed softly, grateful for his attempt to lighten the mood. "Go ahead. Maybe they'll fine me and force me to take a proper break."

Si grinned, nudging her gently. "Or maybe they'll lock you up in the Christmas spirit jail, where the only punishment is eating too many mince pies and listening to Wham! on repeat."

Lyra rolled her eyes playfully, nudging him back. "You're ridiculous. Anyway, I'm working tomorrow, gotta go to the Manchester hub as I'm working with Buzz Campbell on the afternoon show."

Greg "Buzz" Campbell, Lyra knew, was one of the Bee Manic hosts, a 35-year-old who was, like most Manic personalities, equal parts charming and chaotic. Buzz had a reputation for pushing boundaries on air and off, often veering into territory that made HR nervous. But despite his antics—or perhaps because of them—he was a magnet for listeners, especially during prime slots like the afternoon show.

The fact she had never worked with him, and that it was Boxing Day that they were sharing a shift, at a studio hub that she had never visited before, added an extra layer of nervousness to Lyra's thoughts. There were rumours,

Lyra knew, that he, being the most senior presenter at that hub, only got his annual contract renewals as he had dirt on the regional director at Bee Manic. Whether it was true or not, Lyra didn't know, but she wasn't eager to find out firsthand.

"Buzz, eh?" Si said, his tone neutral but with a hint of amusement. "He's the one who did that live cinnamon challenge on-air, right? Nearly choked himself for the sake of ratings?"

Lyra laughed, recalling the infamous incident. "That's the one. He's... an acquired taste, I think. Should be an interesting shift."

Si nodded, his gaze softening as he reached for her hand. "Just don't let him rope you into anything too wild, alright? You've got enough on your plate without becoming another Manic headline."

Lyra squeezed his hand, grateful for his steady presence. "Don't worry, Si. I know how to handle myself. Buzz might be chaotic, but I doubt he can surprise me after what I've seen at the other hubs."

As the conversation turned to lighter topics, Lyra allowed herself to relax, pushing thoughts of James, Kylie, and the chaotic world of Manic Radio to the back of her mind— at least for now. Tomorrow would bring its own challenges, but for tonight, she intended to enjoy the peace and simplicity of Christmas with Si and her family.

****

CHAPTER 18 – The New Rules Apply
Thursday 1st January 2025

Kicked out.

James knew that he had to face the new reality, that his dad had kicked him out of the Smith house. He knew that it was his fault, that he had let his life spiral out of control, and now he was paying the price. Standing in the cold January morning, a rucksack with a change of clothes and his iMac over his shoulder and his breath visible in the icy air, James stared blankly down the quiet suburban street. The festive glow of Christmas lights still lingered on a few houses, but the cheer felt distant—mocking even.

He knew his father's patience had been wearing thin for weeks. The cocaine-fuelled chaos of his Manic lifestyle, the revelations about Kylie and Penny's pregnancies, and the growing tension within the family had all reached a boiling point. Last night's New Year's Eve broadcast—a high-pressure, national show—had been both a professional success for Kylie, who had hosted it with the grace and charm of a seasoned broadcaster, and a personal disaster for James. The mounting pressure had pushed him into a near meltdown during the broadcast's final hour.

He'd stumbled over his words, and though listeners might have chalked it up to exhaustion, his script had been completely different to what Kylie and their producer, Shane Tipton, had been given, and he had messed up badly, even going as far as to call Kylie by Penny's name live on air during a moment of scripted banter. The mistake had been subtle, but Kylie had shot him a dagger-like glare, her professionalism unbroken but her fury unmistakable. By the time the countdown to midnight ended and the cameras stopped rolling, Kylie had pulled him aside, her words icy and measured.

And then there was the fact that he had, instead of snorting a normal dose of cocaine, inhaled three times the normal amount during the final hour of the broadcast. The effects had been immediate and catastrophic—his energy had veered into manic territory, his speech erratic, and his demeanour unnervingly intense. By the time the New Year had rung in, James had become a liability, not just to Kylie but to the Manic brand.

And there was, afterwards, the contract James had signed that Kylie had handed to him and not told him what it was. James knew that he couldn't tell his dad that he'd basically signed himself to be the new hub cum dump for Manic's Dudley hub—an exploitative and degrading role that represented the darkest, most toxic aspects of the station's culture. Kylie's ability to manipulate James into signing the contract had been a masterstroke of her ruthless ambition, exploiting his vulnerability in the aftermath of their disastrous New Year's Eve broadcast. James had been too shaken to question it, too desperate to cling to any semblance of stability, and now he was trapped.

And that if he told Pete, his dad, that he was now to be the plaything for everyone at Manic in Dudley, from Cal, the regional manager, to Clara, the intern who was a sound technician, then Pete would have his show suspended, that as an independent contractor, Pete would lose his income entirely. Manic had made it clear that James's submission to this degrading role was the price of protecting his father's career. It was a chilling reminder of how far the station's toxic culture could reach, how deeply it could manipulate and control.

Looking down the street, James knew that his car was parked towards the end, as he hadn't took it with him to work the previous evening, so he headed towards his Citroën C1, a silver 2019 plate model that seemed to reflect the life he once had—unassuming, functional, and relatively carefree. As he approached the car, the weight of his new reality pressed down on him. He fumbled with his keys, the chill of the morning biting into his fingers, and slid into the driver's seat. The interior was cold, the faint scent of air freshener doing little to mask the lingering odour of late-night fast food and the occasional spilled energy drink.

James turned the key in the ignition, and the engine sputtered to life. He sat there for a moment, gripping the steering wheel and staring out at the empty street. The radio automatically tuned into Midlands Manic, and the bright, cheery voice of Manic Radio South Coast presenter Kyler Thompson, who was doing the mid-morning network show as no local shows were being produced for the two weeks that covered the Christmas and New Year period, filled the car. The upbeat jingles and slick production only deepened James's sense of detachment. It was a cruel irony—he had once been the bright, promising star of Manic Radio, and now he was little more than a puppet in its relentless machine.

James turned the radio off with a sharp jab at the button, the silence that followed almost deafening. He let out a long breath, the weight of his predicament sinking in.

Then he remembered that the contract specified that Kylie was to be his "handler." She held all the cards now—his career, his reputation, and even his autonomy. Every aspect of his life at Manic, and by extension outside of it, was now dictated by her whims. The realisation made his stomach churn.

Kylie had already messaged him that morning, her tone equal parts mocking and commanding:

Kylie Morgan: *Morning, Reevesy. Hope you've had time to reflect on your New Year's performance. Not exactly award-winning, was it? Anyway, head over to Chloe and Cody's place in Brum, and I'll be waiting for you there. Don't keep me waiting.* 🖤

James closed his eyes, the cold creeping into the car despite the engine running. He knew he had no choice but to comply. The terms of the contract were clear: he was Kylie's, and that she could earn money from him being used as a "hub cum dump" across Manic's Dudley hub and beyond. The thought was nauseating, but the repercussions of defiance were worse. Kylie's control over him wasn't just professional; it was deeply personal, an all-encompassing stranglehold that left him with little room to breathe, let alone resist.

James put the car into gear and began driving towards Birmingham. The streets were eerily quiet, the remnants of New Year's Eve celebrations scattered along the pavements—empty bottles, discarded party hats, and faint traces of confetti glimmering in the morning light. The festive debris only heightened the sense of dissonance

James felt, as if the world had moved on to a brighter chapter while he was stuck in the darkest one yet.

As he drove, James's mind churned. How had it come to this? Two months ago, he had signed to Manic, signed to become the newest talent that had signed to the media conglomerate which was, along with Bauer and Global, part of the trio of CHR powerhouses dominating the British radio landscape. He had been brimming with excitement, imagining a future filled with opportunity, fame, and creative freedom. Now, he was nothing more than a pawn in Manic's ruthless game, a "golden boy" tarnished by the very system he once idolised.

James reached the city centre and manoeuvred through the quieter-than-usual streets of Birmingham. Cody and Chloe's flat in the Allegro Living complex loomed ahead, its sleek modern facade as imposing as ever. James parked his car in a nearby pay-and-display bay, knowing that he couldn't afford the fine if he left it unpaid. His hands trembled as he fed coins into the machine and printed the ticket, sticking it on the dashboard with shaky fingers.

The walk to the flat felt like a march to the gallows. He hesitated before knocking, briefly considering walking away, but the grip of the contract—and Kylie's influence—dragged him forward. He raised his hand and knocked, the sound echoing down the sterile hallway.

The door swung open to reveal Kylie, dressed impeccably as always. She wore a fitted blazer over a low-cut blouse, paired with tailored trousers and stilettos that clicked ominously as she stepped aside to let him in. Her icy blue eyes assessed him with a mixture of amusement and disdain.

"Well, look who decided to show up," she said, her voice saccharine with an edge of steel. "Come in, Reevesy. We've got a lot to discuss."

James stepped inside, the warmth of the flat doing little to alleviate the cold knot in his stomach. Chloe lounged on the sofa, scrolling through her phone, while Cody busied himself in the kitchen. The smell of coffee and bacon filled the air, but James's appetite had long since disappeared.

Kylie closed the door behind him and motioned for him to sit at the dining table. As James lowered himself into the chair, Kylie slid a folder across the table towards him. Her lips curled into a smirk that sent a shiver down his spine.

"Your duties, starting today," she said simply.

James stared at the folder, reluctant to open it. Kylie's tone was matter-of-fact, as though she were handing over a standard work assignment rather than detailing the humiliating terms of his new role. He finally flipped it open, scanning the pages with growing dread.

The document was explicit, laying out his responsibilities as the "hub cum dump" with clinical precision. It detailed who could make "requests," the conditions under which he was expected to comply, and the mechanisms for Kylie to monetise his availability. There were even clauses about appearances at Manic events, framed as opportunities to "strengthen team morale."

"You're joking," James said, his voice barely above a whisper. He looked up at Kylie, hoping to see some hint of remorse or humour in her expression. There was none.

Kylie arched an eyebrow, her smirk unwavering. "Do I look like I'm joking, Reevesy? This is the reality you signed up for. And before you start whining, remember—this isn't just about you. Your dad's show, your family's reputation—it's all riding on you keeping your end of the deal."

Chloe snorted from the sofa. "My darling brother finally learning what it's like to be the underdog," she muttered, not bothering to look up from her phone. Cody chuckled from the kitchen, clearly finding the situation more amusing than concerning.

"Oh, and there's some new accessories that you need to wear, slut," Kylie then said with the venom of a viper poised to strike. She reached into an Ann Summers bag to pull out an anal plug, a pair of nipple clamps, a cock ring and a chastity cage.

"This chastity cage is to wear on occasions either me, Cody or Chloe want to fuck you in the arse and we don't want you to get an erection," Kylie continued, her tone both cold and condescending. She placed the items on the table one by one, each addition making James feel smaller and more humiliated. The sight of the chastity cage in particular made his stomach churn. It was a stark symbol of the control Kylie now wielded over every aspect of his life. "Now bend over, Cody wants to be the first in your arse under the new regime," Kylie said, her tone a mockery of professional authority. James's hands trembled as he gripped the edge of the table, his face flushing with a mixture of rage and humiliation.

"Are you serious right now?" he whispered, his voice barely audible, the knot in his stomach tightening.

Cody sauntered over from the kitchen, his grin widening. "Oh, don't look so glum, mate. It's all part of team bonding, isn't it?" he joked, though the malice in his tone was unmistakable.

Kylie leaned closer, her voice dropping to a chilling whisper. "Yes, James. Very serious. You signed the contract. You belong to Manic now—body and soul. And don't forget, if you don't comply, your father's career goes down the drain. Do you really want that on your conscience?"

James's mind raced, the reality of his situation crashing down on him with brutal clarity. He felt trapped, like a cornered animal, with no way out. His thoughts briefly flickered to his dad, his mum, and the life he once had before Manic—a life that now seemed like a distant dream.

And then he undid his jeans, as he knew he had no options, that he had been stripped of agency by Kylie and the contract he had signed. The humiliation burned deep, his cheeks flushing hot as he bent over the table. Cody's laughter rang out behind him, mocking and cruel, while Chloe remained fixated on her phone, only smirking occasionally at the degrading scene unfolding in the flat.

James closed his eyes, trying to block out the sounds, the smells, the feeling of utter degradation. His mind flashed to happier moments—Christmas mornings with his family, carefree days at university, even the brief pride he felt when he first joined Manic. Those memories now seemed like they belonged to someone else, a different version of himself that had been left behind the moment he stepped into the toxic world of Manic Radio.

And then he felt Cody enter him without any lubrication, without a condom, straight in as if he were an object, not a person. The pain was immediate and searing, his body tensing involuntarily as he gritted his teeth to stifle a cry. The degradation was beyond anything he had imagined, and the tears that welled in his eyes were not just from physical discomfort but from the overwhelming sense of hopelessness and humiliation.

Then he noticed Chloe putting a strap-on on and stroking it as if it were a real person's member. She smirked, her eyes gleaming with malicious delight as she observed James's plight.

"Wanna watch this slut get spit roasted, Kyles?" Chloe asked and James could see the grin that his sister had across her face—a grin that spoke of triumph and cruelty. Kylie, still leaning casually against the counter, chuckled darkly and nodded.

"Oh, absolutely," Kylie said, her tone dripping with malice. "After all, it's important for James to understand his new role thoroughly. No shortcuts, no exceptions."

James wanted to scream, to fight back, to do something, but the sheer weight of the situation pressed down on him like an iron cage. He knew any resistance would only make things worse—not just for him, but for his father, whose career hung precariously in the balance. The thought of Pete, oblivious to the horrors his son was enduring, was almost too much to bear.

Chloe approached, her every movement deliberate and calculated, the strap-on in place and gleaming in the cold light of the flat. James could feel the tension in the air, every second dragging out into an eternity. Cody, still positioned behind him, laughed as he delivered a sharp slap to James's back, the sound echoing in the otherwise quiet room.

"Look at you," Cody sneered. "From golden boy to... well, whatever this is. Don't worry, mate, we'll take good care of you."

Chloe positioned herself in front of James, forcing him to meet her eyes. The satisfaction on her face was undeniable, a sickening reminder of just how far she was willing to go to assert her dominance.

"Open wide, Jamie," she cooed mockingly, gripping the base of the strap-on and guiding it toward his mouth. "Let's see if you're good for something after all."

James's body trembled with a mix of rage, shame, and helplessness. Every fibre of his being wanted to fight back, to scream that he wasn't a pawn in their twisted game. But the contract, the threats, the suffocating web of control that Kylie had spun around him—it left him no choice. He opened his mouth, every ounce of his pride and dignity crumbling in the process.

Taking in every inch of the 12 inch fake appendage was a horrifying experience. James's tears streamed freely now, the mixture of physical pain, humiliation, and emotional despair overwhelming him. Chloe's cruel laughter echoed in his ears, every second stretching into an eternity.

Kylie stood nearby, arms crossed, her gaze icy and unrelenting. She was the orchestrator of this nightmare, her manipulations having led James to this moment. Yet, she showed no signs of remorse—only satisfaction at her dominance.

Chloe leaned in closer, her voice dripping with venom. "You know, Jamie, this is what happens when you think you're better than everyone else. Welcome to reality."

James's mind tried to retreat into itself, searching for a shred of solace amidst the horror. Memories of simpler times—sitting in his dad's studio, dreaming of a career in radio—felt like cruel taunts now. He had worked so hard to achieve his dreams, only to watch them mutate into this grotesque mockery.

You brought it on yourself, James.

No... no, I didn't. I didn't. Kylie should be the one humiliated, not me.

But even as the thought flickered in James's mind, it felt hollow. Whatever blame he wanted to place on Kylie, Chloe, Cody, or the toxic culture at Manic Radio, the truth was that he had allowed himself to be swept into the storm. He had made choices—reckless, self-destructive choices—that had led him here.

His body tensed as Chloe pulled back, the strap-on finally leaving his mouth. And then he felt another cock in his arse at the same time as Cody's, and he noticed that Kylie wasn't where she was standing, that she was the other one, that she was wearing a harness with a strap-on.

"You're moving in with me at Great Bridge, Reevesy, and you'll be servicing me every day," Kylie then said as she continued her relentless degradation, her voice cold and commanding. "You'll learn to accept your place, James. Consider this your initiation. Welcome to the real world."

James felt his mind fracturing under the weight of the moment. He was trapped, not just physically but emotionally and psychologically, bound by the contract Kylie had tricked him into signing and the unrelenting humiliation that followed. Each second felt like an eternity, each taunt cutting deeper than the last.

His thoughts turned inward, seeking refuge in the happier moments of his life—the warmth of Christmas mornings with his family, the pride he'd felt when he first stepped into a radio studio, and the dreams he'd once had of making a name for himself in the industry. Those memories now felt like shards of a broken mirror, reflecting a version of himself he could barely recognise.

"James," Kylie said, her tone softening, though it carried no trace of empathy, "this isn't just about punishment. It's about teaching you how to survive in this world. The faster you learn to submit, the easier it will be for everyone."

Tears streaming down his face, James managed to choke out a single word: "Why?"

Kylie's smirk returned, her eyes gleaming with satisfaction. "Because, Reevesy, power is everything in this business. And I hold all the cards now. You're not just a presenter anymore—you're a symbol, a reminder to everyone else at Manic of what happens when you fall out of line. Be grateful I'm letting you stay in the game at all."

The room fell silent, save for the sound of James's ragged breathing. Chloe and Cody exchanged smug glances, their shared satisfaction palpable. Kylie stepped back, adjusting her blazer as if she had just finished a routine task rather than orchestrating one of the most degrading moments of James's life.

"Clean yourself up," Kylie ordered, tossing a towel at James. "And get dressed. You've got work to do."

****

Books by Thomas Brant

Broadcasting Boundaries
Broadcasting Boundaries

www.ingramcontent.com/pod-product-compliance
Lightning Source LLC
Chambersburg PA
CBHW030926120726
47906CB00002B/506